V-Clan Series

Blood Sector

Night Sector

Eclipse Sector

Kodiak Sector

Other Standalone Stories in this World:

X-Clan Series

X-Clan: The Origin

Andorra Sector

X-Clan: The Experiment

Winter's Arrow

Bariloche Sector

Exiled Sector World

Venom Island by Lexi C. Foss

Nightmare Island by Mila Young

Outcast Island by Jennifer Thorn

ECLIPSE SECTOR

V-CLAN SERIES

USA TODAY BESTSELLING AUTHOR

LEXI C. FOSS

This is a work of fiction. Names, characters, places, and incidents are either the product of the author's imagination or are used fictitiously, and any resemblance to actual persons, living or dead, business establishments, events, or locales is entirely coincidental.

Eclipse Sector Discreet Cover Edition

Editing by: Outthink Editing, LLC

Proofreading by: Katie Schmahl & Jean Bachen

Cover Design: Manuela Serra

Photography: Christopher John

Models: Eric Guilmette & Sam

Chapter Headers Created by: Anna Spies (Atra Luna Designs) & Nathan Hansen

Chapter Background Images: Manuela Serra

Chapter Background Photography: Christopher John

Chapter Background Models: Eric Guilmette & Sam

Published by: Ninja Newt Publishing, LLC

Hardback Edition

ISBN: 978-1-68530-368-6

AI Disclaimer: This book does not contain any elements of AI content. All art was designed by real artists, and all of the words were written by the author.

For those who love the moment when the rejector becomes the rejectee…
Because who doesn't enjoy a good grovel?

"One of these days, you're going to ask me to dance, Cillian, and it'll be too late."
—Ivana

ECLIPSE SECTOR

A V-CLAN NOVEL

ECLIPSE SECTOR

I loved an Alpha once.
An unattainable Elite.
A former V-Clan Prince.

I thought we had a connection.
A unique bond founded on our shared values and aspirations.
Then he broke my heart with a few choice words.

He doesn't want me? Fine. I'll search for an Alpha who does. Which is how I find myself on the stage being introduced as Candidate Thirteen of the Eligible Omega Mates program.

Except, there's just one tiny problem—the Alpha who broke my heart is in charge of supervising the mating activities. Which means he's privy to every interview. Every date. Every *kiss*.

How am I supposed to find an appropriate mate when he's watching me with those smoldering irises?
Purring possessive comments in my ear…
Growling at every male who looks my way…
Prowling around my nest…

It doesn't help that someone is attacking the Omegas in the program.

Now my Alpha is even more territorial, his feral nature that much more potent.
Because he's refusing to leave my side.
And he's promised to do whatever it takes to protect me.
Even if it means claiming me for himself.

Author's Note: This is a standalone dark shifter romance with Omegaverse vibes—A, B, O dynamics with kn*tting, nesting, and biting. Check the trigger warnings in the introduction for more details.

A NOTE FROM LEXI

Eclipse Sector is a standalone in the V-Clan universe. No other books need to be read prior to this one to follow the storyline.

This is a shifter romance with strong Omegaverse themes. There are Alpha/Omega dynamics, nesting, purring, estrous cycles, and, of course, *knotting*. If you're unfamiliar with these terms, don't worry—they're explained throughout the book. ;)

Those of you familiar with my X-Clan series will notice these similarities.

However, the V-Clan Alphas tend to be a bit more patient than the X-Clan Alphas. They're still possessive and like to bite, but they very much respect an Omega's right to choose.

Cillian is definitely hero-worship material. He has a long road to travel in winning Ivana back, and there are going to be a lot of curves along the way. But this is a journey of love, heartache, and undeniable chemistry. While there may be bumps, they won't be too triggering.

Some notes that may interest you regarding content:

✔ Consent
✔ No Other Woman Drama (No Cheating)
✔ Minor Other Man Drama (No Cheating)
✔ Pregnancy & Primal Energy
✔ Possessive Over The Top Alpha Male
✔ Touch Her and Die Vibes
✔ Knotting, Nesting, Purring, Growling

Enjoy! <3

INTRODUCTION

Nearly a century ago, a zombielike virus spread across the globe, destroying over ninety percent of the human race. Many of the supernatural species of the world were immune to the plague. Others were not.

Those who have survived—both human and supernatural alike—now rule their own territories, otherwise known as sectors.

You're about to enter the V-Clan world, a breed of shifter wolves with vampiric traits. These beings prefer the night. They thrive on magic. And perhaps most importantly of all, the Alphas of this kind cherish their Omega mates.

PART I

Dear Stars,

I'm in love with an Alpha Prince. Except he doesn't see himself as a prince. He prefers to be called an Elite instead. Primarily because he fancies himself as a protector rather than a royal.

However, I see the real him. I know his heart. And my wolf is determined to make him our mate.

So wish us luck.

We're going to need it.

Because this Elite is a stubborn alphahole.

But he's worth the fight.

I hope...

Love,
Ivana

IVANA

"DANCE WITH ME."

It wasn't a request so much as a demand, one that had Cillian sighing the moment I materialized beside him in the shadows of the ballroom.

Goading the too-serious Alpha was one of my favorite pastimes. It was almost as fun as sniffing out his hiding spots.

The *Elite*—a fancy term for *pack enforcer*—had a penchant for blending into the background, his stealth skills admirable. However, Cillian wasn't the only one who enjoyed being a chameleon.

Which was how I constantly found him—because his mind worked similarly to mine.

"No." His response was flat, his tone brooking no argument.

Typical Cillian, always playing hard to get.

One of these days, I would win this game between us.

Hopefully sooner rather than later, as I'd been waiting a long time for Cillian to decide to take a mate.

Maybe now he would consider it since his two best friends had recently chosen their Omegas. Granted, Lorcan appeared to be in a mating of convenience with Kyra. But it counted in my book. Primarily because it would prove to Cillian that he could be both mated and an Elite.

I respected his choice to protect King Kieran—Cillian's other best friend—and Kieran's mate, Queen Quinnlynn. However, Cillian seemed to be under the impression that he had to choose between his own happiness and his sense of duty.

Now that Lorcan had Kyra, perhaps Cillian would realize how ridiculous his sacrifice truly was and consider mating the Omega standing beside him—*me.*

Alas, that didn't seem to be on the agenda for this evening, something he told me by shadowing to another area of the room.

I followed him, simply to prove a point. "I know all your hiding places, Prince Cillian."

"Not all of them, I assure you," he replied, his Irish lilt thicker due to his frustration. "And it's *Cillian*, not *Prince Cillian.*" He finally looked at me, his dark eyes immediately entrancing me in his spell. "But if you feel the need to be respectful, then you can address me as *Alpha Cillian* and accompany the phrase with, *Have a good night.*"

"Hmm." I considered him for a moment. "For that to be a truthful statement, you would need to dance with me. Otherwise, it won't be a very *good* night."

"For you, perhaps." His gaze left me for King Kieran, his eyebrow winging upward.

"For you, too," I murmured quietly, aware that he and the Blood Sector King were now engaged in a silent conversation.

Cillian's ability to read minds and converse telepathically

was well known in the sector. It was probably why he didn't have many friends.

Or perhaps it was his hard approach that scared everyone off.

He and Lorcan both were incredibly intimidating. King Kieran, too. However, I'd never feared them. Maybe it was a result of how I'd originally met Cillian.

Oh, he'd been terrifying then. *The way he slaughtered…*

I cleared my throat, not wanting to recall the violent memory.

Instead, I glanced at the hero of my past.

Cillian.

His near-black eyes trailed back to me, his ability to hear my thoughts likely catching his attention as I'd mentioned his name.

I simply smiled.

He didn't smile back.

"Go find another Alpha to dance with, Ivana. I'm not interested."

Those final three words packed a punch, one I was used to receiving from him. He'd been claiming that lie for years.

I would believe him if I didn't frequently catch the heat in his eyes when he looked at me. Like now, as he tried not to notice the deep V-neck of my dress.

He clenched his jaw, his irritation palpable as he returned his attention to the Blood Sector King.

"My Queen and I are retiring for the night," King Kieran announced suddenly. "Enjoy the wine. It's spiked with blood."

Cillian snorted beside me while several others startled at the Blood Sector King's abrupt announcement—one he punctuated by promptly escorting his Queen out of the room.

Lorcan joined us in a blink, his intense focus on the room as he inclined his head toward Cillian slightly. The latter grunted, telling me the two were conversing mentally about something.

Likely Kieran's early departure.

The whole point of a coronation was to celebrate the newly crowned King and Queen, but apparently our royals had a different evening agenda on their minds.

"We can still dance," I told Cillian. "In fact, I think we should. How else am I going to test the functionality of my dress?" I twirled to emphasize my dress's skirt, the carefully designed slits meant to allow for fluid movements. "Cameron called this *versatile fashion*. I'd like to show off his creation."

I nearly winced at my ridiculous excuse. Cameron didn't need me to *show off* anything. He was Blood Sector's primary dress designer, one everyone sought to work with. And Cillian definitely knew that.

The Alpha's jaw clenched again as he noted my exposed leg. "I'm in charge of security for the night, Ivana. You're going to have to find someone else to waltz you about the room."

I heaved a long, drawn-out sigh. "Always working."

"Yes," he agreed, his dark eyes burning into mine as he met my gaze once more. "*Yes*, I am. Now go find another Alpha to pester."

I rolled my eyes. "One of these days, you're going to ask me to dance, Cillian, and it'll be too late." It was a lie. I'd wait for him for eternity. My wolf had chosen his, just as I was certain his had chosen mine. I just needed the stubborn man to realize the truth.

"We'll see, won't we?" Cillian murmured.

"I suppose we will," I chirped and shadowed to the other side of the room, primarily to stop myself from shaking some sense into him.

"Still playing hard to get?" a deep voice drawled to my right, causing me to loudly sigh in response.

"Yes." I gritted my teeth like Cillian had a few minutes ago. "He's infuriating, Benz."

My best friend chuckled as he handed me a much-needed

drink. He was the reason I'd chosen this side of the room to teleport to—I knew I'd find his hulking form near the buffet and drinking station.

Although, for the amount of food I knew he could consume, his body didn't show it. The Beta male was pure muscle—all six feet, two inches of him.

Taking a sip of the bubbly liquid, I peered at the shifters moving around the ballroom, my lips tugging into a scowl. "He told me to find another Alpha to dance with."

Benz whistled low, his turquoise gaze running over me with intrigue. "In that dress? He must be in a killing mood."

"Or he just doesn't care," I muttered. *Stubborn fucking Alpha.*

Cillian could probably hear me.

But I didn't care.

He deserved the insult.

"Trust me, darling, he cares," Benz replied, his subtle Germanic accent caressing the endearment. "He's just preoccupied with Kieran's ascension. The minute he sees you twirling around with another male—let alone an *Alpha*—he'll lose his damn mind, and his possessive instincts will take over."

"Hmm, no. I'm starting to think those possessive instincts don't exist." I was talking more to myself than to Benz. However, to him, I added, "And you know I'm not the type to try to provoke him like that."

"Maybe you should be the type."

My eyebrows rose. "Oh? The type to do what, exactly?" I asked, suspicious of whatever idea he'd just concocted in that wicked mind of his. Because Benz had a knack for indulging in pranks, something that often got him into trouble.

"Dance with another wolf," he replied, his dark brown eyebrows waggling with the suggestion. "A wolf like, oh, I don't know, *me*."

I gaped at him. "You want to dance?"

"With you? In that dress?" His gaze ran over me again. "Yes, I very much do."

I laughed. "If I didn't know you any better, I'd say you were trying to flirt with me, Beta Benz."

"Darling Omega, I might be a Beta, but my wolf is too proprietorial to let me flirt with you while you're craving an Alpha's knot." He held out a hand. "But I will absolutely enjoy showing you off on the floor if it means waking up that Alpha's possessive side."

"Didn't you just imply Cillian might kill another Alpha for dancing with me?"

He shrugged. "I'm a Beta, not an Alpha."

I shook my head. "You just want to prove you're right about his *possessiveness*."

"Of course I do," he admitted. "But I also want to show you off." He wiggled his fingers at me. "Indulge me, Sunshine?" The nickname—one Benz had given me—rolled off his tongue in a sugary caress, causing my cheeks to heat. Not because I was necessarily attracted to him, but because I couldn't deny his appeal.

While I might crave a certain Alpha, there was no escaping Benz's alluring traits. Even if some of those traits resulted in devious schemes.

One of which I was considering now as I glanced down at my gown. It was glittery, giving it an ice-blue appearance that matched my eyes. And it made my skin appear that much paler.

"Well, it really is a crime not to show off Cameron's creation," I mused. "Although, we'll need to shadow to the other side of the room to ensure Cillian sees us. Otherwise, he won't even notice."

"Oh, he'd notice you anywhere. But if that's your preference, then I'll follow your lead." He mock-bowed. "After you, my lady." His brown hair tickled his ears, the unruly strands always managing to be artfully sexy.

Blowing out a breath, I shook my head and shadowed to the opposite side of the room again. Only this time, I didn't materialize beside Cillian, just close enough for him to definitely see and hear me when Benz arrived.

Except the sound of Cillian's deep tones had my eyebrows lifting in interest as he said, "Maybe you should just let your wolf knot her, see if that helps cure you of the distraction."

Cillian? Talking about knots? I smiled. *Yes, please.*

If he heard me thinking about him, he didn't show it. Probably because I was one of the many minds he had blocked in the room. I wasn't a potential threat, something he more than knew, so why monitor my mind?

"Are you projecting, Cillian? Is your wolf craving a certain *distraction*?" Lorcan taunted back at him, causing my lips to part.

Because Lorcan *never* spoke out loud.

"I don't crave Ivana or anyone else." Cillian's flat reply had me blinking.

What?

"It's just hard to ignore such a determined Omega, even if she's playing in the wrong league," he went on, causing me to stop breathing.

A snort echoed from someone. Lorcan, maybe? I… I wasn't sure. I was still replaying Cillian's words through my head. *Playing in the wrong league…*

"She really needs to start looking for a more appropriate mate, someone who won't mind her misguided penchant for telling Alphas what to do," he added, each word piercing my chest with a sharpness I'd never known Cillian was capable of.

Except… yes, I did.

He constantly rejected me.

But… but I thought…

I thought he was just in denial.

"I think she enjoys irritating you" was Lorcan's reply, his comment barely registering over Cillian's harsh statements.

"Yes, and that's precisely the problem. She needs to find someone better suited for her childish games. Someone who will actually appreciate her unsavory qualities, such as her boldness and her misplaced confidence."

Unsavory qualities? I repeated to myself, my arms folding around my stomach. *Misplaced confidence?*

How…?

How have I so utterly misread this situation?

I…

I don't…

"My point is, I'm not the one hung up on an Omega, mate. I just happen to have one who is annoyingly persistent. You have one consuming your focus. Those are very different situations."

I flinched as Benz pressed a hand to my shoulder, his presence at my side something I hadn't noticed until now.

One look at his expression told me he'd just overheard everything, too.

And the pity…

No. I shadowed out of the room, incapable of facing him right now. Incapable of breathing, let alone talking.

It felt like Cillian had punched a hole through my chest.

Ripped out my heart.

And *crushed* it beneath his heavy black boot.

I covered my face with my hands, my insides burning as my lungs forced me to inhale. But all I heard was this… this… *wheezing* sound.

Sort of like a sob?

But… but fractured?

Worse.

Destroyed.

"Sunshine," Benz whispered, obviously having followed me.

I just shook my head. I couldn't do this right now. "I'm

fine." Except I didn't sound fine at all. I sounded raspy. Like I'd just run a marathon or something.

But no.

I'd just been run over by Cillian's cruelty.

"That was him convincing himself that he's not into you," Benz insisted. "Trust—"

"*Don't*," I told him, my tone harder than seconds ago. "*Don't* make excuses for him."

"Sunshine—"

"No," I cut him off. "I… I just need…"

Well, I wasn't sure what I needed, but I shadowed back into the ballroom, primarily to escape Benz. Which was stupid. He just wanted to comfort me.

However, I didn't want *comfort*.

I… I wanted…

My jaw clenched, my arms encircling my middle again.

I wasn't sure *what* I wanted.

The Alpha I desired… the Alpha I'd been convinced was meant to be *mine*…

Playing in the wrong league.

Unsavory qualities.

Misplaced confidence.

Childish games…

I winced as the words revolved through my thoughts, my shoulders caving in. *What childish games?* I thought numbly. *I… I thought you were just being stubborn. That you didn't want a mate* —any *mate—and just needed to see that it was possible to be mated while also serving as an Elite.*

But that hadn't been it at all.

Cillian just didn't want *me* as a mate.

I'd been blinded by my wolf's desires, seeing things that didn't actually exist.

All the while, he'd been truly irritated with me.

Annoyingly persistent.

The ballroom around me blurred.

I need to go, I realized. *I need to run. To chase away this… this* agony.

Swallowing, I wrapped myself up in darkness again and teleported to one of my favorite snowy fields at the base of a sleeping volcano.

Blood Sector—former-day Iceland—was full of landscapes like this, making it the perfect place for peaceful retreats.

I ripped off my dress and kicked off my shoes, never wishing to set eyes on the outfit again—an outfit I'd worn with *him* in mind.

Then I fell to the ground and let my wolf take over.

She might not have understood Cillian's words, but she understood my pain. Just as she understood he'd been the one to cause said pain.

A howl spilled from my snout the moment I completed my shift, my animal's torment rivaling my own.

Our chosen mate doesn't want us.

Our hero… isn't a hero.

Our Alpha no longer exists to us.

My paws pounded through the snow, the chill a welcome kiss to my senses.

This is what we need, I thought. *Freedom. Fresh air. A new perspective.*

Each bound and leap took us further into the past and pushed us into the present.

A present where we started over.

A present where we remembered our worth.

A present where we decided the Alpha wasn't in *our* league.

Because no potential mate would ever say that about his Omega.

Omegas were rare. Powerful. Destined to be worshipped. Not belittled with sharp words. Rejected on repeat. Ridiculed for having *confidence.*

Cillian isn't our mate.

We deserve better.

We desire more.

An Alpha who loves us. Cherishes us. Fights *for us.*

It was time for us to move on. To stop wallowing in Cillian's potential.

He really doesn't want us, I thought again, my wolf stumbling a bit. *Well, then we don't want him.*

My wolf yipped as though agreeing with me.

And took off across the icy field.

We're done salivating over Cillian.

He thought I'd been playing a *childish game*?

Well, that *game* had just come to an end.

And Cillian? He'd just lost.

Because the right Alpha would see me as a prize.

The right Alpha will actually want me.

You can have tonight to mourn, I told myself. *But tomorrow, you're going to move on and forget all about the* wrong *Alpha.*

It shouldn't be hard.

It wasn't like Cillian ever sought me out.

He probably wouldn't even notice, would just be glad to be rid of my *annoyingly persistent* presence.

My heart panged in my chest, my wolf stumbling once more.

Tonight, we grieve, I reiterated to myself. *Tomorrow, we step into the future. And begin the hunt for a worthier mate…*

CILLIAN

Several Minutes Earlier

And I've lost him again, I thought, my gaze on Lorcan.

He'd ventured somewhere into his mating bond, making his mind murky and incomprehensible. His connection to Kyra had bolstered his mental defenses in a way I could never have anticipated.

Same with Kieran's connection to Quinnlynn.

It fascinated me, as their minds were ones I knew almost as well as my own, yet I could barely hear Lorcan now. Not that he was the chatty or loud sort to begin with, but I could usually hear him contemplating and analyzing.

However, all I could hear right now was a strange sort of static as he checked in on his mate.

What must that be like? I wondered, my gaze scanning the crowd. *Terrifying? Freeing? Intimate?*

I would never know, of course.

My loyalty was to Kieran. Always. But that didn't stop me from being curious about the concept or what it might feel like.

Which naturally had me searching for the little ash-blonde nuisance that constantly made me question my sanity.

Nuisance might be a bit harsh. *Temptation* was a more appropriate term.

A temptation far out of my league, I mused, scanning the crowd for her. *She needs an Alpha who…* The rumination floated off as I caught sight of Ivana across the room, her shoulders oddly hunched.

I took an involuntary step forward, my instincts firing.

Ivana Michaels *never* hunched.

She resembled a fierce goddess despite her petite stature. The woman could set down any Alpha in her path with a few choice words, something I found both aggravating and alluring.

Ivana. The name in Lorcan's mind almost had me looking at him, but I was too focused on the Omega and the slender arms encircling her torso. She appeared to be trying to *breathe.*

Did an Alpha spook her? Lorcan wondered, the question similar to the one bouncing around in my thoughts. *Who did you send her off to dance with?*

No one in particular. I just told her to find someone else to ask, as I'm not here to celebrate. I'm working.

Do you think someone rejected her? he asked.

I frowned, not liking that concept at all. *If they did, I'll kill them.*

Lorcan glanced sideways at me—something I caught in my peripheral vision—his expression mocking. *Technically, you rejected her. You reject her all the time. Are you going to punish yourself?*

I scoffed at the concept. *That's different and you know it.*

But does she know it? he asked softly, his words causing me to clench my teeth.

Ivana knew I was mated to my position, that my loyalty was to Kieran first and foremost. I'd never lied to her, always voicing the truth in her presence.

Well, most of the truth.

I couldn't take a mate, nor did I want to take a mate. And while she certainly tempted my wolf into a rutting mood every damn time she entered a room, I didn't have any plans or intentions to actually knot her.

I couldn't.

I *wouldn't.*

But Lorcan wasn't wrong.

I did reject her often.

However, tonight hadn't been different from any other night. And she never reacted to my rejection like *that.*

No, someone else must have upset her.

And whoever it was would answer to *me.* Omegas were under the protection of Blood Sector and therefore part of my jurisdiction as an Elite.

Heaving a sigh, I engaged my shadowing ability to join her near the dance floor. *I'll be back,* I told Lorcan as an afterthought.

Except Ivana was already gone when I materialized in the space she'd just been, her citrusy perfume a beacon on the wind. Frowning, I searched for her noteworthy hair—all those silky white-blonde strands.

Nothing.

Not a single hint of that glittery dress—which was way too revealing tonight. My wolf had practically growled with hunger the moment she'd appeared beside me, her sultry voice demanding that I *dance* with her.

No. *Fuck* no. I couldn't trust myself to touch her in that sexy gown of hers.

So I'd told her to find another Alpha to pester. *To tempt. To seduce.*

Except I didn't want to think about her succeeding in *that* plight.

My teeth ground together, my irritation mounting.

Maybe she'd run off with one. I could find out by checking her thoughts, but I wasn't going to invade her privacy. Besides, her mental waves were… unique. For as vocal as she could be out loud, her mind was exceptionally quiet. Peaceful, even.

She was upset, I reasoned. *I should check on her.*

Although, it wasn't really any of my business, was it?

I could try to justify it as a need to protect her from harm, but she'd left of her own volition. And while her shoulders had been hunched in defeat, she hadn't exactly been weeping or physically hurt.

I'm overreacting, I decided, shaking my head. *It's all this mating energy around me. And Ivana's sensual invitation.*

My damn canines ached to bite her. Just as my wolf wanted to *rut* her.

It was a damning enticement, one I'd been fighting for years.

And I wasn't going to lose that fight tonight.

Kieran and Quinnlynn had retired early. It was my job to manage the coronation and everyone in this ballroom.

Take charge as the acting Sector Alpha.

It was my responsibility every time Kieran needed a break.

I didn't mind it.

Although, I wondered what it might be like to have the luxury of playing with a mate instead of running a sector.

I'd have to ask Kieran about it tomorrow. Goad him a bit. Perhaps he'd indulge me in a good spar.

Now *that* would distract me from my tempting little goddess.

Clearing my throat, I refocused on the room, my gaze

instantly searching for said goddess once more. However, she'd clearly left.

If she needed me, she'd call for me. She knew how. *From that day, many years ago…*

Swallowing, I pushed the memory from my mind and returned to where Lorcan still lurked in the shadows.

How long do we have to stand here and supervise these animals? Lorcan asked me conversationally, not bothering to follow up on Ivana. Either he assumed I'd handled it, or he had watched me flounder for the last however many minutes while searching futilely for the Omega.

As long as it takes, I told him, replying to his query.

Hmm. He vanished, only to return half a beat later with two glasses of mortal blood, one of which he offered me.

V-Clan shifters required the human essence to bolster our magical abilities, of which I possessed an abundance. When I was young, I used to have to imbibe blood daily, making me feel somewhat like a vampire.

Fortunately, I was far less beastly now, only requiring a drink every few days or so.

Also, fortunately, Kieran had created a home where V-Clan shifters and humans coexisted. We protected the mortals from the deadly zombielike virus that had annihilated over ninety percent of their kind, and they repaid our efforts by donating blood.

Cheers, Lorcan said, tapping his goblet against mine.

Cheers, I echoed, the word meaningless in my mind. Primarily because I was still stuck on a certain female.

Maybe Lorcan was right.

Maybe I had been projecting a bit earlier.

With an internal growl, I forced the conundrum from my head and returned my focus to the shifters moving about the ballroom. It was my job to keep everyone safe and the guests under control.

And I would not fail the inhabitants of Blood Sector.

Unlike those in Eclipse Sector, a dark part of me whispered.

I took a sip of the blood wine, the liquid thick and tasteless in my mouth.

Rather than entertain my morbid past, I shifted my attention to the present. To the dancing shifters. Lurking humans. Visiting princes.

Leashed them all with my power.

Monitored their intentions.

And concentrated on my temporary job as Sector Alpha.

Tomorrow, I would be Cillian again.

Tonight, I was *Prince* Cillian. Just like Ivana had teased. If only I could consider making her my queen.

Alas, I had to be a good enough king to be worthy of a queen.

And history proved I'd never be that.

I was simply… Cillian.

An Elite.

A failed hero.

The breaker of familial vows.

PART II

Dear Stars,

I'm no longer in love with an Alpha Prince.

Elite.

What-the-fuck-ever.

I'm over him. Done. No longer interested.

Okay, okay. That's a lie.

But I'm going to do what I need to do to move on.

And that includes enrolling in the new Eligible Omega Mates program.

Maybe there I can find an Alpha in my league. An Alpha who actually wants me. Doesn't find me overconfident or annoyingly persistent. A male who sees my traits as admirable qualities, not irritants, and appreciates my wolf's bold pursuits.

So, um, wish my animal and me luck again, please.

We're definitely going to need it.

Love,
Ivana

IVANA

A Few Weeks Later

Ivana Michaels.

Eligible Omega Mate.

I stared down at the card in my hand, my throat suddenly dry.

I can do this, I told myself. *Just step out onto the stage, smile, and maybe wave.*

No. No waving.

Well, maybe waving?

I shook my head, the conflicting thoughts making me dizzy as Queen Quinnlynn—who preferred to be called *Quinn*—announced the next Omega candidate. The petite blonde Omega stepped through the curtains and disappeared from view, making it impossible for me to see her entrance.

All I could do was hear the excited male murmurs in the crowd.

Alphas, I thought, swallowing. *Alphas from various V-Clan sectors.*

As well as a few other regions, too.

Like X-Clan Alphas.

And even one Z-Clan Alpha.

I shivered, that last realization causing my stomach to clench. Z-Clan Alphas weren't known for their kindness, especially where Omegas were concerned.

As a general rule, V-Clan wolves didn't typically socialize with other shifters or supernatural beings. We actually tended to keep our existence a secret, allowing the world to believe we'd all perished during the Infected Era.

However, there was a handful of supernaturals out there whom King Kieran had befriended throughout the centuries, and many of those allies were in attendance tonight.

Fortunately, that didn't necessarily mean they would be participating in the Eligible Omega Mates program. But they could apply to join.

A mating program, I mused, still struggling to believe it was actually happening.

When Quinn had told me about the soon-to-be established protocol, I'd been stunned. Primarily because her reveal had been accompanied by an unexpected explanation.

"For over a thousand years, my family has maintained an Omega Sanctuary out in the middle of the Arctic," she'd told me, not bothering to dance around the truth.

My eyebrows had shot upward, surprised by the information. "An Omega Sanctuary?" I'd never heard of such a thing. Omegas were typically protected by Alphas.

At least in the V-Clan world.

The X-Clan and Z-Clan sectors were entirely different, as were a myriad of other shifters and supernatural realms throughout the globe.

Quinn had nodded, confirming I'd heard her right. "A sanctuary for all types of Omegas. My parents were killed because a sadistic Alpha was trying to seek the location of it. And I'd thought it was an Alpha Prince…"

She'd trailed off, the rest of her explanation hanging between us. "That's why you ran from Kieran."

"Among other reasons, yes," she'd admitted. "But that's a story for another day. What I want to tell you about are the new security provisions we're making for the Sanctuary, including renaming it to Night Sector. Everyone will believe it's a new V-Clan territory, one ruled by Kyra and Lorcan."

My eyebrows had jumped upward again. "Oh?" I'd been intrigued because her words had suggested that Lorcan was taking his mating seriously now.

That realization had inspired a hint of hope inside my heart.

One I'd squashed in the next moment.

Because I'd refused to entertain the strand that led directly to *him*. My former love. The Alpha who'd declared himself as *out of my league*.

Oblivious to my inner turmoil, Quinn had continued by telling me King Kieran's plans for announcing the new sector to those in attendance tonight.

"Due to recent events, we feel this is our best option to help safeguard the Sanctuary's secrets," she'd added, not elaborating on the *recent events*.

Instead, she'd gone on to describe some of the security in place within the Sanctuary, including a brief summary of the enchantment safeguarding the island.

"Only Omegas and Alphas mated to Omega inhabitants can enter," she'd explained. "Which means Kieran and Lorcan can pass through the protective barrier, as well as a handful of recently relocated Omegas and their Alpha mates. But those Omegas and Alphas are too new for the others to trust them, so…"

She'd continued by saying that they'd conceptualized an idea to help bolster protection on the island.

And that idea involved creating a mating program for interested Omegas at the Sanctuary.

"It will allow us to bring in a few more Alphas, ones that should, in theory, earn the trust of the Sanctuary a little faster since they would be mating Omegas who have lived there for a while."

"Trust by association," I'd translated.

She'd dipped her chin in confirmation. "Exactly."

"It's a good idea," I'd told her.

"I'm glad you think so," she'd murmured. "Because I was wondering if you'd like to participate in the program."

I'd blinked at her, dumbfounded by the offer.

"You wouldn't necessarily have to relocate to Night Sector afterward, either," she'd added. "I just wanted to let you know that you're invited to join the mating pool. If you're interested, I mean."

I… hadn't known what to say at first.

But after nearly a week of mulling it over, I'd thought, *Why not? What better way to find an Alpha "in my league"?*

Okay, maybe that was catty.

However, it wasn't like I had a lot of options standing before me. And I needed a way to move on from *Alpha Cillian.*

He didn't want me.

He never had.

I could see that now. I'd misread the situation entirely.

I wouldn't allow that to happen again.

So here I stood, dressed in a shimmery blue gown with slits up both my thighs—another design, courtesy of Beta Cameron—waiting for my number to be called.

Am I crazy for doing this? I wondered for the thousandth time.

"You'll be able to walk away at any time," Quinn had told me. "All the Omegas and Alphas will. This is simply meant as an opportunity to facilitate introductions between wolves who might be ready to take mates. That's it."

She'd made it sound so simple.

But I knew that wouldn't be the case.

Alphas were possessive creatures. Just as Omegas were equally possessive over their chosen Alphas.

One twitch of the nose was all it would take to identify an ideal mate.

Unfortunately, in my nearly three decades of existence, my wolf had only scented one possible match.

Yet he doesn't want us, I reminded myself.

There had to be someone somewhere who would feel differently.

And this mating program might just help me meet him.

I ran my palms along my sequined gown as I forced myself to take a steadying breath. *Forget about Cillian. He's the past. Time to focus on the future.*

As if fate were responding to my thought, I heard Quinn say, "Our thirteenth and final Omega candidate is a late addition."

I glanced down at my card again, noting the number beneath my status as an Eligible Omega Mate.

Thirteen.

I stepped forward, positioning myself right out of sight. Then a Beta swept open the curtain and smiled encouragingly at me to join the King and Queen of Blood Sector on the balcony—a balcony that served as a platform for the entire room to see.

This is it. I squared my shoulders. *No turning back now.*

With my head held high, I moved out into the proverbial spotlight.

Quinn smiled, her expression encouraging.

I returned her grin before glancing around the room below. There were too many shifters in attendance for me to focus on one in particular, so I allowed my gaze to dance around the crowd for a few beats before returning my attention to Quinn.

"Ivana is a V-Clan Omega from Blood Sector," she announced to the attendees. "Her interests are in analytics, advanced technology, and weaponry."

My lips twitched a little at that last point.

What Quinn had meant by that was that I enjoyed playing with guns. Most wolves preferred their claws and teeth. But I was an Omega. Small. *Weaker* than Alphas and Betas. A fact I'd learned at a very young age.

However, certain weapons provided me with an advantage.

Which was why I'd spent years learning how to perfect my aim.

I was one of the best shots in all of Blood Sector. Not that anyone allowed me to do anything with my talents.

Omegas were meant to be protected, not put in the line of duty.

Although, Quinn had mentioned that the Sanctuary would be different. "Your love of firing a gun will make you quite popular with Jas and the others," she'd told me.

We'll see, I thought now as I started down the staircase into the ballroom below.

Benz waited for me at the bottom, his full lips curved upward at the corner. He didn't speak, just offered me his arm as my chosen escort tonight—something I'd designated ahead of time—and led me deeper onto the dance floor as Quinn started laying out the rules for the Eligible Omega Mates program.

I barely heard her over the buzzing in my ears, my dry mouth instantly thankful for the flute of champagne Benz magically conjured.

Well, not *magically*.

He caught a server at precisely the right moment. But it might as well have been magic.

Sometimes I suspected Benz's charm was his hidden power and all his other abilities were just minor side effects of being a V-Clan wolf.

Taking another hefty sip, I listened as Kieran explained how the Alphas could enter the dating pool. They would be reviewed and vetted prior to being allowed to join. Then the Omega candidates—*myself included*—would be given files for review.

"The first official round of meet and greets will commence in a week," King Kieran said. "Tonight is simply a celebration of the future. Behave. Enjoy. And be mindful of your actions."

With that clear warning, he raised his hand to dismiss the crowd, then placed a palm on his mate's lower back and escorted her down the stairs.

Murmurs broke out around the room, the scent of intrigue heavy in the air.

My arms prickled with awareness as the feeling of being studied and admired tickled my senses.

This is just the beginning, I thought, nearly finishing my drink. *Just take a deep breath and enjoy the moment.*

"You look beautiful," Benz murmured against my ear.

"You clean up nicely, too," I told him, my gaze going to his all-black tuxedo. "Thank you for escorting me tonight."

His eyes crinkled. "It's not a hardship, I assure you." He glanced over my shoulder, then to the right. "Although, I do have a few Alphas taking my measure at the moment. And not in the way I'd like."

"And what way would you prefer?" I teased him.

Except he didn't appear to hear me because all he did was hum.

"Benz?" I prompted after an awkward moment of him ignoring me in favor of those around us.

"Well, this should be fun to watch," Benz said suddenly, his arm leaving mine. "I'll be right over there if you need me, darling."

"What?" I asked.

But he was already walking away, my glass somehow going along with him.

Because he'd taken it from my hand.

It'd been nearly empty. However, I hadn't expected him to take it. "Where are you—"

Goose bumps pebbled down my arms, a familiar presence approaching at my back.

Oh. My teeth ground together, my gaze searching for Benz so I could glare at him. But he wasn't *right over there* at all. He'd disappeared entirely. *Traitor.*

I'd told him not to—

"What the hell are you doing?"

—leave me alone in case Cillian found me.

Because I did not want to talk to him, see him, or even think about him.

And now he stood right behind me.

IVANA

Taking a deep breath, I steeled my spine and drew my brows upward as I faced Cillian.

"Excuse me?" Because *what the hell* was his problem?

Demanding that I say what I'm doing…

Isn't it obvious that I'm simply standing here in a ballroom, same as him?

"You enrolled in the Eligible Omega Mates program. Why?" he demanded.

Excuse me? I wanted to repeat.

Instead, I folded my arms across my chest and gave him the haughtiest look I could muster. "How else am I supposed to find someone *more in my league*?" Those were his words the other week, yes?

His eyebrows lifted like mine had seconds ago. "What?"

"You know, an Alpha who might appreciate my… what

was it?" I glanced upward, pretending like I didn't know every word he'd uttered that had broken my heart. "Oh, right. My *misplaced confidence* among my other *unsavory qualities*."

Repeating those descriptions did little to heal my emotional wounds. However, I did rather enjoy the confused expression rolling across Cillian's features. The Elite was rarely caught off guard, but clearly I was surprising him now.

He blinked. "I'm sorry, what?"

"Come on, you're the one who said I needed to start looking for a more appropriate mate, one who won't mind my…" I looked up again, then snapped my fingers. "My penchant for telling Alphas what to do. Maybe I'll find that Alpha through the courtship program. Perhaps he'll like my *childish games*, too."

That had his eyebrows flying upward, realization seeming to have finally cut through the layers of his stubborn mind. "Ivana—"

"It's fine, Cillian," I interjected, not wanting to discuss this further. "I already told Quinnlynn that I'll happily relocate to Night Sector. Soon enough, you won't have to worry about my unsavory company at all."

I gave him a consolatory pat on the arm, then shadowed to the other side of the room before my eyes gave away my true feelings.

Or before I said something I shouldn't.

Something heartfelt. Painful. *Depressing.*

Because just seeing him brought back all the emotions he'd evoked that night.

A night when I realized I'd been hoping and trying in vain to win the attention of an Alpha who would never see me as worthy of him.

Who would never desire me like I desired him.

Stop this, I chastised myself. *Stop thinking about him.*

Of course, this had been the entire point of asking Benz to—

"Nicely done," the Beta interjected, appearing beside me as though conjured by my thoughts. "I don't think I've ever seen Cillian look so out of sorts."

Gritting my teeth, I rotated toward my *best friend* and narrowed my gaze at him. "You had one job as my escort tonight, Benz: Don't let me talk to Cillian."

"You told me not to let you look for him or approach him or talk *about* him," Benz replied. "You said nothing about keeping him from approaching you."

My lips parted, prepared to offer a retort.

Except…

Except nothing came out.

Because he was right.

I'd told him not to let me go anywhere near Cillian. It had never even crossed my mind to tell Benz to stop Cillian from talking to me.

Because Cillian *never* sought me out.

Not once in our entire six years of knowing one another.

Unless I counted the first night we'd met, but he hadn't actually been there for me. I'd been an unexpected part of the situation. So that hardly counted.

Cillian came up to me, I marveled. *How… strange.*

And how incredibly frustrating, too.

Because now he was very much on my mind. On an evening when I'd vowed to move on. To step into my future. To stop fretting over an Alpha who didn't want me.

My fingers curled into fists, my jaw clenching as irritation sizzled along each of my nerve endings.

"Prince Cael," Benz greeted suddenly, his tone taking on a regal quality that he complemented with a bow.

"Hello," a cultured voice said in response, his accent holding a touch of English to it. "Am I interrupting?"

"Of course not," Benz replied, his head still lowered. "I'm simply Omega Ivana's escort for the evening."

"A friend, then?"

"A friend," Benz echoed.

"A *best* friend," I corrected him.

Benz's lips curled just slightly. "Yes, a best friend."

"That is a very important distinction," Prince Cael murmured. "Beta…?"

"Benz," my best friend replied, finally lifting his head.

"Cael," the Alpha said in return, the two of them shaking hands. "It seems I need to impress you almost as much as Omega Ivana."

I blinked at that, my focus shifting to the Alpha Prince.

Prince Cael and I had never met, but I knew of him. He'd attended the coronation a few weeks ago. As had Prince Tadhg, Prince Lykos, and a handful of other high-ranking V-Clan wolves.

Of course, I knew of Prince Cael before that evening, too.

He was an Alpha Prince.

Everyone knew of him.

His blue-green eyes captured and held mine as I openly evaluated him. I should probably bow or curtsy, but my wolf seemed too intrigued by this male's nearness to cower or submit.

Which was precisely the wrong way to react to an Alpha Prince.

However, he didn't admonish me for it. He merely smiled, the action making his handsome features that much more alluring.

"Why would you need to impress either of us?" I asked him. It was typically the other way around where Alpha Princes were concerned.

"Because I'll be joining the mating pool," he replied softly.

My eyebrows lifted. "But you can't relocate to Night Sector."

He chuckled and shook his head. "Indeed, I cannot. However, Kieran has given me special permission, as I require a mate for Lunar Sector."

"Oh." My brow furrowed as I considered what he was saying. "You don't have any eligible Omegas?"

"There are a few in Lunar Sector, but none that are suitable," he replied. "I'm either related to them, or they're too young."

"Hmm, I suppose that would pose a bit of a problem," I agreed, cocking my head. "Good thing King Kieran discovered more, then."

Benz cleared his throat beside me, causing me to glance at him. His turquoise eyes seemed to be trying to convey some sort of warning, one I didn't quite understand.

Had Prince Cael not been standing beside us, I'd have been tempted to demand, *What the hell is that look for?*

Except, just thinking about it provided me with the answer.

I was speaking to Prince Cael as I would anyone else.

Although, he wasn't *anyone else*. He was an *Alpha Prince*. A visiting royal from another sector. A being who required respect, exuded authority, and no doubt expected me to *submit*.

Especially as an Omega.

"Forgive me, Prince Cael," I said immediately, falling into a curtsy. "You caught me by surprise."

"On the contrary, I think you caught me by surprise," he replied, holding out a hand. "Formalities are unnecessary, as are apologies. I find your candor refreshing."

"Refreshing?" I repeated dumbly, my gaze on his hand while I maintained a curtsied position.

"Yes, *refreshing*." He waggled his fingers in my view.

I swallowed, unsure of what to say now. *What does he mean by "refreshing"?* It sounded like a compliment. But surely I'd misunderstood him.

And why is he moving his hand like that? Is he trying to tell me to stand?

"Would you like to begin anew?" he asked, causing my brow to furrow. "Perhaps I can properly introduce myself and you can return the favor? Then you can give me your beautiful gaze again rather than wasting the view on my hand."

I glanced up at him, his words so unexpected that I couldn't help it.

A pair of dimples framed his elegant smile, his eyes crinkling a bit with the action. "Hello. I'm Cael."

I straightened. "Seriously?"

"Quite serious. And you are?"

Arching a brow, I deadpanned, "Ivana."

He smirked and held out his hand again. "Lovely to meet you, Ivana."

I gave him my palm, purely because it felt natural to do so. Then I felt my own lips curling as he bent to press a kiss to the back of my hand. It was a very formal gesture, if a bit intimate. "I thought you said formalities are unnecessary?"

"They are," he said, his blue-green irises swirling with secrets as he held my gaze. "But I'll never turn down an opportunity to kiss an Omega."

"Unless you're related to the Omega, or if the Omega is too young," I replied, reiterating his claim regarding the Omegas in his sector. "Correct?"

He chuckled, releasing my hand as he stood up once more. "I like you, Ivana."

"That's not exactly an answer," I pointed out.

"When I kiss an Omega I'm related to, it's on the cheek in a brotherly kind of way." He paused, his gaze flicking upward. "Well, I suppose the same could be said about Lunar Sector's two little five-year-old hellhound Omegas, too. But that's more so because they demand kisses from me."

I smile again, entertained by his description. "So you've already been claimed, then?"

"It seems that way some days," he replied. "They're probably not going to be too enthused by me joining the mating pool."

"No, I bet not."

He lifted a shoulder. "Maybe they'll forgive me if I find a more age-appropriate mate to help me create an Alpha pup for them to fight over."

"Already planning for your future children?" I asked, my eyebrow inching upward again. "What if you and your mate create an Omega instead?"

"Then my mate and I will have to try for an Alpha the second time around," he returned without missing a beat.

"So you want multiple pups?"

"Of course. What Alpha doesn't?"

"Hmm," I hummed, considering the question. "Well—"

I very nearly replied "Cillian"—because of course my mind went *there* first—but Benz cleared his throat, interrupting my thought.

"I'm going to grab a blood champagne. Would either of you like one?" he asked. It was a smoothly delivered line, one anyone else would assume was innocently voiced.

However, I knew better.

Benz had absolutely known what I'd been about to say, and he'd effortlessly stopped me from mentioning a certain Alpha's name.

"Ah, you're taking my line," Prince Cael said, his amusement palpable. "Shouldn't I be offering to find the lovely female a drink?"

Benz grinned. "I think the *lovely female* is enjoying your conversation too much to part with your company. So I'll go handle the drinks, like a proper escort." He shot me a wink before stepping away, leaving me alone on the edge of the ballroom dance floor with the Alpha.

"Well, I daresay your best friend is rather charming," Prince Cael mused.

"I think Benz would say the same about you." Because this Alpha was clearly cut from the same cloth as Benz.

"Oh?" He feigned surprise. "You think I'm charming?"

"I think you know you're charming, My Prince," I told him.

"Just 'Cael,' please." He gifted me with another one of those alluring smiles. "We've already agreed to forgo formalities, yes?"

"Then you'll need to call me *Ivana* rather than *lovely female*," I told him.

He laughed, the sound so infectious that I couldn't stop myself from smiling in response.

Yep. Definitely a charmer, I thought, surprised by how comfortable I felt in his presence. Only Benz had ever managed to accomplish such a feat this quickly. And even he took a little bit of warming up to.

"Kieran told me I would like you," Cael said, his gaze dancing over me in obvious merriment. "He wasn't wrong."

"King Kieran told you about me?"

He nodded. "Yes. He suggested I come talk to you tonight, and I must say, I'm glad I listened."

"Why did he tell you to talk to me?" I wondered aloud.

He shrugged. "I think he was trying to ensure I joined the mating pool."

"By introducing us?"

"Yes." He cocked his head a little to the side, causing his dark locks to fall playfully across his forehead. "If it was his goal to entice me, he's succeeded."

"I thought you were joining because you need a mate?"

"I do need a mate, and I fully intend to join the pool," he replied. "But I didn't tell Kieran that. He's an ally, not a friend. Although, I'm starting to question the latter. He's proving to be quite intuitive where my needs and desires are concerned."

My cheeks heated as Cael looked me up and down, his insinuation clear.

"I hope I'm not being too forward," he said after a beat of silence. "I just don't see the point in hiding my intentions or dancing around the truth. And something tells me you feel similarly."

"I do," I admitted, swallowing.

Benz chose that exact moment to return, causing the Alpha to grin widely once more. "Ah, perfect timing, mate." He accepted one of the flutes from Benz and gave it to me before taking a second for himself.

"Thank you," I said to them both.

Benz flashed me a grin.

Cael issued his own thanks to Benz, then returned his focus to me. "A toast, then?" he asked. "To the mating games?"

Mating games, I repeated to myself. *An interesting turn of phrase.*

"Yes," I agreed, clinking my crystal glass against his. "To the mating games."

His smile was positively dazzling. "Cheers, then."

"Cheers," I returned, tapping my flute to Benz's as well.

I took a sip, the blood-laced alcohol easily sliding down my throat—an action Cael watched with interest before following suit.

It all felt so natural.

So *easy*.

And yet… I could *feel* Cillian's eyes on me.

Maybe it was just in my mind. Some hopeful part of me not wanting to let him go. My wolf *refusing* to acknowledge defeat.

I couldn't say.

But I swore I could almost hear him growling in my mind.

A fantasy, I decided. *That's all he ever was.*

However, Cael—*Prince* Cael—might just be the true fantasy.

Only time would tell.

Mating games, I thought once more. *Mating games indeed…*

CILLIAN

Fuck.

My fists clenched at my sides, my feet threatening to pace.

No. Not pace. *Run.*

Because Prince Cael was talking to Ivana.

Mine, my inner beast seemed to growl.

Not ours, I grated back at him. *Not ours at all.*

Something I'd made painstakingly clear on countless occasions. Yet seeing the hurt in her eyes mere moments ago had unnerved me.

It was as though she hadn't fully believed me… until now.

Until she overheard my conversation with Lorcan, I thought, grimacing. *Fuck. Is that why she's doing this? Why she enrolled in this social experiment between Omegas and Alphas? Because I pushed her into it through my careless words?*

"Come on, you're the one who said I needed to start

looking for a more appropriate mate," she'd said. And then she'd ended it all with, "I already told Quinnlynn that I'll happily relocate to Night Sector. Soon enough, you won't have to worry about my unsavory company at all."

That all suggested I might be to blame for her joining the Eligible Omega Mates program.

Shit. I need a drink.

Shadowing to the bar, I took a glass from the shelf and poured myself a healthy serving of amber liquid laced with blood. The bubbly crap being passed around the room definitely wouldn't be strong enough to quell my mounting mood.

"You're making the Lunar Sector Elites nervous." The words resembled a whisper on the wind as Lorcan materialized beside me. "Is there a threat I should be concerned with?"

Rather than reply, I swallowed some of my drink, my throat feeling far too dry.

Lorcan arched a brow, his expression imperious. "Cillian?"

"I'm fine." The words came out through my teeth, the bite in them unintentional, yet there.

"That's not what I asked."

"I know." I took another gulp, then grabbed the bottle to refill my glass. "Everything is fine." There, *that* was a better phrase.

But also complete and utter bullshit.

Because everything was *not* fine.

Not only did it seem that Ivana had enlisted herself as an Eligible Omega Mate because of me, but Kieran had invited me to join the eligible Alpha pool.

Feckin' bastard, I thought, irritated all over again.

He'd stopped by moments ago, his humored state clear in the cocky set of his mouth.

A mouth I'd wanted to punch.

Because he'd let Ivana join this farce of an experiment.

You look ready to kill Prince Cael, Kieran had murmured as he'd shadowed to my side. *Has he done something I should be concerned about?*

My teeth had ground together as I'd narrowed my gaze at my oldest friend. *He's flirting with Ivana.*

And?

And nothing, I'd snapped. *She's an eligible Omega, right?*

Right, he'd agreed. *Unless she's not…*

I'd said nothing. Because what was there to say? She wasn't mine. She was free to be courted. Hell, I'd *encouraged* her to pursue other Alphas.

I just hadn't expected it to be here and now.

Well, the next few weeks should be fun to observe, Kieran had mused next, his Irish lilt heavy in my mind. *Let me know if you want to be added to the suitor list. You have until tomorrow to decide…*

My fingers squeezed around my glass now as I recalled his offer, my urge to throw my drink against a nearby wall all-encompassing.

What the fuck kind of option is that? I wanted to demand, my mind nearly connecting to the Blood Sector King's.

Kieran knew I didn't want a mate.

And especially not Ivana.

She deserved so much better than a distracted Alpha who could never put her first.

Fuck. I downed my drink again and went to refill it once more, only Lorcan's hand was suddenly in the way.

"Have you heard a word I've said?"

My teeth gnashed together. That phrase was the exact same one I'd used on Lorcan just weeks ago during the coronation. He'd been too busy thinking about Kyra to listen to me. Which I'd teased him about at the time.

And then he'd taunted me about Ivana.

A conversation she apparently overheard.

Sighing, I set my empty glass down and focused on Lorcan. "I'm a little distracted."

"Clearly," he deadpanned in response. "By Ivana and Prince Cael."

Hearing him group their names together immediately had me glancing at the couple in question.

Couple, I repeated to myself. *Not. A. Fucking. Couple.*

Although, they were fucking dancing now.

When the hell did that happen?

I took a step toward them before my mind could stop me, only for Lorcan to suddenly be there, his expression darkening. "Don't. His Elites are already on edge by the way you keep staring down their prince. Think about what we would do if one of them was looking at Kieran like this."

We'd kill them on sight, I thought flatly, the words ones I allowed to enter Lorcan's mind.

Exactly, he replied, switching to a mental conversation. *They're in the back corner of the room to your left. Glance over there. See what I'm seeing. And fucking get it together.*

How would you feel if Prince Cael was waltzing around with your Omega? I countered before I could consider my words.

My Omega isn't an eligible mate, he returned. *And last I checked, you didn't consider Ivana to be* your *Omega.*

I grimaced. *It was a turn of phrase.*

He snorted. *Right.*

I just mean that an outsider is flirting with one of our Omegas. We should be protecting her, yes? It was a weak explanation, one Lorcan likely didn't accept.

Fortunately, he took pity on me and said, "This will take some getting used to." He shifted back to speaking aloud, his gaze flicking to the far corner he'd mentioned previously.

Obviously, his words were more for the Lunar Sector Elites than for me.

A way to appease them and let them know I wasn't about to kill their Alpha Prince.

My jaw ticked as I followed Lorcan's gaze to the Elites in

question. *Granger and Dixon.* Alphas. Old. But not nearly old enough to stand a chance against me.

Although, a quick sweep of their minds told me they were contemplating how to take me down should I become a problem for them.

At least, Granger's mind indicated that. Dixon's, however, was harder to hear, his thoughts murky at best.

Interesting, I mused. *It seems Dixon is capable of blocking my gifts.*

Oh? Lorcan's intrigue was piqued. *Similar to Orion? Or is he fighting you like Myon?*

The two Alphas Lorcan referenced were ones I'd interrogated a few weeks ago regarding a potential murder. Both of them had proved difficult to read. An anomaly for one in my position.

Similar to Orion, I replied, referring to the Alpha's natural ability to keep me out of his mind.

Myon had been able to thwart my attempts because he was old and powerful. However, as I wasn't currently interrogating Dixon, he had no cause to shove me out.

Hence, his talent appeared to be more intrinsic in nature.

Just like Orion.

But not like Ivana. The thought came to me unbidden, causing my gaze to return to the gorgeous blonde twirling in the arms of another Alpha. *Her mind is simply… quiet. Not a block, just soothing. Calm. A beautiful place to merely exist.*

Only, now her thoughts were wrapped up in the male waltzing her across the dance floor.

She smiled up at him, her expression a bit shy. It wasn't the same smile she often bestowed upon me—the one that brimmed with confidence and knowledge. The one that had me scowling back at her each time.

Because I hated that I couldn't have her.

That she tempted me to want to break all my rules.

That she made me want to be selfish for once in my life.

Gritting my teeth, I tore my gaze away from her. *I need to go for a run.* The words were for Lorcan. *Between Kieran's offer to let me join the mating program and Ivana's…* I trailed off, not wanting to talk about what Ivana had overheard.

Because it didn't matter.

What's done is done, I told myself, careful not to send that statement to Lorcan's mind.

Kieran and I can supervise, Lorcan murmured in reply, his gaze already on the crowd. *Everyone seems to be behaving. Even Tadhg is putting forth an effort to appear charming, and we both know how brutish he can be.*

I followed Lorcan's gaze to Tadhg as he bowed to kiss an Omega's wrist. *Sylvia,* I recognized from the candidate introductions earlier. I didn't know much about her, just that she was one of the Sanctuary Omegas.

If anything changes, we'll howl for you to return, Lorcan added, his words encouraging me to depart.

My fingers curled into fists at my sides, my throat suddenly tight.

With a stiff nod, I teleported to the other end of Iceland.

It was completely out of character for me to leave in the middle of an assignment, to allow Lorcan and Kieran to handle such a large event on their own. But I recognized that my mental state was compromised. That I couldn't focus on being a good Alpha at the moment, nor could I be trusted to protect my people.

Not when all my attention was consumed by a single Omega.

Damn it. I tore off my clothes and shifted in a blink, my wolf's massive paws landing on the ice as a growl ripped from my animal's throat.

My wolf was *furious.*

He wanted to charge back to the party and rip Prince Cael's head from his shoulders. To sink his teeth into Ivana's delicate shoulder and declare her as *his.* Then howl his claim for all the V-Clan sectors to hear.

Not going to happen, I told him, earning myself another snarl. *Run it out. Pound your frustration into the earth. But we are* not *going back for Ivana.*

He growled again, not fully understanding my words but clearly interpreting the meaning behind them.

Fortunately, he knew better than to try to challenge my authority.

However, that didn't stop him from tearing across the icy landscape on an unknown trajectory.

Fury and frustration echoed in our wake, my animal's aggression an untamable beast.

This was why I needed to run. To escape the stuffy confines of that celebration. *To turn my back on my responsibilities.*

Fuck.

I'm not this Alpha, I told myself. *I'm stronger than this.*

Yet, in this moment, I'd never felt weaker.

This—right here—is the reason I can't take a mate. Why I had to let Ivana find someone else. Because I couldn't afford to disregard my responsibilities for another wolf. Even one as beautiful and strong as Ivana.

I have to let her go. Entirely.

But for tonight, I would allow myself to mourn the loss.

Tonight, I would be selfish.

Let my wolf free.

Run off this wild energy.

And say goodbye, once and for all.

She already hated me for what I'd said. While most of it had been out of context, I wouldn't try to explain myself. I wouldn't apologize. I'd just let her… be.

My punishment for those words would come in the method of having to watch her fall for another Alpha. One who would be a better fit for her. Take her away from Blood Sector. Make her his in every way.

And leave me to my solitary fate.

The way it should be.

The way it has to be.

I would agree to help with the Eligible Omega Mates program. To guard the Omegas involved while they considered Alphas mates. But I would not be among the eligible pool—something I confirmed to Kieran now with a brief thought.

His only reply was a hum in response, the sound not saying much at all. But I didn't need his commentary. Because I would not be changing my mind.

I'd resigned myself to a solitary fate long ago.

Ivana deserves better, I reminded myself as my wolf continued to tear across the cold ground. *Ivana deserves the* best.

Something I would ensure she found since Kieran had placed me in charge of Omega security. Ivana Michaels would not settle for anything less than perfect. I'd make sure of it.

There was no other choice.

She was a prized jewel. A beauty unlike any other. An Omega with the spirit of an Alpha. And any potential mate who didn't see that—who didn't *respect* and *adore* that—wouldn't be permitted to go anywhere near her.

Because she was still mine to protect for now.

And I would protect her until someone worthy enough stepped into her path…

IVANA

A Week Later

Prince Cael.

Home: Lunar Sector.

Age: Too old to need to answer this. But if I'm asked nicely, I may give away a number.

Languages: English, Norwegian, Swedish, Russian, German, and French.

Hobbies: Ice fishing, expensive cars, technology.

Likes: Anything that makes me smile.

Dislikes: Anything that makes me frown.

A snort escaped me at those last two items sprawling across the screen, causing Quinn to glance at me. "Interested or not interested?"

"He's an Alpha Prince." I shrugged. "I think that means every Omega is interested by default."

"I'm not asking about every Omega; I'm asking about you."

"I'm not going to judge an Alpha by his profile or a little quiz he was given upon entering the dating pool," I informed her. "Courtship is too personal for that."

She nodded. "True. So should I stop showing you all these interviews, then?"

I studied the photo of Prince Cael on the screen, noting the devilish twinkle in his blue-green eyes.

The other Omegas were reviewing the same slides today, only they were looking at them in Night Sector with Kyra. Quinn had volunteered to show me the Alpha candidates here in Blood Sector, probably because she wanted to see if I reacted favorably to any of the potential mates.

Or maybe because she was just being a good friend.

The beginning of our relationship had been rather rocky since I'd despised the former princess on sight. She'd abandoned her people, something I had little respect for. But then Quinn showed me the claws beneath her gentle veneer, thus changing my mind about her almost immediately.

And now that I knew the truth about her supposed abandonment, I liked her even more.

"Ivana?" she prompted me, her near-black eyebrow arching as she held her pointer over an icon that read *Exit*.

"No, I want to see the slides." I cleared my throat. "It'll help me remember all the names for the commencement dinner tomorrow."

Thirteen Omegas.

Over thirty Alphas.

The odds were… intense. But not all that surprising. Alphas outnumbered Omegas in general, making it expected that there would be more Alpha candidates than Omega candidates.

What if none of them find me worthy enough, though? I wondered. *Would they all see me as Cillian does?*

I winced, that name one I'd told myself to stop thinking about. Yet I couldn't help it. Being here, in Quinn's private quarters, reminded me of King Kieran. And when I thought of King Kieran, I thought of his Elites.

My jaw clenched, my eyes scanning the screen before me. Only, I wasn't actually reading a word of it. Which entirely defeated the purpose of this exercise. "Can you go back a slide?" I asked, frustrated with myself for my inability to focus.

Quinn flipped back to Alpha Hawk, his almond-shaped eyes highlighted by thick, dark lashes that matched his head of black hair.

"He's Prince Tadhg's second-in-command," Quinn informed me softly. "I've met him a few times. He's quiet but seems kind."

"I assume Prince Tadhg won't be joining the program?" I guessed.

Quinn snorted. "No. He has no interest in taking a mate."

"Really?" I asked, surprised by that.

"He told Kieran, and I quote, 'I'm not interested in tying my knot anytime soon.' "

I scoffed at that. "Charming."

"Indeed," she muttered. "He's polite, but there's something about him that's never sat right with me." She shrugged. "Anyway, Alpha Hawk seems lovely, though. He'll be a good addition to the program."

I wasn't sure what to say to that, so I just nodded, then scanned the facts about him and committed them to memory. Or tried to, anyway. The mention of him being the second-in-command naturally had me thinking of another second-in-command.

A sigh nearly escaped me, but I swallowed it.

And forced myself to read the next slide.

Quinn shared several more, then paused as Alpha Grey

appeared. His glacial eyes captured mine, the intensity of them stealing the breath from my lungs.

"Wow," I whispered, rather stunned by his appearance.

His physical attributes redefined the meaning of perfection. Sculpted cheekbones. Full lips. Thick lashes the color of sand. Light blond hair that fell tousled to his broad shoulders.

"I… I don't remember seeing him last week." And I was pretty sure I would have noticed him. He was too striking in nature to forget.

"That's because he didn't attend," Quinn replied. "He remained in Lunar Sector as the acting Sector Alpha."

"He's Prince Cael's second-in-command?" I asked, surprised and also irritated. Because of course that reminded me of Cillian. *Again.*

"Sort of." She considered the screen. "I think he's more of an enforcer. He's part Z-Clan Alpha, which makes him ineligible to be a V-Clan Prince."

"Z-Clan?" I repeated, almost choking on the term. "He's part Z-Clan Alpha?"

Stars…

Z-Clan Alphas were deadly creatures. Positively violent. *Vile.*

Yet his features were almost angelic. Too beautiful to be real.

Are all Z-Clan Alphas like that? Deceivingly light to mask all the darkness inside?

"He's also part V-Clan Alpha," Quinn clarified. "His mom was a V-Clan Omega, one Prince Cael's parents saved while she was pregnant with Grey."

I swallowed. "I see."

"So he's ineligible to lead, but he's very powerful. Which is why Kyra accepted him as an Alpha for the mating program—she and Lorcan feel he could be an asset for Night Sector's security."

That made sense. His mixed heritage would certainly make him an asset.

"We'll see how the Sanctuary, erm, I mean, *Night Sector* Omegas feel about him," she said, correcting herself.

The Omega Sanctuary used to be a MacNamara family secret. Alas, the events of late had forced Quinn to share her family's legacy with the world, hence her mate announcing the creation of *Night Sector*. I suspected there was a lot more to the story than Quinn and King Kieran were letting on, but I didn't press my friend for details.

"Regardless, I agree with Kyra and Lorcan about his potential," Quinn concluded. "So we'll see how he's received."

As I hadn't yet met Alpha Grey, I didn't have an opinion. However, I did wonder how Ashlyn—a Z-Clan Omega candidate—would react to him. While I didn't know her background, I assumed she'd sought refuge in Night Sector for a reason. And that reason was likely related to her escaping a Z-Clan sector.

"Anyway," Quinn murmured, flipping to the next slide, which showcased a muscular male with dark skin and beautiful black eyes. "Alpha Ransom, Glacier Sector."

I shivered, not from the attractive man on the screen, but at the thought of his homeland. From what I understood, it was appropriately named.

It also happened to be the first sector the Eligible Omega Mates would be visiting during our upcoming V-Clan tour.

"The Alpha Princes are all supportive of our Eligible Omega Mates program, but they've expressed a desire to host the Omegas in their home sectors," Quinn had explained to me earlier today.

Apparently, it served as a way to make sure the Omegas—myself included—were comfortable with our potential mate's homeland before mating. Just in case we were called back for a visit or opted to move later in life.

It made sense.

But some of the V-Clan sectors intimidated me.

Especially Glacier Sector.

"He definitely looks like a Viking," I mused aloud, commenting on Alpha Ransom.

Quinn considered it for a moment. "The Viking Alphas I've seen have all been bigger. More intimidating. White fur, not black fur."

"You've met Viking Alphas?" I asked, surprised. "From old Europe?"

Her features darkened, her gaze narrowing slightly. "Not directly. But I've witnessed their brute strength. Alpha Ransom is much more civilized."

"Not all Viking Alphas are uncivilized," King Kieran said as he materialized in the room, his wolf ears obviously allowing him to hear our conversation before he entered.

The hairs along the back of my neck inched upward as Cillian appeared beside him, his hands clasped behind his back in that elegant way of his.

I studiously ignored him and focused on what King Kieran was saying about Viking Alphas. "Don't let the Savage Sector name fool you, darling. The Alphas there cherish their Omega mates. Perhaps not as much as we do here, but I'm guessing the two you're thinking of are anomalies among their kind."

"Like the V-Clan Alpha I scented," she muttered, causing my brows to furrow.

"Yes, him as well." King Kieran palmed her cheek and pressed a kiss to her forehead. "I still intend to hunt him for you."

"I haven't sensed him."

"I know."

"You've been listening?"

"I'm always listening, little trickster," he replied, a twinkle in his dark eyes as his hand drifted down to the noticeable bump in her abdomen. "You know that."

Quinn huffed. "It's not like I can shadow."

"We both know you're far more inventive than that."

"I think I've proved that I intend to stay."

"You have." He leaned down to press his lips to her ear. "But I've heard you thinking about hunting that Alpha, darling. To protect your Omegas. To protect our unborn child. Don't think for one second I'd allow you to go alone."

"You won't *allow* me to do anything." She sounded petulant, like they were having two entirely different conversations.

"I told you we could visit them, Quinn. Just say when, and I'll ready the jet."

She bit her cheek, her eyes still narrowed. "I have to finish preparing the Omegas."

"I know."

"Then we'll go." She sounded pleased. Not that I had any idea what they were talking about now. It seemed like they'd jumped through three or four unrelated discussions.

"All right." He brushed his lips against her temple, his expression indulgent. "I'm yours to command, My Queen. Always."

She nodded, her arms curling around him as she buried her face in his neck.

I glanced away, suddenly feeling very out of place in this obviously intimate moment between them.

In the time I'd known Quinn, she'd always been well poised and regal in nature. She was a take-no-shit Omega who stood up for those in need. But right now, she needed her Alpha's purr—something he gave her with a loud rumble of his chest.

Displays of affection were normal between them.

But this… this felt even more affectionate than usual.

She's pregnant, Cillian said into my mind. *Pregnant Omegas are often emotional.*

I glanced sharply in his direction. *Why are you in my head?*

Because your thoughts are particularly loud today, he growled. *I felt obligated to reply.*

I nearly snorted. *You can choose what to listen to.*

Yes, and I do. But you happen to be thinking about two of the names I'm always listening for—Quinn and Kieran.

Obviously, I'm not a threat, I fired back at him. *So tune me out.*

I wish I could. Irritation glittered in his near-black irises, the expression one I was all too familiar with.

Because Cillian always glowered at me this way—like I was a menace to his sanity.

How did I ever mistake this glare for anything other than disdain? I wondered, searching his expression now. *How did I ever think there could be more between us?*

A hint of something else crossed his features. An emotion that looked a hell of a lot like *pity*.

Ivana—

Don't, I snapped. *Get out of my head.*

It was the last place I wanted him to be. He didn't need to hear about my heartbreak or my ridiculous thoughts about what I'd hoped we would one day be. It was none of his business.

I was an Eligible Omega Mate now. Determined to find a new Alpha. Hell-bent on leaving this sector. On leaving *him*.

"Can you send me the rest of the files, Quinn?" I asked, my attention returning to her. She was no longer hugging King Kieran but glancing back and forth between me and Cillian. "Or I'll just review the ones I've missed with the others before the commencement dinner tomorrow?"

The suggestion was phrased as a question because I was already backing away toward the door.

"I appreciate you letting me see the profiles, but… I…" I

cleared my throat. "I know you have better uses for your time."

She frowned at me. "I really don't mind, Ivana."

"I know you don't. But…" I trailed off, my gaze flitting to King Kieran before flickering over to a scowling Cillian.

I winced.

It wasn't like me to run away from an altercation. Hell, I used to crave them with Cillian. But now… now I just… I just wanted to move on.

"I'll email them to you," Quinn said softly. "Let me know if any strike your fancy."

I wouldn't be doing that. However, I nodded anyway. Primarily because I wanted to disappear. "Thank you." I turned, only to run into Cillian's chest.

Because the bastard had shadowed across the room to block my exit. "I'll walk you home." His deep tones were underlined in authority, his words not an offer or a request but a demand.

A month ago, that order would have made me ecstatic. It would have inspired hope that Cillian finally saw me as a potential mate.

But now I knew better.

Cillian didn't want me. He considered me to be an irritation, an Omega full of *unsavory qualities* and completely out of his league.

And fuck if I was going to trouble him further by accepting his version of a "pity pat." "I'll escort myself home, thank you." I gave him a brief curtsy—a show of formal respect—and attempted to move around him.

Except he caught my hip in his unyielding grasp. "Ivana."

"Have a good night, Alpha Cillian," I whispered.

Because I didn't want to hear what he had to say. It would probably just be another placating statement. Or worse, a demand that I let him walk me home.

Soon, I'll be part of another sector, I thought, aware he could likely hear the words. *And you'll never have to put up with me again.*

With that, I blinked out of existence and shadowed myself to my apartment.

I had better things to do than worry about Cillian's pity.

Such as figuring out how to stop comparing every candidate to the Elite in question.

Stars, I muttered to myself. There were over thirty Alphas interested in taking a mate. And one of them was even a Sector Prince.

Prince Cael.

Handsome. Cunning. Flirty. Entertaining.

A perfect catch.

If only my inner wolf agreed…

Sighing, I collapsed onto my bed and closed my eyes.

Forget Blood Sector, I told my animal. *Forget Cillian. That's our past. It's time to focus on the future.*

CILLIAN

Soon, I'll be part of another sector. And you'll never have to put up with me again.

Ivana's thoughts from yesterday lingered in my mind, primarily because I hadn't expected them to pack such a punch.

It'd taken physical restraint not to shadow after her and explain myself to her. To make her understand that I didn't find her irritating. I found her to be far too enticing, which irritated me—an entirely different concept than I'd led her to believe.

And I also didn't dislike her presence or feel she was beneath me. Rather, I considered her *above* me, and I hated how much I craved her.

The female tempted me into distraction. *Constantly*.

And now was no different.

How a woman could be this alluring while eating soup was beyond me. But I could hardly keep my eyes off of her. Which was a problem because I had a room full of Alphas to monitor and supervise.

I had most of them under my control already, my power curling around them like an invisible leash. My usual list of words I monitored for mentally had increased exponentially, my mind scanning the room for any hint of a threat.

So far, the only alarming thoughts were around *mating*.

Primarily because some of those thoughts swirled around Ivana's name.

Alpha Ransom had taken a particular interest in her, choosing to sit beside her for the meal while Prince Cael sat across from her.

Both men were trying to engage her in conversation. Cael appeared to be winning, his charm highlighted in the tilt of his lips as he gazed fondly in my Omega's direction.

Not my Omega, I corrected myself, my jaw clenching as I forced myself to scan the rest of the room.

Thirteen Omegas.

Thirty-one Alphas.

Technically, there should be thirty-two Alphas in attendance. However, Grey had stayed behind in Lunar Sector. Prince Cael hadn't elaborated on why, just stated that Grey was still interested and intended to attend future events.

Hence, the thirty-one eligible Alphas seated around the massive dining hall of The MacNamara—a renovated entertainment venue that Kieran had rebuilt to honor his mate's family. It was a suitable location for this commencement dinner, not just because of the size, but because of the layers of hidden security inside.

There were cameras everywhere.

All of which were being monitored by Lorcan right now. He'd chosen to remain hidden with Kyra, leaving me as the primary guard on duty. It was a show of power, one meant to underline my authority and the confidence both Lorcan and Kieran had in my ability to control thirty-one Alphas.

Of course, I had two lieutenants on staff, neither of whom I'd personally vetted.

One was Fritz, an Omega Sanctuary Protector. He'd recently royally fucked up by letting a Vampire Alpha manipulate his mind.

Letting might be the wrong term. More like he'd been taken advantage of and used against his will.

Regardless, that hint of weakness made me wary about trusting him. His assignment here was meant as a way to earn back some favor among his fellow Omegas. Or maybe he felt this was his penance. Either way, he'd volunteered to assist, and Lorcan had granted approval for the request.

Benz was the other one in the room under my command. The Beta had offered his services to Kieran—not to me—and my best friend had obliged him without my consent.

Not that he actually needed my consent. It took balls to offer oneself up to the Blood Sector King like that. But it would have been a sign of respect to also speak with me on the topic.

Of course, the last hour in his presence told me why he hadn't bothered to speak to me. When it came to respect, that didn't exist for him where I was concerned.

Because I'd hurt his best friend.

Ivana.

My gaze instantly returned to her just in time for her to giggle at something Ransom had just said. Or *muttered* was likely a more appropriate term because the Alpha seemed to speak in dry tones rather than smooth ones.

It marked him as quite opposite to Prince Cael, making me morbidly curious as to whom Ivana preferred. Or if she even liked either of them.

But I refused to poke inside her head.

I didn't trust myself not to react violently.

Clearing my throat, I once again scanned the dining hall, my mind registering all the thoughts and cataloging them as required.

No threats.

No dark intentions.

Just a hum of mating potential. One that leaves me with an odd sense of longing deep inside. Because I would never experience this. I couldn't allow it.

I forced my expression to remain neutral as I stood along the sidelines, observing, listening, *secretly wanting*.

Time ticked by too slowly, my wolf pacing inside with the need for a long, hard run.

This was the life I'd vowed to lead. The punishment I deserved. Even if the sins I sought penance for weren't necessarily my own.

Anything of importance to report? Kieran drawled into my mind, pulling me from the void known as my past.

If there were, I would have reported it, I replied.

He snorted. *Someone's in a mood.*

I've been listening to Benz assassinate my character for the last three or four hours, I growled, pulling on the first excuse I could muster. *How am I supposed to rely on him for security assistance when he despises his superior?*

I'm certain he's not the first disgruntled Beta to step into your path, my oldest friend returned. *Earn his respect like you have the others'.*

I'm not sure that's possible. He's under the misconception that I've led his best friend on and hates me for rejecting her.

Benz is best friends with Ivana? Kieran deadpanned. *Fascinating. I had no idea.*

I nearly grunted out loud. *Liar.*

Would I lie about something so trivial?

Yes. Because Kieran loved to meddle. At least when it came to my life. Politics, he despised. Fucking with me, he adored.

Hmm, he hummed into my mind, the sound

noncommittal. *How is Ivana faring? Do you think she'll find a suitable mate?*

Your goading isn't going to work.

I'm not goading. I'm inquiring about a female under my protection.

All Omegas are under your protection, I immediately pointed out. *You're the fucking King.*

Indeed. He sounded far too amused. Probably because he could hear my irritation. Which meant his goading was working, despite my claim to the contrary.

I need to focus, I muttered at him. *Kindly fuck off,* Sire.

His chuckle rolled through my mind, causing my hands to fist at my sides.

He was one of the few minds I constantly remained connected to, and I was seriously regretting that instinct right now. If his security wasn't my primary priority in life, I'd block him.

Alas, I had to remain open to him in case he needed me.

The evening is almost over, Cillian, he murmured, ignoring my request for him to fuck off. *Go for a run afterward. You clearly need it.*

I didn't bother replying. There was nothing important to say, nor was I in the mood for more bantering.

Leaning against the wall behind me, I scanned all the minds again. Most of the Omegas and Alphas were standing now, socializing around the room over dessert drinks—many of which were laced with blood.

Ivana was in the center of a group, conversing with Cael again. His two Elites were right behind him, their gazes as vigilant as my own.

Which naturally meant they kept wandering to me, as I was the biggest known threat in the room. Someone who could easily challenge their prince for his sector.

Not that I had any desire to play in the land of Alpha Princes.

But no matter how many times I proclaimed that out loud, no one believed me. Kieran included.

Maybe if I voice it directly into Dixon's and Granger's minds, they'll believe me, I thought darkly.

However, Dixon still remained blocked.

I studied the muscular male, noting his similar features to Cael's. One could definitely tell they were related, only Dixon's eyes were solid green, not blue-green like his brother's.

And both men appear to possess natural barriers within their minds, I realized as I scanned the surface of Cael's thoughts.

I could hear bits and pieces, enough to know he harbored no ill will toward Ivana. But the mental musings were mere fragments, not complete statements.

My ability ignited, the challenge tempting me to dig deeper.

Only for Cael's voice to suddenly pierce my thoughts. *I can feel that, Cillian. I believe my intentions in your sector are clear. However, if you require further vetting of said intentions, I'll be happy to remain behind to discuss them in depth.*

My gaze narrowed. *You're blocking me.*

I am.

Why?

Because my thoughts are my own. His blue-green gaze lifted to meet mine, his irises flickering with mild irritation. *While some Alpha Princes may be a threat, I am not one of them.*

That's an interesting take, I replied. *Which Alpha Princes are threats, in your opinion?*

A conversation for another day, perhaps, he returned. *All you need to know right now is that I'm not a threat.*

You are, I told him without missing a beat. *The biggest one in the room.*

He arched a brow. *Do you wish to measure our knots, Cillian?*

I'm not challenging you, Cael. Just stating a fact.

Then allow me to reciprocate, he drawled. *You're an equal threat, yet I'm not letting that ruin my evening. I suggest you do the same.*

He dismissed me by returning his focus to a frowning Ivana, his lips curling into an apologetic smile. "I'm sorry, love. Where were we?" He reached forward to tuck one of her stray white-blonde strands behind her ear.

I wasn't sure what bothered me more—his choice of endearment or him touching her.

"You were telling me about your underground roads," she said slowly, her gaze dancing from him to me and back again. "Is Cillian bothering you?"

Cael chuckled. "No. He's just being protective."

Her brow furrowed. *Over what?* she wondered.

You, I nearly answered.

But instead, I left them to their conversation and shadowed to a darker part of the room. I didn't want to be seen or heard or *felt*. I wanted to disappear and observe in silence.

Which was precisely what I did for the next two long hours until finally the commencement event was brought to an end.

I left Fritz and Benz in charge of escorting the Alphas to their guest quarters—several of them were remaining in Blood Sector for the week. Some already lived here. And a few were traveling back to their home sectors.

Thankfully, Cael was among that latter group.

He shot me a wink before shadowing off with his two Elites. I didn't outwardly reply. But inside, my animal growled.

Something about that had felt like a challenge.

And it was a challenge I did not want to entertain.

He could keep Lunar Sector to himself. I was perfectly content here in Blood Sector.

Well, mostly content.

Ivana had left without an escort, choosing to shadow herself back to her nest. Presumably, anyway.

Ignoring the desire to chase after her, I led our visiting Omegas back to their guest suites within Kieran and

Quinnlynn's palace—which was more like an apartment building than a traditional royal residence.

Once they were secure, I mentally informed Kieran of the uneventful night and shadowed back to my den.

Except nothing felt right down here.

There were too many foreign Alphas in our sector. *On our land.*

And Ivana had chosen to sleep apart from the other Omegas.

"Fuck," I muttered, running my fingers through my hair. I should have pushed harder to have her room with the others. It made the most sense from a security standpoint, especially with the thirty-one visiting Alphas.

My leash around said Alphas tightened, my mind scanning all of theirs for ill intentions out of habit.

Nothing.

Not a single bad thought.

And yet, I couldn't shake the feeling something was wrong.

Pacing, I tried to reach for Ivana's mind. But it was quiet. Like always. Peaceful. Not giving me a single statement to focus on.

She was safe.

Unless someone is interfering, I thought, pausing mid-stride. *No. That's impossible.*

And yet, Cael's and Dixon's capabilities of thwarting my natural talents had me second-guessing my entire existence.

My jaw clenched. *You've lost the plot,* I told myself. *Stop with this nonsense.*

Yet that irritation in my chest wouldn't abate. It just kept thrumming. Prickling at my instincts. Causing my hands to curl and uncurl.

I growled, my eyes slamming closed as I fought the urge coming over me to shadow.

Checking my watch, my teeth only ground harder.

It'd been nearly ninety minutes since I'd last seen Ivana.

Maybe if I just… checked on her… I'd feel better. I could rid myself of this sensation.

"Fine," I growled, shadowing to the street outside of her building.

The sun was already inching up over the horizon, the commencement dinner having run into the early hours of the morning.

We were night creatures by nature, preferring to sleep during the day. However, the sun didn't bother us like it did other beings in our world.

If anything, the sun merely served as an irritant to our eyes.

Sighing, I leaned against the building and tried to focus on Ivana's mind again.

Still silent, I muttered, my gaze narrowing.

Without thinking it through, I shadowed to her floor and listened again.

When it was still too quiet, I went to her door and lifted my hand to knock.

Only to hear a soft moan from inside, one that put my enhanced senses immediately on alert. The world disappeared and reappeared around me in a blink, the hallway instantly replaced by Ivana's inner sanctuary.

While I knew where she lived, I'd never actually visited her here before. However, my nose led me right to her nest.

And the petite Omega curled up in the sheets.

My lips parted at the stunning sight, her hair tousled in a brilliant golden halo that practically glowed despite the darkness of her room.

Fuck. I was instantly hard at the sight, my knot pulsing with a need to join her. *Shadow,* I commanded myself. *Leave. Now.*

Except another one of those delicious sounds parted her full lips, the beckoning call lighting my veins on fire.

My chest tingled with the need to purr.

And my dick…

No. Fuck no. I took a forceful step backward. *Not happening.*

This mating program was fucking with my head.

I needed to go for that run. To embrace my animal's desire to shift and—

"Cillian," Ivana whispered, causing my eyes to widen.

Shit. I swallowed, my mouth suddenly dry. Because I didn't know how to explain why I was here. Why I was standing next to her nest with a fucking hard-on. "Ivana, I—"

"*Ohhh, Cillian…*" She curled into a tighter ball, the scent of her slick hitting me with the force of an avalanche, stealing the breath from my lungs.

A growl tightened my chest, overtaking the urge to purr, my instinct to *rut* almost overwhelming my sense of reason.

Ivana moaned again, her lips parting in a gasp as she tossed her head back, her nostrils flaring.

Yet her eyes remained closed while she whispered my name once more.

A dream, I realized through the haze of arousal clouding my thoughts. *She's dreaming of me…*

Fuck, I really needed to shadow out of here before I took advantage of her mind and observed her inner fantasies.

Or worse, stayed here and made her dream come true.

With another growl, I forced myself to leave.

Except I couldn't get farther than her living room.

I hovered by the door, incapable of teleporting through it, and inhaled her alluring scent.

Reveled in it.

Pretended for just a second that it was truly meant for me. That her sweet slick could be mine. That those fantasies of hers could become a reality.

But as her pulse escalated, I broke free from the intoxicating lust chaining me to her presence.

Shadowed to an ice field.

Ripped off my clothes.
Shifted.
And *ran*.

PART III

Dear Stars,

I keep dreaming of Cillian. What's even stranger is that his scent seems to be clinging to my nest.

I'm not sure why.

He's never been in my room before.

Not like I haven't invited him, though. Every heat cycle, he was the only Alpha on my list. But he never came. Never once visited.

Because he never wanted me like I wanted him.

Maybe I'll be mated for my next heat cycle.

Maybe I'll finally experience a proper knot.

Maybe I'll finally experience... love.

Yours,
Ivana

IVANA

A Few Days Later

I STARED at my last journal entry, my pen tapping the page. Hoping for love seemed a bit extreme. Maybe *lust* was a more accurate term.

But that was entirely my problem.

I'd met several Alphas now, all of them handsome and charming and interested in taking a mate, yet Cillian continued to star in my dreams.

And his scent, I thought, shivering. *His scent has been everywhere.*

All over my nest.

My rooms.

Almost as though he'd visited my personal space.

Which was insane. Oh, he'd been invited there countless times, but he'd never accepted the offer. He'd left me to suffer my heats alone instead.

Part of it was my fault. Blood Sector Omegas were allowed to make a list of Alphas to help satisfy our estrous cycles, and I'd only ever noted Cillian as my choice.

But he never showed up, I muttered to myself, wincing. *He just left me there to suffer, year after year.*

I tried not to blame him. Not completely, anyway.

I could have asked for another Alpha.

However, I'd never wanted anyone else.

And this whole mating program was making me wonder if I would ever desire another man.

Dear Stars, I wrote after turning to a clean page. *Maybe I'm destined to be alone. Prince Cael is perfectly lovely. But I just don't feel that spark. Not like I do with—*

I angrily crossed out the entry and flipped my journal over on the table, irritated with my inner musings.

This is ridiculous, I told myself.

I hadn't seen Cillian in five days. Not since the commencement dinner, where he'd glared daggers at Prince Cael.

"He's just being protective," Prince Cael had said.

Protective of what? I'd wanted to ask.

Instead, all I'd managed was an ineloquent "Oh."

Then our conversation had returned to discussion of the underground road system in Lunar Sector—something I very much wanted to see.

Unfortunately, Lunar Sector was stop number three on our program tour.

Glacier Sector was up first.

I glanced out the window beside me, intrigued by the fluffy clouds in the sky around us. They glittered in the moonlight, providing an almost eerie glow. This was only my second time traveling in this manner, my ability to shadow rendering flying an unnecessary mode of transportation.

However, not all the Omegas in the program could teleport.

Hence, we were flying to Glacier Sector instead of shadowing there.

All of the Eligible Alpha Mates were invited to meet us on-site, but the Glacier Sector Alphas were given first dibs on selecting their "dates" for the week.

Alpha Ransom had selected me.

My lips pursed to the side as I refocused on my journal once more.

Dear Stars, I started again. *The Omegas on the jet feel nervous. Or maybe it's just me. I've never really "dated" an Alpha before. But Alpha Ransom seems nice. Quiet, too. However, his eyes—*

"Do you mind if I sit here?" a soft voice asked, drawing my attention away from my pen and up to a pair of big blue eyes.

Ashlyn.

I blinked at her, somewhat surprised she'd chosen my quiet booth-like corner in the back of the jet. All the other Omegas were busy chatting on the sofas near the front, their excitement a hum of electricity in the air. I'd been too caught up in my thoughts to join them.

"Um, no. Go for it," I said, gesturing to the open seat across from me.

She gave me a small smile and slipped onto the oversized chair, her petite form practically engulfed by the beige leather behind her. "Thanks." She pulled out a notebook and a pen. "I have a vision that's driving me crazy. I need to write it down, and this seemed like the best place to do that."

"A vision?" I repeated.

"Mm-hmm," she hummed, already scribbling on a blank page.

Z-Clan Omegas were known to be intuitive by nature,

capable of reading auras of those around them. It was a unique talent, one that their Alphas tended to abuse.

While Z-Clan Omegas were gifted with rare psychic abilities, the Z-Clan Alphas were blessed with dominance and strength. Which made them more feral in nature, especially when it came to mastering their Omega mates.

I'd never had the displeasure of meeting a Z-Clan Alpha, and I hoped to never experience it in my life as well.

However, Ashlyn… I suspected she'd known several in her existence.

"I can feel your concern, but I'm fine," she murmured in that soft voice of hers. "The past is the past. It's the future that concerns me more." She paused then to look up at me. "Can I tell you a secret?"

She had a dreamlike quality to her gaze, one that had me wondering if she was actually seeing me or something else. "Uh, sure," I offered, a bit confused by this unexpected interaction.

"I love to journal." She sounded quite pleased with this *secret* of hers. "I have so many notebooks filled with musings back in my nest. But only someone who knows where to look can find my diaries."

"I see."

She smiled. "You don't, but you will." She leaned forward. "I hide my journals beneath my nest, under the floorboards. That's my secret."

"And you're telling me this because…?"

She shrugged. "In case you ever need to know something."

I stared at her. "Is there something I should know?"

"A great many things, I'm sure," she sighed. "But that's the problem with visions. I can only see, never share. However, just in case…" She trailed off and returned to her journal as though she hadn't just been in the middle of a statement.

I was half tempted to lean forward and read her cursive-like scrawl. Alas, that would be rude.

What a strange Omega, I thought, observing her as she scribbled words in her journal. I would have to mention this to Quinn.

Unless this was normal behavior for the Z-Clan Omega?

I really didn't know.

When she made no move to continue speaking, I returned to my own musings about Ransom's handsome features.

Dark hair.

Brown skin.

Kind eyes.

Full lips.

Broad shoulders.

I chewed the inside of my cheek, my pen tapping against my jaw as I tried to define his quiet personality in my head. Except that was all I could say—*he's quiet.*

Maybe our date this week would awaken something more profound inside my mind.

Cillian would be forced to keep his distance. Not that he would have an issue with that. He'd done a fine job all week and hadn't even acknowledged me upon boarding the jet. Now he was at the helm with Benz, sitting in a copilot seat while my best friend flew the jet. I couldn't see them from back here.

Good riddance, I decided, forcing my thoughts to return to Ransom.

Only, I could sense Ashlyn staring at me again, which caused me to peek up at her in kind. "Can I tell you something else? A warning, more than a secret?"

I frowned, the latter statement—which she worded as a question—sounding rather ominous. "Um, yes?"

She glanced around, then slowly rotated her notebook toward me so I could see the words on the page.

Be careful of Prince Cael, her elegant scrawl read. *He's surrounded by darkness.*

My eyebrows rose. "What?"

She brushed her finger over her lips, then looked over her shoulder while pointing at her ear.

My brow furrowed. "I don't understand."

She sighed and picked up her pen again to write, *Wolf ears, Ivana. Everyone can hear us. And this is not something that can be heard.*

I nearly responded out loud but decided to play her game and jotted down a few words of my own. *If Prince Cael is dangerous, then you need to tell Quinn.*

She shook her head. *He's not dangerous,* she replied with her pen. *The darkness around him… I don't know how to explain this. Just… be careful, okay?*

I stared at her, then pointed to my statement once more.

Her blue eyes narrowed. "You really are a stubborn wolf."

My lips parted. "Excuse me?"

She smiled. "It's not an insult, Ivana. It's a compliment. If we had more time, I think we would be great friends." She glanced out the window. "Alas, we're about to land."

With that, she gathered her journal and flounced off to the front of the jet, her long white-blonde hair flowing in her wake.

I blinked at her. *What the fuck just happened?*

She tried to warn me about Prince Cael, then blatantly ignored my… I blinked down at my notebook to see the page I'd been writing on torn off at the edges.

She'd taken my reply.

How…? I hadn't even heard the paper rip.

Ashlyn's giggle traveled back to me as one of the other Omegas whispered something into her ear. I met the female's brown eyes, her name something that began with an *S.*

Whatever she was saying, it was clearly about me.

And Ashlyn found it humorous.

I narrowed my gaze. I was all too familiar with the mean-girl mentality, having shared a building with several of them these last few years.

Miranda, an unmated Omega with her heart set on

landing an Alpha Prince, had tried to make my life a living hell when I'd first arrived in Blood Sector. She'd made it quite clear that Kieran belonged to her and no one else.

Except he hadn't belonged to her at all.

He'd been chosen by Quinn over a century ago. Only, the princess had run away before their mating was complete, leaving Kieran in charge of Blood Sector in her absence.

That had made Kieran eligible in Miranda's eyes. Unfortunately for her, he hadn't been interested.

But that hadn't stopped her from being the mean-girl queen of the Omegas in Blood Sector.

And now it seemed I'd met a few more.

Be careful of Prince Cael, Ashlyn had written.

I nearly snorted now.

I'd been worried for a second, but clearly the little Z-Clan Omega was playing a game with me. She probably wanted Cael for herself. And what better way to claim him than to chase away any competition?

Cael seemed perfectly fine to me. Charming. Handsome. *Interested in mating.*

Yeah, I wasn't going to avoid him. If he continued to seek me out, I'd answer in kind.

Maybe a kiss will help ignite some of those butterflies in my belly, I mused.

Of course, Cillian had never needed to kiss me to create that feeling. He had simply needed to exist.

My teeth ground together as my attention shifted from the tittering Omegas to the front of the jet. I still couldn't see him or Benz, which was probably a good thing.

But I would be seeing them soon.

Because Ashlyn hadn't been lying about us descending.

The cabin pressure was changing with each passing second as we angled downward in the sky toward our frosty destination.

I ripped my gaze away from the closed door at the front

and looked out the window to see an endless sea of water. Even from here, I could tell it was cold.

We'd flown northeast, heading toward what used to be known as the Russian Archipelago. I wasn't alive during that time period, but I'd learned about it after arriving in Blood Sector.

It's going to be so cold, I thought as ice caps appeared in the distance. *Very, very cold.*

I swallowed, my nerves twisting as the jet angled for the frozen land ahead.

I hadn't left Blood Sector since I'd arrived all those years ago. There hadn't really been an opportunity to travel. But even if there had been, I wouldn't have left.

Not after how hard I'd fought to find safety.

Away from my family.

From my evil father.

My eyes closed, my past threatening to assault my mind. *Blood. Tears. An array of violence. Cillian's face as he found me nearly frozen in that frigid hole.*

He'd been like a dark knight, kneeling above me, his near-black eyes glittering with concern.

His arms had been so warm. So protective. So *right.*

I'd known right then and there that I belonged to him.

But he'd never really been mine.

That thought haunted me as the jet settled on the ground, the sensation causing several of the Omegas to gasp about the "updated technology." I wasn't sure what they'd meant. My one and only flight had been just like this.

"More like a rocket ship than a plane," I overheard one of them whispering.

"I told you it would be fun," another said.

"Your definition of *fun* differs from mine," someone else groused.

I really needed to learn their names, but I'd always been more of a loner. The only reason I knew Ashlyn's identity was because of her origin—she was the only Z-Clan Omega in the group.

Kimmi was a Vampire Omega.

And Jane was a W-Clan Omega.

Everyone else was a V-Clan Omega like me. Those were the names I was struggling to memorize. The Alpha identities had felt more important, but these Omegas were my future neighbors. So I really should focus on them.

Except that brunette talking to Ashlyn, I decided. The mean-girl clique could go kick rocks for all I cared.

The door to the pilot cabin opened, causing goose bumps to pebble down my arms as Cillian appeared. His eyes instantly scanned the interior, though he didn't quite reach me before he focused on the exterior exit.

All the Omegas fell quiet, their focus on Cillian.

A few of them stared at him with open interest, his dominance a palpable presence that seduced everyone and everything in his orbit.

He ignored them all, his mind likely scanning all of those outside.

I could practically hear him leashing all of Glacier Sector with his power, taking control of every single being with a thorough sweep of his mind.

His power hummed along my skin, his abilities bordering on terrifying.

He was an Alpha Prince without the title, his ancient bloodline evident in his quiet prowess.

After a long, tense moment, he moved to the exterior door and pressed a button. A series of locks disengaged as the cabin fully depressurized around us. Then a jolt of icy air assaulted the cabin. That was *without* the door even being open.

"Coats," Cillian said, his voice quiet yet underlined with authority.

Everyone inside obeyed, grabbing the jackets we'd been provided before takeoff and pulling them on. Only, he didn't bother to don one himself. He merely opened the door in his jeans and long thermal sweater.

It was a show of strength. A way of saying without words that he felt completely unaffected by this sector's chilling energy.

Part of me had wondered if the point of these sector visits was actually a way of forming political alliances with the other V-Clan Princes. It seemed like something Kieran would orchestrate under the guise of a mating program. And Cillian would absolutely be the one he'd send to deliver his quiet message of authority.

Because Cillian was the politically savvy one of the trio. He also served as a unique symbol of power. He could be a prince, yet he chose to serve Kieran. Which essentially meant Blood Sector had two very capable Alphas at the helm, thus securing their position at the top of the V-Clan hierarchy.

"Prince Lykos," Cillian greeted.

"Alpha Cillian," a cool voice replied from outside.

Silence descended, creating an even more violent chill in the air.

Because the Alphas were evaluating one another.

Or perhaps even engaged in a silent conversation.

My stomach twisted as I studied Cillian's features, noting the subtle tic in his jaw. Otherwise, his expression gave nothing away. As calm as ever. *The quintessential politician.*

But he wasn't looking away from the other man. No nods. No signs of subtle submission.

Prince Lykos might be in charge here, but Cillian wouldn't bow to him. Because he didn't have to. He was a being of equal power, something I felt him highlight with a not-so-subtle sweep of his mental presence.

I could almost always sense his gift. It resembled a warm caress I constantly craved yet very rarely felt. However, I reveled in it now, loving the way it calmed my inner wolf.

Protected, she seemed to say. *Safe.*

Because that was how Cillian had always made us feel from the very first moment we'd met.

I nearly closed my eyes, lost to that warmth. But it left my mind in the next instant as Prince Lykos said, "Welcome to Glacier Sector. Shall we start with a tour?"

CILLIAN

Ivana's natural perfume wrapped around my neck like a fucking noose.

Every inhale reminded me of the other morning in her room.

And each morning since, I thought darkly.

Because yeah, I kept going back. Like a damn lunatic, I'd shadowed to her building every morning under the guise of checking on her.

Then I'd waited and listened for those beautiful moans of hers.

Moans that resembled *my name*.

Moans that I took home with me.

Moans that haunted my mind while I'd grabbed my knot and created my own fantasies of her within my mind.

It was… a problem. An addiction. *Fucking. Wrong.*

Ivana had always been my one temptation, and this mating program had worsened my craving for her.

My jaw tightened as I forced my mind away from the temptation walking behind me and scanned our surroundings for threats once more.

Prince Lykos hadn't appreciated me leashing his Alphas upon our arrival, but fuck if I cared about his comfort. I had thirteen Omegas to protect in a foreign land, one I'd only visited a handful of times before. The landscape was a bit too cold for my taste. And the magic here irritated my senses.

My wolf bristled inside as though to agree, his desire to run chilled by the frigid air clawing at my exposed skin. No amount of fur could fight this frozen climate.

Only enchantments would do.

I'd already woven one across my being, the shield thin yet functional. If I didn't have an entire island of Alphas to monitor, I might have expended more energy in thickening the barrier. Alas, I had to keep some residual power inside me in the off chance I needed to fight.

Of course, Prince Lykos would be a fool if he tried to harm the Omegas under my care. I was here as an extended arm of the Blood Sector King. An assault against me would serve as an assault against Kieran himself.

And no sane wolf wanted to challenge Kieran O'Callaghan.

Well, a few had considered it once upon a time. Prince Tadhg, for example. He'd expressed his doubt at Kieran's ability to rule. He hadn't been too keen on Quinnlynn's choice for King, either. But so far, he'd stayed in Alpha Sector—his home to rule—and hadn't posed any true threats.

If and when he did, he'd die.

Because while he was powerful in his own right, he was no Kieran. No one compared to Kieran.

"This place reminds me of home," one of the Omegas whispered behind me.

Sylvia, I recognized, her mind loud and filled with awe as she took in the ice-like buildings before us.

"Yeah," another replied.

Prince Lykos glanced backward with curiosity but didn't comment. He'd clearly overheard the comment and likely understood the compliment underlying it.

These Omegas were used to ice and snow. They loved it.

Well, almost all of them, anyway.

Ivana remained quiet, her mind giving nothing away.

I nearly looked at her, my desire to know her innermost thoughts grating against my instincts. *Would those icy eyes of hers give something away? Would she tell me her thoughts if I asked?*

Gritting my teeth, I forced the inane concept from my mind and focused on the task at hand—protecting the Omegas.

I barely listened to anything Prince Lykos said as he explained the sector infrastructure, talking about enchantments that kept the ice from melting while allowing the inhabitants to flourish.

Alphas, Betas, and a handful of Omegas met us in the town square—a spacious ice rink in the middle of the frost-covered town—and a welcome party ensued.

Nothing too extravagant.

Just some drinks featuring Glacier Sector's specialty, blood-laced vodka, along with a few mystic snacks. The latter were basically appetizers kept warm with spells.

I indulged in a few bites but declined the alcohol. Not because it would impair me, but because I didn't particularly care for vodka.

Benz and Fritz followed suit, their eyes on the crowd as our Omegas mingled with the inhabitants of Glacier Sector. Most of the Alphas from the mating program were here, but a handful were notably missing. Prince Cael being among those on the short list.

Ivana didn't seem to mind, though. She was too busy chatting with Ransom to notice.

Although, *chatting* might be too loose a term. She wasn't really talking, just standing near him and observing the crowd alongside him.

It seemed his verbal skills from dinner the other night were indeed not outshined by Prince Cael; the Alpha simply didn't speak.

Not a good match for Ivana, I thought with an internal snort. She needed someone who enjoyed her voice, not someone who would tell her to be quiet.

I grabbed a water from a nearby tray and downed it, then forced my gaze away from her to focus on the crowd once more.

Time seemed to tick on at a snail's pace. However, when Prince Lykos finally called an end to the celebration, only two hours had actually passed since our arrival.

This is going to be a long fucking week, I muttered to myself as Prince Lykos led us all to our accommodations.

"Don't let the ice fool you," he said before stepping onto a street lined with igloos. "Inside, you'll find the living quarters to be warm and comfortable."

Several of the Omegas expressed excitement in response.

"Each lodging accommodates two guests," Prince Lykos went on. "I've already assigned your igloos for the duration of your stay, based on the information Queen Quinnlynn provided. So up first, we have Ashlyn and Sylvia."

He gave the Z-Clan Omega a doting smile before searching for Sylvia. When the petite blonde stepped forward, he grinned at her as well and waved them off to their igloo.

"I'm going to need a copy of that accommodation list," I told him as we continued forward.

His dark brow inched upward. "Your King and Queen didn't provide you with a copy?"

My jaw threatened to tick at that question. It insinuated something I didn't appreciate—*distrust.*

"No." I flashed him a tight smile, one I knew he saw right through. But just in case he didn't, I added, "Kieran focused more on security. Therefore, he provided me with interior schematics for your sector, not the Omega housing arrangements."

Now it was Prince Lykos's turn to mask the tic in his own jaw. Only, he didn't hide it nearly as well as I had. "I see."

He said nothing for a long moment, my words clearly having met their mark. I'd purposely referred to Kieran without his title because I could, something Lykos and I both knew he could not do.

Because he wasn't best friends with the Blood Sector King.

That said, nothing I'd told Lykos had been a lie. Kieran and I had reviewed the layout for Glacier Sector, as well as outlined any and all potential threats. Temporary living assignments had been the furthest from our minds. I'd known where we would be staying in Glacier Sector, just not who would be paired with whom.

"You can have this sheet when I'm done," Prince Lykos finally muttered before assigning the next igloo to Benz and Fritz.

I glanced at my two men. "Keep walking with us. You can return once we know where everyone is staying."

They both nodded in agreement, trailing along as the Omegas were paired off into their accommodations. As we neared the final few igloos, however, a sense of foreboding hit me in the gut.

Because I had a feeling I knew exactly how this was going to end.

Perhaps Kieran was more in tune with the temporary living assignments than I originally thought, I realized, my teeth grinding together for an entirely different reason now.

A reason that became a reality as Prince Lykos said, "And that last igloo over there belongs to you and Omega Ivana."

I'm going to fucking kill you, Kieran, I growled.

Not that the bastard could hear me. He was too far away for my telepathic ability to reach him. But I would absolutely be texting him soon.

"Oh, I…" Ivana trailed off, her icy gaze flitting to me and then back to Prince Lykos. "Okay."

The Glacier Sector Alpha cocked his head. "Are you sure, little one?" he asked her softly, his tone grating on my nerves. "I'd originally questioned the pairing, but your King and Queen said you and Cillian are comfortable with each other. If that's not the case, then—"

"Then what?" I interjected, arching a brow. "You'll give her a guest suite in your personal quarters?"

Irritation flashed in Prince Lykos's gaze as he looked at me. "I was going to suggest that you go sleep on your jet."

I snorted. "That's not happening. I'm staying near my charges and protecting them."

"Are you saying you can't protect them from afar, Cillian? Because I think we both know that's a lie." He tugged on the mental leash I'd lassoed around his sector the moment we'd arrived, his power almost rivaling mine.

Almost being the operative word there.

Because I was stronger. Faster. And more than capable of bringing Glacier Sector to its proverbial knees.

"It's fine," Ivana interjected before I could reply. "I was just surprised. But I don't mind. Truly." She cleared her throat and stepped forward, her pretty gaze capturing mine. "Let's go, Alpha Cillian."

That was the second time she'd called me *Alpha Cillian* this week. The first time had been when she'd told me to have a good night—something I'd known was intentional.

Because I'd said that to her several weeks ago when I'd suggested she say that phrase to me and leave me alone.

Now… now I didn't like it. At all.

However, rather than comment, I nodded and gestured for her to lead the way. "Thank you for the accommodations, Prince Lykos. I'll be sure to pass along my praise to Kieran as well."

With that, I left the Glacier Sector Alpha behind me and pressed my palm to Ivana's lower back.

It was a step further than I really needed to go, but my wolf demanded that I stake my claim. *This one is mine to protect,* my hand placement said. *Kindly fuck right off.*

Trying to suggest I stay on the jet. What sort of proposal was that? And to imply Ivana might not be comfortable with me…

I swallowed the urge to growl.

If that asshole knew our history, he would never have questioned my intentions where Ivana was concerned.

Ivana entered the igloo first, her ash-blonde hair catching on the low interior lighting and providing her with a golden glow. One I admired for all of two seconds before she shadowed across the room and turned to glare at me.

A large bed stood out in the center of the tight space, the object one that sat between us like a protective shield.

And it's the only bed in this room, I realized with a sweep of my gaze. *Why the hell—*

"Are you suddenly interested in becoming a Sector Alpha?" Ivana snapped, her question jolting me from my thoughts.

"What?" I frowned and closed the door behind me. "Why are you asking me about being a Sector Alpha?" She knew better than almost everyone that I had no desire to lead.

She pointed outside. "That's why."

I blinked at her. "You've lost me, Ivana."

"You were basically challenging Prince Lykos," she told me through her teeth. "So I'm asking if you've suddenly adopted an urge to become a Sector Alpha, because last I checked, you weren't interested in doing anything other than worshipping King Kieran."

My eyebrows hit my hairline, her tone catching me completely off guard, along with her accusation. "I wasn't challenging anyone."

She gave me a look that said, *Sure you weren't.* Or maybe that was the thought traveling through her head. I couldn't exactly focus enough to determine what she was thinking, too floored by her chastising glare. Omegas *never* glowered at me. Especially not Ivana.

"What the hell is your problem?" I demanded. "I'm not the one who came up with these living arrangements, so don't take it out on me."

She barked out a laugh that lacked humor. "*Wow.*" With that profound statement, she walked over to our bags on a nearby couch—the items likely having been delivered here while we were on our tour and at the party—and ripped hers open.

I waited for her to say more.

She didn't.

She simply yanked out a smaller bag and some clothes, then stomped off into the adjoining bathroom.

The door slammed behind her with a finality that left me gaping at the dark-colored wood separating us.

You think a door is going to stop me from talking to you? I asked into her mind, somewhat amused, and a whole hell of a lot annoyed.

No reply.

Not even a thought.

Because of course I couldn't hear anything. Ivana lived in a perpetual state of peace, one I fought not to disturb.

Ivana.

Nothing.

I growled. *You have three seconds before I shadow in there and make you talk to me, Ivana.*

I'm merely complying with your desires, Alpha Cillian, she drawled back at me.

My desires? I repeated, utterly consumed by this female's madness.

Yes. I'm refraining from irritating you with my misguided penchants for telling Alphas what to do. Wouldn't want to bother you with my overconfidence, after all.

My head fell back on a sigh that I was sure she heard through the door. *Ivana—*

Just leave me alone, Alpha Cillian. I would like to take a shower and go to sleep.

Stop calling me Alpha Cillian, I growled back at her.

Silence. No acknowledgment. Not a single musing or even a muttered acceptance.

My fingers curled into fists, my irritation mounting with each passing second.

But rather than shadow into the bathroom like a dark part of me wanted to do, I forced myself to go outside instead.

My goal had been to inhale deeply and calm my nerves.

But I found Benz and Fritz waiting for me instead. The latter of which appeared to be holding a piece of paper, one I suspected was the accommodations list from Prince Lykos.

Fuck. I'd left my two lieutenants out here without a single order.

Because I'd forgotten they were here.

Sharing a damn igloo with Ivana was going to cost me my sanity.

And my pride.

"I'll take the first shift," I told Benz and Fritz. "Go get some rest."

"What time do you want us up?" the Beta asked.

It was a simple question.

However, it had me wanting to snarl at him in reply.

Maybe because I could hear the thoughts rolling through

his mind, too. All of them revolved around me lodging with Ivana and his blatant disapproval.

Well, he wasn't the only one who disapproved of the room assignments.

But it wasn't his fucking problem to handle. It was mine.

Still, my instinct to lash out at him was a problem. Because who the fuck cared what he thought?

I sure as hell shouldn't.

Yet my wolf was practically pacing beneath my skin, determined to break free and make this Beta submit.

Shit. I couldn't remember the last time I felt this close to losing control of my animal.

It's Ivana. Her scent. Her sass. Knowing she's probably naked in the shower right now…

I swallowed. *Hard.* And focused on Benz. "I'll wake you if I need you. Until then, sleep."

Rather than wait for his acceptance, I shadowed back to the jet and pulled up a screen from my watch. Prince Lykos had been right—I could monitor the Omegas from here.

But that didn't mean I wanted to sleep on the damn jet.

However, I did want to have a private chat with my oldest friend. Specifically about that *accommodations list*—which I'd left with Fritz. Or I assumed I had, anyway. I had no idea what other paper he could've been holding.

Doesn't matter. I'll get a copy from the asshole who created said list.

Kieran picked up seconds after I selected his name on the translucent screen, his concerned expression appearing in an instant. "What's wrong?"

"Don't you think Benz would have been a better roommate for Ivana?" I asked him, not bothering to address his query or offer him a greeting.

Everything was fine.

Mostly.

Except for the fact that the igloo has one fucking bed, I thought, recalling the schematics of the room. I'd barely noticed it upon entry because of Ivana's open irritation. She'd distracted me from the sleeping arrangements—arrangements I very much wanted to discuss with Kieran now.

"You also could have roomed her with Fritz, who happens to be an Omega—just like her," I added.

"Am I to understand that you just interrupted my nesting time with Quinnlynn to bitch about some sleeping arrangements?" Kieran inquired, a hint of mild irritation coloring his tone. But it didn't quite match the amusement dancing in his dark gaze.

"I know what you're doing," I informed him, ignoring both his tone and his question. "Stop fucking with my personal life, Kieran."

"Would I do that?"

"Yes." Absolutely no question he would. "For a moment, perhaps consider how Ivana feels about this arrangement. Forget me. Think about her and her discomfort."

"I highly doubt Ivana is uncomfortable," Kieran replied without missing a beat. "If she is, that's your doing, not mine."

My gaze narrowed. "I've done nothing."

"Then I'm sure she's fine." He shrugged, his shoulders bare rather than clothed. "As to your questions, Fritz was recently mind-fucked by an Alpha. I doubt he would appreciate sharing a room with a renowned telepath. And you've expressed concerns that Benz wishes you bodily harm, so I assumed you wouldn't want him as a roommate."

He paused, but I sensed it wasn't because he wanted me to reply. He seemed distracted by something—or, more likely, *someone*—in the distance.

Still, I felt it necessary to say, "I expressed my objections to Benz's assignment because his violent thoughts toward me make it likely that he won't respect me as his commander. At no point did I express fear or concern for my personal safety. That excuse is a stretch and you know it."

"Hmm, well, if I'm wrong, then make the switch," he

replied distractedly. "Now, if you'll excuse me, my Omega is pregnant and requires my knot."

The focus of the camera shifted away from him, the wall of his bedroom suite coming into view as Quinnlynn said something in response to Kieran's crass commentary.

"I want an electronic copy of the room arrangements," I interjected before he could hang up.

It would save me from having to ask Fritz about that piece of paper. I wasn't even sure it contained the information I desired anyway. For all I knew, it'd been a random report of some kind. Or a letter.

Kieran's face reappeared. "Seems like a waste of time, but fine. I'll send it this evening."

He might find it to be a waste of time, but I sure as hell didn't. I needed to figure out a way to fix this so I could properly concentrate on my assignment.

The scene changed once more on the screen, showing the wall again before Kieran's face returned to view.

"Oh, and, Cillian," he went on. "If you ever needlessly bother me again while I'm in my Queen's nest, I'll drop you in the middle of an Infected pit."

"I would just shadow out of it," I pointed out.

He shrugged again. "I would do it all the same."

"*Kieran*," Quinnlynn chastised in the background, her tone reminding me of Ivana's from moments ago.

He merely smiled. "Coming, darling."

The screen went dark, leaving me shaking my head at the other man as I pulled up a keyboard to type, *Matchmaking doesn't suit you.* I hit *Send* and closed the screen.

My wrist buzzed a second later.

I almost ignored it.

But my pride forced me to read Kieran's reply.

And I immediately regretted the decision.

Because his words hit me right in the fucking heart.

Being a martyr doesn't suit you, either, old friend.

IVANA

This has got to be a joke, I thought, glaring at the bed.

Sure, it was a nice size. A king. Maybe even a little bigger. But it was a solitary fixture. Single. Only one.

A growl escaped me as I paced before it, my silky pajama pants swishing with each step. *I can't share this bed with Cillian. I just can't. Not with all the dreams I've been having about him.*

Gods, how embarrassing would it be to fantasize about a mind reader while sleeping beside him? He'd hear every word. Witness every detail.

Then he'd pity me even more.

Probably lecture me to my face about playing in the wrong league or something.

"Ugh," I groaned, my palms covering my eyes. "This is horrible."

Not only had I chastised him, but I now had to live with him. *For a week.*

"This is a nightmare. A complete and utter *nightmare.*"

I'd been tempted to beg Benz to switch roommates with me, but I hadn't wanted to appear weak.

And maybe a small, tiny, inconsequential part of me had wanted to share an igloo with Cillian.

But I hadn't realized there would only be one bed. I'd expected at least two. Preferably in separate bedrooms.

Then Cillian had started posturing with Prince Lykos, something he'd been doing since we'd arrived, and I'd reacted. Their mounting Alpha testosterone had been wreaking havoc on my senses, making my legs feel weak. I'd felt my slick building, my insides roaring with the need to be *claimed* by the Alpha I'd stupidly considered mine for far too long.

Which had led me to responding in the only way I'd known how—acceptance of the lodging assignments.

It was that or suffer public embarrassment by begging Cillian for his knot.

Stars, why is he even here? Couldn't King Kieran have assigned another Alpha to protective duty?

But of course he couldn't have; there was no one else. Lorcan had to protect Night Sector. And Cillian was the only other Alpha that could be trusted with this task.

Another growl rumbled in my chest as I dropped my hands and glared at the mattress. "I'm not sleeping next to him. I'm just not."

And the couch was far too small for him to rest on, which meant I had to sleep there.

Because the only other option was to share the bed and that wasn't happening.

I crept forward to test the couch cushion with my palms. It was firm, but not too firm.

"Hmm," I hummed as I relocated our bags to the floor—Cillian's was notably light—and considered the throw pillows.

There was a blanket tossed haphazardly across the back of the sofa as well. Alas, it wouldn't be enough to keep me warm in this sector.

Magic might have warmed the interior of the igloo to a more palatable temperature, but it was still chilly.

All the Omegas kept commenting on how it reminded them of home—a home I intended to move to with my future mate.

I shivered at the thought. The moment my skin felt the subzero climate here, I'd felt… ill at ease. Like I didn't belong here. I'd been okay with that realization until I'd overheard all the Omegas excitedly chattering about how "homey" it felt in this sector.

Does that mean I won't feel at home in Night Sector? I'd wondered. *Will I hate it there?*

The realization that I might not fit in… had left me feeling out of sorts.

That, on top of being paired with Cillian, had basically rendered me an emotional mess. One I'd taken out on him.

Blowing out a breath, I returned to the bed to take off the comforter and grab a pillow. "This will have to do."

Thankfully, Cillian was nowhere to be found. The jerk would probably argue with me. Or worse, demand that I *talk* to him again—something I did not want to do.

"Stop calling me Alpha Cillian" had been his final words.

Gods, the things I'd wanted to say back to him in that moment.

How many times have you demanded I call you just that?

Trust me when I say "Alpha Cillian" is the nicer form of what I'd prefer to call you right now.

You're chastising me for being formal now? How ironic.

Would you prefer "Prince Cillian"?

Don't tell me what to do. You lost that right when you broke my heart.

Fuck you, Alpha Cillian.

Stop bothering me.

Stop growling at me.

Stop existing.

Stop haunting my dreams at night.

The list was endless. Each statement had percolated through my mind during my shower and continued to do so now as I lay down on the couch.

If only my brain had an off switch.

The entire evening scrawled across my mind as I closed my eyes.

The flight to Glacier Sector. Ashlyn's weird behavior. Me trying to write in my journal. The welcome party. Ransom's soft dominance as he'd stood beside me without saying much. Cillian's not-so-soft dominance as he'd basically challenged Prince Lykos.

The words I'd exchanged with Cillian in this igloo.

The words I wished I had said in return.

The words I was glad I hadn't said in return.

I punched the pillow beside my head as I tried to get more comfortable.

Stop, I told my brain. *Just stop. I need to sleep.*

Ransom had asked me to go ice-skating with him tomorrow, something I'd never done before. *Maybe it'll be fun*, I thought. *Or maybe I'll break my neck.*

Good thing I'm basically immortal.

Oh my Gods, stop thinking.

La. La. La.

I pictured Ransom and his gentle smile. *Ice-skating will be fun. I mean, it's going to be absolutely freezing. But… but I'll like it.*

I have to like it.

I have to like this environment. It's my future. Not Cillian. Not Blood Sector.

Night Sector.

I can do this.

I can do this.

I can do this.

The chant echoed in my head, drowning out my uncertainties.

Or so I'd hoped.

But when I finally dreamt, it was of a time long ago. A time when I'd been cold. Alone. Frightened. *And nearly dead…*

A time when Cillian had been my hero.

"I've got you," he'd whispered into my ear. "You're safe now."

Warmth unlike any I'd ever experienced had touched my heart in that moment. A warmth I'd reserved solely for him.

My intended mate.

My wolf's obsession.

My Alpha.

His scent—peppermint tinged with something masculine, something that was all Cillian—swathed me in a blanket of protection.

I inhaled deeply. Lovingly. *Longingly.*

Mine, my wolf purred.

Except Cillian's words from the Blood Sector coronation night soon followed in my mind, stirring me from this strange sleeplike state. And I woke in a sea of unfamiliar darkness. I drew my knees up to my chest as a violent tremble overtook my spine.

Where am I? I couldn't possibly be back in that hole. The softness beneath me was nothing like the cold, hard ground of that savage pit.

Still, I felt the need to sniff the air, to ensure the stench of copper and dirt didn't fill my senses.

Instead, all I scented was Cillian. *A refreshing peppermint kiss.*

Just like every other morning recently.

Only, I hadn't dreamt of him like I had then; this dream… this dream had been too realistic. Too reminiscent of our past.

I blinked, confused, and rolled to my back on the soft mattress.

My lips curled down then, my gaze scanning the unfamiliar bed.

How…? Where…?

Memories of last night—or perhaps earlier this morning—assaulted me at once, reminding me that I was in Glacier Sector. In an igloo. *And I went to bed on the couch.*

Only… only I was no longer on the couch. I was wrapped up in the blankets on the bed.

And Cillian… Cillian was nowhere to be seen.

All I sensed was his residual scent and the heat he'd left behind.

Against my back, I realized, my palm touching my spine. It was hot, like I'd been pressed up against another body for hours.

The bed… I moved my touch to explore it. *The bed's still warm beside me.*

Cillian had been here.

He'd moved me to the mattress.

And then… *Did he hold me? For how long? Is this even real? A dream? What does it mean?*

My mind raced with so many questions, my imagination threatening to overwhelm me with too many hopeful images.

I shook my head, forcing myself to clear it. I would go mad if I started considering the what-ifs of the situation.

Cillian had put me in the bed.

I'd slept.

End of consideration.

I checked the time on my watch and noted that it was still a little early to be up, but I left the bed anyway. Sleeping was no longer an option. I'd just… get ready.

For my date.

With Alpha Ransom.

CILLIAN

I WASN'T sure what pissed me off more—Ivana attempting to ice-skate or Ivana sleeping on the couch.

Both activities threatened her health and safety. The latter problem I'd been able to solve by moving her to the bed. The former issue, however, I was currently being forced to observe from the sidelines.

While another Alpha put his fucking paws all over her in an attempt to keep her from falling down.

Each time the asshole failed had me nearly shadowing to the ice rink to handle Ivana myself.

Alas, my job tonight was to supervise and guard from afar. Not teach Ivana how to balance on deadly blades.

She giggled as Ransom caught her by the waist, her arms flailing around while she fought for balance.

My wolf growled inside, irritated over the sight before us.

Another Alpha has his hands on our female, my inner beast seemed to be saying. *Kill him.*

She's not ours, I thought at my animal half.

Holding Ivana all day while she'd slept had been a bad idea. But when I'd found her curled into a tiny ball on that couch, a part of me had broken inside.

A part that hadn't liked the touch of blue painting her lips or the goose bumps decorating her arms. She'd been cold and shivering and *alone*.

And it'd reminded me of the night we'd first met.

A night when I'd purred for her on instinct and cradled her body against mine for hours.

She'd looked so young. So fragile. So *shattered*.

And last night, she'd exuded a similar appearance.

Or maybe it had all been in my mind.

Still, I hadn't been able to stop myself from carrying her to the bed and purring for her while she slept. It'd felt so unbelievably right despite being so incredibly wrong.

I didn't deserve her or any other Omega. *Not after what I let my father do to…*

Rolling my neck, I shook off the ancient memory before it could encapsulate my mind. The last thing I needed was another distraction. Ivana was quite enough.

If that Alpha touches her one more time… My teeth ground together as Ransom caught Ivana again before she could face-plant on the ice.

Her responding laugh went straight to my gut, the sound one I hadn't heard from her before.

Because she never laughed in my presence.

Oh, she'd smiled and flirted with me. But she'd never laughed. Only ever fake-giggled at some of the other Blood Sector Omegas—an action she'd usually accompanied with a roll of her eyes.

Ivana had always reacted that way around Miranda and her crew of mean-girl types.

I'd admired that about Ivana—her ability to just not care.

Fuck, I admired a lot of things about Ivana. Like the way her hips looked in those tight jeans of hers right now.

So fucking breedable, I thought, my knot pulsating in response.

I ripped my gaze away from her to focus on some of the other Omegas skating around the rink with their Alpha dates for the evening. My wolf instantly calmed, not interested in any of those pairings at all.

My fingers curled and uncurled at my sides, my mind scanning the entire sector for any notions of a threat and finding none.

Other than myself.

Never in my entire existence had I ever felt this close to losing control.

Well, no. That wasn't quite true.

I'd lost control once. Over a thousand years ago.

On the night I betrayed my entire family.

I gritted my teeth, the memory once again threatening to overwhelm me. A memory I rarely ever considered, yet that was twice in a short span of time that it had nearly—

Cillian. Fritz's mental call immediately caught my attention, as I'd been loosely in tune with both him and Benz all evening.

Yes?

Ashlyn fell into the ice pond. She's fine, but—

I shadowed to his side before he could finish, my gaze instantly landing on the shivering blonde curled into a ball on the bank of the frozen pond. Grey hovered nearby, his ice-like gaze narrowed at Henrik—one of Glacier Sector's Alphas.

Imbecile, I overheard Grey thinking. *Z-Clan Omegas aren't built like V-Clan Omegas. Their powers are mental, not physical.*

My brow furrowed. *What happened?* I asked Fritz. *And when did Grey get here?*

I hadn't even been aware he'd intended to join us today.

Thus far, he'd missed all the mating events. It seemed a little strange for him to visit for group dates today, especially since this wasn't even his home sector.

Ashlyn fell into one of the fishing holes, Fritz replied.

Yes, I'm asking how *she fell in,* I rephrased.

I'm not sure. I was grabbing some poles when—

You weren't watching? I interjected, facing him.

"Henrik asked me to *fetch*—his word—some extra fishing rods from the shed," Fritz answered out loud, his arms folding before him. "So I shadowed over to *fetch* them. When I heard Ashlyn shriek, I immediately teleported back, but Grey had already jumped in to grab her."

"I d-didn't shrie-eek," Ashlyn muttered, her teeth chattering over the words.

"He appeared out of fucking nowhere," Henrik growled.

"Who did?" I demanded, not following his comment.

"The half-breed." He gestured sharply at Grey, who simply arched a brow in response to being called a *half-breed.* "One minute, we're fishing. And the next, he shadows in uninvited and Ashlyn falls in."

"I'm one of the candidates," Grey reminded him coolly. "By definition, that means I'm invited, not uninvited."

"I'm fine," Ashlyn interjected. "No harm. Just a little swim. But I'd like to go change my clothes now." She started to walk away, but I stepped into her path.

"I'll escort you," I told her, my tone as soft as I could manage, given the situation. Henrik and Grey were throwing down a lot of testosterone that my wolf very much wanted to respond to, but now wasn't the time to assert dominance.

I needed to ensure Ashlyn was okay first.

Then I would deal with the two simmering Alphas.

Find out how she actually fell in, I told Fritz, wanting him to gather statements from Grey and Henrik.

Meanwhile, I'd focus on Ashlyn's point of view.

Waving a hand forward, I said, "After you."

She stared at me for a beat, her blue eyes seeming to see right through me. Then she nodded and started walking.

I trailed behind her, my mind still locked on the Alphas behind me. They were too busy sizing each other up to care about me taking the Omega from them.

But that left Fritz to deal with their aggression.

He was big for an Omega, and apparently quite skilled with a gun. However, I wasn't sure that would be enough to put Grey down.

Henrik, maybe.

Grey… Grey might actually prove difficult for me to take down. His Z-Clan half made him an unknown. And his mind didn't feel all that vulnerable.

I could hear his surface thoughts, but nothing too deep.

Granted, that could be because he was currently consumed by Henrik throwing insults his way.

You shouldn't even be here.

You're not one of us.

Just because she's a Z-Clan Omega does not mean she's yours. So don't get any ideas about dragging her off to some cave and claiming her against her will.

The words rolled through Grey's mind on repeat, his own mouth seeming to remain shut during the onslaught of negative statements coming from Henrik.

So, what? You're just going to stand there? All silent and brooding? You pushed *her into the fucking pond!*

I did not, Grey thought, but from what I could tell, he didn't voice the statement out loud.

Which just further pissed off Henrik.

See? He's not even denying it. Make him leave.

I snorted, unsure of whether that whining tone was just Grey's mental interpretation of Henrik's voice or an accurate depiction. Regardless, it was amusing.

"He didn't push me," Ashlyn said quietly, her gaze catching mine as she glanced back at me. "I just didn't see him coming, so his appearance… surprised me. Which is rather uncommon, to say the least."

"You knew he was part of the mating pool, though, right?"

Her lips curled slightly. "Yes. Quinn asked me if I was okay with him joining. I'm not one to fight destiny, so I agreed." She shrugged. "Although, I thought our paths would cross later. Not today."

She picked up her pace a little, her gaze no longer on me, leaving me to study her from behind.

Her cryptic words swirled in my mind as I tried to piece them together.

Z-Clan Omegas were extremely rare, primarily because their Alphas didn't cherish them the way they should. Quinnlynn asking Ashlyn for permission to add Grey to the list of suitors made sense—if anyone would object to a part Z-Clan Alpha joining the mating pool, it would be a Z-Clan Omega.

Ashlyn allowing him to participate meant that either she felt his V-Clan side would balance his Z-Clan heritage, or she'd seen something that made her comfortable with him.

Her words just now made me suspect the latter.

"Don't think about it too hard, Alpha Cillian," she murmured. "Alpha Grey's intentions here are noble. He's just hunting."

"Hunting for what?" I asked, frowning.

"What do most good Alphas hunt for?" she asked, a curious note to her voice. "Mates, yes? Although, I suppose they also hunt down villains with penchants for stealing precious relics. Hmm."

I arched a brow. "Are you purposely being cryptic?"

She shrugged. "I'm pointing out that thinking isn't needed. Not about this. Besides, you have your own future to consider. One you're not going to enjoy if you continue on the path you're on right now."

I frowned at her back. "That sounds ominous."

"It should." She turned down the street that led to our guest igloos, still not looking at me.

I waited for her to elaborate, but she didn't.

Z-Clan Omegas were known for their unique sensitivities to auras and emotions. However, it seemed this one might also have a proclivity for fortune-telling.

Or perhaps it was all instinct based?

Something told me I wouldn't find the answer within her mind, but I was suddenly tempted to try. I'd focused my ability on the Alphas in Glacier Sector, not the Betas or Omegas, because I'd been concerned with threats.

My leash around the Omegas was for protection only, my mental connection to their minds scanning for words of fear more than anything else.

However, I hadn't picked up anything from Ashlyn at all. No fear. Not even a hint of surprise when she'd fallen into the ice pond.

Now I wondered if I hadn't been in touch with her mind at all.

"Don't," she said as we reached her igloo. "If you push, you won't like what you find. And as I said, you should be more concerned with your own future. Not mine."

She faced me then, her expression one that seemed underlined with age and experience, like she'd seen millions of timelines that were not just her own.

"I'm fine. I fell because I was startled. Grey and Henrik don't mean me any harm." She reached out to grab my hand, her fingers resembling ice against my skin. "I'm not yours to worry about, Cillian. While I appreciate your protective instincts, they're unnecessary."

"Why do I feel as though I'm being scolded for simply walking you back to your igloo?" I asked her, my eyebrow arching at the tiny Omega before me.

"Maybe because you need to be scolded," she said,

squeezing my hand before releasing it. "You do realize that you're not the only one being punished by your actions, yes?"

Now both my eyebrows inched upward. "Excuse me?"

"Hmm, I see that you don't realize that at all." She gave me a thoughtful look. "Choosing to suffer out of some misguided need to repent doesn't just impact you, Cillian. That choice—the one where you put everyone else first—impacts her, too. If you remember anything I've said, please remember that."

With that profound statement, she let herself into her igloo and shut the door before I could even fathom a reply.

I'd just been thoroughly chastised by yet another Omega, and I wasn't even sure I understood what she'd just chastised me about.

It felt like it was something I hadn't even done yet. Something I *might* do.

Unless she's talking about leaving the ice rink to check on her at the fishing hole? I wondered, staring at her ice-laden door before glancing at the empty street behind me.

With a renewed sense of urgency, I shadowed back to the ice rink and found it mostly empty, the Omegas and Alphas having chosen to retire for dinner.

A quick mental scan told me Ivana was sitting with a silent Ransom, eating a freshly smoked salmon.

Then what the hell was Ashlyn going on about?

I gripped my nape, my head tilting back as I stared up at the moon, Ashlyn's words repeating through my mind. There'd been something prophetic about her statements. Something… *threatening.*

Pulling up a screen from my watch, I shot a message off to Kieran, asking about Ashlyn's background and penchant for fortune-telling. Perhaps Quinnlynn could share some of the Z-Clan Omega's history with him, then he could give me an idea of how seriously I needed to take her warnings.

Pushing thoughts of the tiny female from my mind, I

shadowed to the dining hall and leaned against the wall. *I assume Henrik and Grey have been taken care of?* I said to Fritz.

Grey left without uttering a single word, Fritz replied. *Henrik…*

Whined like a baby? I guessed.

For a moment, amusement touched Fritz's mind. *Something like that.* He sobered then as he asked, *Is Ashlyn okay?*

She was a bit cryptic but seems all right.

Fritz chuckled into my mind, his amusement returning. *Did she fall into oracle mode?*

Is that a common activity for her?

Only when she sees something worth warning about, he drawled.

Now you're being the cryptic one, I muttered back to him.

Trust me. No one is more cryptic than Ashlyn. But her warnings are usually important, so if she said something, listen to her. She's a lot more powerful than people realize.

A Z-Clan Omega with foreseeing abilities, I thought back to him. *No wonder she sought refuge in the Sanctuary. I'm surprised she's trying to take a mate.*

I don't think she intends to take a mate at all, Fritz replied, sounding serious again. *She's participating for reasons that I've yet to decipher.*

I stood up straighter. *Does Quinnlynn know this?*

Yes. He didn't elaborate, but I heard the whisper of a memory in his mind—a conversation between him and the Blood Sector Queen about Ashlyn's intentions.

Hmm, I hummed, eyeing my watch.

If Quinnlynn knew—which it seemed evident that she did—then Kieran might as well.

Once these dates finished, I'd call him to discuss it.

Until then… My gaze drifted to Ivana's silent form as she quietly chewed her meal. She seemed content enough, if a little shy. Very unlike the Omega I knew who loved to run her mouth at me.

What can you possibly see in that Alpha? I nearly asked her. *He's clearly boring you, darling.*

Her eyes lifted to mine, like she'd heard my comments. Or perhaps she'd just sensed my focus on her.

I quickly looked away.

But I didn't lose sight of her in my mind.

I… lingered. Listening. Waiting for any sign of trouble.

Or that was what I told myself, anyway.

What I forced myself to believe.

Because there couldn't be any other reason for linking myself to her mind.

No other reason at all…

IVANA

Ransom walked quietly beside me, his steps not making a sound. Had his hand not brushed mine every few paces, I wouldn't have even known he was there.

He sort of reminded me of Lorcan, except Ransom just seemed to be perpetually thoughtful, while Lorcan's silence always felt ominous. Maybe because Lorcan was more intimidating by nature, his power palpable whenever in his presence.

Ransom didn't strike me as all that daunting. Sure, he was big like most Alphas, but he had a gentleness to his touch that made him more teddy-bear-like than beast-like.

Cillian's definitely not a teddy bear, I thought darkly, his energy swathing my being despite him walking over a hundred yards behind us.

The Elite had throttled the entire sector with his gifts the moment we'd arrived, and he'd yet to release anyone from his hold.

I hated it. That damn aura of his made focusing on Ransom all the more difficult.

"Would you like to watch a movie tomorrow?" Ransom asked me softly as we arrived at my igloo door. "Maybe one of the old ones? From before the Infected Era?"

Those three questions were more words than he'd said in the last hour. But the way his black eyes lit up with interest told me these *old movies* were important to him.

"I would love to," I told him.

It was a bit of an exaggeration; the cinema had never really appealed to me. I preferred outdoor activities, like fencing, shooting, and running in wolf form. I also enjoyed playing computer games, especially puzzle-like ones that required me to think.

However, I understood that mating meant I needed to indulge in my partner's desires, too.

"Okay." He gave me a small smile, his hand lifting to caress my cheek.

It was a tender graze of his fingertips, one that drew his eyes down to my mouth. I parted my lips, wondering if he intended to kiss me already.

Do I want that? I marveled. *Maybe. Yes. I… I think I do.*

A kiss would help me determine how much chemistry existed between us, if my wolf desired him, if *I* liked him.

He seemed nice enough. But could I mate him?

I licked my lips, suddenly eager to find out.

His nostrils flared, his head angling toward mine.

I closed my eyes, waiting.

Then waited some more.

What…? I peeked at him, confused as to what was happening. I could feel his breath on my mouth, his face close to mine. But his gaze was no longer focused on me.

He was staring behind me.

At Cillian.

I couldn't see him, but I knew he was there. Just like he'd been the entire way back to the igloo.

Our igloo, I realized. *Fuck.*

Ransom cleared his throat, his palm leaving my face as he took a step backward.

Double fuck, I growled in my mind.

"See you tomorrow, Ivana," he said quietly.

Then shadowed before I could reply.

I narrowed my gaze at the space he'd just occupied, then slowly turned to find Cillian standing at the end of the path that led up to the igloo.

"You couldn't have waited a little bit down the street for five minutes to give us some privacy?" I demanded, irritated as hell by him interrupting the end of my date.

He arched a brow and leaned against the dimly lit light post, the top of it dangling off over the vacant street to provide an ominous glow behind him. "I wasn't aware that I needed to *wait* for anything."

I couldn't swallow back my responding growl, my irritation inflamed by the condescension underlining his tone. "No Alpha is going to want to date me with you hovering over me like this, Cillian. I need space so I can be properly courted."

"My existence shouldn't impact your courtships, Ivana. If an Alpha is worthy of you, he won't care if I'm five feet away or a thousand feet away. Because I won't even exist in his orbit."

I blinked at him. "What?" That didn't make any sense. "The Alpha energy is practically pouring off of you. Of course they'll care that you're here."

He pushed off the post to walk toward me. "You're wrong, Ivana."

"Clearly, I'm not," I argued, gesturing at the space

Ransom had just stood in moments ago. "He vanished because you scared him off."

"He disappeared because he's not worthy of you and he knows it."

My eyebrows shot upward. "Excuse me?"

"You heard me, Vana," he said, only a foot away now. "He's not worthy of you."

I ignored the random nickname—one I'd never heard him use before—and focused on the latter part of his statements. "And who are you to decide that?"

"If he were good enough, he wouldn't have cared that I was here. Fuck, he wouldn't have even noticed. He'd have been too taken by you to sense my presence." He cupped my cheek, his palm singeing my skin in a way that Ransom had not.

Stars, Cillian's touch felt like a brand. An imprint. A *claim*.

Why couldn't Ransom have felt that way?

Why was it only this way with *him*?

"You deserve an Alpha who will only ever see you, Ivana," Cillian went on, his thumb brushing my bottom lip. "An Alpha so obsessed with your presence that he forgets everything and everyone else around him. An Alpha who will kiss you without caring who is or isn't watching."

"Cillian…" I shivered, his name leaving me on a breath.

Because he was so close now.

So… so warm. So strong. So *Cillian*.

His dark eyes smoldered with hidden secrets, his intense gaze holding me captive as he bent his head to brush his lips against mine.

A soft touch.

An unexpected one.

And yet, it sent electricity humming through my being.

The hairs along my arms stood on end, my neck prickled, and my heart… my heart felt like it had just beat for the first time.

His mouth met mine once more, this time for longer than a beat. He lingered, inhaling and exhaling against my lips.

"Vana," he whispered, the nickname sounding reverent on his tongue.

I couldn't move. I could hardly even think. Too swept up in Cillian's aura, his dominance, his *claim.*

I'd waited so long for this, dreamt of it, craved it since the night we'd first met.

Yet nothing compared to the experience of finally feeling his mouth against mine.

His palm left my cheek to grasp my nape, his tongue parting my lips as he deepened our embrace. I shuddered, lost to him. His scent. His commanding presence. His sensual taste.

I'd never been kissed like this.

Never been touched like this.

Never been *consumed* like this.

This was… this was…

Stop thinking, Vana, Cillian murmured, his tongue tracing mine. *Just kiss me.*

My pulse raced, my mind seeming to shut down as my body caved to Cillian's will.

He owned me now. My mouth. My tongue. My sense of being.

Our kiss was no longer tender or soft, but passionate and all-encompassing. He set the pace and I matched it, my lips learning and memorizing his movements, perfecting my own skills to rival his.

It was divine. Fated. *Written in the stars.*

This male was mine.

I was his.

And in this moment, everything was right. Everything was perfect. Everything was… *magical.*

Stars, I must be dreaming. But I didn't care. I wanted more. I never wanted this to end. Cillian tasted minty. Refreshing. Like dawn on a cold winter's day.

So crisp and perfect.

I moaned against him, my tongue dueling his in a way I'd never anticipated. He met me in kind, his hand on my nape a reminder of his dominating presence while his opposite arm cradled my lower back, holding me as though I was the most precious being in the world.

The contradiction left me winded, my body shaking with a need that reminded me of my estrus. It wasn't time for me to go into heat. Wasn't time for me to require a knot.

But I wanted his.

I wanted *him*.

"Cillian," I breathed, my arms encircling his neck as I pressed myself tighter against him, ready for more. Ready for him. Ready for *us*.

Only, his mouth left mine, his lips trailing a hot path to my ear. "That's how an Alpha should kiss you, love," he murmured, his Irish lilt thicker than I'd ever heard it before. "Like you're the most important woman in the world. Like he's yours and only yours. Like he couldn't give a fuck as to who might be observing from nearby."

He pressed a kiss to my thundering pulse, then extracted himself from my arms and took a step back.

"Now go get some sleep." He turned to leave, then paused and faced me once more, his palm finding my nape again. "*Not* on the bloody sofa, Ivana. Sleep in the bed. Understand?"

I blinked at him, too confounded by the last few minutes to fathom words, let alone a response.

Did he just… kiss me… to prove a point?

Not kiss me because he wanted me.

But to… to show me *how* I should be kissed.

In front of our igloo. Out in the open. Where everyone and anyone might have seen us.

"Cillian—"

"Go to bed, Ivana," he interjected. "You have a busy schedule tomorrow—a movie date with Ransom and before that, a brunch date with Prince Cael."

What? I was struggling to understand. *A… what?*

"Prince Cael sent a message a bit ago saying he intends to take you out to brunch at nine," Cillian explained, likely having heard my confusion.

Except he hadn't understood my question at all.

I wasn't even sure *I* understood. Because this… this didn't make any sense. Us talking about Ransom and Cael. Right after… right after…

Cillian kissed—

"You need sleep," Cillian said, interrupting my thought. "And I need to do my security rounds. Good night, Ivana."

Rather than shadow, he simply walked away.

Without a backward glance.

I almost called out after him, but I couldn't seem to catch my breath. My heart… was no longer beating.

A movie date with Ransom.

Brunch at nine.

With Prince Cael.

Cillian's words made it sound like he expected me to allow the other Alphas to court me.

Why would he want that after kissing me?

Unless… unless that kiss didn't mean what I think it meant.

Which suggests…

I swallowed, my mind slowly piecing together everything that had just happened.

"That's how an Alpha should kiss you."

"Like you're the most important woman in the world."

"Like he's yours and only yours."

"Like he couldn't give a fuck as to who might be observing from nearby."

That bastard…

Cillian had been *demonstrating* what I should expect from the Alphas courting me. He hadn't kissed me because he'd wanted to, but because he'd wanted to set my expectations.

What the fuck? I thought, glaring in the direction he'd walked off in. It was too late for me to ask that question aloud. I couldn't even see him now, my mind having taken too long to process his kiss.

And hell if I was going to try to talk to him telepathically.

The last thing I wanted was for him to be inside my mind. To hear the chaos floating around. The *hurt.*

He'd just given me a *pity* kiss.

After telling me that Ransom wasn't good enough for me because he hadn't been able to kiss me in front of Cillian.

I growled. "You've got to be kidding me."

How the hell was I supposed to find an Alpha mate with Cillian bestowing pity kisses on me? Not only did I smell like him—thanks to sharing this damn igloo—but he'd basically branded my mouth.

And for what?

To teach me a lesson on sensuality.

Out of pity.

I shoved the door open to our igloo and stomped inside, livid with myself for giving in to his touch. Yeah, I'd dreamt of it for years. And yeah, that kiss had been far better than any fantasy I'd ever concocted.

But the cruel reality of *why* he'd kissed me destroyed everything about the moment.

Stripping off all my layers of clothes, I went to take a shower.

"Sleep in the bed," he'd said.

Fuck you, I thought in reply. *Fuck you and your mouth and your hands and your demands. Fuck. You.*

Telling me not to sleep on the couch.

Well, joke's on him.

I'll sleep in the fucking bathtub instead.

It was the only way I'd rid myself of his *scent.*

And it wasn't like I would be resting much anyway.

IVANA

I DIDN'T END up sleeping in the bathtub.

It was too uncomfortable, and the water wasn't warm enough for living inside an igloo. I also didn't want to drain whatever enchantment was used to heat up the interior.

Instead, I took over the entire bed, choosing to sleep sideways across the mattress.

I'd been childishly proud of myself until I woke up in a little corner of the bed with Cillian's cologne suffocating my senses.

My gaze narrowed as I looked over my shoulder, but the Alpha in question was nowhere to be seen. Just like yesterday.

I reached for a clock on the nightstand and glared at the time. It was only five in the afternoon, which meant I'd slept a mere six hours. But hell if I could rest any longer. The sun would be setting right about now anyway.

Time for a run, I told my wolf.

Stripping out of my pajamas, I knelt on all fours and willed my animal to take control. The shift came over me in a rush of adrenaline, the hairs along my skin morphing into fur as my body changed shape.

A huff escaped my snout when I completed the transition, causing me to giggle inside. My wolf loved her freedom and wasn't pleased that I'd kept her locked up for the last few days.

Let's go sightseeing, I murmured to her as we shadowed outside the igloo.

I'd seen enough of the town area to somewhat know my way around, but I'd yet to explore any sort of countryside.

Although, I doubted there was much to see other than snow and ice.

I shivered inside, not all that enthused by the lack of landscaping here. *Better get used to it,* I muttered to myself.

Because all the Omegas kept saying how Glacier Sector reminded them of *home*—a home I would be calling my own soon enough. *With an Alpha mate.*

That last thought had me swallowing with unease. Cillian's kiss had been everything I'd ever dreamt of. At least until it'd ended and the words that had followed.

Still, it'd set an expectation I wasn't sure the other eligible Alphas could meet.

None of them gave me butterflies the way Cillian did.

Why can't I just get over this stupid crush on him? I wondered while my wolf sniffed around, searching for a field to run in. *This is ridiculous. He doesn't want me. He's made that more than clear. I need to stop thinking about him. Craving him.* Wanting *him.*

I growled, the sound one that had my wolf perking up with interest as she scanned the snowbank ahead of us.

Sorry, I murmured to her. *I'm growling at Cillian, not at any sort of threat.*

She couldn't understand my words, but my tone placated her.

No danger, she'd basically translated. *Safe to continue onward.*

Our paws moved silently across the cold ground, leaving little imprints behind as we trekked along a flat stretch of land. My wolf kept glancing behind us and all around, vigilant and aware—like always.

The setting sun painted a pretty glow on the horizon, one that glittered off the icy earth.

I suppose that's a pretty sight, I thought, admiring the colors. *Although, Blood Sector has similar views during the winter.*

A sigh built deep in my chest, my heart beating a slow, morose rhythm.

When I'd agreed to the mating program, I'd thought moving to Night Sector wouldn't be bothersome at all. But I was beginning to realize that I hadn't thoroughly considered what it meant to leave the land my wolf and I considered to be our home.

We can start fresh. Make new friends. It's not like we have many in Blood Sector anyway.

Except it wasn't just about *friends.*

It was about the environment. The trees. The lush volcanic sand. *The way the grass feels against my paws.*

My wolf grunted at that last part and kicked at the snow beneath us, clearly understanding my thought process. She wasn't a huge fan of this environment either.

But maybe we can learn to love it, I said to her. *Let's... let's just try...*

She released another grunt—one that expressed doubt—and started forward at a trot.

The white blanket on the ground went on for miles. It wasn't entirely flat, but the hills were covered in snow, too.

Perhaps summers are—

My wolf paused, the fur along the back of my neck dancing.

We'd been alone on our stroll. But now... *There's someone coming.*

My animal's pointy ears swiveled, our senses on high alert as my wolf slowly glanced to our left.

Oh, it's you. I should have known *he* would interrupt my early evening adventure. *What do you want, Cillian?*

Unfortunately, my wolf's reaction to seeing Cillian's beast didn't quite match the irritation underlining my tone.

Because she was practically salivating at the sight of his massive form, nearly twice the size of our own.

His beast prowled forward with a confidence that had my wolf's tongue lolling from her mouth, her tail swishing in open delight.

Stop it, I demanded.

She didn't.

Not that I was surprised. My wolf followed her mating instincts, which were all homed in on the approaching Alpha—the one she had considered to be hers for far too long.

Cillian and I had never actually spent time in animal form together. Oh, I'd seen his beast, but always from afar. And I doubted he'd ever actually observed me as my wolf.

Why would he? I thought darkly. *I'm not in his league.*

Do you think it's wise to be wandering a foreign land alone, Ivana? Cillian asked, a chiding tone accompanying his words.

Wise? I repeated as my wolf cocked her head to the side. She'd picked up on his tone, too. And she wasn't sure she liked it. *I'm stretching my legs, Cillian. Going for a run. Surely you understand that as a fellow shifter?*

You're a guest here, Ivana. An unmated *Omega,* he said slowly, his words grating on my nerves. Because what the fuck did that have to do with anything?

I'm fully aware of my mating status, I growled back at him. *But thanks for the reminder.*

You're missing the point.

My animal huffed at his voice while I muttered, *Clearly.* Because why should it matter? *We're in a V-Clan sector. I'm safe here.*

Are you? he countered, his animal circling mine. *Out here? In the open air where anyone could drop in and snatch you away?*

My wolf and I snorted at him. *Who would possibly want to* snatch me *away, Cillian?*

His beast paused right in front of me. *Were you this confident when you ended up in that hole?*

Had I been in human form, my mouth would have dropped open at the cold reminder of how we'd met. *You're going to bring that up? Now? Here?*

I'm making a point.

And what point is that? I demanded. *That you're an asshole?*

A low rumble of sound left his beast, one that usually would have had my own animal taking a step back. But my wolf and I had never feared Cillian.

I'm pointing out that being in V-Clan territory does not mean you're safe, he snapped into my mind. *Why do you think I had to accompany all of you here? To* protect *you. This place is an unknown. Fuck, this entire experiment is an unknown.*

My wolf gritted her teeth, her tail no longer swishing. Not only did she not appreciate his tone, but she also wasn't a fan of his Alpha posturing.

You're an Omega, Ivana. Vulnerable. Small. Easy to catch. And this world is dangerous, he went on. *I would think you, of all Omegas, would know that.*

I can take care of myself, I bit back at him, irritated by his belittling statements.

Vulnerable.

Small.

Easy to catch.

Fuck. That.

His wolf released another rumble, the growl seeming to reverberate through the telepathic link he'd established with my mind as he uttered two words—*Prove it.*

What?

You heard me, Vana. You think you're safe out here? That you can take care of yourself? Then prove it. Show me what you can do. Show me how you would defend yourself against an Alpha. Fight me.

Had I been in human form, I might have laughed.

But I could hear how serious he was, could see it echoed in his wolf's stance.

No, I told him. *I'm not going to fight you.*

Because you know you'll lose.

Because that's not what I would do if an Alpha tried to attack me, or snatch *me, as you said.* My wolf released a huff of agreement. Or perhaps she was reacting to his nearness and the intimidating wave of energy swirling around him.

She was not impressed.

And neither was I.

I know better than to fight an Alpha in wolf form, Cillian. I would shadow somewhere and find a weapon to use—from a distance.

His beast started prowling around me again, that energy intensifying and causing my animal to whine in response. She didn't like the oppressive feel of his aura against ours, his presence no longer a welcome warmth, but a chilling caress.

What happens when you can't shadow, Omega? he asked me, his mental voice taking on a dark tone. *Will you end up in a hole again? Used and abused and waiting for someone like me to rescue you?*

I flinched inside, his words lashing against my heart and unleashing a myriad of memories. Of a time when I should have been safe. Of a time when I'd naively trusted those who'd been meant to protect me. Of a time when I ended up in the ground, unable to move. Unable to shadow. Unable to *scream*.

My wolf shuddered as well, no doubt feeling the haunting nightmare of our past creeping across my consciousness.

Or she was responding to the repressive energy weighing down on her being, demanding that she *kneel*.

Cillian…

If you wanted to go for a run, perhaps you should have mentioned it to Ransom. Asked him for an outdoor date instead of a movie date. He resumed his pacing, his power pressing down on me even more as he moved. *Or maybe you could have waited to ask Cael to escort you.*

My wolf's jaw clenched, her legs nearly giving out beneath the onslaught of his Alpha prowess.

He was making a point. Pushing my animal into the ground with mere thoughts rather than brute strength. He wanted me to *feel* his power. To scare me. To… to point out what an Alpha could do to me.

But I knew that better than most.

I was fully aware of the brute strength his kind possessed.

I'd just never expected Cillian to use it against me.

Especially after what I'd been through, how he'd found me, what he'd *seen.*

Running without a proper guardian is foolish and unsafe, he went on, seemingly oblivious to the turmoil he'd stirred inside my mind, the pain gouging at my heart.

This was the Alpha my wolf had chosen for herself. The Alpha she'd trusted.

But now… now he was using his power against us. Sharpening his energy like a weapon and making us *hurt.*

All while throttling my ability to shadow, I realized, his earlier question finally registering.

What happens when you can't shadow, Omega? he'd asked. *Will you end up in a hole again? Used and abused and waiting for someone like me to rescue you?*

I shivered inside, the reality of being grounded forcing my mind to push inward to a place I feared. A place I hadn't visited in six very long years. A place I'd created when my father had wrapped me up in an invisible noose and forced me to live in that *hole.*

Cold.

Alone.

Waiting for my *betrothed.*

A monster my father had sold me to.

A Gold Sector Alpha.

My wolf snarled, her instincts firing as she felt me retreat within our mind. She didn't want me to hide. She wanted me to *fight.*

Cillian had been talking, saying something via the telepathic link he'd established, but I hadn't heard a word of it.

I'd… shut him out. Wandered into that empty space inside my head, a place I'd resided in for what had felt like months while being trapped inside the ground, unable to move. Strapped down by an Alpha's mental restraints.

Just like now.

With an Alpha I thought I could trust.

And all for what? Going on an evening jog as a wolf?

Cillian had wanted to prove a point—that I wasn't safe here.

Congratulations. I believe you, I thought, not caring at all if he could hear me or not. *The only one I can trust to protect me is myself.*

Yet I couldn't shadow. He'd lassoed me with his strength, ensuring I was trapped before him.

Oh, my paws could move. But what would he do if I ran? Flatten me to the ground like my brother and father had? Force me to obey? Truly make me kneel?

Are you even listening to me? Cillian demanded, his words piercing through the fog of my thoughts.

No, I replied, both in answer to his question and in response to his dominant air. *No.* I would *not* be tied down again. I was a free Omega now, allowed to make my own decisions.

But not free to shadow, apparently, I growled to myself. *Likely not free to run, either. Because it's not safe here. And Cillian, the Alpha I thought would always protect me, just proved that he can't be trusted.*

Throttling my ability to shadow.

Chastising me.

Kissing me out of pity.

Sharing an igloo with one fucking bed.

Saying I wasn't in his league.

Rejecting me.

It… it was all too fucking much. I'd spent years pining for this Alpha, wanting to be his mate, thinking he was just playing hard to get.

But now…

Now I understand who you are, I muttered, my wolf's gaze meeting his dark orbs. *And I won't fucking bow.*

Vana… The nickname trailed off in my mind, his voice a mere whisper, one I shoved from my head before he could finish whatever profound statement or threat he'd intended to make.

Because I was done.

Done being rejected.

Done with his pity.

Done with being grounded by his power.

Done. With. Him.

My animal roared as I screamed inside my mind, needing to be *free*. Free of the burden of his presence. Free of this obsession. Free of this childish crush. Free of his oppressive energy.

Free. Of. Him.

"Ivana," he said, having shifted back into his human form.

I didn't even care that he was standing before me. Didn't care that he'd shifted in the blink of an eye. Didn't care that he was fucking naked.

Didn't care at all.

Because I wanted nothing to do with him.

Not anymore.

We're done.

I shadowed myself back to the igloo and directly into the shower, my wolf instantly giving me my body back. I wasn't sure if Cillian had released me from his oppressive energy or if I'd somehow fought him off.

It didn't matter.

I was alone.

And all I wanted to do… was cry.

I flipped the water on and lay on the heated tile floor.

It wouldn't stay warm for long, but I probably wouldn't even notice.

Because all I felt inside was ice.

Might as well freeze on the outside, too.

CILLIAN

What the fuck just happened?

I couldn't feel Ivana. Couldn't sense her mind. Couldn't even determine her location.

It was as though she'd just *died*.

I scanned Glacier Sector, searching for her presence. *Nothing*.

My inability to sense her suggested she was no longer within reach of my powers. Which could only mean she'd left Glacier Sector.

Did she go back to her nest? I wondered, bewildered and a whole hell of a lot concerned. *Did she shadow somewhere else entirely?*

Fuck. I ran my fingers through my hair as I scanned the frigid landscape. *Fuck!*

I pulled up a screen on my watch, my finger hovering over a phone icon.

Kieran would be able to tell me instantly if Ivana had returned to Blood Sector.

Or I could shadow there myself.

Except that would mean leaving the other Omegas.

Fritz and Benz weren't strong enough to guard them all against a pack of lust-crazed Alphas. Not that such a pack of Alphas currently existed, but the potential for one kept me rooted to Glacier Sector's ice.

How the hell did Ivana break my hold on her? I marveled. She shouldn't have been able to shadow, let alone leave this sector.

I'd been harsh. Cruel, even. *But wandering around without a guardian…* I nearly growled at the foolish concept. *What the fuck had she been thinking?*

For once, I couldn't even attempt to answer the question.

Because I couldn't fucking feel her anymore.

I uttered another curse and selected Kieran's name.

He picked up after the second ring, his face cast in shadows as he said, "Someone had better be dying, Cillian…"

"Is Ivana in Blood Sector?" I asked, ignoring the warning note in his tone.

He sat up, instantly more alert. "Last I checked, she was with you."

"Can you sense her in Blood Sector?" I reiterated, not in the mood to banter with my best friend.

Kieran fell silent for a beat. "No."

"Fuck." I hung up the phone and wiped my hand over my face. "*Fuck.*"

Where the hell did she go? My mind instantly pictured that hole I'd once found her in. *Starving, naked, bruised, and going into heat…*

I'd never forget that night for as long as I existed.

The images of a broken Omega on the verge of her first estrus assaulted my mind as my wrist buzzed with an incoming alert. I didn't even have to look at the screen to know it was Kieran phoning me back.

Growling, I shadowed back to the igloo before accepting his call. "I…" I trailed off, my nose twitching as Ivana's scent washed over me instantly. "I found her."

I hung up again before Kieran could reply, my focus entirely on the Omega I could *smell* but not *feel* in the igloo. I'd shadowed back here with the intention of finding my pants, but now all I could focus on was Ivana and the mental wall she'd somehow created between us.

That's new, I thought. Alphas had been able to block my ability to read their minds before, but never their *auras*. I could always sense their nearness, as well as their power.

But Ivana…

I sensed nothing other than her scent.

Sweet Omega perfume. Like an orange garden warmed by the sun.

Only there was an undercurrent of something sour in her fragrance. More like a grapefruit than an orange.

It inspired the memory of our first meeting to deepen in my mind, my nose twitching with the remembrance of her tainted scent.

So much sadness.

Devastation.

Fear.

The hairs along the back of my neck rose as I checked our perimeter, searching for any sign of a threat. Anyone or anything that could have made her feel this way.

But the only presence I sensed—other than hers—was my own.

And I'd been with her just moments ago, I thought. *When she'd vanished from the—*

My wrist buzzed again, Kieran's name scrawling through the air like a bad omen.

Taking a deep breath—one filled with that grapefruit-like perfume—I answered his call. "I'm sorry I disturbed your sleep," I told him before he could speak. "But I need to focus on Ivana right now."

His face hovered before me in a translucent shadow, his gaze searching. "I'll call Lorcan. He'll shadow in to cover for you while you fix whatever you fucked up."

This time, Kieran ended the call before I could reply.

Who says I fucked something up? I would have thought at him had he been close enough to hear me.

Except, I was pretty sure I had fucked up.

And the evidence of that fuckup was souring Ivana's scent.

Gritting my teeth, I followed her fragrance into the bathroom and froze just outside of the glass-doored shower.

My confident, mouthy Omega was currently curled up into a tiny ball on the floor while water rained down over her.

Another image of that fateful night washed over me, one of her doing that very thing in the shower I'd taken her to after rescuing her from that hole.

"Please, I'll… I'll do whatever you want," she'd whispered. "J-just don't ground me again."

"I'm not going to ground you, *macushla*," I'd promised her.

I broke that promise today, I realized, a pang splicing through my heart. *Fuck.*

All her thoughts—the disjointed ones that had caused me to shift back into my human form—suddenly made sense.

I believe you.

Not free to shadow.

Not free to run.

Not safe.

Can't be trusted.

I winced all over again, realizing that she'd likely been referring to me with those last two lines. The simple act of *grounding her* had destroyed her faith in me.

And rightly so, given our history.

"Vana," I murmured, kneeling beside the shower. "I'm so sorry, macushla." The endearment was one I hadn't used since the night we'd first met. It'd been reserved for her after that day.

Just like my purr, I thought, the rumbling sensation roaring to life inside me.

Oh, I'd purred for Omegas before her. But only when they were hurt or needed comfort.

However, that wasn't the reason I purred for Ivana now.

Or why I'd been purring for her all fucking week.

While she'd slept.

It'd been a temptation I should have ignored. A desire I had no business indulging in. A need I'd repressed for far too long.

This female would be my undoing. I'd known that since the moment her icy blue eyes had captured mine.

I just hadn't expected it to go down quite like this—with me on my knees while she silently wept on a barely warm shower floor.

It wasn't just my grounding her that had upset her. I'd gathered that much from her broken thoughts.

She was finally done with me.

Over her crush.

Over what we could have been.

Now, she was in mourning.

I had two options: Let her hate me and move on. Or beg her for her forgiveness and…

And what? I wondered. *And try to have a relationship with her? Could I be that selfish?*

She would never be able to come first. I'd devoted my existence to helping Kieran. It was the honor and respect he was due.

Ivana didn't understand that. She didn't understand me or my history. *Because I've never told her.*

Instead, I'd spent the last six years trying to push her away. To guide her toward a more reasonable future. One where she would be happy. In love. Properly worshipped.

Yet the woman before me now was none of those things.

Because of me.

"I never meant to hurt you," I told her softly. "Fuck, Vana, hurting you is the last thing I've ever wanted. It's why I've refused to let anything happen between us. I'm not good enough for you, love. I've never been good enough. And I'll never be good enough."

Uttering the truth aloud was agonizing in a way I hadn't anticipated. Because the truth was that a deeply buried part of me wanted to be good enough for her.

"You're the first one to ever tempt me from my fate," I confided to her. "But I'm not in your league, darling. That's what I was saying to Lorcan that day—you're in a league far above my own. And I need you to see that. To find someone better suited. Someone who can give you everything. Someone who…"

I trailed off, swallowing.

Because I hated everything about this conversation.

"Fuck, I'm trying. But it's…" I closed my eyes, my wolf growling furiously inside. He absolutely understood the gist of what I was trying to say, and he didn't agree.

Mine! he practically roared.

"It goes against every instinct for an Alpha to try to convince his Omega to pick someone else," I said through my teeth. "But it's the right thing to do. I'll never be right for you. Pretty sure I proved that this morning."

I'd grounded her in a way I shouldn't have.

All because I couldn't seem to control myself around her.

The moment I'd felt her wandering off without a chaperone, I'd lost my mind. She could have been taken. Hurt. Or a myriad of other things.

Was it likely something would happen to her? No, not really. Not with me here.

But just the mere concept of it had sent my beast

shadowing toward her. Because she was his to guard. *Until she finds another Alpha to protect her.*

I ran my palm over my face and finally opened my eyes, ready to comment further on what Ivana needed to find in a mate. But I found myself unable to utter the words as I took in the heartbreak etched into her expression.

She'd finally uncurled from her ball, and I truly wished she hadn't. Because the sadness in her features caused my heart to shatter into a thousand pieces.

I did this to her.

I hurt her.

I broke my promise.

"I'm sorry," I whispered again, my purr still radiating from my chest. "I should never have throttled your shadowing ability. I knew better. I…" I shook my head, cutting off what I'd been about to say. "I'm not going to insult you with an excuse. I shouldn't have done it. End of discussion."

She stared at me, her mind still eerily silent. If she weren't right in front of me, I'd worry she might be dead.

Because that was how this felt—this separation from her aura.

This is how it'll feel when she finds a mate and moves to Night Sector, I thought, my throat working to swallow.

I'd known losing her would hurt, but I hadn't realized just how painful it would be.

Yet this was worse. She'd chosen to lock me out. I had no idea how she'd done it. The ability was miraculous, and under any other circumstance, I'd be enthralled.

But right now, I'd give anything to sense her again. Even if her surface-level thoughts were all filled with hatred toward me, at least I'd be able to *feel* her.

"I thought you hating me would help you move on," I admitted aloud. "I was willing to accept the pain of your hatred if it meant your inevitable happiness." I ran my fingers through my hair and blew out a breath. "I'm still willing to accept that hatred, Vana. But this…" I trailed off, my gaze taking in the sadness etched into her porcelain features.

She wasn't happy at all.

She was downright miserable.

And that made two of us.

"I've said and done some things I'm not proud of, Ivana."

That was a fucking understatement.

However, I didn't voice that unnecessary addition aloud.

Instead, I went on by saying, "I thought I was making things easier on both of us. But nothing about this feels easy or right. I don't know what else to say, other than I was wrong. I'm here to protect you, not hurt you."

The words *I'm sorry* lingered on my tongue, but I'd already voiced them twice. She was going to either forgive me or tell me to fuck off.

The latter was more likely. And probably more warranted as well.

Still, I purred for her. Because it was all I could think to do. I remembered the hellhole I'd found her in all those years ago. I could only imagine the horrors threatening her mind now.

Her father had promised her to a Gold Sector Alpha. A fucking *dragon*. Not a wolf.

And her brother had done nothing to help her. Hell, when he'd told me about the arrangement, he'd *laughed*.

"What's with the Omega in the hole outside?" I'd asked while pretending to drink the blood-laced beer he'd offered me at his pack's version of a bar. It'd looked more like a cave.

I'd pretended to be a lone wolf, just passing through on my way to gods only knew where. The Alphas hadn't thought anything of it, the mixed pack filled with all types of wolves.

Ivana's brother and father had been the only V-Clan shifters.

And her mother had passed long before I'd arrived,

probably because her father had shared her with the other Alphas. I'd never asked, and Ivana had never mentioned it.

"She's a prize," Ivana's brother—*Chip*—had said, a smile in his tone. "For Alpha Oros."

"Alpha Oros?" I'd repeated, certain I hadn't heard that right.

"Gold Sector Alpha." Her brother had smirked. "He's paying for her with some of that mystic rock shit. The kind that creates barriers." He'd shrugged, obviously not fully aware of what Dragon Alphas could actually do with *mystic rock shit*. "She wasn't wantin' to uphold her part. So." He took a long swig. "Dad put her in the hole."

"She's about to go into her first heat," a growly W-Clan Alpha had added. "Chip here can't play for obvious reasons. But Jinx said we can knot the Omega bitch until the dragon gets here. If you want a turn, you'll have to get in line. Should be able to start sometime tomorrow, and I hear it'll go on for a month."

The excitement in his tone had been palpable.

And it'd disgusted me to my core.

We'd been close enough to where Ivana had been mentally chained for her to hear every word with her wolfish senses.

Which had consequently allowed her to overhear my reaction to her intended fate.

I'd been exceptionally violent, taking everyone down with a quick wave of power that none of them had anticipated. They'd assumed I was just a nomad passing through. A unique V-Clan wolf from a sector that had long been extinct.

Because that was what we'd led the majority of the supernaturals in the world to believe.

Eclipse Sector burned and all the wolves died.

Some powerful beings knew it was a lie. Most of those were either our allies or like-minded creatures who kept to themselves.

Regardless, I'd taken advantage of Jinx—Ivana's father

and the self-appointed small-pack leader—and his ignorance and killed all the Alphas in that run-down cave.

Then I'd freed Ivana and taken her back to my lair, where I protected her through her first heat.

She'd started in the shower—curling in a ball similar to moments ago—and quietly begged me not to ground her again.

When I'd promised not to throttle her abilities, she'd begun to sob.

For hours.

And hours.

Until finally, she grew quiet. Somber. *Curious*. That was when she'd first tested my words.

I'd sat in the hallway near the bathroom and waited patiently as she shadowed around my lair. Remained quiet as she'd shifted into her wolf and prowled through my personal quarters. Then cooked her dinner when she'd finally returned to her human form.

"Why am I no longer burning?" she'd asked, her voice barely audible. "How did you stop my estrus?"

"I didn't stop anything; Prince Kieran is using his healing power to shield you from your heat," I'd informed her.

Then I'd explained that Kieran would release her at any time. He'd only been helping her through the situation because he'd wanted her to understand she was safe before her estrus hit.

"In Blood Sector, we protect our Omegas during this vulnerable time. We don't *use* them or *trade* them. We cherish them. Kieran felt it necessary for you to understand that before…"

"Before losing my mind and potentially going insane," she'd finished for me, her expression astute and her words precise. "Will he be the one knotting me?"

I'd nearly choked on the bite of steak I'd just put in my mouth. *No,* I'd answered into her mind. *Kieran's betrothed.*

She'd blinked at me, seemingly unsurprised by my mental reply. *You're a telepath?*

Yes.

And you read minds?

Yes. I'd finished my steak. "But I try not to pry."

She'd cocked her head. "What am I thinking right now?"

I'd narrowed my eyes. "Are you doubting my abilities?"

"Yes."

My eyebrows had lifted in surprise.

Only for my power to sweep her mind and find that she was teasing me.

Except that wasn't the only discovery I'd made that day. I'd found Ivana's thoughts to be soothingly peaceful.

At least until she'd started thinking about asking me if I intended to knot her during her heat.

I might not mind that, she'd decided, her blue eyes dancing over me with interest. *In fact, I think I would like it.*

"No," I'd told her. "If you want an Alpha to help you through your first estrus, I can introduce you to a few. I won't be able to do that."

"Why not?" she'd boldly asked me, the cowering female from the shower nowhere in sight. A confident goddess had taken her place.

And she'd remained inside her until today.

Until I'd shattered her faith in me.

I shifted to lean back against the wall now, my legs tucked up so my arms could wrap around my knees. It was the same position I'd taken out in the hallway during her shower in my lair. Only this time, I was in the bathroom with her. Both of us naked and staring at one another.

I'd never answered her question that day. *"Why not?"*

Because the truth was that I'd been tempted to seduce her. To knot her. To make her mine.

Which had been so fucking wrong.

She'd been nineteen at the time, a young Omega on the verge of her future.

I hadn't wanted to destroy it by tying her to me for eternity.

Yet somehow, I'd managed to harm her anyway.

As evidenced by her continued silence.

At least she isn't crying anymore, I thought, admiring her clear eyes.

I continued to purr while holding her gaze. Time passed. At some point, I'd felt and ignored Lorcan's arrival.

I hear you fucked up, he'd said.

When I hadn't replied, he went about taking over my tasks.

All while Ivana and I continued this strange staring contest.

If the water had gone cold, Ivana didn't react to it. I almost reached forward to test it for myself, but I didn't want to risk spooking her.

She needed time.

I would give her time.

And my purr.

For as long as—

"What are my other unsavory qualities?" she asked, her question so unexpected that I couldn't stop my eyebrows from flying upward.

"What?"

"You told Lorcan that I need to find someone who won't mind my childish games, boldness, misplaced confidence, and other unsavory qualities. What are those unsavory qualities?"

Fuck. The fact that she remembered the precise phrasing I'd used, when even I couldn't recall all of what I'd said, spoke volumes about what my words had done to her.

"Ivana, I said those things out of frustration. If I tell myself your traits irritate me, maybe I'll one day believe it and stop wanting to…" I trailed off before I could finish the statement. But I'd already revealed too much.

"Wanting to what?" she asked, one haughty eyebrow inching upward as her inner goddess peeked at me through her beautiful eyes.

"It doesn't matter what I want, love. What matters is, I said some things that day that weren't fair. I meant, you need an Alpha who will adore your confidence and boldness and won't mind you setting him down when it's warranted. You deserve an Alpha who can put you first. Love you. Worship you. Exist in your goddess-like league."

Unfortunately, that Alpha would never be me.

But I could be good to her right now. Tell her the absolute truth. And hope that she was confident enough to believe it.

"There's nothing unsavory about you, Ivana," I told her, my accent thickening my voice. "You're perfect, macushla."

IVANA

"YOU'RE PERFECT, MACUSHLA."

Cillian's praise reverberated through my mind, conflicting with the pain and heartache he'd inspired over the last few weeks.

Everything he'd said—his explanations, his words, his *claim… "It goes against every instinct for an Alpha to try to convince his Omega to pick someone else."*

My belly flipped as his statement played through my mind once more.

His Omega.

He'd referred to me as *his* Omega.

Sort of, anyway. It'd been implied. Or maybe I was thinking too deeply about that single phrase.

I nearly sighed, irritated with the hope sparking to life inside me. I knew better. This Alpha didn't want me.

And yet…

He says I'm perfect.

But he also called me overconfident and annoyingly persistent.

Because he wants to believe that? I wondered, recalling everything he'd said to me this morning. *Because he thinks I'm in another league. A goddess-like league.*

That seemed too good to be true.

Just like when he kissed me…

I narrowed my gaze. "You're taking pity on me again, aren't you? Saying what I want to hear as some sort of lesson, similar to this morning, right?"

My eyes rolled, irritation prickling at my nerve endings.

Nothing he'd said was true. He simply wanted me to move on, find another Alpha, and leave him alone. Which I couldn't do while moping in the shower.

"You can stop trying to make me feel better, Alpha Cillian," I told him, cutting off whatever reply he'd just been uttering. "I don't need or want your pitying remarks, or any more pity kisses, or whatever else you feel you need to bestow upon me. I accept your rejection. Just leave me alone."

I forced myself to stand in the shower. Because it was time to focus on today.

And stop sulking over a man who doesn't want to be with me.

Closing my eyes, I allowed the water to wash over my face and drown my ears. Cillian was speaking, but I didn't want to hear him. I didn't want to see him. I didn't want to be near him.

He'd made his feelings clear.

And I was done—

His hand on my nape sliced through my thoughts, causing my eyes to pop open. "Cill—"

He yanked me around into his body with a force that left me winded in his arms, my startled reply dying on my lips in an instant.

"I do *not* pity you," he growled, his chest a hot wall of masculine flesh against my breasts. "And I've certainly never rejected you, Ivana."

Despite my breathless state, I managed a snort and muttered, "Six years of suffering through heat cycles alone says otherwise."

Both of his eyebrows flew upward. "*Ivana.*"

"What?" I demanded. "What are you going to do? Kiss me again? Maybe you think the earlier lesson didn't stick. Or, I know, maybe you'll give me a pity knot this time, hmm? Demonstrate how another Alpha should properly fuck me, right?"

His dark eyes resembled midnight storm clouds, his expression positively thunderous. "If I knotted you, Omega, there would never be another Alpha. I promise you that."

I huffed a laugh and rolled my eyes again. "Whatever, *Alpha Cillian.*" I tried to step back from him, but his grip tightened on my neck as his opposite arm encircled my lower back.

"I hurt you. I'm sorry. But if you keep sassing me, Omega, I will bend you over my knee and teach that sweet little ass of yours a *lesson* you won't soon forget."

Now it was my turn for my eyebrows to leap upward. "*Excuse me?*"

"You're being disrespectful and you know it."

"I'm being truthful," I bit back at him. "You keep doing all these things out of pity and—"

"I do not pity—"

"*No,*" I snapped, my palms landing on his chest in an effort to shove him away from me.

But he wouldn't budge.

The stubborn Alpha simply *growled.*

"Stop *lying* to me," I told him furiously. "Your actions and your words prove that you pity me, Cillian. I mean, you kissed

Ransom didn't, just to show me what an Alpha ... You offered to walk me home the other day from Quinn's palace, which you've never done before. Tonight, you chase me down out of some misconceived notion to protect me. Then you… you…"

I closed my eyes, my own growl emanating in my chest.

Because *how dare he* ground me.

But that wasn't the point here.

"I don't need or want your pity, Cillian," I said through my teeth. "I'm a big girl. I can handle your rejection. So just… stop doing whatever it is you're doing and let me move on."

I tried to push away from his grasp once more and found myself suddenly sandwiched between his hot form and the cold shower wall.

"Does this feel like I pity you, Ivana?" Cillian asked, his tone holding a lethal edge to it that caused goose bumps to scatter up and down my arms.

I swallowed, his heat a brand against my skin, specifically the hard part of him pressed up against my lower belly.

"Cillian—"

His palm slid from my nape to my throat, his gaze ensnaring mine and forcing me to submit. "It's my turn to talk now, Omega."

I shivered, his dominance washing over me in a welcome caress, one that had my wolf whimpering inside for more.

Her desired mate was naked, aroused, and had us pinned to a wall. There was only one outcome she could imagine in this situation.

Unfortunately, I knew of too many other ways this could end.

That knowledge was all that kept me from moaning out loud as Cillian drew his thumb in a circle against the throbbing pulse point of my neck.

"I kissed you because I wanted to," he said, the violent undercurrent of his tone still very much present. "It wasn't a lesson. It wasn't because I pitied you. It was because I *want* you. Because I've considered you mine for six very long years. And I'm struggling to do the right thing and let you go."

His words echoed in my mind, stirring a tidal wave of confusion. "If you—"

His grip tightened. "I'm not finished talking, Omega."

My wolf quivered at the way he said that, all dominance and grace, an Alpha taking charge and forcing his mate to *listen*.

But the woman inside me was stronger, causing my eyes to narrow in defiance.

"*That*," he growled, the storm churning in his dark irises. "*That* right there is why I find you so fucking irresistible, Vana. You're not afraid of me even when you should be. And you don't put me on a bloody pedestal either. You challenge me every damn day, surprise me constantly, and provide me with the most unique sense of peace, all at the same time."

He pressed his forehead to mine, his eyes falling closed as he inhaled deeply.

"Fuck, Vana. You have no idea what you do to me. How hard this is. How much I wish I could make you mine. But I'm not good enough for you. It's taking all my strength, all my *power*, to let you move on. Hell, to *force you* to move on. Except it's the right thing to do. *For you*."

"Why?" I whispered, my fingers lifting up to grasp his bare arms. "*Why* is it the right thing to do? If you want me, then why…? Why fight it?"

I didn't understand.

None of this made any sense.

"Because I can never put you first." He pulled back, his eyes open once more as he gazed down at me. "You deserve someone who will make you his world, Vana. Someone who

will always choose you over everything and everyone else. I can't be that someone."

"Who says I want that someone," I told him. "Who are you to decide what or who I should want?"

He sighed. "I'm doing what needs to be done to ensure your happiness."

I frowned at him. "Why do you get to decide what will and will not make me happy?"

He studied me. "Ivana—"

"No, Cillian. You said you don't pity me. Then you told me you want me. And now you're saying you can't have me because I deserve better. But I'm the one who decides who and what I deserve. Not you."

He released my throat and took a step back.

So I followed him.

"Either you're lying or you're making excuses. I can't tell which. But this is bullshit, Cillian. If you want me, prove it." Those were the two words he'd used outside when I'd said I could take care of myself. Might as well return the favor now.

Because if he meant any of this, then he needed to act on it.

"Don't tell me what I deserve or what kind of Alpha I should want. Respect me enough to let me make my own choices, and fight for me."

He drew his fingers through his thick, damp hair, the showerhead having rained down over his head and broad shoulders when he'd entered the shower. "I can't fight for you, Ivana. I can't take a mate."

"Why?" I demanded. "Why can't you take a mate?"

He gave me a hard look. "You already know the answer to that."

"Then tell me again."

"Kieran owns my fealty. He will always come first."

"Okay. And he doesn't want you to take a mate?"

"That's not what I said."

"You said you can't take a mate because Kieran will always come first. If he hasn't ordered you to remain single, then why can't you take a mate?"

"Because he comes first," he said through his teeth. "I won't take a mate just to make her the second most important wolf in my life. That's not fair to her. It wouldn't be fair to *you*."

"What isn't fair is for you to tell me what's good enough and what's not. Have you asked me if I mind being second to Kieran on your priority list?"

"Vana—"

"Answer the question, Cillian. Have you asked me how *I* feel?"

He clenched his jaw. "I won't let you sacrifice your happiness, Ivana."

"Do I look happy to you?" I asked him. "Have I seemed happy at all these last few weeks?"

His jaw tightened again. "You were laughing with Prince Cael."

I snorted. "Really? That's your answer?"

"It's a response to your question, Ivana."

"It's a deflection," I retorted. "You're making decisions on my behalf, and I don't appreciate it."

"I'm making a decision for both of us. I won't mate you or anyone else. And nothing you say will ever change my mind."

He turned to leave, causing me to gape at his back. "You're a coward," I realized out loud.

Cillian froze. "What did you just say to me?" His voice was deathly quiet, the shower nearly making him inaudible.

"You're a coward," I repeated. Because there was something he wasn't telling me. A reason he refused to give. "I would understand being second to Kieran. You know I would. Yet you won't even give us a chance. Because we might actually work. And that terrifies you."

I had no idea *why* it scared him, but it did. I was certain of it.

"It's either that or you're lying to me about everything in some ridiculous attempt to make me feel better. But I don't think that's it at all. My wolf has wanted you since the moment you took us back to your lair. And for six long years, I was certain you felt the same way. Until I heard you talking to Lorcan…"

I trailed off on a wince, the memory one that was still too raw for me to ignore.

However, everything he'd said to me tonight… it suggested my instincts were right. That Cillian *did* fancy me. He just didn't want to like me.

Because he feels he's unworthy of me.

Because he thinks I deserve better.

Because he's decided that we can't be together.

"Coward," I breathed once more, my gaze dropping to watch the water swirl down the drain. "I… I never realized that about you until now."

It… it changed things.

If Cillian was too afraid to fight for me—to fight for *us*—then maybe… maybe he'd been right from the beginning. *Maybe we shouldn't be together.*

"Say that one more time, Omega," Cillian said, a strange note in his tone. "I dare you."

"You're a coward," I repeated without bothering to look at him.

What's the point? I marveled, feeling defeated all over again. *If he's not going to try, not even going to* consider *being with me, then—*

Cold tile met my shoulder blades as a hard, masculine form pressed into my front. I gasped as his fingers tangled with my hair to yank my head back, his molten irises capturing mine. "That's a very dangerous thing to say to an Alpha, Ivana."

I stared back at him, feeling nothing inside just like I had when I'd first stepped into this shower. "Dangerous, perhaps. But that doesn't make it any less true."

He growled. "Do you think I enjoy watching you with other Alphas, Ivana? Because I don't. Not one fucking bit. But I'm willing to suffer if it means you'll inevitably be happier. There's nothing *cowardly* about my sacrifice."

"Who are you trying to convince here, Cillian?" I wondered aloud. "Me or you?"

CILLIAN

IVANA'S ABILITY TO challenge me drove me mad in the best and worst ways.

"You're a coward."

Those three words haunted me. I'd witnessed the sudden understanding in her features as she'd voiced that statement. She hadn't meant the proclamation to be cruel; she'd simply been vocalizing a realization.

And it was a realization I did not like.

Not one fucking bit.

Because a small part of me was now whispering, *Is she right? Am I a coward?*

Ivana seemed to think so, and that belief was changing everything. I could see it in her eyes, the way she seemed to look at me now. It'd all changed in a blink, the natural glow of intrigue disappearing from her gaze as a disappointed glimmer took its place.

My stomach twisted.

I didn't appreciate this change. It bothered me almost as much as watching her date other Alphas.

What happens when that amorous glitter appears for one of them? I wondered, a growl building in my chest.

A base part of me understood that this had all been tolerable because, despite everything, deep down, Ivana had still wanted me.

That had appealed to me on a level I hadn't fully analyzed, which naturally made me an asshole. I couldn't push her away while secretly being pleased that she never left.

Fuck.

Ivana sighed, her gaze leaving mine. I felt that departure deep in my soul, this moment profound in a way that had my wolf pacing inside me.

If I left her now, it would be the end.

She'd finally be free of her crush.

And I would be alone.

For good.

"I need to get ready for my date with Prince Cael," Ivana said softly, her demeanor and tone confirming my fears.

She shifted sideways, attempting to free herself from my grasp. My hands automatically tightened around her in response, my body refusing to let her go.

This… this can't be the end.

She's mine.

She's not.

She is.

The voices warred in my head, the thoughts swirling in a cacophony of insanity. This Omega… this woman… *Ivana…*

"*Fuck,*" I breathed. My grip in her hair forced her head back once more, causing her gaze to clash with mine. "I'm not afraid, Ivana. Not… not in the way you think. I… I made a vow to myself over a thousand years ago to never take a mate. To never be my father. To ensure his line ended… with me."

It was more than I'd ever voiced aloud to anyone.

Oh, Kieran no doubt knew. Lorcan, too.

But I'd never vocalized my intentions to them.

However, Ivana… I wanted her to understand. To not see me as a coward. To realize that I was trying to protect her—*from me.*

"He was a tyrant," I told her. "The former Alpha Prince of Eclipse Sector. Kieran took him down when I couldn't." Because I'd been too weak to finish the job. "That's how Kieran became an Alpha Prince." She might have heard about that in passing already. Or maybe she hadn't. Most wolves in Blood Sector weren't old enough to know the history of Eclipse Sector.

Because my father killed most of the Alphas and raped their Omegas.

And that had happened after exterminating every Beta in Eclipse Sector.

I winced at the graphic history unfolding in my mind. My bastard father had murdered many of my brothers and sisters, too. As well as all of their Omega mothers.

Including my own.

"My father was insane," I confided softly. "And I don't mean that as an exaggeration. I mean he was driven to insanity by bloodlust." I swallowed. "I don't know what triggered it, but whatever it was likely exists in me. So when you talk about fear, Ivana, *that* is my phobia—becoming my father."

Which was why I'd devoted my life to saving Omegas from troublesome situations.

My father had created a harem of unwilling Omegas, knotting the women without regard to their consent and sharing them with Alphas from other clans around the world. He hadn't fraternized with V-Clan kind; he'd preferred the mentality of Z-Clan and X-Clan wolves.

I repeated some of that aloud to Ivana, withholding the violent details. Then added, "He killed everyone in Eclipse Sector who was over the age of fifteen, as well as all of his Alpha sons—except me. The only reason I survived was because he saw himself in me."

A fact he loved to comment on every time we locked eyes. "It's like looking in a mirror," he'd say, pleased. "Just need to toughen you up, my boy."

My grip in Ivana's hair loosened, my stomach churning with the memories of my past. Memories of *him*.

"I was thirteen when he finally died," I muttered. "It took me far too many years to take him down, and in the end, I hadn't been able to finish the job." That was when Kieran had taken over and severed my father's head from his body.

Lorcan had then tossed the remains into my father's pride and joy—his dungeon incinerator.

The stench of that damn place still haunted me today, despite it having been long destroyed.

"I was a coward that day," I admitted aloud. "But I'm not a coward with you, Ivana. I'm trying to be strong, to encourage you to find a better mate, to ensure you're not tied in any way to my darkness."

I released her hair to palm her cheek.

"I'm not worthy of an Omega mate, love. It's a fate I've long accepted. Although you've certainly tempted me to reconsider, I can't allow myself to be that selfish. Because I don't deserve to have such a beautiful gift in my life." I brushed my lips against hers in the softest of touches. "If I could have you, I would in a heartbeat. But it would be wrong, Vana. Very, very wrong."

My heart felt somehow lighter now that I'd revealed the truth to her.

I wished she could be mine.

But she couldn't.

"I vowed long ago that I would dedicate my life to

protecting the remaining inhabitants of Eclipse Sector and their kin. That vow expanded when Kieran took over Blood Sector and brought all our wolves with him. I serve at his side willingly because he earned my fealty. And I will spend my existence making amends on behalf of my bloodline."

It was my due. Too many wolves had lost their parents before they even knew them, all because I hadn't been able to take my father down on my own.

I'd needed Kieran.

"That sounds lonely," Ivana whispered, drawing my gaze to her mouth. There was something in her tone that hypnotized me. Or maybe it was just the female herself.

Everything she did captivated me. Made me question my fate. Had me longing for something I shouldn't. Forced words from my mouth that I shouldn't say…

"Being alone has never bothered me," I murmured. "It's my life."

"That doesn't have to be your life, Cillian." Her palms skimmed up my sides, the warmth of her touch causing my wolf to freeze inside me. Anticipation hummed through my veins, my inner beast curious as to what she might do.

Her fingers danced over my chest, causing me to hold my breath.

I didn't want to move.

Didn't want to frighten the exploring Omega.

Didn't want to destroy this unique moment between us.

I'd told her things I hadn't said to anyone else. Provided her with a history that left me feeling inferior as an Alpha. Gave her all the reasons why we couldn't be together.

Yet she was… moving closer to me.

"You don't have to be alone," she told me, her gentle voice a kiss to my senses. Her warmth moved up to my face, her palm cradling my cheek. I leaned into her hand, desperate for more. Utterly lost to her display of affection.

My hands fell to her hips, my fingers gripping her with a need I could barely suppress.

Fuck. I had no idea what was happening here, but it was profound. Powerful. *Us.*

And I really didn't want to fight anymore.

I just wanted to indulge in her soft, feminine touch. Let her pet me. Absorb her words. Believe them, if only just for a few precious seconds.

Ivana's fingers trailed up into my hair while her opposite palm remained against my cheek.

I swallowed, feeling oddly vulnerable. It was… strange. Very unlike me. But I just wanted to melt into her, accept every ounce of her affection.

It was selfish.

I didn't deserve this or her.

But I let her lead. Let her press her lips to mine. Let her breathe me in as though I was the oxygen she craved.

Or maybe it was me breathing her in.

Because I suddenly felt anchored to her. Reliant on her to hold me in place. To ground me. To *center* me.

"Vana," I said on a reverent exhale, my lips brushing hers.

"Shh," she hushed me. "Let me show you what it could be like, Cillian. Let me be with you. Just for a minute."

I shuddered, a hint of alarm sounding from somewhere deep within my mind. *Stop this*, that part of me demanded. *Stop this before it's—*

Her tongue traced my bottom lip, silencing my thoughts.

For the first time in my life, I relinquished control.

I gave my Omega what she craved—a piece of me.

No, not a piece. *All* of me.

If only for a second, I would grant her access to my mind, body, heart, and soul. She was the first Omega to ever tempt me. The first Omega to ever make me consider an alternate path.

And I'd responded by pushing her away.

All while my wolf had pined for her.

Our Omega.

Our mate.

Our Vana.

I groaned as her tongue slid into my mouth, her kiss far more tentative than the one we'd shared after her date.

That had been about hunger.

This… this was about something so much deeper. A connection I'd fought for far too long. A yearning that existed between our souls.

But as her tongue touched mine, it awoke something much less tentative inside me. Something visceral. Something *feral.*

My fingers dug into her hips as I pulled her more firmly against me, my mouth taking charge of hers in the next breath.

I needed more.

I needed her.

I needed *this.*

Her taste. Her tongue. Her willingness.

This wasn't about teaching her what she deserved or showing her how an Alpha should kiss an Omega. It was about how *I* would embrace her. How *I* would touch her. How *I* would worship her.

She moaned as I pressed her up against the wall once more, my palms sliding up her wet, naked body to cup her firm breasts. They fit perfectly in my hands, her curves made for my touch. For *me.*

Because she's mine.

My wolf growled inside, agreeing with the claim. His rumble grew so loud that I couldn't hide it, my chest vibrating against Ivana as I kissed her harder. More thoroughly. More *intently.*

Cillian. The mental voice didn't belong to my Omega, so I ignored it.

Only Ivana mattered.

Her touch. Her heat. Her *slick*.

Sweet fuck, I groaned, my inner animal practically rabid with the need to taste our Omega between her thighs. Her citrusy scent had blossomed into an aroma that suffocated every single one of my senses.

My knot throbbed.

My stomach tightened.

My heart raced.

I just wanted to kneel and lick every fucking inch of her.

But her fingers were tangled with my hair, her tongue dueling with mine.

This was no longer soft or sweet or emotional; it was intensity personified.

She wrapped a leg around my hip, her moan an invitation against my mouth.

I lifted her up without thought, my pulsing cock instantly finding her weeping cunt. "Vana," I growled, sliding against her, reveling in the heat bathing my shaft.

She arched in response, her clit rubbing the head of my dick as she whimpered with need.

Too fast, I thought. *Too fucking fast.*

Yet we'd been dancing around this for years.

"*Fuck.*" I was losing control again. But I couldn't tell if I was handing the reins to Ivana or to my wolf.

I wanted to be inside her so damn bad.

To *rut* her.

Knot her.

Claim her.

Her nails scratched down my back as her sweet pussy ground against my aching cock. "*Cillian.*"

I didn't even know if she was ready to take me. *Has she ever been taken by an Alpha*? I wondered.

And instantly wished that I hadn't.

Because the thought of anyone else fucking her had me wanting to murder whoever had dared touch *my* Omega.

It also had me wanting to drive inside her and claim what was meant to be mine. To make sure she forgot everyone and anyone who might have touched her before me. And to ensure no other Alpha would ever be good enough for her in the future.

So fucking wrong.

Feels too damn right.

My hands skimmed up her sides to once more palm her perfect tits. I teased her hard nipples with my thumbs while my lower half firmly pinned her against the wall.

It wouldn't take much to enter her.

But an insistent pull in my mind held me back, reminding me to be gentle with her. To cherish her as an Alpha should.

My wolf grumbled inside, his need for her bordering on violence. It'd been six very long years since I'd taken a woman to my bed.

I hadn't meant to fall into a bout of celibacy, but after meeting Ivana, I'd simply lost interest in everyone else.

She'd consumed every ounce of my attention, dragging me into one of the hardest battles of my life.

It was a battle I was currently losing.

A battle I no longer wished to take part in.

Not with the pliable, willing Omega pressed up against my hard, aroused flesh.

Ivana caught my bottom lip between her teeth, causing my eyes to flash open and collide with her dangerous gaze.

If she bit down, it would initiate a mating bond between us. A bond that required me to bite her in return.

Don't tempt me, macushla, I thought at her, belatedly realizing that I could access her mind again.

Whatever block she'd created had long since crumbled to dust, allowing me to hear the sensual intentions dancing through her thoughts.

Gods, I groaned, enthralled by her imagination. Yet the underlying hint of innocence told me she wasn't experienced.

And that…

That forced me to slow down.

To take a breath.

To gently remove my lip from her teeth so I could trail kisses across her cheek.

She needed tenderness. Adoration. *Worship.*

My hands returned to her hips, my lips going to her ear. "Have you ever been knotted, Vana?"

Her fingertips skated down my torso, nearing my groin. "Not by a real Alpha, no."

I frowned. "Are you being coy with me, darling?" Because that certainly seemed like a very Ivana thing to do.

"I have a toy," she whispered. Her blue eyes lifted to mine, only to drift to the side a heartbeat later as she added, "For my heat cycles. Because… you never…" She swallowed and shook her head. "I don't think it's the same as a real knot, but it… helps."

A note of sadness haunted her mind, pushing away some of her lustful thoughts.

He never came, she was thinking. *He left me to suffer alone. Because he never wanted me.*

"Fuck, Vana, I—"

A loud knock against the bathroom door interrupted me mid-sentence. My power instantly locked on our intruder, my gaze narrowing as I spun in his direction.

I should have sensed his entry, should have known he was here by his *scent.*

But I'd been so consumed by Ivana and her sweet fragrance that I'd failed to properly monitor our surroundings.

Of course, the *Beta* had just shadowed into the igloo—something I knew with a sweep of his mind.

At least I hadn't been so far gone that even my wolf had failed to detect his physical approach.

Alas, I should have been aware enough to catch his mental intentions.

That was a problem I'd fix *immediately*.

You better have a damn good reason for interrupting us, Beta, I telepathically said to Benz.

Lorcan sent me was all he said in reply. But I heard—and *felt*—his underlying irritation.

He didn't like that I was in here with Ivana.

And he really didn't approve of the alluring scent of her slick in the air.

I ignored his presence and connected to Lorcan's mind. *You sent Benz for me?*

You weren't responding to my calls. The stoicism that typically underlined my old friend's voice was notably replaced by annoyance. *We have a situation.*

What kind of situation?

Lorcan went straight to the point, replying, *Omega Sylvia was found unconscious thirty minutes ago in her igloo.*

I froze. *What?*

Someone drugged her, Cillian. I'm healing her, but it's an estrus stimulant. When she wakes up, she'll be in heat.

A growl escaped me. A growl born of unadulterated *fury*.

Stimulating an estrus was common for other types of wolves. Some Alphas didn't want to wait to breed their chosen Omegas.

However, that wasn't how we did things in the V-Clan sectors. We respected our Omegas and their cycles.

One of these Alphas isn't playing by the rules, I thought to myself, my hands balling into fists. *And that asshole broke those rules while I was otherwise occupied.*

"What is it?" Ivana asked, pulling me from my thoughts and forcing me to look at the heart of my distraction.

"I need to go," I told her, the words a rumble in my chest.

Fuck. I shouldn't have even been here at all.

It was my job to watch the Omegas.

My *duty* to protect them.

And I'd been too caught up in Ivana to focus on my task. On my *vow*.

This… this was precisely why I couldn't mate her. She was a dangerous distraction. A tempting fate. *An unattainable ideal.*

"Cillian," she said, grabbing my arm. "Tell me what's going on."

"Benz can explain," I replied as I shadowed out of the shower to grab a towel. The Beta opened the door, causing me to glare at him. "You can explain *after* Ivana is dressed."

"You act as though I haven't seen her naked before," he drawled, leaning against the doorjamb and blocking my exit. "She's my best friend, Alpha Cillian. We run together as wolves often. She's like a sister to me."

The way he said that sounded like more of a warning than an explanation. Like he was trying to tell me to be careful with her or he would make me pay for hurting her.

I would have laughed if I weren't so concerned with the situation at hand. "Move, Beta."

He held my gaze for a beat too long, then sighed and stepped back to allow me to pass.

"Cillian," Ivana called as she grabbed a towel to trail after me.

By the time she entered the main room, my pants were already on. "I have to go," I told her again as I grabbed my shirt.

Then I shadowed before she could try to stop me.

I'm sorry, Vana, I whispered into her mind. *But I can't be yours.*

Not now.

Not ever.

Because I was married to my duty first.

Everything else had to come second.

Or bad things happened.

Bad things… like this.

IVANA

Cillian's apology caused my teeth to grind together in annoyance.

You can be mine, I snapped back at him. *You just have to fucking communicate with me.*

Either he ignored my reply or he'd tuned me out, because he said nothing.

Stubborn Alphahole, I muttered at him.

"What's going on?" I asked Benz without looking his way. I was too busy trying to find clothes. I hadn't actually washed my hair or my skin, but I'd showered last night. So I should be fine.

"Sunshine," Benz said slowly. "Are you sure you want to do this?"

My brow furrowed as I glanced at him. "Do this, as in…?"

He gave me a look. "You know what I mean."

"No, I really don't."

"I'm a wolf, Ivana. I may not have seen what you were doing in there, but I could smell it," he told me, causing my cheeks to burn.

"*Benz.*"

"What?" Both of his dark brows shot upward. "That asshole broke your heart. And you finally have a chance to maybe find someone else. But if you let him play with you like this…"

"He's not playing with me," I argued. "He…" He'd *confided* in me. Told me things I could tell were personal to him. Things he hadn't said to many others, if anyone at all. "Cillian's complicated."

Benz snorted. "No shit."

I tugged on a pair of jeans. "I don't want to debate Cillian right now, Benz. Just tell me what's going on."

Because I could use the distraction from my thoughts—which were all basically whirling with frustration.

Cillian had finally kissed me.

Then he'd apologized.

For shadowing off after kissing the hell out of me? For kissing me in general? For something else entirely?

I wanted to growl, scream, and cheer, all at the same time. It was a mingled mix of emotions that I forced to subside as I yanked on a shirt and waited for Benz's response.

When he didn't say anything, I met his incredulous gaze and arched a brow.

He sighed in response and shook his head. "If he hurts you…"

"Then he hurts me," I replied, not wanting to discuss it further. "Now tell me what has Cillian jumping into Alpha mode."

"When is he not in Alpha mode?" Benz muttered as he ran his fingers through his thick brown hair.

"*Benz.*"

"Has anyone ever told you that you're demanding for an Omega?"

I narrowed my gaze. "Stop stalling and spit it out." Because I recognized a deflection when I saw one.

The flicker in his turquoise irises told me I was spot-on, too.

As did the curse that slipped through his lips as his head fell back for him to stare up at the ceiling. By the time he looked at me again, his expression had turned somber, telling me something was really wrong. "Lorcan found Sylvia unconscious in her igloo."

I frowned. "Did someone knock her out?"

His mouth twisted. "Sort of."

"What do you mean, *sort of*?"

"She's going into heat," he replied. "A forced one."

I blinked, not understanding. "Because someone knocked her out…?" That wasn't how a heat cycle was provoked. Besides, Sylvia was a V-Clan wolf. "Our heat cycles aren't set to begin for a few more months."

We only went into estrus during the summer. It was one of the reasons our kind chose to thrive at night—Omegas hibernated in our nests during the sunny months.

Because of our cycles.

If Sylvia was going into heat now, then…

I swallowed.

Then someone or something forced her cycle to begin.

Which is what knocked her out.

"Oh," I breathed. "*Oh.*" This was bad. Very, *very* bad.

And worse… *This happened on Cillian's watch. While he was with me.*

I'm sorry, Vana, he'd mentally told me. *But I can't be yours.*

Because he was no doubt blaming me for distracting him from his job.

He'd laid it all out for me, explaining why he felt he didn't deserve an Omega, why he wasn't good enough for me, why he'd devoted his life to protecting others while living alone.

Cillian carried the weight of the V-Clan world on his back, shouldering the blame for his father's sins.

And now Cillian was out there trying to fix whatever had happened to Sylvia, all while likely blaming himself for spending time with me.

I nearly growled in frustration.

Stubborn. Fucking. Alpha.

I hoped he heard that.

But he'd probably already blocked me from his mind.

Too bad, I thought at him. *Because I can be just as stubborn.*

He liked me. Wanted me. Felt I was too good for him. Desired more, but told himself he couldn't have it.

Which made it my job to prove him wrong.

We could be good together. Perfect, even. I didn't need to be his first priority. Would it be nice every once and while? Sure. However, I understood his need to protect others. I respected that need, too.

And this was the perfect time to show him that.

"Let's go see what we can do to help," I told Benz as I pulled on a pair of snow boots.

I didn't wait for my best friend to agree—he knew better than to argue with me when I set my mind to something anyway—and shadowed outside.

My nose told me where to find Cillian, as well as Sylvia.

Because Benz had been right—she was definitely going into heat.

My stomach twisted at the notion of being forced into an estrous cycle against my will. Some clans did that to their Omegas. V-Clan wolves did not.

That made this situation even more troublesome.

Several Omegas were outside, arms folded around their middles, eyes concerned.

Ashlyn stood among them, her crystal-blue eyes meeting

mine as I approached. She and Sylvia were friends, yet she didn't appear all that concerned. "It's started," she murmured softly once I was a few feet away. "Remember what I told you, please."

I frowned at her. "About what?"

All-consuming Alpha energy surrounded us before she could reply, the strength and vitality preceding Prince Cael's arrival as he materialized across from me.

"Ivana," he greeted with a soft smile that instantly froze on his handsome face.

He slowly looked toward Sylvia's igloo as his two Elites shadowed in beside him, the intimidating males immediately scenting the air and following Cael's gaze.

"What the hell…?" Prince Cael trailed off, his blue-green irises flickering to his brother, Dixon. "You came by ninety minutes ago for a security sweep and said everything was fine."

His brother's jaw tightened. "It was. This is obviously a recent development." His sharp green eyes drifted across the crowd, landing on me for a split second before skipping along the other Omegas. "We should—"

Cillian appeared between me and Prince Cael, cutting off Dixon's commentary and my view of the three males. "Kieran is on his way. He wants to have a word with all participating Alphas, including you."

Another wave of masculine intensity accompanied Prince Cael's reply of "I see."

Silence.

I shivered, Cillian's magnetic energy mounting with each passing second. He appeared to be measuring his powers against Cael and his two Elites.

Or maybe he and Cael were engaged in a mental conversation.

Regardless, it left an uneasy current in the air, one that made some of the Omegas squirm in response.

I cleared my throat and glanced at the other women. "Perhaps we should all go have breakfast?" I suggested, trying to remind the two Alphas of their audience.

Cillian, I added in a mental whisper. *You and Cael are making the Omegas even more nervous than they already are.*

He didn't reply.

"Evening breakfast sounds like a good idea," Benz said, acknowledging my commentary. "Let's go to the main lodge and see what's—"

"No," Cillian interjected. "The Omegas are returning to Night Sector with Lorcan. The jet is already being prepared."

"But it won't be ready for another hour," Fritz added as he stepped out of Sylvia's igloo. "Breakfast might be a good idea."

It was a daring move to question an Alpha's judgment. But Cillian's focus remained on Cael, the two males refusing to look away from each other.

This isn't helping.

Tired of their posturing, I shadowed between them and gave Cillian my back so I could look up at Prince Cael. "Can you escort us to breakfast?" I asked him in the softest tone I could muster.

Cillian firmly grabbed my hips, an action Cael didn't miss.

But I pretended not to notice as I added, "I think the Omegas would feel more comfortable if an Alpha Prince accompanied them."

Because whatever was happening here between him and Cillian was having the opposite impact, and what the Omegas needed most right now was a distraction.

"Please?" I pressed, finally catching the prince's gaze. The sharp quality of his features gentled as he refocused on me, an indulgent expression loosening his tightened jaw.

"It would be my honor," he replied, his voice as smooth as ever.

"Thank you." I gifted him with a small smile before glancing at Benz. "Can you lead the way?"

Since when do you command my men? a velvety voice inquired in my mind, the words paired with a subtle squeeze against my hips.

I took a page out of Cillian's book and ignored him, my focus on Benz and the Omegas.

"I'll be there in a moment," I told Benz. "I just need to have a quick word with Cillian first."

Now isn't the time for this, Vana, Cillian telepathically replied. *I realize I left abruptly, but I have—*

Shh, I hushed him. *I'm trying to focus.*

"Oh, and, Ashlyn, if there's any smoked salmon, can you save me a piece?" I asked, doing my best to sound completely normal. Like the fact that an Omega was going into heat in the igloo didn't faze me at all.

The light-haired Z-Clan Omega's lips tilted up like she understood what I was doing and nodded. "Yep. A cream cheese toastie, too?"

"Yes, please." I was surprised she knew I liked that side with my salmon. But then, it seemed there was a lot more to Ashlyn than just a few cryptic comments.

Such as the one about Prince Cael and his darkness, I recalled, glancing at him now.

He didn't seem all that *dark.* If anything, he appeared quite relaxed and almost bored.

Except his gaze kept shifting down to where Cillian's hands clasped my hips.

A subtle tic started in his jaw as Cillian's thumb moved in a possessive circle, the Alpha behind me no doubt fully aware of his movements.

Or maybe it was subconscious.

I'd have to ask him about it later. For now, I just wanted the testosterone-filled air to dissipate and the Omegas to relax.

"I'll save you a seat, Ivana," Cael said to me.

I smiled. "Thank you, Cael."

He winked at me—likely pleased by me addressing him informally—and turned to help Benz escort everyone to the lodge in town for breakfast.

Once they were all well out of earshot, I shifted to face Cillian. His hands followed the movement, allowing me to complete my rotation before settling once more on my hips.

"Look, I'm sorry for what happened between us, but—"

"Stop," I interrupted. "We can talk about that later. What I want to know is when the jet will be here, who will be piloting it, and is it going straight to Night Sector, or will it be stopping in Blood Sector first?" Because those were the questions that the Omegas would want answers to.

He stared down at me somewhat warily as he replied, "In an hour, Lorcan, and straight to Night Sector."

I nodded. "Do all of us need to go to Night Sector, or can Blood Sector be an option?"

"You don't want to go to Night Sector?"

"I would prefer my own nest," I admitted. "But if I'm permitted to go to Blood Sector, others may want to go there, too. So before I make any decisions, I want to know what all the options are."

"I imagine all the others will prefer Night Sector since it's their home."

"I agree," I told him. "But on the off chance anyone suddenly decides they would prefer to go to Blood Sector, I want to know if it's even an option."

He stared at me. "You can go back to your nest in Blood Sector, Ivana. And if anyone else wants to go there, that's fine, too."

I nodded. "Okay, good. Now, what can I tell them about Sylvia, because they're going to ask about her?"

He shook his head. "I don't know anything yet. She's… unconscious. Lorcan's trying to heal her, but whatever is in her system can't be reversed." The frustration in his tone grew with each word, ending in him releasing me to run his palm over his face. "This is my fault. I was distracted and—"

"Did you drug her?" I demanded, cutting him off.

"What?" He looked at me as though I'd physically slapped him. "No. Of course not. How could you—"

"If you didn't drug her, then this isn't your fault," I snapped, interrupting him again. "So stop blaming yourself and focus on mitigating the situation. What I need are details I can share with the others to keep them calm. What can I tell them?"

He just blinked at me.

"Great, that's very useful, Cillian. Thank you."

His eyes narrowed. "You're choosing now to sass me, Omega?"

"I'm always going to sass you, Alpha. Now stop stalling and answer my question so I can take care of the Omegas while you focus on finding out who hurt Sylvia."

Cillian gaped at me for a beat, his shock palpable. However, he quickly recovered with a subtle clearing of his throat.

"Tell them the truth—Sylvia's heat isn't natural. Kieran will be here soon to evaluate her, then we'll be questioning all of the Alphas with access to this sector. Because one of them dosed her with something. And that Alpha will be removed."

I didn't need him to elaborate on what *removed* meant.

"Thank you. I will do my best to relay all of that in the softest way possible," I promised him. "I'll also ask if anyone has seen or heard anything suspicious."

And I'd start with Ashlyn.

With the plan set in motion, I stepped around Cillian to head toward the lodge.

But I found myself suddenly unable to move because my nape was caught in his palm.

He gently pulled me back to face him and pressed his

forehead to mine for a long, silent moment. *We'll talk soon,* he promised into my mind.

There's nothing to talk about, I countered, my palm lifting to his cheek. "This is what it feels like to have a partner, Cillian," I added aloud. "You don't have to do this alone." I went up onto my toes to brush a kiss against his mouth.

Then I shadowed to the lodge before he could reply with a contradictory statement or something snarky.

He didn't get to have the last word this time. I did.

And I would show him what I meant about having a partner.

By taking care of the Night Sector Omegas and trying to put them all at ease.

Easier said than done.

However, I had to try, not only for them but for Cillian, too.

CILLIAN

I STOOD DUMBFOUNDED on the icy street for too long a second after Ivana vanished.

When I'd sensed Cael's arrival, I'd shadowed out here to stand between him and Ivana. It wasn't that I suspected him of drugging Sylvia; I just didn't want him near Ivana. She was mine to protect. Mine to… Well, just *mine*.

I couldn't seem to stop my wolf from trying to claim her, even though I knew I shouldn't.

"Fuck," I muttered, my palm running over my face. This day was not turning out how I'd expected at all.

"Mate her," Lorcan said as he appeared beside me.

I glanced at him, my eyebrow arched. "What?"

"You heard me. *Mate. Her.*"

I didn't need to ask him whom he meant. "You sound like Kieran."

He lifted one big shoulder in a shrug, his expression saying nothing at all. Lorcan rarely ever spoke, which made his commentary all the more important. Because he'd felt it necessary to voice it aloud, something he would never do unless he truly meant it.

"Speaking of," I began, changing the subject. "What did Kieran decide?" He and Lorcan had been discussing how to handle Sylvia when I'd felt Cael's arrival. I'd shadowed outside on instinct, leaving Kieran and Lorcan to debate next steps without me.

It'd been an unusual reaction for me, but my wolf had demanded that I shadow to Ivana. And I'd been too caught up in the sensation to fight it.

If it had bothered Lorcan, he hadn't said anything.

Just as he didn't comment on my shift in topics now.

"He wants me to shadow Sylvia to Blood Sector. I've made her as comfortable as I can; Kieran will need to do the rest."

"Blood Sector and not Night Sector?" I asked, clarifying.

Lorcan dipped his chin. *He doesn't want to leave Quinnlynn unguarded*, he informed me mentally.

I see, I replied, a frown tugging at my lips. *He's concerned this is just the beginning of something nefarious, isn't he?*

Lorcan shrugged again. *If it is, we'll handle it.*

Indeed, I agreed.

"Mate her," Lorcan said for the third time, causing me to narrow my eyes. *You're not the only one adept at abrupt topic changes*, he thought at me, his expression and mental tone devoid of emotion.

"She deserves better than me," I bit back at him.

"I know," he agreed, voice still flat. "So do better."

With that, he vanished. And a second later, the scent of an Omega in heat began to dissipate, telling me he'd taken Sylvia to Blood Sector.

"He's right," another voice said, preceding Cael's arrival as he shadowed into Lorcan's place. "She deserves better."

My eyes narrowed once more for an entirely different reason. "Let me guess—you believe you're better for her?"

"Oh, I know I am," he drawled, making my hands curl into fists at my sides. "But I think you could be best for her, if you could manage to take your head out of your ass."

My eyebrows flew upward, his words rendering me momentarily speechless. I was both flattered and insulted, and above all, shocked.

"Ivana is an ideal mate," he went on. "She's intelligent, confident, witty, fucking stunning, and she wants pups. She'd be perfect for me if it weren't for one very serious flaw."

My teeth ground together. *She has no flaws.* The words flowed from my mind to his, primarily because I couldn't hold them back. *She's perfect.*

"She's in love with you," Cael stated matter-of-factly. "And while I can handle a lot of flaws, that's one my wolf can't accept."

My jaw tightened even more. *It's a crush, not love*, I wanted to argue. *And it's not a flaw, asshole.*

Although, truly, it was. Because I wouldn't be able to mate an Omega who coveted another Alpha, either.

"So get your shit together, Cillian," he continued, not giving me a chance to speak. "Otherwise, I'm going to be really fucking tempted to show your female how a real Alpha treats his chosen mate. And I can guaran-damn-tee you that that little flaw of hers will become a distant memory—one she'll eventually forget, while it haunts you for eternity."

I swore my jaw was going to break from clenching it so hard. "Why does that sound like a challenge?" I asked him, my inner beast pacing inside me, ready to teach this *Alpha Prince* a lesson in dominance.

Cael was powerful, and we'd be evenly matched.

But on this, I'd win.

"Because I'm threatening to take what's yours," Cael said,

his blue-green eyes flashing with promise as he all but plucked the words from my mind.

I'd win this fight because it involves Ivana.

"Either treat her right," he told me, "or fuck off."

"It's not your job to protect her," I growled at him. "So if anyone should fuck off, it's you."

He snorted. "You're right. It's your job. So do *better*, Cillian." His inflection on the word *better* brought us full circle to how this strange conversation had begun.

However, rather than shadow off like Lorcan had, Cael simply turned away from me, the action making my inner wolf claw at my insides in fury.

I'd just been *dismissed*.

And the Alpha who had done the dismissing wasn't concerned at all about presenting me with his fucking back.

"If I didn't know any better, Cael, I'd say you were trying to pick a fight with me, perhaps to distract me from the events of this evening?" I taunted, the theory popping into my head before I could properly think it through.

Cael froze.

Then slowly faced me once more.

"If you think I had anything to do with Sylvia's condition, then you've not been paying attention, *Elite*."

His reference to my position was intentional. A reminder. One that had me meeting his gaze without flinching.

"Then why are you suddenly so concerned with my personal affairs, Cael?" I asked, purposely leaving off his princely title.

"I couldn't give two shits about your 'personal affairs,' Cillian," he returned, his wolf dancing in his eyes and turning the blue-green irises to a darker shade of blue. "Ivana, however, has piqued my interest. She deserves better. So if you don't figure your shit out—and soon—then you're going to lose your Omega to a real Alpha Prince."

The air chilled around us, our wolves staring each other down. "There you go challenging me again."

"I only challenge worthy opponents." His pupils flared as he looked me up and down. "And I certainly don't see one standing in front of me."

I took a step forward, my animal raging inside. "You see your better standing before you."

"No," he bit back. "I see a fucking coward. So fix your shit, Cillian. Fight for your Omega. Treat her right. Or I'll show you what a real challenge looks like."

The bastard shadowed before I could respond, leaving me growling at the empty space in front of me. *And you call me a coward,* I snarled into his mind.

A snort was his only reply, his mental thoughts instantly turning to the Omegas standing nearby.

Or one Omega in particular.

My Omega.

For just a second, he let me hear his appreciation as he met Ivana's gaze. Then he shut me out with a mental shove that nearly knocked me on my ass.

My gaze narrowed. Either this was all meant to be some sort of distraction from the issue at hand or…

Or he really meant everything he said.

My hands fisted at my sides. First Kieran, then Lorcan, and now Cael. Kieran and Lorcan's concern with my personal life made sense—they were my best mates. But Cael? Cael and I… we weren't exactly friends. But we'd never been enemies to one another either. Actually, he tended to serve as an ally when I needed him to.

He also had a fondness for games. Typically, political ones, which I also excelled in. Hence our undefined relationship. One that was about to be severely tested if he tried to take Ivana from me.

Except she wasn't really mine.

Not yet, I thought.

No. Not ever. I shook my head, a growl vibrating my chest as my inner wolf adamantly disagreed with the direction of my thoughts. Or maybe my animal was reacting to the knowledge that Prince fucking Cael was near our Omega right now.

Because I could hear the thoughts of those observing Ivana and Cael as they started distributing meals to everyone in the room.

They look good together, Ashlyn was thinking, her voice abnormally loud and grating on my nerves. *I wonder what their pups will look like.*

My jaw clenched as I shut her off, only to be sucked into Ransom's mind as he internally groused about unfair competition, how he couldn't compare to an Alpha Prince.

I snorted. *With thoughts like that, no, you'll never be able to compete,* I nearly said to him. But I swallowed the mental words and instead shadowed to the dining area that Ivana had escorted all of the Omegas to.

I leaned against a wall shrouded in darkness, the shadows seeming to gravitate toward me as I took in the room.

Almost everyone was seated, most of the Omegas quiet and huddled together while Alphas sat at other tables, their postures guarded as they watched the exits.

No one noticed my arrival, primarily because I hadn't allowed my presence to be felt. I always preferred to linger and to listen without being seen. Situations such as this were why I'd perfected my stealth-like abilities.

I tuned in to the surrounding mental voices, sifting through them and listening for any hints of what might have happened to Sylvia.

All the while, my gaze remained on one focal point in particular—*Ivana.*

She stood by a table of Omegas, her blonde head bent as she calmly said, "Sylvia will be okay. King Kieran is a healer. He won't let anything happen to her."

"But she's in heat," a dark-haired Omega named Glory whispered. "And there are unmated Alphas in Blood Sector."

Ivana nodded. "Yes, true. But Blood Sector has a system in place that guarantees consent."

"What system?" Glory asked, her thick brows furrowing.

"Blood Sector Omegas make a list of Alpha candidates for our estrous cycles," Ivana explained softly, causing my heart to squeeze.

Because I knew all about Ivana's list.

And the only name she had noted there.

Mine.

"Only those Alphas are allowed near our nests during our times of need," she added.

"But Sylvia doesn't have a list," Omega Brie chimed in, her dark complexion appearing somewhat pale from the low lighting above. "And she can't make one in this state. She wouldn't even know who to choose."

"Not all Omegas have a list," Ivana told her. "There are places with, um, appropriate accommodations, for those who don't have an Alpha to help them through their heat."

Glory frowned even more. "What kind of accommodations?"

"The kind that provides relief," Ivana said carefully.

"Toys," Brie inserted.

Ivana's cheeks pinkened a little as she said, "Yes."

And my knot instantly pulsed to life.

"I have a toy," she'd told me. *"For my heat cycles. Because… you never…"*

I winced, recalling where our conversation had been headed right before Benz had interrupted us. *Fuck. I owe Ivana an apology. An explanation. Something. Anything, honestly.*

My throat suddenly felt tight, my ears straining as I returned my focus to Ivana and her conversation with the Omegas.

"At the Sanct…?" Glory was saying, only to trail off on a

cough, the action not at all masking her intended words. "I mean, in, um, Night Sector?"

"I… I don't know what you use there," Ivana hedged, "but I imagine they're similar."

Fuck, they're still talking about toys. I really should shift my attention to the others in the room. But my throbbing knot held me captive, my gaze glued to Ivana and her alluring mouth. Her tongue slipped out to lick the plump lower lip, almost as though she could feel my eyes on her.

Knowing Ivana, she probably did.

The little vixen always seemed to sense me. It was a miracle she hadn't glanced my way yet.

"Is that what you've done, then? Used toys?" Glory asked Ivana. "Do you not have a list?"

I swallowed as Ivana murmured, "No, I… I have a list. But only one…" She pinched her lips to the side. "Just because an Omega gives an Alpha consent doesn't mean he'll take advantage of the permission."

Glory and Brie gaped at Ivana.

"Alphas say no to knotting an Omega in need?" Brie sounded shocked.

"Stubborn ones do," Ashlyn chimed in from across the table, the Z-Clan Omega having remained quiet throughout the entire exchange until now. "Ones who don't realize the gift that's standing right in front of them can be quite blind sometimes."

Cael stopped behind Ashlyn, his lips quirking upward. "How right you are, sweetheart," he murmured before setting down a tray of beverages in the middle of the table. "But most Alphas of worth fully acknowledge that gift and accept it without hesitation." His gaze fluttered up to Ivana as he spoke, causing my Omega to blush in response to his open appraisal.

My jaw tightened, my wolf raging once more. *You must have a death wish,* I told Cael. He might be able to keep me from reading his mind, but he couldn't block my telepathic ability. *I can't see any other reason why you continue to provoke me.*

Maybe I find it fun, he returned, the words loud and clear, almost as though I were reading his mind. But no, he'd just allowed the surface thought to pass through whatever magical barrier he possessed inside his head. *Or maybe I want you to find happiness. Depends on how altruistic you find me to be, hmm?*

His gaze snapped up to me in the shadows just for a second before he returned to the long spread of food and beverages to grab a drink.

Kieran and I were going to have a lengthy chat about *Prince Cael* when he arrived. While I didn't think the Alpha Prince was responsible for Sylvia's condition, he'd very clearly grown in power over the last century. And that was something worth discussing.

Because Lorcan, Kieran, and I had always kept an eye on Cael and the other princes. However, we'd categorized Cael as an ally with reasonable abilities.

Now, I wondered if he was an ally with profound abilities.

Or an impressive enemy masquerading as a docile ally.

He lifted a glass my way in a false *cheers* motion, almost as though he could hear my calculative thoughts, then tipped the water into his mouth and downed it like one would a shot of liquor. Then he set it aside, picked up another tray, and took it to a table next to where Ivana had stood moments ago.

Only, she wasn't there now.

I glanced around, then froze as she materialized beside me in the shadows, her body seeming to blend in with mine despite her fair features.

CILLIAN

Have you picked up on anything noteworthy? Ivana mentally asked as she took a sip from the drink in her hand. The liquid was pale yellow in color, the sweet yet sour scent suggesting it was lemonade in her cup. *About Sylvia, I mean,* she clarified.

I admired her long, delicate fingers wrapped around the stem of her glass, as well as the way her throat lightly bobbed with each swallow. A myriad of sensual images danced through my mind, each of them involving her lips wrapped around something much larger—and harder—while her throat created a similar motion.

It was wrong.

The timing was absolutely inappropriate.

And yet, I couldn't seem to halt the stream of thought.

Such a dangerous distraction, I told myself. *Which is why I can't have her.* Shouldn't *have her.*

Cillian? she prompted, her gaze on the room despite her thoughts being directed at me.

Yes?

Her lips curled down a little. *I asked if you'd found anything.*

Oh. Right.

I'm still working on it, I lied. Well, it wasn't technically a lie. I was trying to work. I just… *Fuck, Ivana, I'm sorry. I—*

Her free hand grabbed mine, giving it a squeeze. *Don't. Not here. Not now. We both have a job to do. You figure out who drugged Sylvia while I keep the Omegas calm.*

And who is going to keep you calm? I asked, at a loss for what else to say to this marvelous creature.

She faced me, one blonde eyebrow inching upward. *Do I need to be calmed?* she asked, her tone underlined with a profound patience that I couldn't help but respect. *Because I feel pretty calm, Cillian.*

How? I asked her. *How are you so calm?*

She lifted a shoulder and took another sip from her glass, the picture of nonchalance.

I know you'll figure this out and protect us, Cillian. And I know Sylvia is safe in Blood Sector. My only concern right now is regarding the Sanctuary Omegas. They don't have the same experience and faith that I do. This is all still very new to them. They need reassurances right now, which I can provide. And you'll do the same when you determine who hurt Sylvia.

Her hand squeezed mine once more before slipping away.

Or she attempted to, anyway.

I intertwined our fingers before she could and tugged her back to me, her warmth a welcome sensation against my skin.

For whatever reason, I wasn't quite ready to let her go.

Maybe it was her calm aura.

Maybe it was the fact that I didn't want her to go anywhere near Cael.

Or maybe I simply needed her.

Who the fuck knew? I just couldn't release her. Not now.

Not after she'd found me lurking in the shadows. She'd done this countless times before, but something was different now. I wasn't sure if it was our time in the shower or the forbidden kiss I'd stolen from her, or some combination of both.

All I knew was I couldn't release her. Not physically or mentally.

Cillian? she asked, her mental voice tentative.

I need a minute, I told her, my thumb running along her hand. *Just sixty more seconds.*

Okay, she replied, not asking me to explain.

Instead, she stood quietly beside me while finishing her drink, her mind as peaceful as ever. She exuded a serenity unlike any other, her mere presence allowing me to breathe a little deeper.

I'd spent so many years fighting this pull between us, this urge to just sink into her embrace and allow her to care for me. So many tense moments. So much physical and mental strain.

It was like I'd been drowning for years and had refused to let her tug me up to the surface for air. But I'd been drowning for her. Protecting her from my turbulent undertow. Ensuring she could remain in the blissful sun without me anchoring her to the ocean floor.

Some might say I was selfless.

Others might call me selfish.

I supposed it was all about perspective, because right now, I felt more selfish than I'd ever been, holding her hand and keeping her away from all the Alpha suitors in the room. Staking a claim I shouldn't be allowed to stake.

Yet it felt too good. Too right. Too *necessary*.

I swallowed, my eyes scanning the area before us and noting the quiet murmurs occurring between the Omegas, as well as the guarded looks among the Alphas. They were all questioning each other's intentions, wondering if one of the others had tried to hurt Sylvia.

The general undertone of fury suggested they were all innocent. None of them were pleased that Sylvia had been drugged.

It was an anger I shared with them all.

An anger the Omega beside me miraculously quieted.

Our minute stretched into two minutes. Then five. And on to ten. All the while, Ivana remained by my side without uttering a word, allowing me to focus my mind and continue scanning everyone around us, including the inhabitants of Glacier Sector not in this dining hall.

A myriad of emotion-filled thoughts swirled through my mind, allowing me to filter them out as I searched for useful information.

Concern. Rage. Fear. Some irritation.

But no guilt.

And the fear was coming from the Omegas, not from an Alpha afraid of being caught.

I clenched and unclenched my jaw. There were only three Alphas I couldn't read at all—Cael and his Elites.

Kieran's not going to be pleased, I told Ivana. *We're going to spend days questioning everyone.* Which meant he would be away from his pregnant mate.

Everyone? she repeated.

I haven't been able to find a single clue or hint in anyone's thoughts, which means I'm missing something. A fact that had me questioning everything. Sylvia had been assaulted on my watch while I'd been distracted. And now, I had no proof.

Or no one here is guilty, she murmured. *Maybe whoever hurt her shadowed in and out before anyone could sense them. Or perhaps this was done before we even arrived.*

I startled at her thought. *Before we arrived?* I echoed, considering her words.

Suppressants take weeks to build up in an Omega's system. She glanced at me. *Couldn't a heat inducer work similarly?*

What do you know about suppressants? I asked, the concept causing the hairs along my arms to stand on end. *You—*

I've never taken them, she interjected before I could finish my next question. *But I know all about them. Just like I know a lot about the drugs used in Bariloche Sector. Quinn would probably be a good resource to ask about heat inducers.*

My stomach twisted at the mention of the hellhole Kieran, Lorcan, and I had pulled Quinnlynn from a few months back. Fortunately, she'd been mostly unharmed—just drained of energy from healing all the Omegas around her.

But some of the other Omegas had been in much worse shape, many of them having been drugged repeatedly by the former Alpha of Bariloche Sector and his merry band of sadistic supporters.

I'll talk to Quinnlynn, I informed Ivana and moved to face her, placing the room at my back. But these next two words needed to be spoken aloud, not whispered into her mind.

She needed to understand the importance of what she'd just offered me. Not just the ideas in her thoughts, but also the quiet comfort she'd provided when I'd needed it. And the show of leadership she'd displayed when taking over with the Omegas.

"Thank you," I told her softly, my palm reaching up to cup her cheek as I bent to press my forehead to hers. "Thank you, Ivana." It was worth repeating.

You don't have to thank me, Cillian.

I do, I admitted into her mind. *When this is done, we'll talk.*

Her responding sigh touched my lips, her agitation momentarily glittering in her mind. However, I pressed a kiss to her mouth before she could reply to my comment.

Because we would talk.

About what had happened today. Before today. After today. Just… *everything.*

Alas, for now, I left it with a brief kiss, trying to display my intentions and my emotions without words.

Then stepped back to finally let her go.

Lorcan will be here soon to pilot everyone to Blood Sector. I expect you to get on that plane, Ivana.

Her blue eyes held mine for a long moment before she nodded. *Okay*.

Okay, I echoed, my palm still cupping her cheek. I brushed my thumb against her bottom lip, my gaze following the action. *Be safe, macushla. But call me if you need me.*

She stared at me for another beat, her eyes searching. Then she dipped her chin again in a small nod and disappeared to rejoin the Omegas.

Ashlyn instantly moved over, making room for Ivana. My Omega studied her for a second before setting her empty glass on the table and sliding onto the open chair. She almost seemed wary, the exchange a bit strange.

However, everything surrounding the Z-Clan Omega seemed off. Even her thoughts—which were once again surface level and seemed to be directed right at me as she thought, *That's much better, Alpha. Much better indeed.*

I didn't reply, instead wrapping myself even deeper into the shadows. Then I pulled up a screen from my watch and typed a message to Kieran, one I knew he wouldn't like. But Ivana's point had been extremely valid.

Ask Quinnlynn to evaluate Sylvia. Specifically, see if the condition reminds her of anything from Bariloche Sector.

She'd once said a V-Clan Alpha had been visiting the captive Omegas. And we'd yet to determine who that Alpha had been.

It was a long shot, but if the condition was similar, then it could be the same Alpha.

And Ivana's comments about how the serum might have been given to Sylvia before she'd arrived in Glacier Sector could hold merit.

My wrist buzzed as Kieran replied with, *I'll talk to Quinnlynn.*

Let me know what you learn. I have nothing to report here.

Well, except for Cael's growing powers.

But that was a discussion Kieran and I needed to have in person.

Minimizing my screen, I leaned back against the wall and resumed my lurking.

Let me know if you need any food, Ivana thought at me. *I'll sneak something over to you.*

My lips almost curled. *I'm all right for now, but thank you.*

Okay, but even stubborn Alphas need to eat, Cillian.

The only thing I want to eat right now is you, Vana, I answered before I could stop myself.

A loud clatter drew my gaze to her at the table where she was apologizing for dropping her fork.

My lips truly curled now. *Careful, love. You're supposed to be calming the Omegas, not startling them.*

Cillian, she practically growled into my mind, causing my smile to grow. *You can't… don't… ughhh.*

I can't what? Eat you? I canted my head a little. *Pretty sure I could devour you, macushla. Several times.*

Stop, she hissed. *You're distracting me.*

Hmm, I'm quite familiar with the problem, I drawled. *Very pleased to return the favor now.*

She growled again but didn't say anything. Out loud, she was asking Ashlyn about the notebook on the table. The Z-Clan Omega murmured something about it being her doodling journal.

"The real ones are… well, I already told you about all that. Hopefully, you remember," Ashlyn concluded.

I almost interjected again, just to make Ivana blush once more, but I decided to let her be.

Because she'd been right—now wasn't the time for this.

Maybe later.

Or maybe never, I thought, my smile disappearing as I ran a hand over my face.

I had a job to do first.
Then… then I would… figure this shit out.

PART IV

Dear Stars,

Alas, I'm on the plane again, heading home to Blood Sector.

Honestly, this all feels very strange. I... I don't really know what to say other than that. Mostly because my solace and peace are being interrupted by an interloper. Ashlyn. Yeah, I see you looking over my shoulder. Why are you intruding—

Ivana,

Has anyone ever told you it's rude to write about other people? I've been told that. Though, I suppose, sometimes it's necessary. Sometimes it helps. And sometimes it hurts. Of course, you don't know what I mean yet. Alas, you will. Soon.

Please don't forget what I told you. Under the floorboards, Ivana.

Oh, and tell Cillian that a new life is more important than an old one. I'll be fine.

Sweet dreams (or is it all real?),
Ashlyn

Stars... Or should I just write this to you, Ashlyn?

I don't even know what to say to any of that. So I'm closing my journal now.

Ivana

IVANA

Several Hours Later

Home sweet home.

Only it didn't feel all that *sweet* to be here.

Sighing, I fell back into my nest, my gaze on the ceiling. It'd been a long flight home. I could have shadowed myself back to Blood Sector, but I hadn't wanted to leave the other Omegas. They'd needed someone—*a local*—to soothe their nerves.

I'd done the best I could. Now, the Sanctuary Omegas were with Quinn and Kyra. They'd be better at providing comfort, mostly because of their shared histories.

Rather than stay, I'd opted to come back here. Alone. Primarily to think about Cillian.

He'd remained in Glacier Sector where all the Alpha

candidates were gathering for a meeting. Kieran would be off to join them any minute now. He'd chosen to wait for all the Omegas to settle in his palace before leaving. As soon as he did, Lorcan would become the acting Blood Sector Alpha. Or King, I supposed.

Or is it the Blood Sector Prince? I grunted. *Who the hell knows the right term anymore?*

Yawning, I curled into a ball and shifted my focus to Cillian. Primarily his *knot.* Because now I knew what it looked like. How it felt. And yeah, my toy—I glanced at the drawer housing said instrument—wasn't nearly accurate enough.

My thighs squeezed together as I recalled the way his knot had felt against my core, how hot and thick he'd been between my legs.

Stars, this wasn't the time to be thinking about this. Not after everything that had occurred tonight.

First Sylvia.

Then all the Omegas being concerned about what had happened and what might happen next.

And then there'd been Ashlyn.

She was… interesting. The Z-Clan Omega had been mostly quiet the entire way home, except for when writing in my journal. I'd wanted to snap at her for it, but something in her gaze had made me bite my tongue.

Forlorn, I thought, picturing her again now. *She had looked so forlorn.*

Sylvia was her friend. Of course Ashlyn was worried. Yet it'd felt deeper than that, almost as though she'd given up hope.

Rather than lecture her on journal etiquette, I'd tried to convince her—and several others—that Blood Sector was safe. That Sylvia would be okay. That the Alphas here would protect all of them, not hurt them.

Are Quinn and Kyra repeating all of that to them right now? I wondered.

Probably.

I blew out a breath and closed my eyes.

I'd never been great at making friends, but I'd tried to be one today. If the other Omegas hadn't believed me, they'd believe Kyra and Quinn.

If that didn't work, then this whole program would probably go up in flames.

"If it hasn't already," I muttered to myself as I pushed away from my nest. "I need a distraction. Maybe food."

And now I was talking to myself.

"Good job, Ivana," I grumbled.

Shoving aside my bout of quirkiness, I focused on fixing a comfort meal. *Noodles. Cream cheese. Tomato sauce. Mozzarella cheese. And bake it for thirty minutes.*

The minute the buzzer rang, I devoured a good portion of my pasta-bake casserole.

All while thinking of the night and Cillian. *Has he gotten any closer to determining what happened?*

I'd ask him, but I didn't want to interrupt him. Not yet, anyway.

Now that I knew how he really felt about me, and how he considered himself to be unworthy of an Omega, I was determined to fight for him. To fight for *us*.

So if he tried to push me away—which I had no doubt he would—I'd chase him. I'd give it my all. And if he still refused me…

I swallowed.

I… I didn't want to consider that outcome. Not yet. Not now.

Forcing the thought from my mind, I cleaned up the kitchen while the sun rose outside. No way was I going to sleep anytime soon. I didn't even feel tired. Which was strange, as I'd barely slept yesterday.

What I needed to do was relax.

I glanced at my nest and beyond it to the nightstand.

That's one way to relax, I thought, shivering as I pictured the toy in the drawer.

But after feeling Cillian's knot, the way it pulsed heatedly against me…

My throat worked once more.

Yeah, no. No toy. But maybe a bath.

Thirty minutes later, I found myself lounging in the tub filled with my favorite salts, and still thinking about Cillian's cock.

I growled.

The pent-up need I felt for him had been stoked to a roaring fire in that shower, only to be instantly doused in ice water upon Benz's arrival.

However, the flames licking through my veins were reigniting now that I was alone with my thoughts. *Thoughts of Cillian. His long, muscular form. Naked. Wet. Aroused.*

I closed my eyes and pictured all the hard lines of his exquisite form, the little dimples by his hips, the defined planes of his abdomen, up to his impressive pecs.

Oh, who was I kidding?

I wasn't looking up; I was looking *down*.

At his knot.

Throbbing.

Beckoning my touch.

I wanted to wrap my hand around him and stroke. Slowly. Memorizing the path. *Owning* him.

My Alpha. My wolf. My Cillian.

You can try to run, but I'll chase you, I warned him, aware that he couldn't hear me here because he was probably still in Glacier Sector. *You're meant to be mine, Alpha. None of this "unworthy" bullshit. Mine. Mine. Mine.*

Only, he wasn't here for me to growl at. Yet his scent was everywhere. It was so strange because he'd never been in my home before. However, I swore I could smell him here.

He's embedded in my skin. In my heart. In my damn soul.

Oh, but how I wished he were embedded in me somewhere else. Somewhere between my legs. I moaned at the thought, my body inflamed all over by the prospect.

I'd been on edge all day, the other Omegas barely distracting me from the yearning deep within me. A yearning Cillian had awoken with a vengeance after pinning me to the shower wall.

Stars, I'd been so close to exploding. So close to experiencing Cillian's Alpha touch.

Or maybe his mouth, I marveled, recalling the words he'd said into my mind, the ones about *devouring* me.

He'd been flirting with me in that dining hall, treating me like a desired Omega rather than a rejected one.

And I'd loved it. Perhaps it hadn't been the most appropriate time for his mental commentary, but it'd given me hope.

Remembering it now didn't inspire hope so much as lust because I could picture his face between my thighs and his tongue against my slick core.

Cillian, I moaned in my mind, my palm gliding down my belly toward the place I ached most.

I should have brought my toy into the bathroom. Should have known I'd end up touching myself.

Gods, I want your knot inside me, I wanted to tell Cillian. But he wasn't here. So I thought it to myself instead as my fingers explored my damp flesh. *This isn't the same…*

My touch wasn't hot enough or hard enough.

I almost felt like I was going into heat with how badly I craved my Alpha. That was how pent up I felt from our shower escapades. All amplified by six years of wanting a man I couldn't have.

A man who'd desired me the entire time yet fought his attraction under some misguided notion that I deserved better.

You're mine, Cillian, I growled in my mind. *I won't let you reject me again.*

"I never rejected you the first time, Vana," he replied, causing my eyes to spring open.

He stood in the bathroom entrance, one shoulder propped up against the door frame, muscular arms folded, dark eyes smoldering.

"Cillian," I breathed, my lungs ceasing to work.

"Ivana," he returned, those sinful irises skating down my naked form—a form he could obviously see through the water. I found myself suddenly wishing I'd made a bubble bath instead of just using salt.

My hand instantly left my core, my cheeks warming in response.

"Don't stop on my account," he murmured, eyes slowly tracking back up to my face. "I was very much enjoying the show."

My hand curled into a fist. "What are you doing in here?" I sputtered, ignoring his commentary regarding the *show.*

"Well, I was in the hallway and about to knock, but then you threatened to chase me if I ran, so I shadowed inside instead." His lips curled slightly. "If you'd like to chase me right now, in your current state, I think you'd catch me very quickly."

I swallowed, my cheeks burning even hotter than before. "You heard all that?"

"Kind of hard not to, macushla," he replied softly. "You were shouting at me, then moaning." His gaze dropped once more. "Please continue. I'd like to see how this ends."

I was so flustered that I didn't even know how to respond to that.

Naturally, I chose the first thing on my mind and said, "You're supposed to be in Glacier Sector."

"Hmm," he hummed. "I was there, yes. But there's nothing left to discuss. The Alpha candidates all appear to be innocent. Thus, we need Sylvia to tell us what happened, and it's going to be a while before she's coherent enough to speak. So, I think I'll pass the time by watching you come."

"*Cillian*," I choked out, at a loss of how to even begin reacting to his abrupt topic change.

"Yes, preferably with you saying my name as you climax." He pushed away from the door and sauntered toward me. "Show me how you pleasure yourself, Vana. Perhaps I'll reward you with a similar demonstration."

My heart seemed to beat harder in my chest, creating a thudding sound in my ears. There was so much promise in his words, so much unveiled *intention*, that all I could do was stare up at him.

"Touch yourself," he told me, a hint of dominance underlining those two words. "I want to see how you like to be stroked." He stood right over the tub, his arms loose at his sides. "Teach me, Vana. Show me what pleases you."

CILLIAN

I didn't come here for this. I'd simply wanted to check in on her before heading home.

Hell, I'd expected her to be asleep.

But no.

She'd been loudly thinking about me. Captivating me with her thoughts. And any notion of doing the chivalrous thing, such as letting her go once and for all, dissolved into dust.

She was beautiful. Naked. Wet. Aroused. And craving *my* knot.

It took physical strength to stand here above her, fully clothed, and not touch her. But I wanted her to finish what she'd started. I wanted to watch her lose control. Hear her breathing change. Smell her need. *Her slick.*

"Touch yourself," I repeated. "Now, Ivana."

Because I needed to see her fall apart. To witness every

excruciating second of it. To know what I'd been missing all these years. To determine how far off my fantasies had been from reality.

It would be a punishment and a gift. Sweet torture. Savage passion.

I'd been a fool to deny us both this connection. Or perhaps I was a fool to give in to it now.

The nuances no longer mattered. Reality could fuck off right along with my past vows.

Because all I cared about in this moment was Ivana's hand and the tentative shift of her touch toward the slickness between her thighs.

"Be bold, macushla," I told her. "Show me what I've been missing these last six years."

Her nostrils flared, a challenge igniting in her gaze.

There's my vixen. My Omega. The one who has never feared me.

I let her hear my thoughts, my mental voice open to her mind. It seemed only fair given everything I'd overheard from her.

Her furious need.

Her threat to chase me.

Her begging for my knot.

Her claim.

It was madness. Intense. A fucked-up fate.

But this Omega wanted me, even after everything I'd told her. She was determined to show me what we could be together. To embrace what little I had to give.

I didn't deserve her.

So do better, Lorcan and Cael had said.

Gods, I would need to accomplish more than just *better*. And I had no idea where to start. If I even wanted that future. If I could even attain it.

However, that uncertainty—what little there was left of it—fled as Ivana's finger brushed her clit. She jolted in response, her back bowing and bringing the tips of her beautiful tits into view above the water.

Fuck, I wanted to bend down and lick her. Nibble her. *Bite* her. Mark every godsdamn inch of her body. Scent her. Ensure everyone else knew she was *mine.*

This all-encompassing desire was going to slay me. Shred my control. Demolish whatever resolve I had left to do what was right. Hell, I couldn't even define what was right or wrong anymore.

And that hand between her thighs wasn't helping matters.

Gods, she looked amazing.

All flushed and panting.

Her mind begging for more. For my knot. For me to fuck her the way an Alpha should.

"Keep going," I told her, my voice holding a touch of a growl to it. Because I was both loving and hating this demonstration. I wanted to help her. Touch her. Kiss her. *Claim* her.

But I needed this punishment. I *deserved* it.

Six long fucking years, I'd denied us both. I'd denied *this.* Her parted lips. Lust-blown pupils. *Dripping* sex. I could see her so clearly through the water, her finger sliding inside herself with ease. Every time she brushed her little clit, she tensed, then moaned inside her mind.

"Talk to me," I demanded. "Don't keep it to yourself, macushla. Torture me with your words."

"Cillian," she breathed, arching once more. "You're the one who's…" She trailed off on a sharp inhale, then exhaled the rest of her sentence with, "Torturing me."

My eyebrow lifted. "How am I torturing you, Vana?"

"By not touching me," she whispered, her eyelashes fanning along her cheekbone. "By denying me for years. By *rejecting* me."

A growl caught in my chest as my knees bent toward the floor. "I never *rejected* you," I told her again as I settled beside the tub, my hands grabbing the porcelain edge as I leaned over her.

"You did. You have." Her eyes started to close as a shudder visibly trembled through her.

"Look at me, Vana." I ensured my tone held the right edge of dominance. Sensual, not threatening. Because while her words infuriated me, that wasn't why I desired her gaze. I wanted to watch her, see the moment she approached the precipice of no return, witness her in the throes of climax.

Her blonde lashes fluttered as she reopened her eyes, her alluring blue irises darkening to show her inner wolf.

"You're so beautiful, love," I whispered, my irritation disappearing in a blink. Her cheeks were pretty and pink, her eyes were filled with yearning, and her plump lips were parted in expectation. "Fuck, Vana. I could never reject you. You're the only one I've wanted for six very long years."

She started to shake her head, an argument already forming in her mind.

But I was done debating semantics. I wanted to watch my beautiful Omega come.

I pushed the long sleeves of my long shirt up to my elbows.

"But you—"

I grabbed the tub again and slipped my other hand into the water, effectively silencing her. Her eyes widened as I touched her wrist, then she gasped when I stopped her from pulling away from me. "If you're not going to finish the job, darling, then I'll help you," I said, sliding my fingers alongside hers.

She moaned long and loud as I pressed her palm onto her clit, our hands realigning together to allow me to push one of her fingers—along with one of mine—into her slick channel. "*Cillian*," she breathed, her lower half bowing up out of the tub and into the pressure created by our joint touch.

I gently nudged her back down, then curled our fingers

together inside her. "You're very tight, macushla," I said softly. "We'll need to work on that if you want my knot."

Her sheath tightened around me in response, her mind seeming to fracture from my words alone. Mostly because she couldn't believe I was here, touching her, and talking about fucking her.

Rejected me for so long, she was thinking to herself.

I nearly sighed at her use of that word again. I just didn't care for it in relation to Ivana. Had I told her to look elsewhere? Yes. But I'd never used the word *reject* with her.

However, in this case, my actions and words…

I bowed my head. "You're right," I admitted, hating myself a little more. "I have rejected you in a way, but not because I didn't want you, Ivana. I hope that much is at least clear. And if it's not, I'm about to make it *very* clear to you just how much I want you."

I slid a second finger inside her, trapping her single digit there as her thighs clenched in response. "Cillian," she moaned, her lower half attempting to leave the tub again. But this time I was ready for her, my palm already pressing her hand down right into her clit.

"You're going to come for me, Ivana," I informed her. "Then I'm going to pull you out of this tub, take you to your nest, and lick every fucking inch of you while you come again and again." Because I owed her six years of orgasms. Six years of pleasure. Six years of *companionship*.

"Oh, stars…" The hiss of words escaped her on an exhale as her free hand jolted downward to wrap around my wrist. Then she pressed up into our joined touch below and released the most exquisite sound I'd ever heard from her, one I memorized in an instant and trapped in my memories for life.

Part scream, part moan, and one hundred percent Ivana.

Her body shook with the force of her climax, her inner walls clamping down so hard around my fingers that my knot physically pulsed in response. Because fuck, I couldn't wait to be inside her while she did that. She'd be so tight, so perfect, so *mine.*

I released her as soon as her spasms subsided and lifted her from the tub, causing water to splash out everywhere. But I didn't care. I needed to taste her. To claim her with my tongue. To force that sound out of her as soon as fucking possible.

She yelped as I tossed her wet body into her nest, my name leaving her with a chastising tone, one I was far too familiar with from her.

But I ignored her.

Spread her legs.

And pressed my mouth to her swollen clit.

Ivana screamed in response, her hands finding my head as she tried to push me away. "Too much," she said. "Too soon."

I huffed a laugh against her soaked pussy. "You can take it, Vana. Trust me."

Whatever argument she was about to toss my way died in a jumble of words as I sucked her pulsing little bud into my mouth while sliding two fingers back inside her.

My Omega reacted just as I'd expected—by releasing a fresh wave of slick all over my hand. *Gods, Ivana, it's like you're in heat,* I told her, loving her reaction to my touch. *Your body is just begging for me to knot you.*

Yesss, she hissed back into my mind, her body squirming beneath me.

I pressed my unoccupied palm to her belly to hold her in place while I devoured her. Licking every inch, just like I'd vowed to do. Nibbling gently. Kissing her intimately. Memorizing the taste of her sweet cunt. Finger-fucking her tight channel.

She chanted my name, her fingers yanking on my hair while she also pushed me even more into her hot flesh. Those chants turned into shrieks that could probably be heard all over the damn sector as she fell apart again, her body shaking almost violently from the onslaught of her ecstasy.

When I didn't stop licking her, she began to cry, her hoarse voice resembling a soft little whimper of protest.

But that protest died within minutes of me pushing her further, her Omega form more than capable of withstanding my sensual assault.

You were made for this, Omega, I reminded her, my tongue gently lapping at her weeping slit as I indulged in her citrus-like flavor. *And as your Alpha, I was made to pleasure you. I'm sorry I've waited so long to introduce you to oblivion, love. So fucking sorry.*

I'd spend the next several hours—*days*—making it up to her.

And I allowed her to see that in my mind, my licentious promises loud and detailed, as I pushed all my fantasies into her head.

She vibrated in response, her pussy strangling my fingers as I resumed my pace against her clit.

Stars, stars, stars, she was thinking.

The word slowly shifted into something else entirely. Something incomprehensible. Because all she could do was feel. Embrace. *Take.*

As she fell apart a third time, I smiled, loving how utterly incoherent she'd become.

I pressed my lips to her sensitive flesh and whispered sweet words of praise, telling her how good she was, how much I loved making her come, and thanking her for letting me taste her. "You're positively decadent," I murmured, kissing her again and chuckling as she tensed. "Worried I'll force another orgasm out of you, love?" I trailed my lips over her neatly trimmed mound to her hip bone.

"Y-yes," she stammered, quivering.

"Hmm, that was a fairly coherent answer," I mused. "You definitely need more orgasms. Plural, Vana. Many more."

She attempted to close her legs, but I was between them, preventing it from happening.

"No, love. If I'm your Alpha, then you're my Omega. And I fully intend to brand myself on your very fucking soul, macushla." I sank my teeth into her skin, leaving a mark on her hip. She hadn't bitten me before, which didn't make this a claiming bite. But it certainly displayed intent.

And it was an intention that she understood, because she instantly froze beneath me, her eyes going wide. "Cillian…"

I laved the mark I'd left on her hip, drawing the blood onto my tongue, then crawled up her body so she could watch me swallow it.

"If we're doing this, then we're really doing this, Ivana. Because once I knot you, you're mine." I'd promised her that in the shower—that if I knotted her, there would be no other Alpha for her. "I don't share."

It'd been hard enough to watch her date those other Alphas. There was no fucking way I'd be able to let that continue after I'd claimed her with my knot.

"So you'd better be sure this is what you want," I went on. "You said in your mind that I'm yours, that you wanted my knot. Now I'm saying out loud what it'll mean. If I fuck you, I will make you mine. Even if you don't bite me first."

Because doing this meant breaking every vow I'd ever made to myself.

I'd sworn to live alone.

To never take a mate.

To ensure my father's legacy died with me.

To protect the descendants of Eclipse Sector until my dying breath.

But having Ivana—*knotting her*—would give my wolf full control of my instincts. He didn't care about my personal vows; he cared about *her*. And I couldn't fight my animal. Not on this. Not when I wanted and craved Ivana just as badly as he did.

I'd been so close to letting her go, so close to *losing* her. I'd seen it in her eyes when she'd called me a coward. Felt it in the way she'd slipped away from me mentally a short time before that. And I'd realized that I didn't want to live without her. I didn't want to watch her fall in love with another Alpha. I wanted her to be mine.

Such a selfish fucking desire.

But she wanted me, too.

She'd fought for me endlessly these last six years. Never giving up on me until recently. And that had hurt more than I ever wanted to admit.

"I don't deserve to love you, Ivana," I admitted on a breath, needing to speak my truth. "And loving you makes me selfish. It makes me want things I shouldn't, things I've never been worthy of in my entire life. It fucking terrifies me."

I cupped her cheeks, my upper body balancing on my elbows on either side of her head.

Her eyes had misted with my words, some of the drunken pleasure having melted from her features.

"I don't say any of this to hurt you," I went on. "I just want you to understand how complex this is for me. I know I'm not good enough for you, Vana. Hell, the last six years are evidence enough of that. What kind of Alpha rejects his perfect Omega?"

I purposely used her choice of terminology since it was technically accurate, at least on the surface.

"One who thinks he's doing the right thing for his people," she whispered, surprising me while also proving yet again how perfect she was for me.

Because she understood me.

Not only that, but she *forgave* me. I could hear it in her mind that despite all the pain, she didn't hate me the way she should. Instead, she acknowledged my reasons and considered those reasons to be valid.

"I really don't deserve you," I repeated, more than aware

that I'd uttered that phrase, as well as thought it, a million times.

But rather than push away from her like I should, I opted for a new route.

A new way forward.

A tentative step.

Because I wanted to be good enough for her. To her. *With* her.

However, to do that, she needed to understand what I could and couldn't offer her.

"I've spent all these years saying you needed a better Alpha, one who would put you first and love you the way you should be loved. And I may never be able to do that." In all likelihood, I could never do that.

I could handle breaking my vow not to take a mate.

But I refused to break my vow of protection for the former inhabitants of Eclipse Sector and their heirs. Thus, Ivana would always come second to my Elite responsibilities.

I admitted all that out loud before continuing with, "It's utterly selfish of me to want to keep you. Acknowledging and accepting that fact is how I've been able to fight the inclination to claim you. I can still fight that inclination, Vana."

She swallowed, yet a hint of challenge entered her gaze, telling me she was planning a retort.

However, I wasn't done.

I needed her to understand what would happen between us if we continued down this path. How things would change. What I would be forced to do. Because I wasn't a one-night-stand kind of Alpha. Not with her. Not *ever* with her.

"If you tell me to knot you, Vana, I won't be able to ignore the need to bite you. I will claim you, even if in just name alone, and I will challenge any Alpha who tries to take you from me."

That much I knew for certain.

If I fucked her, she would be mine. End of discussion.

"So you'd better be sure, love," I said, my lips brushing hers. "But you don't need to decide right now. Take your time, think about it, and I—"

Her teeth sank into my lower lip, drawing blood in an instant.

I started to pull back, mostly in response to the unexpected bite, only for her to suck my wound into her mouth.

And swallow.

IVANA

Mine. I shivered. *Mine. Mine. Mine.*

Cillian's blood coated my tongue and throat. He tasted like a refreshing day. Crisp. New. *Inspiring.*

I pulled on his lip, desiring more of his addictive flavor. All strength and masculinity, yet underlined with a sense of refreshment. A sense of freedom. A sense of renewed life.

Vana, he groaned into my mind.

Mine was all I said in reply.

As though I'd even needed to think about his offer. Such a humorous notion. I'd craved this Alpha for six very long years. I wasn't going to waste a second longer than necessary in making my decision.

"Fuck," he growled out loud, his mouth claiming mine in the next beat.

It wasn't a tentative kiss or a soft one. It was harsh. Hungry. *Punishing.*

Naughty little Omega, he telepathically said. *You didn't even let me finish talking.*

I was tired of waiting for you to get to the point, I sassed back at him. *Besides, there was nothing left to say.*

He growled.

I rumbled in return.

His palm encircled my throat, his tongue dominating mine. His blood mingled with the taste of my arousal on his lips, providing an erotic undertone for our embrace.

This male had just forced three orgasms from me, and yet I was ready again. *More than ready.*

Stars, I'd never experienced anything like this. It was more intense than my heat. More impactful. More *meaningful.*

Cillian squeezed my throat. "Always trying to tell me what to do."

"It's one of my flaws," I returned, causing him to grin against my lips.

"It's one of your strengths," he countered, then took my mouth with a renewed vengeance.

Molten need heated my veins, lighting me on fire from within. Every part of me burned, my skin pulled tight as my nerves tingled with want.

Cillian stoked my inner flames with his tongue, each stroke somehow making me that much hotter, to the point where I felt like I might combust from his mouth alone.

But just before I could, his thumb circled my pulse and his mouth left mine to trail a path of kisses to my ear. "I'm going to knot you, Omega. And then, I'm going to bite you."

I shuddered, the words reminiscent of a dream. "Yes," I moaned. "Yes, Alpha." I wanted him deep inside me, pulsing and claiming and branding me as his.

Except he was still clothed.

I could feel his heavy arousal through his pants, but it

wasn't nearly enough. I needed him closer. Naked. Hard and insistent against my skin.

He must have read my mind, or perhaps felt the same way, because he went up to his knees to remove his long-sleeved shirt. My mouth watered at the sight of his sinewy strength, his muscles rippling with the motion of pulling off the fabric.

Then his hand went to his pants, his thumb flicking open the button and guiding the zipper downward.

I swallowed, my eyes tracking over every exposed inch of him.

A small whimper escaped me as he moved off the bed, my skin suddenly bereft from his missing touch.

He grinned, clearly having caught the sound. "I think I would enjoy hearing you beg for my knot, macushla. But not this time. We've both waited far too long already."

And whose fault is that? I nearly asked out loud. Instead, it remained a thought in my mind, one he definitely heard.

Because he aloud replied, "Mine. And I'm about to spend all day apologizing to you for it. So I hope you didn't plan on sleeping anytime soon because we won't be resting much at all."

A shiver traversed my spine, the sensation heightening the heat within me.

"You're about to become mine, Omega," Cillian went on. "There will be no going back after this."

Stars, this all felt like a dream. A fantasy. *Unreal.*

Alphas were possessive, but Cillian… Cillian had always pushed me away. Told me to find another Alpha. Refused to dance with me. Argued with me.

But now… now he was threatening to *own* me.

And I welcomed that ownership by spreading my legs wider for him. "Knot me, Alpha," I told him. Only it came out as a plea, not a command. One that had his cock growing impossibly larger in response.

This was going to hurt in the best way.

Fortunately, his mouth and fingers had me more than ready to receive him.

Only, he didn't immediately climb over me and slide inside me.

No.

He picked up one of my legs and pressed a kiss to my ankle instead. Then he trailed his lips upward to my inner knee as he shifted forward. His teeth skimmed the inside of my thigh, making my heart beat a little faster.

Will he claim me there? I wondered dizzily.

I'm claiming you with my knot before my teeth, Omega, he whispered into my mind. *This is me worshipping you. Loving you. Ensuring you're truly ready for me to* fuck *you.*

My legs clenched in response, my core suddenly desperate for friction. This man… the things he was saying… *Gods, Cillian…*

Just Cillian will do, he replied as his mouth met my weeping heat once more. He gave me a long lick, his chest rumbling with approval. *You taste so fucking good, macushla.* He ran his tongue against my sensitive flesh again, causing my toes to curl in response.

Then he slid two fingers into me, and my entire world turned on its axis. Because all I could feel was him, his touch, his intimate kiss, his everything.

Another growl touched the air, this one slightly more feral. A warning. One I saw reflected in his dark gaze as he stared up at me from between my thighs. His wolf was on edge, threatening to take over entirely.

I understood because my animal was pacing inside me as well, demanding that our chosen mate return the favor with his bite.

But rather than sink his teeth into my skin, he licked me. Long. Hard. *Thoroughly*. All while stretching my channel with his fingers. A third one joined his efforts, making me flinch a little in response.

Maybe I wasn't as ready as I'd thought, I mused as I arched into his touch.

Almost ready, he murmured back to me, clearly having heard my mental voice. *It's still going to burn, love, but I'll give you time to adjust.*

I won't need it, I promised him. *I've waited too long for you, Cillian. Too long for your knot. I want all of you. Every damn inch. Every violent thrust. I was made for you, Alpha. Let me have you. Please let me have you.*

"I was right," he growled. "I do enjoy hearing you beg for my knot." He crawled upward, his lips glistening with my arousal. "Next time, though, I'm going to make you kneel while you beg. Then I'm going to fuck this beautiful mouth of yours and make you suck my cock."

I gasped against his damp lips, the visual his words provoked making me even wetter below. But he didn't give me a chance to respond to his request—or ask him to do just that now—because he was kissing me again.

Passionately.

Possessively.

Purposefully.

Cillian…

Vana, he returned, his hips settling against mine. "Wrap your legs around me, love."

My limbs moved before he even finished speaking, my damp core instantly meeting his hardened flesh. I wanted him inside me. Claiming me. *Knotting* me.

He balanced himself on one arm, then grabbed my hand and led it downward between us. My fingers tingled as they met the base of his shaft—right against his knot.

"Grab my cock, Ivana," he demanded. "And show me where you want me."

Every part of me lit up even hotter than before, his words filled with command while also ensuring my consent.

This Alpha didn't want to *take*; he wanted to *give*.

And I very much wanted to *receive*.

I guided him to my entrance, my insides squeezing in anticipation of his size. *So big. So Alpha. So—*

Mine, he interrupted, his hips punching forward and forcing me to accept him in a powerful thrust.

I instantly stilled, the shock of his entry leaving me breathless.

But the pain only lasted a second before bliss overtook my being, my world suddenly feeling exquisitely *right*.

Because he filled me completely, his head touching a place so deep inside me that it almost felt forbidden.

So much better than my toy, I thought on a mental exhale. *Gods, so, so much better.*

Cillian purred in response, the sound quickly morphing into an intimidating rumble as he slid out to the tip and back in again. "You're never using a toy again," he informed me, his hand trapping mine on the mattress beside my head. "Only my cock, Ivana. Only ever *my cock*."

My thighs tensed against his hips, my body more than on board with that new rule. "Only ever your *knot*."

His chest vibrated with his approval, then his mouth captured mine in a bruising kiss as his pace increased below.

My fingers threaded with his, my opposite hand grabbing his muscular shoulder. I dug my nails into his skin, my insides clenching and pulsing around his sensual assault.

It was intense yet tender. I could feel him holding back some of his strength, his body seeming to cradle me beneath him rather than owning me entirely.

I wanted to make him move, force him to take me harder.

But I couldn't.

Mostly because this felt right. It felt *good*. There was so much emotion caught up in this embrace, so much history, so much *want*.

His kiss turned molten against my mouth, his tongue distracting me from his movements below. All I could do was breathe him in, let him devour me, submit to his dominance, and just... *exist.*

It was freeing.

Liberating.

Enlightening.

I'd never felt so cherished and protected before, his strength surrounding me in a way that left no doubt as to his claim.

He's going to bite me, I marveled, excited to feel his teeth in my flesh. To experience his possession. *Oh, but first... first he's going to knot me...*

My core clenched, my body primed and ready for his erotic claim.

Stars, this was better than anything I'd ever experienced before, better than the intense pleasures brought on by my heat cycle.

And it was because of Cillian being inside me. My chosen mate. The Alpha of my dreams.

"You feel incredible," he said against my mouth. "Fuck, I want to stay here forever, never leave the warmth of your sweet, tight pussy."

He drew my bottom lip into his mouth and nibbled it lightly, then released my hand to palm my breast.

"I want to mark every damn inch of you," he went on. "Cover you in my seed, then parade you around in front of all those other Alphas, just so they know you're mine."

His mouth went to my neck, his teeth sinking into my pulse.

Only, he didn't break the skin, just bit down hard enough to leave an imprint.

Or maybe it would bruise.

I didn't care. I loved this possessive side of him, his dark words, his intimate vows.

"I'm going to bite you here," he whispered. "Then again on each tit." He tweaked my nipple as he uttered the threat.

"And finally between your legs. I'm going to fucking claim every part of you, Vana. And then you're going to do the same to me."

His palm slid up to my throat, his thumb tracing my jaw as he returned his lips to mine.

"I want you to bite my knot, then suck my cock." The words resembled a wicked demand against my mouth, his dark eyes intense. "You're going to own me, Vana. Every fucking inch. And I'll reward you by coming down your pretty little throat."

I shuddered, his dirty words undoing me. "Gods, Cillian..."

"Just Cillian," he reminded me, his hips thrusting forward to punctuate his words. "*Your* Cillian."

My core tensed around him, his words striking a chord inside me. I loved that he was mine. Now I wanted to be *his*. "Please, Cillian. Give me your knot. *Please*."

He nipped my lower lip. "Always telling me what to do," he mused, laving the indent he'd just left on my mouth. "Fuck, you're perfect, macushla. So damn perfect."

His tongue silenced any sort of reply I could have made, his hands roaming down my sides. I jolted as he grabbed my hips, my legs squeezing him as he took control of my lower half.

A strangled sound escaped me as he started to pound into me, his cock going impossibly deeper.

Stars, I'd thought he'd been fucking me before. But no. That had been tender compared to this. A slow introduction of his power and prowess.

This... *this* was Cillian taking charge and unleashing his beast. This was an Alpha taking his chosen Omega. This was... *rapturous bliss*.

I bowed off the bed, my body his to command. And my mouth opened to receive his dominating tongue.

Yes, yes, yes, I chanted in my mind, reality slowly slipping away as passion took hold of my being.

Cillian growled, the sound one that resonated deep within —an Alpha call. A claim. A way to provoke even more slick from an Omega. It was a natural response, a type of domination, and it sent me cascading into a whirlwind of sensation.

Dark.

Light.

Heat.

So. Much. *Heat.*

His name left my mouth as I screamed inside my mind, my limbs shaking as I broke beneath an avalanche of unadulterated ecstasy.

Too much, I thought wildly. *Oh, stars, it's too much…*

The pressure inside…

The pain…

His knot, I realized with a start. *That's his knot.*

He'd followed me over the precipice into an oblivion of sweet relief, only to secure us both with his impressive bulb. I could feel him throbbing inside me, his seed filling me with the intent to breed.

Although, I could only become pregnant during an estrous cycle.

So we were safe.

Except…

I frowned.

Except this feels too intense…

Cillian whispered my name, but he felt far away despite being above me. I stared up at him, his face a blur due to the tears in my eyes.

I tried to respond, to utter a question, but a spasm shook my core with such vigor that all I could do was moan.

Oh, Gods, I needed *more.* His knot was no longer

throbbing inside me, yet he was still there, locking us together in an agonizingly still embrace.

Move, I begged him. *Oh, please, move!*

Because I needed him to come again. To drive me over the edge once more. To fill me so completely, so utterly, that I could *taste* him.

He said my name again, this time with a harsher undertone.

But I couldn't focus on him. I just wanted to come again. And again. And *again.*

This was so much worse than my heat. It… it *hurt.*

Tears filled my vision, these ones born of pain, not pleasure.

Cillian held my face between his palms, his expression furious.

I'm sorry, I tried to tell him. *I… I don't… I don't know what's happening.*

If he heard me, he didn't respond. Or maybe he did and I couldn't hear him over the rushing sound in my ears.

Everything *burned.* And I felt empty. So, so empty…

Like I always did during my heat cycles.

Oh, Gods, Cillian isn't going to help me. He never helps me. He's never here…

Years of torture filled my mind, all those moments where I tried to satisfy myself with the toy, only to end up screaming in my nest. Alone. In agony. Without an Alpha to properly care for my needs.

I'd put Cillian on my list because he was the only Alpha I trusted, the one Alpha I desired.

But he never came.

He never comes.

He doesn't want me.

He's never wanted me.

I closed my eyes, lost to the torment of my past, swimming in a sea of solitude.

I need my toy. I need the fake knot. Something to relieve this pressure. Something to help me through this hell!

I squirmed, my nest no longer comforting. I needed… needed… *Stars!*

Did I scream that out loud?

Because my throat… it felt… raw.

Why is this happening? It's too soon, a logical part of me recognized.

But another spasm yanked me under a wave of lava that left me gasping for air that no longer existed.

I'm drowning.

It's just the heat, I told myself. *It's… it's going to be okay.*

But he isn't coming.

He never comes.

Cillian… never… comes.

CILLIAN

What the fuck is going on?!

One minute, Ivana was reveling in pleasure, and the next, she was screaming.

Crying.

And suddenly in the throes of an intense estrus.

Kieran, I said, tapping into my best friend's mind. Before he could reply or chastise me for interrupting his sleep, I told him, *Ivana just went into heat.*

So did three other Omegas, he replied without missing a beat. *I was just about to call for you.*

Fuck. I held Ivana's face between my hands as I tried to keep her beneath me. But she was squirming almost violently, her mind chaotic and desperate. She kept thinking about her toy, how she needed it to help.

Because *I* wouldn't come to help her.

"I'm right here, love," I told her. Yet she didn't seem to hear me. She was too lost in her thoughts, her past experiences replaying loudly through her mind.

"Ivana, I'm right here," I tried again as Kieran said my name.

Sorry, can you repeat that? I asked him, my gaze on Ivana's tear-stained face. She seemed to be looking right through me, not at me.

I have Lorcan on the phone—two of the Omegas in Night Sector just went into heat as well.

I frowned. *Two candidates?*

Yeah. A small group decided to shadow back to their respective nests rather than stay in Blood Sector.

They don't trust us, I translated.

No, they don't. And this isn't helping, he muttered. *We need—*

He abruptly stopped talking, making me stiffen. *Kieran?*

No response, causing me to sink deeper into his mind.

Where I learned right along with him that another Omega candidate had just gone into heat in Night Sector.

"Fuck," I breathed, only for Ivana to still beneath me.

"C-Cillian?" she whispered, her eyes seeming to clear for a moment.

But that moment was short-lived, because in the next instant, she was back in the darkness of her past, her thoughts instantly telling her not to hope. *He never comes,* she told herself for the thousandth time. *Stars, he* never *comes.*

"Iv—"

She shadowed out from beneath me to clumsily land on the floor beside the bed, her ability short-circuiting due to her vulnerable state. Omegas often lost control of their talents while in estrus; all their bodies wanted to do was *breed.*

Ivana yanked open the drawer on her nightstand, her hand curling around a thick dildo that she promptly pulled toward her slick cunt.

I growled as she shoved it inside herself without so much

as a warm-up, her entire body curling onto her side on the bare floor as sobs racked her body.

"Fuck, Ivana," I whispered, seeing her come undone in a way I *never* wanted to witness again.

But I couldn't help gaping at her for a prolonged period of time as the reality of what I was seeing—what I was *learning*—slashed right through my heart.

This was how she endured her heat cycles. How she'd *always* endured them.

Because I'd never come.

I'd left her to this fate.

Left her in this agonized state.

For six fucking years.

Cillian! Kieran shouted into my mind, clearly having tried to grasp my attention for however many minutes had passed. He said something now about Alpha Carlos—the former leader of what used to be Bariloche Sector—drawing me slightly into his thoughts, only for Ivana's pained mewl to yank me right back out.

"Gods, macushla..." She sounded so distraught and broken. So unlike the Omega I knew and loved.

I shadowed off the bed to the floor and scooped her up into my arms, my chest instantly igniting with a deep, resounding purr.

"I'm sorry," I told her. "I'm so fucking sorry." I pulled her back into her nest, my body wrapping around hers as she continued using that damn thing between her legs while furiously stroking her clit with her thumb.

Not enough. Not enough. Not enough. The words were a chant in her head.

I pressed my lips to her neck, my purr loud and demanding against her back. She didn't even seem to notice I was here, her body contorting into a tighter fetal position as I cocooned her from behind.

"Vana," I breathed, my teeth skimming her raging pulse. I

hadn't bitten her yet, because the moment I'd been about to, she'd gone into a full-blown heat. "I'm right—"

Cillian, Kieran said again, drawing my attention back to his mind. *Did you hear what I said about the estrus parties?*

Estrus parties? I repeated more to myself than to him. Then I shook my head. Because it didn't matter. *Kieran, I can't do this right now,* I said to him for the first time in our very long friendship. *Ivana… Ivana needs me. I can't focus on what you're saying while she's…* I trailed off, swallowing. *She needs me,* I repeated, my arms tightening around her.

You're choosing to focus on Ivana instead of our present issue? Kieran asked slowly, his mental voice holding an edge to it that had my teeth grinding together.

She's part of that "issue," as you call it, I argued. *And someone has to take care of her.* Something I'd failed to do for far too long.

And that someone is you? he pressed, that edge still underlining his tone. It wasn't incredulity, but it was definitely an emotion of some kind.

However, I really didn't have the patience to determine what that edge meant or why he was being a dick about this.

Yes, I snarled at him. *She's mine. And she needs me. So fuck off.*

Silence met my words, making me relax only marginally.

Because Ivana was still sobbing and using that damn toy on herself instead of my knot.

Instead of *me*.

Because she had yet to realize I was here despite my purr at her back.

"Iv—"

Cillian, Kieran interrupted again, a thousand years of being connected to his mind making it very easy for him to call for me.

What? I demanded.

It's about fucking time you claimed that female, he said to me. *Now give her your complete focus and stop listening to me.*

I blinked. Then I snorted back at him. *You're an asshole.*

Likewise. Now go take care of your woman. A mental wall seemed to slam down between us, one I didn't even know he could create.

Or perhaps I'd done it.

I'd evaluate it later. *After* I helped Ivana.

Pressing another kiss to her throat, I slid one hand down her body to where her hand was working between her thighs. "Take out this fucking dildo, Omega," I said into her ear as I grabbed her wrist. "And get up on your hands and knees."

Her entire body jolted against mine, her mind seeming to clear once more. "Alpha?"

"Yes, I'm here, and I want to fuck you. So get rid of this poor excuse for a knot and let me mount you."

Ivana released a sound that was part whine, part relief, and pulled the contraption from between her legs.

Only to freeze in the next instant as her mind rebelled, telling her this was a fantasy, that I wasn't really here because I never come for her.

Overhearing all that chaos—and the residual pain those thoughts caused—had me growling against her neck in a way only an Alpha could. "*Now*, Omega," I demanded. "Get that sexy ass of yours in the air, spread your fucking legs, and present yourself to me."

She shivered in response to the dominant wave of energy I released onto her, the cloud in her mind subsiding in an instant.

You're really here, she thought at me.

Yes, I am. And my knot is so damn swollen that I'm about to take you just like this. So either get yourself into position, or grab on to the mattress. Because I'm going to fuck you, Omega. Hard.

Another tremble worked its way through her, this one causing her to finally move the way I wanted.

Every part of her shook as she went up onto her hands and knees, her slick running down her inner thighs. I palmed her there, my fingers instantly finding her aching channel and soaking my skin.

"I was just inside you, Omega," I reminded her. "Filling you with my seed. Don't you remember?"

I pulled my hand away and positioned myself behind her on my knees, all while bringing my palm around to her mouth.

"Lick my fingers," I told her. "Taste us."

Because my cum had mingled with her essence, providing an erotic mixture I knew she would enjoy. Especially in this state.

Because Omegas in heat loved the flavor of anything related to sex with an Alpha. And her tasting our combined pleasure would prove to her that I was here. That I hadn't abandoned her like all those other times. That her Alpha had finally joined her in her nest.

Her tongue tentatively touched my skin, reigniting the purr in my chest.

That purr turned into a low growl as she wrapped her plump lips around my finger and sucked it deep into her mouth.

I grabbed her hip with my opposite palm, my lower half aligning with her pretty little rump as my cock easily found her weeping entrance.

Gripping her jaw, I forced her to take my second finger into her mouth as I thrust deep inside her.

She screamed around my hand, her nails digging into the bedding in response to my abrupt movements. Then she sucked hard on my fingers while her ass moved against me, begging me to properly take her. To fuck her. To force her into oblivion.

I didn't go easy on her like I did before. Earlier had been about finally giving in to our instincts and experiencing each other for the first time.

This was about an Alpha satisfying his Omega.

She was vulnerable, in pain, and needed my knot. Not to mention all the other care and affection she would require for however long this forced heat would last.

She whimpered in reply, her tongue swirling around my fingers to take in every drop of our shared essence.

He's here, she told herself on repeat. *My Alpha's here. He's here.*

I leaned over her, my lips finding her nape as I gently bit down, dominating her in a way I knew she needed to feel safe.

Yes, I'm here, I confirmed into her mind. *No more toys, Vana. No more solo heats. I'm fucking* here. I punctuated that last word with my hips, forcing her to feel my throbbing knot at the base.

Her responding mewl had my palm leaving her hip to dip between her thighs, my thumb finding her swollen clit and giving it some overdue attention.

She came immediately, her estrus-primed form forcing her to live on the perpetual edge of pleasure in her current state.

A soft cry escaped her, the sound muffled by my hand.

Not enough, she was thinking. *Not enough.*

I growled against her nape, my hips moving faster and harder against her. "You want my knot, Omega?"

"Yessss," she hissed, causing my fingers to leave her mouth.

I wrapped my damp hand around her throat and squeezed, my other palm still between her thighs as I fucked her into oblivion.

It'd been a long time since I'd experienced the pleasure of an Omega's pussy. A long time since I'd knotted anyone.

Until tonight.

Until finally taking Ivana.

"Over six years," I panted against her nape, aware that she probably had no idea what I was saying or why. "I haven't seen an Omega through her heat in over six years, Vana. Since the day I found you, I've wanted no one else. Only you."

It was an admission I would likely have to reiterate later.

Or maybe she'd remember.

Heats varied for every Omega, their minds and bodies handling the experience in different ways.

Ivana responded by pressing back against me, her small form quivering violently beneath me.

"Don't worry, macushla," I said, my lips moving to her ear. "I might be out of practice, but I have years of fantasies for us to explore."

So. Many. Fucking. Fantasies.

"You're going to be so sore when I finish with you," I warned her. "But I'll make it all better, Vana. I'll kiss every bruise. Every mark. Lick your sweet cunt until you pass out from coming. Bathe you. Feed you. Then fuck you again."

Her pussy spasmed around me, another climax taking her under from my words alone.

She wanted all of that and more.

If only she understood what *more* meant. But by the time she woke from her heat, she would grasp the meaning entirely.

Then I'd officially make her *mine.*

The thought of mating her had my knot shooting out of me in a primal claim, my animal roaring within as I growled out my release.

Fuck, I groaned, the orgasm stealing through me in an intense wave of delicious agony.

Ivana joined me in the downward spiral, her climax eliciting a scream of pleasure followed by violent spasms as she fell into a powerful rapturous state.

My knot throbbed in her, my cum filling her to completion. Each pulsation stirred orgasmic ripples that kept her satiated and content, her body pleased with our connection.

Alas, it wouldn't last for long.

She needed constant relief, her overheated form obsessed with one goal—*procreation*.

I had no idea if she could even breed in this state, as this wasn't a normal heat cycle. And it was far too late for me to do anything about preventing a pregnancy. The males of our kind had pills that we could take, but they required planning.

There was no planning here, just desperate yearning.

A renewed yearning that Ivana was beginning to feel again now.

She started to growl, her little cunt squeezing my knot as she attempted to squirm away from me and force us to begin again.

My teeth clamped down on her nape, my hand leaving her heat to wrap my arm around her middle.

"Don't move," I told her. Because if she tried to pull away right now, my knot would rip out of her. And while she might not notice the pain in her current state, she would absolutely notice later.

Ivana snarled in response, causing my wolf to snarl right back at her.

She whimpered then, her body submitting to mine, her instincts fully overtaken by her animal's wants and needs.

I purred, telling her without words that I appreciated her listening to me and that I would reward her for it. *Soon.*

"Please, Alpha," she said after several more minutes.

I hushed her, my purr still rumbling against her back as I kissed her nape. "You're doing so well, Vana. So very well."

I was no longer coming, but my knot held us together. Neither of us could control it, as my body was made to breed her.

Fuck, I didn't want to create a pup. My bloodline was supposed to die with me.

And yet, the notion of Ivana pregnant… It did something to me. Elicited a feral need to keep myself lodged inside her until I was certain my seed had taken root.

I pressed my lips into her nape, these ideas making me dizzy.

It's her scent, I told myself. *Her heat. I'm not thinking straight.*

Except I'd never felt more certain of anything in my life. I wanted this female. I'd wanted her for years. And now I had her beneath me.

My pretty Omega.

My daring little vixen.

She might be submitting to me right now, but I knew she would challenge me the moment her heat ended.

Which meant I needed to enjoy this to the fullest. To stop thinking and just let our beasts fuck one another.

My knot finally returned to the base of my shaft, my body clearly getting the memo from my mind.

I immediately pulled out of Ivana and flipped her, my desire to see her eyes a yearning I couldn't ignore.

"Look at me," I demanded, a growl underlying my tone.

Ivana's long blonde lashes fluttered, her gaze positively drunk on endorphins as she gazed up at me. "Yes, Alpha."

Godsdamn, those words had me instantly aroused. "I'm going to enjoy fucking you, Omega. In every way imaginable."

Her legs encircled my hips, her slick heat pressing against my groin. "Yes, Alpha," she repeated, making me shudder.

"Grab my shoulders, macushla," I told her. "And don't be afraid to use your claws."

Because I was going to fuck her into oblivion. Put her in a pleasure coma. Then I'd force her to hydrate and eat when she eventually woke up.

And knot her again and again…

IVANA

My Alpha is here. But he's being a dick.

A snort sounded in response to my thoughts. *Finish your sandwich,* he said into my mind.

My wolf growled, irritated by our Alpha's insistence that I eat. All we wanted was to *fuck*. But every time I put my rump in the air, he slapped my ass instead.

"I won't fuck you again until I'm satisfied that your basic needs have been met," he informed me for what felt like the hundredth time. "Stop being stubborn, Vana."

Me? Stubborn? Now I snorted at him. *You're the one obsessed with food.*

He kept doing this to me—pausing and demanding that I eat.

"It's been seven days, macushla. You have to stay hydrated. I wouldn't be doing my job if I didn't feed you."

"Hmph," I grumbled in reply before taking another forced bite of the food. It tasted dry in my mouth. Boring. Lacking in the flavor I desperately craved.

My gaze dropped to his groin and the impressive knot at the base of his dick. I licked my lips, longing for a taste.

"Take three more bites and I'll let you suck my cock, Omega," he told me.

My eyes lifted to his dark orbs, my nipples tightening at the look I found waiting for me there.

He was just as aroused as I was, yet he was playing hard to get. Or maybe he just enjoyed delayed gratification.

Regardless, I forced my mouth to close around the sandwich, then chewed and swallowed before setting the food back down and crawling toward him on the bed.

"No, Vana. Two more bites."

I growled at him in response, tired of this game. "Knot. Now."

His lips curled. "I should have known you would continue trying to tell me what to do, even while in heat." He leaned forward then, his nose meeting mine. "And no. Two more bites, then we'll fuck."

He lifted his own meal to my mouth.

My nose crinkled, the scent not at all appealing. But I forced myself to obey, to satisfy my Alpha.

"Good girl," he praised, making my wolf preen inside. "I really hope you remember this later, macushla. It's been most entertaining."

Why wouldn't I remember it? I wondered. *Silly Alpha.*

He also kept calling me *macushla*. I had no idea what it meant, but my wolf seemed to like it. I preferred *Omega*.

"One more bite, *Omega*," he said, like he could read my mind.

Maybe he could.

He grinned again like he was amused by something. I liked that expression, so I did what he asked and swallowed.

"Such an obedient little Omega," he mused, his knuckles brushing my cheek. "I think I like you in this state, Vana. All sex crazed and obsessed with my knot. It's quite enjoyable."

All I cared about was him mentioning his knot. *Mine*, I thought, eyeing the impressive bulge. *My knot.*

He chuckled.

I ignored him and crawled between his sprawled legs so I could lick the object of my affection.

Something shuffled above—him setting down that irritating plate of food?—and he grabbed the back of my head. I moaned as his fingers threaded through the strands of my hair, his thick cock a brand against my lips.

"Get me ready for you, love," he told me. "Make me so damn hard I can't think of anything other than knotting you."

Mmm, that was a challenge I understood and accepted.

My tongue traced the underside of his impressive length, all the way to the tip. Some precum waited for me there, making me hungry for more.

I took him into my mouth, sucking him all the way down as far as my throat would allow. But my lips didn't even graze the top of his knot. He was too long and wide for me to swallow him completely, making me mewl around him in frustration.

"Shh," he hushed. "Use your hand, Omega. Massage my knot while you stroke the rest of me with your mouth and tongue."

I shivered, loving the way he coached me.

He'd done that the last few times as well, almost as though he knew I wasn't experienced in this area.

Some part of my mind registered that realization, a deeper part of me beginning to surface. A part of me that understood history.

Cillian, I thought, tasting the name. *Mmm, my Cillian.*

Your Cillian, my Alpha echoed, confirming I was right. *It seems your heat is starting to subside.*

Hmm? I hummed, confused by his meaning.

Better keep sucking, love. I want to knot you a few more times before you're coherent enough to feel how sore you are.

Sore? I repeated, my nose crinkling. I wasn't sore at all, just *empty*.

Something I intended to fix by making my Alpha give me his knot.

I ran my teeth along his sensitive skin—an action that had him growling in response—and wrapped my palm around his wide base. His growl deepened as I applied pressure to his knot, causing my wolf to dance excitedly inside me.

My insides clenched in anticipation of awakening my chosen beast. Gods, he was fierce and protective and *strong*.

I laid my free hand over his thigh, my nails digging into his muscular leg as I sucked him hard to the tip. Then I pushed back down again, desperately trying to take more of him.

"You know how I feel about you choking yourself," he gritted out. "I want you breathing and panting, Omega, not suffocating and coughing."

I eased back a bit, listening to my Alpha's command, and swirled my tongue around his tip—a trick I'd learned the other day, one I knew my chosen mate liked.

"Good girl," he praised, his fingers releasing some of their pressure in my hair. "So fucking good, Vana."

My legs clenched, my inner thighs slick with need. I enjoyed pleasing my beast. And I loved it when he expressed his appreciation of my actions.

I squeezed his knot again and groaned as he rewarded me with more precum.

Then suddenly I found myself on my back and looking up into a pair of dark, intense eyes. "You've gotten very good at sucking my cock, Omega," he informed me, his dick already at my entrance. "But I want to come inside your pussy, not down your throat."

A scream escaped me as he slammed inside of me, his abrupt action leaving me winded in the best way.

I grabbed his shoulders, my claws embedding in his skin to mark him with little crescent moons, as my hips rose to meet his violent thrusts.

Yes, yes, yes, I panted, utterly lost to my Alpha's claim.

Except it wasn't a true claim because he hadn't bitten me back yet.

Why hasn't he bitten me? a part of me wondered, stirring confusion in the pit of my gut.

But that confusion dissipated in the next instant as heat bathed my insides, a searing pain echoing from my womb that quickly morphed into the most delicious pleasure of my life.

His knot, I thought dizzily, my body spasming around his in incredible waves of euphoria.

The world disappeared. Reality melted away. And all that mattered was his knot pulsing inside me.

I settled into the bed—*our nest*—on a sigh, reveling in each rapturous pulse, until too soon it disappeared. But the ache from before didn't immediately return. Instead, I felt replete.

Finally, I thought, exhausted. *Finally, I can sleep… at least for a little while.*

I must have closed my eyes, because the next thing I knew, I was tucked into the hard body of my Alpha, his strength having cocooned me while I dozed.

My lips curled, contentment unlike any other warming my heart and soul. *He's here. Cillian's here.*

I slowly slipped back into unconsciousness, only to awaken a beat later—or maybe it'd been several hours—with a pang in my belly.

Something sweet touched my lips in the next instant, causing me to open my mouth, chew, and swallow. Some part of me registered that I was eating fruit. *Berries*, to be exact.

After a few minutes of savoring the flavor, I peeked out through my lashes to find Cillian kneeling by the bed with a strawberry poised in his hand. I took it from him with my teeth, then sat up to evaluate the room.

Our nest was a mess.

Frowning, I started patting around the fluffy bedding to fix it. First the pillows. Then the sheets. But it wasn't enough. It… it needed something.

I crawled out of the soft refuge, noticing a few more pangs in my body as I did, and searched for what I needed.

My nose led me to a pile of fabric in a basket on the floor near the foot of the bed. Sniffing, I bent and started rummaging through the silky goodness inside, my wolf instantly appeased.

An offering from our Alpha, I recognized, his peppermint cologne a welcome scent.

I gathered up all the material to begin remaking my nest, keeping my pillows but replacing the sheets with these peppermint-smelling ones. After smoothing out the wrinkles, I deposited the soiled linens in the basket and sat back to evaluate my improved safe haven.

Hmm, hmm, hmm… I need something else. Something…

I slowly turned my head toward my waiting Alpha. He hadn't moved from his spot on the floor, his naked form kneeling beside the bed. The only thing he'd done was put the bowl of fruit on the nightstand.

He arched a brow at my open appraisal. "Yes, macushla?"

I pointed to the nest. "Lie down."

His lips curved upward in open amusement. "Only for you will I obey such commands." He carefully crawled into the center of my new haven, sprawled out on his back, and tucked his hands behind his head. "Come ride me, Omega."

Only for you will I obey such commands, I parroted back at him in my mind, causing his eyes to narrow in challenge.

"You'll do a lot more than *obey*," he returned as I straddled him. "You'll beg and crawl, too."

He thrust up, filling me in one punch of his hips, then rolled to take me to my back.

"Now kiss me, macushla," he demanded. "Because your forced heat is ending and I want to spend the rest of our time together fucking."

I wrapped my legs around his hips, my body his to command.

But my mind… my mind held on to his words, a small part of me wondering what he meant by *ending* and *rest of our time*.

However, his cock hit me so deep in the next instant that I lost focus on the words.

And all I could think was *More, more, more…*

IVANA

Warm.

Safe.

But, oh my stars, ow!

I made the mistake of stretching my legs, and now I never intended to move again. *What the hell did I do last night?*

Me, a deep voice replied. *Or rather, I did you. Repeatedly. For nearly nine days.* Sensual lips met my neck, then my ear, as Cillian whispered, “You’re welcome.”

I froze. *What?*

My eyes fluttered.

My heart skipped several beats.

And my mind… my mind started replaying several very hot, very *intense*, intimate embraces.

All of them involving Cillian’s knot. His hands. His tongue.

My hand flew to the space between my legs, then started to roam toward my backside, but I couldn't reach much more due to his groin being pressed against my ass.

"Yes, I took you there," he confirmed against my ear. "I took you everywhere, Vana."

A shiver traversed my spine as I desperately clawed at the memories swirling through my thoughts. I tried to put them in order, to understand how this had happened.

I went into heat. That much is clear.

I just had no idea *how* I went into heat.

Nine days ago, I marveled, sifting through various snippets of sex while trying to pinpoint the origin of my estrus. *Were there hints I missed? Some sort of…* My thought trailed off as I recalled sinking my teeth into Cillian's lip. *Oh, no…*

I'd claimed him.

I'd… I'd made him *mine*.

Except it wasn't complete.

He didn't bite me back, I realized in the next beat. *This can still be undone*.

Cillian shifted behind me, his mouth leaving my ear as he pulled away slightly. I nearly rolled with him, my body naturally drawn to his, but I couldn't move.

Because our mating wasn't complete.

He hadn't claimed me as his.

If another Alpha knots me, I started thinking, only to squash the thought before I could finish it. Just the notion of taking another Alpha's knot had me sick to my stomach.

Cillian was the only Alpha I desired, the only Alpha I could ever mate.

But he didn't claim me… our mating isn't permanent.

A wave of nausea hit me in the gut, some of it inspired by the realization pelting my mind and some of it caused by…

My eyes flew open. "I'm pregnant," I breathed, my throat raspy with the words. *Oh, stars…*

I'd bitten Cillian.

He'd fucked me through my heat.

Didn't claim me back.

Yet left a… a *child* in my womb.

"There wasn't time for birth control," he told me, a hint of remorse in his voice.

That remorse nearly undid me—because it suggested regret.

Which made sense.

What was it he'd said to me? About his father?

"I made a vow to myself over a thousand years ago to never take a mate. To never be my father. To ensure his line ended… with me."

I swallowed, his words clear as day in my head.

He'd vowed to never have children, to never take a *mate.*

Yet I'd bitten him.

I'd forced myself upon him.

Why? I wondered now, my head spinning. *Why did…?* The question trailed off in my mind as I recalled some of what Cillian had said about not being able to control his animal if we fucked, how he would bite me. *But he… he didn't. Why didn't he…?*

Cillian sighed behind me, the sound hurting my heart. "I'm sorry, Ivana."

I winced, his words slicing through me even more than his sigh had.

"Actually, no, I'm not sorry," he went on, causing my lungs to stop working. "Even if I could have done it, I don't think I would have."

The world spun around me, his admission dismantling my soul. "Why?" I breathed out, releasing the rest of the oxygen inside me. "Why, Cillian?"

"Because I wouldn't have wanted to," he answered without hesitation.

Wouldn't have wanted to, I repeated in my mind.

He hadn't bitten me because he wouldn't have wanted to bite me.

That… that…

I swallowed, my chest burning.

Cillian didn't want to claim me.

I knew that. He'd said that so many times. But to choose him—to *bite* him—and have him not return that claim…

Stars, it hurt.

It really fucking *hurt.*

And now I'm pregnant, I thought, my palm going to my belly as my lungs demanded that I inhale. *Oh, Gods…*

What did this mean?

I… I was an unmated Omega, carrying the baby of an Alpha who didn't want her.

Why did you see me through my heat? I wanted to ask him. *Why are you here?*

"Vana." The way he said my name—with another damn sigh—had me wanting to shove him out of my nest. "I thought you wanted me here. I'm on your list. Hell, I'm the only one on your list. And you were thinking about all the times I wasn't here, how much it had *hurt.* I'd… I'd wanted to help."

My nostrils flared, my walls inside seeming to slam upright, just like they had after he'd grounded me.

Because this had been about pity again.

A fucking pity knotting.

Just like the kiss.

Just like everything else.

"Ivana."

"I don't want to talk about this anymore," I growled out, my mind trying to turn off the memories of my unexpected—and *unwanted*—estrus.

There were pieces that didn't make sense. Pieces about him vowing to bite me. Something about love.

Made up or real? I wondered.

But I didn't want to sort it out. Not now. I was too exhausted, too *sore*, to give it proper evaluation.

I needed a shower. *Or a bath.*

The thought made me still. *That's where it started… in the bath.*

No. I'm not reliving this right now.

It hurt too much.

Shower. Eat. Figure out… everything else.

I started to push away from him, then winced as agony shot up from my core.

Gods, he really knotted me good…

And I sort of hated him for it.

"Let me take care of you," Cillian said softly. "I—"

"I think you've done enough," I grumbled, cutting him off. "I'll be fine on my own."

I'd have to get used to it now anyway. Because no way in hell was I allowing him to raise our child out of pity for our situation.

"Ivana," he growled.

"I don't want to talk about this anymore," I repeated harshly, nearly shadowing out of the nest, only to remember in the next breath that I *couldn't* shadow.

Because I'm pregnant.

I palmed my belly, then curled into a ball before releasing a frustrated sob.

"Fuck, Vana," he breathed, his arm coming around me. "I…"

He trailed off, leaving us in silence as I tried to control my raging emotions.

Part of me knew this was a residual result of my heat, the fog in my mind clouding my better judgment. The pregnancy wasn't improving matters, either.

Gods, I was a mess.

I needed to calm down, think this through, speak my frustrations aloud. But I wasn't even sure where to start.

The memories swirled together in a chaotic cloud of lust, pleasure, and strong emotions. All culminating in a baby.

Our pup.

"I need to talk to Kieran," Cillian said in a low voice. "We… we'll figure this out when I get back, okay?"

Of course he was leaving me for Kieran. Why wouldn't he leave me for Kieran?

"I can never put you first," Cillian had warned me. "You deserve someone who will make you his world, Vana. Someone who will always choose you over everything and everyone else. I can't be that someone."

I'd fired back with, "Who says I want that someone?"

At the time, I'd believed that.

Now? Here? I… I did want that someone. An Alpha who would choose me. Bite me. *Mate* me.

But Cillian wouldn't be that mate. He'd said it clear as day just moments ago—*"I wouldn't have wanted to."*

He wouldn't have bitten me because he wouldn't have wanted to.

What more was there to say to that?

"Ivana?" Cillian prompted.

"Yes?" I asked almost robotically.

"Did you hear me?"

"Yes," I repeated. "You need to go to Kieran." Because he was Cillian's first priority. He would always put the King of Blood Sector first, as well as all the wolves under Kieran's protection.

I would be last.

A low priority.

Would our pup be treated in a similar manner? I wondered. *Would Cillian even want him or her in his life?*

Gods, I couldn't allow that to happen.

But our mating wasn't permanent yet. I could… I could find another Alpha.

Assuming any of them would even want me now.

Carrying another wolf's baby certainly wouldn't make me very popular among the possessive males of my kind.

I curled tighter into myself, barely hearing Cillian's voice as he said something behind me. Something about coming back.

I just shrugged.

It didn't matter when he came back or if he came back. "Do whatever you need to do," I told him, my voice sounding far away.

He pressed a kiss to my neck that I barely felt, the sheets moving around him as he left the bed. *My nest.* Except, it didn't feel right now. It felt… foreign. Infiltrated by his minty scent.

I pressed my nose into the sheets and winced, realizing that at some point I'd changed the linen. I'd probably wanted to make my safe haven smell like the Alpha I'd chosen.

But he hadn't chosen me.

He'd rejected me.

Said he would never bite me.

Only… only a memory nagged at my mind, one where he'd said if we did this, if he knotted me, he'd claim me.

Was that real or a dream?

A fantasy or reality?

He kissed me again, only on the temple this time. "I'll bring back something to eat in a bit," he told me.

I snorted. The notion of food did not appeal to me.

Which brought on a few more strange memories of Cillian forcing a sandwich on me, as well as fresh fruit.

"Maybe rest a little, macushla," he whispered now, his lips hovering against my forehead.

Rest, I thought, grunting a little. *Yeah, sure. That'll help the situation.*

He heaved another of those horrible sighs and disappeared, leaving me inside my strange nest.

Pregnant.

Unmated.

Alone.

He warned me, I thought sadly, curling into an even tighter ball. *I didn't listen. And now, I only have myself to blame…*

CILLIAN

My wolf growled inside me, furious with my decision to leave our chosen mate. I'd originally planned to bite her the moment she became coherent enough to understand my intent, but then things had gone horribly wrong.

I hadn't been able to hear every thought—her natural block seeming to be in place between us now that her heat had subsided. However, I'd overheard enough to know how she felt about being pregnant, that she blamed me for her current condition.

And rightfully so.

She hadn't consented to becoming a mother. Of course, most Omegas desired pups as much as, if not more than, their Alphas did. But this was all so new between us. We'd barely even discussed what mating one another would mean.

And I'd been pretty clear about not wanting to continue my familial line.

However, now that Ivana was pregnant… I couldn't imagine life any other way.

I'd meant what I'd told her—I wouldn't have wanted to use birth control, even if I could have. I'd wanted to breed her. To make her mine in all ways. To start a future together.

Which apparently made me an asshole because Ivana hadn't wanted any of that.

Oh, she'd claimed me. But after hearing her response to the pregnancy and all her thoughts about our mating not being permanent, I was starting to wonder if she'd been in the right frame of mind when she'd bitten me.

That was why I needed to talk to Kieran, to find out more about her forced heat and the mental state that had accompanied it.

If I bit her, our connection would be final. There would be no going back. I wasn't sure I could do that to her, knowing that she might not really want this. Not yet, anyway.

I had a lot of work to do where Ivana was concerned, primarily with proving myself worthy of her. I knew that. I just hadn't expected her to react this way to being pregnant.

But I'd never asked her how she felt about pups.

She'd told me she wouldn't mind coming second to my responsibilities, had pointed out a few times that I had never really considered her feelings on the topic of us, that I'd just made decisions for us.

Was this another one of those decisions?

I growled, irritated not just with myself, but also with her. Because I didn't understand her reactions. And then she'd said she didn't want to talk about it anymore, basically dismissing me with her words.

Most Omegas wanted love and affection after a heat cycle, requiring the gentle side of their Alpha to help care for them as they healed.

But not Ivana.

No, never Ivana.

Why would she be normal?

Because she was never fucking normal. She was a goddess. A puzzle I'd never quite solved.

Running a hand over my face, I bit back another growl and focused on finding some clothes. I'd left my clothes from last week in Ivana's room, leaving me stark naked as I'd shadowed back to my den.

It felt cold here. Isolating. And the smell was all wrong.

Maybe I should go back and bring Ivana here, I thought. *Have her roll around in my sheets while I go talk to Kieran.*

I would have smiled at the notion had my Omega not been so upset with me at the moment.

Gods, I would never have thought she'd react this way to being pregnant. *Did I just not know her at all?* I wondered.

How had we ended up on such opposite sides of the spectrum?

I'd never wanted a pup, the very idea of spreading my seed making my balls want to shrivel up inside.

Yet everything had changed during Ivana's heat. Part of me had been obsessed with the concept of breeding her. I'd wanted her so full of my seed that she could taste it. And I hadn't for an instant regretted that decision or choice.

But now… now I very much did. Because I hadn't given her a choice.

I should have known better. This heat hadn't been planned or even expected. She'd had no way of preparing for it.

No wonder she'd so eagerly claimed me.

"Fuck," I muttered, yanking on a pair of jeans. I grabbed a black sweater—the color matching my mood—and pulled it over my head.

There was no way in hell I was showering. I wanted Ivana's scent all over me. We might not be mated yet, but she was mine, and I very much wanted everyone else to know about us.

She might be mad at me right now, but she'd forgive me.

Hopefully.

Swallowing, I finished getting ready by adding socks and boots to my feet, then checked my watch. It was a little past midnight, which explained the rumble in my stomach. Ivana had to be hungry, too. Yet she'd scoffed at my promise to return with food.

Then she'd said resting wouldn't help with anything.

That thought had been loud and clear.

Meaning rest wouldn't help make her any less pregnant.

I'd tried to apologize, only to realize it wasn't heartfelt. Because I liked her being pregnant. And that made me an asshole.

At least I'm an honest asshole, I told myself.

Running my fingers through my hair, I headed toward my door.

Then I thought better of it and mentally connected to Kieran's mind. That wall he'd created during Ivana's heat was still there, but I could feel how tentative it was, the structure flimsy at best. More like a temporary barrier to keep me from being distracted.

Kieran, I murmured, attempting to break through the barricade he'd erected. *I need to talk to you.*

How's Ivana? he replied a few seconds later.

That's what I want to talk about.

Hmm. I'll meet you in my office in two minutes. His mind remained open after he finished speaking, allowing me to overhear him thinking about Quinnlynn.

I quickly escaped his thoughts, not wanting to intrude, and shadowed to his lair to wait by the desk. Having nothing to do other than wait, I reached for Ivana's psyche, wanting to hear her mental voice. But she was silent.

Maybe she chose to follow my advice and rest? I hoped.

But another part of me was concerned that she'd blocked me out again, just like she had after I'd grounded her abilities.

I gripped the thick mahogany wood of Kieran's desk and glared at the nearby window, my reflection staring back at me thanks to the light inside the office.

How did I fuck this up so badly? I wondered.

I'd demanded her consent before I'd even knotted her, and I hadn't realized she'd been on the verge of her heat.

A heat I still didn't know anything about, such as what had caused it, why it'd only lasted for nine days, how it had made her fertile, or what impacts it might have had on her mental state.

Bowing my head, I stole a deep breath, my wolf pacing inside me. He didn't like that our chosen mate had cut us off mentally. He also didn't like being away from her. But I had to talk to Kieran, to see what he'd learned about the other Omegas over the last week.

What caused the sudden heat? Did it alter Ivana's ability to consent? Is there anything else I need to know before I return to her? They were all questions I needed answered.

As well as a few regarding how this dynamic would work going forward.

Because I'd chosen Ivana over my duty to Blood Sector, and it hadn't felt wrong to do so. Actually, it'd felt natural. Like there hadn't been a choice at all.

The wood creaked under my palms, my muscles flexing as my frustration mounted.

"Careful with that," Kieran said as he materialized near the window. "That desk is one of the few relics I kept from Eclipse Sector, and I would like it to remain intact."

My teeth ground together as I forced myself to release the mahogany and straighten my spine.

"You're in a strange mood for a man who just spent the last week and a half playing in an Omega's nest," he drawled as he settled into his chair. One dark eyebrow arched upward.

"I can smell her all over you, so I know you did your job. Dare I ask why you feel the need to obliterate my desk? Has it wronged you in some way?"

I narrowed my gaze at him. "Your sarcasm isn't appreciated."

"Your surliness isn't appreciated either," he returned. "What's going on, Cillian? Why haven't you claimed Ivana?"

Of course, he would be able to smell that, too.

Her mark was embedded in my skin, but not the other way around.

Any Alpha of power would scent it immediately.

"She's pregnant," I managed to say through my teeth.

"That's a natural result of an Omega's heat, yes. I believe you knew that before you chose to see her through the process?" he phrased it as a question, one that had me wanting to punch him in the face.

But really, that would just be me using him as an outlet for my aggression—something I suspected he was attempting to offer if I needed such an outlet. Otherwise, he wouldn't be purposefully goading me in this way.

"I need you to tell me what you've learned about the heat accelerant or serum or whatever it was that caused this. I..." I took a deep breath, willing my racing heart to stop trying to escape my chest. "I need to know that Ivana claimed me for the right reasons."

Kieran stared at me for a long moment, his expression shifting from curious to incredulous. "You're fucking joking, yes?" he demanded in our ancient tongue rather than English. "That Omega has been obsessed with you for six years, and you're questioning her *claim*?"

I blew out a breath and collapsed into the leather chair across from his desk, my head falling back so I could take in the dark beams decorating his coffered ceiling.

Kieran switching to our ancient tongue meant I'd pissed him off. He typically preferred conversing in English or modern-day Irish. To anyone else, his decision to change languages would be a warning.

My wolf just saw it as a playful challenge.

This was my best friend, one of two men I trusted more than anyone else in this world.

Which was why I felt comfortable enough to reply, "Ivana isn't reacting well to the pregnancy." Swallowing, I finally looked at him. "In fact, she seems downright livid with me for not using birth control. But there hadn't been any time. And honestly, I wouldn't have wanted to use any even if I could have."

Kieran grunted. "You waited six fucking years to knot her, so I'm not surprised." He leaned back in his chair and canted his head. "But I don't understand why Ivana's angry about it."

"Because I took the choice away from her?" I suggested. "Because she wasn't in the right frame of mind when she claimed me? Because she was drugged?"

"Did you actually ask her?" he countered, that damn eyebrow arched once more.

"No. I came here to talk to you."

He stared at me. "You know, I've always considered you to be an expert when it comes to political negotiations and shifter affairs. I had no idea you were this bad with women, but I suppose I shouldn't be surprised since it took you six fucking years to claim Ivana. And you still haven't fucking done it."

"Are you going to keep repeating yourself?" I demanded. "I'm aware it took me six years to figure this out."

"Apparently, you haven't figured anything out," he shot back. "Ask Ivana why she's upset. Don't assume. That's like Women 101, Cillian. For fuck's sake, it's like you've never knotted a female before."

"I'm starting to think you want me to punch you in the face," I growled at him. "Are you in the mood for a fight, Kieran?"

His resulting grin was the epitome of wolfishness.

"Actually, I am. It's been a fucked-up week and a half, and I could use a punching bag."

Now it was my turn to grunt at him. "You won't land more than two hits on me before I have you flattened on the ground, *King*."

"So you do want to be an Alpha King," he drawled.

I rolled my eyes. "Stop fucking goading me and tell me what you know about this damn serum."

He sobered a bit, some of his amusement dying. "Well, first, it's not a serum. It's a drink."

I frowned. "A drink?"

"Yeah. Apparently, the late Alpha of Bariloche Sector —*Carlos*—developed a drug that can be imbibed. He liked to do it for his infamous estrus parties."

Estrus parties, I repeated to myself, recalling the term from my mental conversation with Kieran last week. "Do I even want to know what that means?"

"I'm rather sure you can guess," he ground out, all signs of his previous good mood disappearing behind a cloud of fury.

It was a cloud I understood.

Because yeah. I could fucking guess what that meant.

However…

"I need every detail you've learned, Kieran." That was the only way I'd be able to properly talk to Ivana. "I need to understand exactly what was done to my Omega. Then I can work on fixing whatever I broke."

IVANA

I STARED AT THE CEILING, my palm on my belly.

The Alpha had told me to rest.

I didn't want to rest. But I didn't want to move either. I just wanted to… *exist*. Except my nest smelled wrong. *Very, very wrong*.

Too pepperminty.

Too masculine.

Too much like *him*.

My Alpha.

The one I'd chosen as a mate.

The one who had constantly rejected me.

And now, he was rejecting our child.

I drew my thumb across my flat belly, the life inside me too small to even be felt. Yet I sensed the spirit growing there, the very real understanding of the soul blossoming inside me.

Don't worry, I whispered to my unborn child. *Mommy won't let anyone hurt you.*

Including me.

Which meant I needed to eat.

The Alpha had said he would bring back some food, but that had felt like hours ago. Maybe it'd only been thirty minutes. I really had no way of knowing.

And I didn't trust him to follow through on his promise.

Certain memories swirled in my mind, one repetitive and insistent.

"If you tell me to knot you, Vana, I won't be able to ignore the need to bite you. I will claim you, even if in just name alone, and I will challenge any Alpha who tries to take you from me."

His voice rolled through my mind, making me snort aloud now.

Because he'd *lied.*

Just another act of pity, I thought angrily.

"Well, fuck him," I rasped out, my throat raw from days of fucking and screaming.

The Alpha had left some water beside the bed, but I hadn't wanted to touch it. I didn't want anything from him. Not anymore.

Done. I pushed myself upward to a seated position. *I. Am. Done.*

But I had to think about more than myself.

For you, I'll get up and eat, I told my little one. *For you, I'll do everything.*

My limbs protested as I moved, my inner thighs particularly sore.

"This is going to take some getting used to," I told myself, wincing as my feet met the ground.

Being a V-Clan shifter typically allowed me to heal almost instantly.

But I was pregnant.

And pregnancy came with a whole slew of fun complications.

"It'll be worth it, though," I told my unborn baby, my palm finding my belly again as I glanced down at my naked form.

I was surprised to find that I was actually pretty clean, suggesting the Alpha had bathed me recently. *Well, that was kind of you, I suppose*, I thought darkly at him.

Not that he could hear me.

I'd put up another wall, this one reinforced with every mental block I could imagine.

He couldn't expect me to remain open to him after he tricked me into claiming him, impregnated me, and then punctuated my lack of importance by just leaving me while still weak from my heat cycle.

No.

Done, I repeated as I forced myself into the bathroom for a quick shower.

The hot spray against my shoulders felt nice, the muscles along my arms seeming to loosen slightly.

My *quick* shower turned into a *long* shower as I just stood there, staring at the marbled tile wall.

But eventually the pang in my belly reminded me of why I'd left the nest.

"Fine, fine," I grumbled before grabbing a towel.

I didn't bother with clothes, just headed into the kitchen. Then growled at the empty contents of my fridge.

The Alpha had cleaned me out, probably to feed us both during my heat. I supposed I wouldn't have had much in my kitchen anyway since I'd just been in Glacier Sector before this.

A frown taunted my mouth. *How did Cil*—the Alpha—*feed me during my estrus?*

I remembered fresh fruit.

A sandwich.

Even a pasta dish.

Someone must have brought him meals.

Although, my recently run dishwasher—and the items inside it—suggested otherwise.

Did he cook for me? I wondered, my palm finding my belly again as my frown deepened. *That suggests he cares.*

Unless I was reading into the action too much.

Or maybe I was overreacting to his responses earlier.

Except… except he'd blatantly stated he had no interest in biting me. Well, not like that. But he'd said he wouldn't have done it even if he could have.

"Because I wouldn't have wanted to," he'd said, the words lashing at my heart as I recalled them now.

The Alpha had never wanted—and would never want—a mate. He'd made that perfectly clear in the cruelest of ways.

I leaned against my refrigerator and huffed out a breath. "Then we don't want him either," I said, speaking on behalf of myself and the little one inside me.

Alas, my need for food still prevailed.

So I trudged into my room, found some suitable clothes, and left my condo to find something to satisfy my aching stomach.

Unlike Glacier Sector, Blood Sector had multiple places to shop, eat, and socialize. However, we shared most of our space with the humans under King Kieran's protection, which made the city a little more populated.

The mortals tended to stick to themselves, a preference that made sense to me. To live here, they had to donate blood—which my kind then imbibed to maintain our connection to our V-Clan magic.

That made for some awkward social moments.

Although, there were a few humans who didn't mind at all and in fact seemed to fancy the idea of donating blood in sensual ways.

A group of those humans stood just outside my favorite

pizza place now, their eyes on a pair of Betas standing across the street.

"Gods, what I wouldn't give to feel all that power inside me," one of them was saying.

"I wonder if Beta Yuko will offer to bite me again if I invite Yasmina to join us?" another asked, causing my brow to furrow.

"I bet it feels so, so good. But I'll never know. I'm not pretty like Isla is."

Blinking, I glanced at the group, trying to figure out who had said that last one.

"Pepperoni sounds good," a slender woman was saying, her voice reminding me of the one who had just commented on Beta Yuko. *But not as good as Beta cock,* I heard her add without her mouth moving. Her black eyes went to the Beta in question as her tongue dampened her lower lip. *Gods, what I wouldn't give to have his fangs in my neck again.*

"Can we add sausage?" another girl asked, causing my gaze to shift to her. *I'm suddenly in the mood for it after seeing that Alpha shift into his wolf earlier. Talk about impressive.*

I gaped at the blonde. *How are you doing that?*

She jumped, her brown eyes flying toward me. "Excuse me?"

I blinked again. *You heard that?*

Her eyes widened even more. "I… I…" A blush stained her pale cheeks, her *thoughts* suddenly an endless string of words.

She can talk into my mind. Oh, Gods, she read my mind. She heard me thinking about that Alpha. Gods, I hope it isn't her *Alpha. She's an Omega, right? I… I need to go. I need to say something. I need to—*

"Stop," I begged, my hands holding my head as I fought off a headache.

Only, the others around her started thinking at me, too. Or just thinking in general. They were all suddenly concerned, their thoughts of the Betas disappearing into a cloud of bizarre judgment.

What's wrong with her?

Why is that Omega clutching her head?

What's going on?

Should we call someone?

She doesn't look so hot.

I pushed through their group, my hands still on my head as I tried to shove them all *out*, and started running down the street to get away from them.

Eventually, the voices faded, but my head was still spinning. *How is this possible?* I wondered. *What's happening to me?*

I leaned against a wall, the cool siding bleeding through my thin sweater. It felt good against my overheated skin.

Breathe, I told myself, inhaling slowly and reveling in the wintry air. *Just breathe.*

Several minutes passed.

Or maybe it was seconds.

Regardless, my head felt a little clearer.

At least until I overheard a voice that made my skin crawl.

"Pathetic," Miranda spat at me, her tone akin to nails on a chalkboard.

I closed my eyes tighter, not at all in the mood to deal with her mean-girl bullshit right now.

"Looks like she finally got Cillian to knot her," one of her wicked sidekicks—Chastain—mused. "Or maybe another Alpha did the job?"

"Oh, Gods, is she *pregnant*?" Miranda went on.

I could practically hear her sniffing me.

Or maybe it was in my head.

My head, I repeated to myself as I looked up to find Miranda, Chastain, and Mindy standing almost a block away, all three of them staring right at me.

She is! She's pregnant! Miranda practically yelled, yet her mouth didn't move. *But she's… she's not claimed.*

Which Alpha could it be if not Cillian? Chastain was thinking at the same time, her thoughts clear as day as though she were speaking them aloud. Except her mouth remained shut, just like Miranda's.

Oh. My. Gods. Pregnant and unclaimed. She's even more pathetic now than she was before. Miranda's words resembled a slap across my face, one I would normally return in kind.

But I didn't have the energy to try. Nor did I want to put forth the effort.

Because what was the point? Miranda wasn't wrong. Cillian had knotted me during a heat and hadn't returned my bite.

It was pathetic.

I am pathetic, I told myself. *And stupid. And naive. And so, so… tired.*

My knees shook as my legs threatened to give out beneath me. All the while, I heard Miranda and Chastain judging me. Mindy, too.

I clutched my head once more, uncertain of when I'd stopped, and tried to cease the tremble working its way through my limbs.

But I couldn't… I couldn't stop shaking.

I… I couldn't turn off the voices.

Unmated.

Pregnant.

Poor thing.

Guess she finally got what she wanted—the only part of Cillian he'll ever be willing to give.

Stop, I begged, trying to turn off all the voices as the world swam dangerously around me. *Please, stop.* Concrete met my shins. Or maybe my knees? I was struggling to feel, to understand my surroundings. It was just so *loud*. So *intense*.

Look at her. She's practically breaking down in the street.

Something is really wrong, Mindy was thinking, her statement underlined with fear. "Ivana," I heard her say out loud.

Or maybe it was in her head.

"*Cillian!*" she screamed, eliciting a wince from inside me, the source of it my heart.

Don't, I wanted to tell her. But I… I couldn't… *I can't… Oh, Gods…*

Cillian! Cillian! Cillian!

Each shriek resembled a bullet to my heart. I didn't want to hear his name, but it was screeching across my mind, engraving its presence in my very soul.

Tears clouded my vision, my head spinning with unwanted thoughts. Unwanted shouts. *And wolflike snarls.*

A loud growl echoed from deep within me, the vibration so intense that I hugged my knees to my chest in an attempt to quiet the sound.

Except I hadn't been the one to unleash it.

Cillian, I heard several people think.

"Ivana." His voice rumbled through me like he was hovering over me. Surrounding me. Filling me with his warmth. "*Ivana.*"

A purr followed, causing my wolf to mewl with want. We wanted an Alpha to purr for us. To care for us. To nurture us.

An Alpha who loved us.

Who wanted us.

Who *chose* us.

But I was alone. *We* were alone. Me. My wolf. *The baby.*

My arms curled around my belly protectively, my mind seeming to fracture beneath the intense uncertainty surrounding me.

The voices. So many voices. Too many voi—

Listen to me, one of them demanded. *Only me, Ivana. Hear my thoughts. My words. Only mine.*

I tried to shake my head, but I seemed to be immobilized against something hard and hot. *The sidewalk? No. Too warm for that. I… I…*

Ivana. The deep tone carried through my head, causing my

wolf to whine at the dominance of that voice. *Focus on me, macushla. Pretend there are doors in your mind and slam all of them shut except for the one connected to me.*

No, no, I thought, trying once more to shake my head. Because no. No, I didn't want to hear him at all. *He doesn't want us. Me or the baby.*

My heart stuttered, the last vestiges of my strength seeming to disappear as heavy bands of muscle wrapped around me. Or maybe they'd been there for a while?

I wasn't sure.

And I no longer cared.

Because everything had finally gone quiet.

Peace, I marveled, thankful for the mental reprieve. *Finally… some peace.*

CILLIAN

A Few Minutes Earlier

I STARED AT KIERAN, both disgusted and shocked by everything he'd just said regarding Alpha Carlos and his infamous estrus parties.

Kieran shared in my disgust, his mind telling me just what he would like to do to Alpha Carlos. Alas, the bastard was already dead.

But there had been plenty of Alphas who had attended the parties, several of whom were still alive. Such as the V-Clan Alpha Quinnlynn had scented on a few occasions.

Unfortunately, none of the Alpha candidates matched the notorious scent. Apparently, Kieran and Quinnlynn had checked this while I'd been busy with Ivana.

"So then it's none of the candidates," I said now. "What about the Glacier Sector Alphas?"

"She's met about twenty of them thus far—all of them brought here by Lykos—and none of them are a match," Kieran replied, his irritation palpable. "Even Tadhg brought a few Alphas over. All of them were just as charming as their damn prince."

His dry sarcasm wasn't lost on me. Tadhg wasn't known for his charm, even if he had mustered a little magnetism during his recent visits to Blood Sector. But it was all a façade. A pleasant face for the political arena.

Beneath it all, he was a warrior.

And a powerful one at that.

Fuck.

I could only imagine the restraint it had required of Kieran to just sit back and observe while his pregnant mate sniffed other Alphas. When—or *if*—one of them ended up emitting a scent she recognized, Kieran would kill the wolf on the spot.

"Lykos intends to bring another five Alphas with him tonight, but I'm beginning to think—"

Lorcan appeared in the office, effectively cutting off Kieran's statement. Surprise registered in Lorcan's features, then a frown etched its way across his face. "You're unmated," he said, stating the obvious.

"Yes, I am," I drawled, doing my best to ignore the sensation clawing at my gut. 'Thank you for noticing."

His frown deepened. "Why?"

"Because he's an idiot who doesn't know how to properly communicate," Kieran interjected. "What did you find out about Ashlyn?"

I started, not just at Kieran's offhanded insult but also at the comment about Ashlyn. "What's wrong with Ashlyn?"

"She's gone missing," Kieran said distractedly. "Lorcan?"

"Missing?" I repeated before Lorcan could reply. "An

Omega has gone *missing*, and you didn't feel the need to tell me that?"

"I can only deal with one Omega concern at a time, and Ivana is the one I want you focused on, not Ashlyn."

"That's not your call to make."

His dark eyes flashed as he met my gaze. "Actually, Cillian, as your *King*, it is my decision to make."

My jaw clenched, the arms of my chair creaking much like Kieran's desk had moments ago. Only this time, I was squeezing wood encased in leather.

"If you'd like to challenge me for the role, I'd be more than happy to entertain the request," he went on. "But as you've shown no desire to lead, then I'll lead for you. Ivana is your priority right now, not Ashlyn."

"Ashlyn is my priority," Lorcan interjected. "She's an Omega in my sector. And to answer your original question, Kieran, no. No one knows anything about where she went or how she disappeared."

Kieran leaned back in his chair, a curse littering the air between us.

"Was she in Night Sector when she went missing?" I asked, trying to catch up on what I'd missed.

Kieran's answer was promptly drowned out by someone screaming my name in my head.

Fuck! I instantly searched for the source of the voice. *Mindy*.

Cillian! Cillian! Cillian! she shrieked.

What the hell is going on? Where are you? I demanded, only to catch the location a half a beat later as several more thoughts assaulted me.

"Ivana," I breathed, shadowing to a street a few blocks away from where she lived. "Oh, Ivana." I picked her up off the pavement, a growl vibrating through my chest. "What happened, macushla?"

She said nothing, her mind silent.

Until it wasn't silent at all.

But *loud*.

With all the mental voices of everyone around us.

"Oh, shit." I should have expected this. Sometimes Omegas—especially powerful ones—inherited their Alpha mate's talents during the bonding process. It didn't matter if I hadn't bitten her back yet; the process had already started.

The same thing had happened to Quinnlynn and Kieran. She'd received a portion of his healing ability, allowing her to help all those Omegas in Bariloche Sector for nearly a century.

Had Quinnlynn slept with another Alpha, the bond would have been broken. But she'd remained faithful to him, thus her power had remained intact as a result.

Just as Ivana would now be able to read minds, and possibly communicate telepathically, too. Both talents would only deepen once I bit her.

Assuming she even wants that.

"Ivana," I said, ignoring the unwanted thought. I held her close, intent on safeguarding her. Supporting her. *Helping* her. "*Ivana.*"

A purr ignited in my chest, my need to soothe her flourishing inside me.

Ivana relaxed for half a beat, then winced and instantly covered her abdomen. I frowned down at the motion, aware that she was attempting to protect our unborn child. I just didn't understand who she was protecting the baby from.

The voices?

From me?

I wasn't sure because I couldn't hear her over all the other thoughts echoing in her head.

Listen to me, I demanded. *Only me, Ivana. Hear my thoughts. My words. Only mine.*

She shuddered in response. Or perhaps she'd been trying to move.

Ivana, I tried again, this time reinforcing my tone with my wolf's dominance.

A subtle whine echoed in response, her animal acknowledging my presence and my power.

So I kept going.

Focus on me, macushla. Pretend there are doors in your mind and slam all of them shut except for the one connected to me.

No, no, she replied, her voice soft. Too soft. Like she was lost down a long, dark tunnel. *He doesn't want us. Me or the baby.*

I frowned. *Why do you think that?* I asked her, confused by her thoughts.

Nothing.

Ivana, why do you think I—

She went limp in my arms, her mind quieting once more.

Sighing, I pressed my forehead to hers. "You and I are going to have a very long talk when you wake up, Vana."

"That would be wise," Kieran drawled from behind me. He and Lorcan had followed me here, anticipating a threat. I hadn't noticed, too caught up in Ivana and the chaos in her mind. But I heard Kieran and Lorcan clearly now.

"She needs food, too," Kieran went on.

No shit, I thought, already aware that my Omega needed food. I'd intended to bring some back to her after talking to Kieran.

"Pregnant Omegas are always hungry," he continued, like I was completely inept at understanding the needs of my female.

I slowly turned to face my oldest friend while tightly clutching Ivana to my chest. "Any other relationship advice you'd like to share?" I asked him darkly, not at all amused by his blatant teasing.

"Just to communicate," he said with a quick grin. "Go take care of your Omega."

We'll update you as we learn more about Ashlyn, Lorcan added with a thought.

Thank you, I telepathically replied to both of them.

I started toward Ivana's condo—walking rather than shadowing since she was pregnant—and ventured more than a block before realizing I'd just prioritized her over everything and everyone else. It'd been a natural response.

My intended mate needs me. How am I supposed to focus on anything other than her?

I winced, another thought swiftly following. *This is why I never took a mate. It's changing everything.*

Except… is that change so bad? I wondered, frowning.

I'd spent over a thousand years alone, atoning for my inability to kill my own father. I'd vowed to never extend his familial line. To never take a mate.

But what if creating a new life is actually the solution?

Living beneath my father's constant shadow made it impossible to truly escape his ghost. However, with Ivana, I felt… renewed. Like a different man entirely.

Perhaps the true way to demolish my father's past was to replace it with a brighter future.

A future with Ivana, I thought as we neared her building.

She was still silent and unmoving against me, her skin paler than I liked. Given where I'd found her, it seemed clear she hadn't rested like I'd suggested, and she also likely hadn't eaten.

Benz, I called, the telepathic link one I'd used several times over the last two weeks. First, in Glacier Sector. Then, in Blood Sector.

I hadn't trusted anyone else to bring us supplies while Ivana had been in heat.

Yes? he thought back at me, his irritation palpable. I swore I heard the term *Master* follow that response, but he seemed to be trying to fight the sarcastic title.

Ivana passed out, I told him, instantly grabbing his full attention. His mind started firing questions, but I ignored them and added, *She needs something to eat, and quickly. Can you pick up a cheese pizza with pepperoni and green olives from San Marinos?* I knew from observing Ivana in the past that it was one of her favorite meals.

And now that she was no longer in heat, I could properly feed her.

Before, it was all sandwiches and a few light meals I'd prepared with the groceries Benz had brought for us.

Just tell Diego to charge my account. And if you can get some strawberry lemonade for Ivana, I would appreciate it. Because Ivana loved fresh strawberry lemonade, too.

Benz didn't reply immediately, his mind processing everything I'd just requested. A hint of surprise colored his thoughts, as well as a note of respect. *Okay* was all he said. *Give me thirty to forty minutes.*

Thank you, I replied to him, then refocused on my Omega.

She didn't stir as we entered her building or moved up the stairs, her head resting against my shoulder as she slept.

I shuffled her a bit to find a key tucked haphazardly into her jeans pocket and unlocked her door, then settled us both inside on her couch.

"I never said anything about not wanting our child," I told her, recalling her thoughts from before. "Why would you think that, macushla?"

My mind tracked through everything that had happened when she initially woke from her heat, recounting all our comments and twisting them around in my head.

"I thought you didn't want our baby," I continued out loud while combing my fingers through her damp hair. She must have showered before heading out. My wolf and I weren't too fond of that notion, our scent notably missing from our Omega's skin. "I thought you were upset with me for not using any birth control."

Still nothing.

No sound.

Not even a thought.

Unless she's blocked me from her mind yet again.

If I bit her now, I would solve that issue. But I wanted her coherent—and accepting—when I staked my claim.

"Oh, but it will happen," I added out loud. "I'm going to bite you, Vana. Even if I have to beg you for weeks or years to let me do it. You're mine, macushla. I think you've been mine since the day we first met."

Which explained why I'd taken her back to my lair that day rather than to one of the many temporary homes we had in Blood Sector.

It explained why no other Alpha was ever good enough for her; why none of the Alphas in Blood Sector had even *tried* to court her.

"I've been a fool to avoid this for so long," I admitted to her, my gaze on the wall across the room while I processed everything out loud.

I'd have to repeat it all to her once she was awake, but I wouldn't mind. I'd do anything and everything for her. Fuck, I already had. I just hadn't realized it.

"You're my priority, Vana. I think you always have been, but keeping you at arm's length just made it easier for me to focus on Blood Sector. Or perhaps it just made it easier to trick myself into thinking I was doing the right thing for both of us." I swallowed, my fingers still gliding through her hair.

She felt so fragile in my arms.

So small and still.

I wanted to feel her fight, hear her voice, explore her *mind*.

Instead, I continued talking, hoping that maybe my voice—underlined with my purr—would help comfort her.

"I realize now how wrong I'd been. Because the right thing is what I'm doing now—putting you first. Even when it's killing me not to help Lorcan and Kieran track down Ashlyn, I know this is where I need to be. And I know I can trust them to find her. Just like they would—"

"Find her?" Ivana repeated, causing my gaze to snap

down to her in my arms. I hadn't even realized she was awake, let alone looking at me. She'd been so motionless and silent that I'd assumed she was still unconscious.

"How long have you been awake?" I asked.

"Long enough," she replied, her gaze searching. "What's happened to Ashlyn?"

"Don't worry about Ashlyn," I murmured. "Lorcan and Kieran are handling it."

She tried to push away from me, to sit up, but I clutched her tighter.

"Ivana—"

"No, I want to know what's going on with Ashlyn," she said, putting a little more strength into her hands as she shoved again.

This time I let her move, taking the hint that she didn't want to touch me.

But rather than scramble off my lap, she just repositioned herself and grabbed my shoulders. "Tell me about Ashlyn."

I shook my head. "I don't know much," I admitted. "Just that she's missing and no one knows how or when she disappeared." I ran my palm down her back, away from her hair. "Lorcan was in the process of bringing Kieran up to speed when Mindy started screaming for me. I left to help you."

Ivana blinked at me. "Is that why Kieran needed you earlier? Because of Ashlyn?"

My brow furrowed. "Kieran didn't need me."

"But you said you had to talk to him. I assumed he'd called you."

"No, I needed to talk to him about your heat and the serum—or I guess it was a *drink*—used to provoke it."

She stared at me. "You left me to talk about me?"

"To talk about the serum used on you, yes. I wanted to know if it altered your ability to consent." My palm fell to her hip, my gaze holding hers. Rather than play with words, I decided to be direct. "I wanted to make sure you didn't claim me because of the serum."

Her eyes widened. "*What?*"

"Well, you were upset about me not using birth control, which is warranted. I should have asked how you felt about pups before…" I trailed off, wincing. Kieran was right—*I am acting like I've never knotted an Omega before.*

Clearing my throat, I attempted to start over.

But Ivana started speaking first. "I wasn't upset about the lack of birth control. I was—*am*—upset that you didn't claim me, Cillian. That you *don't want to* claim me. That you said you wouldn't have, even if you could have. And—"

I slanted my mouth over hers, silencing her with my lips.

Which turned out to be the wrong thing to do because the little vixen *bit* me again. Hard. Drawing blood in the same place she'd bitten me last week.

Don't you dare kiss me, she snarled into my head. *You rejected me and our child. You don't get to kiss me anymore or ever again.*

I pulled back to gape at her. "I did *not* reject you."

She rolled her eyes, her full lips parting on what I knew would be some sort of argument.

I grabbed her nape and forced her to look right into my eyes as I repeated, "I did not reject you, Ivana Michaels. And I certainly didn't reject our child."

"You said you weren't sorry and that you wouldn't have bitten me even if you could have."

"I said I wasn't sorry about the lack of birth control and that I wouldn't have used it even if I could have," I corrected her immediately. "Which makes me an asshole, I know. But the notion of you being pregnant with our child makes me so fucking hard that I can barely think straight. And you being in heat? Yeah, there's no way in hell I would have even wanted to try to prevent the outcome because it's all I could possibly want."

Her eyes widened, her lips parting as she attempted to form words.

But nothing came out.

"And all I've wanted to do for nine fucking days is bite you," I decided to tack on. "But I wanted you coherent and willing. Not moping and upset about me impregnating you without permission."

She blinked. "Moping and upset…?" She shook her head, some of her thoughts seeming to escape her in the process.

He wants the baby.

He wants to bite me.

He… he isn't sorry about impregnating me.

I bit back the urge to growl at that last line, but Ivana's mouth was suddenly on mine, her tongue tracing the wound she'd left on my lip.

My arms came around her, my wolf purring with approval inside as she straddled my hips and pressed her heated center against my groin.

It was such a stark contrast to moments ago when she'd looked ready to kill me. Now she just seemed to want to devour me.

I let her lead, giving in to her kiss as she encircled my neck with her arms, her tongue dancing with mine in a quest for something more. Something profound.

My hand slid up her spine to her nape, holding her to me as I opened my mind, allowing her to hear my innermost thoughts. My fears. My past. My desires. My *love.*

She shuddered, part of her overwhelmed by the wealth of information blossoming before her, while an intrinsic side of her latched on to the truth—*my* truth.

I want you. I want this. I want us. I want our child. Our future. Our lives together. I had no idea how alone I was until you. How meaningless life was until you. You're my world now. My priority. My purpose. I love you, Vana. It's only ever been you for me. Only you.

She started to cry, causing my palm to shift to her cheeks. But she wasn't sad. She was… *relieved.*

Because she understood me. She understood everything.

"You're mine, macushla," I whispered. "Just as I'm yours."

A bite didn't prove that; our souls did. Our hearts did. Our bodies did.

But as she licked my lower lip once more, I felt my wolf growl, longing to repay the favor, to finally *taste* her.

I allowed her to hear that need, that stark *yearning.* The clawing sensation inside me demanding that I finish this, that I claim her once and for all.

"Yes," she whispered. "Please."

It was on the tip of my tongue to tell her to *be sure* when a knock sounded through the living area, drawing a growl from my chest.

Benz entered in the next moment, choosing to shadow rather than open the door.

And my head fell to Ivana's shoulder.

Fucking Beta. "Your timing is as impeccable as ever."

IVANA

I BLINKED out of my erotic haze, my focus falling on my best friend. "B-Benz?" I stammered, confused by his appearance in my space.

"Servant Benz at your service," he drawled, bending at the waist while holding a pizza box in one hand and a drink in the other. "Glad to see that you're somewhat more coherent, though, Sunshine. Wish I could say the same for your Alpha."

Cillian narrowed his gaze at Benz. "Careful, Beta."

Benz looked at him and said, "You're welcome, *Alpha*," before setting the items on my kitchen counter. "Is there anything else you need, *Alpha*?"

Cillian bristled beneath me. "You're lucky my Omega favors you as much as she does, Benz. It's the only thing keeping me from teaching you a very important lesson."

Benz grinned. "Perhaps I would enjoy the lesson, Alpha. Ever consider that?"

My snarky friend vanished before Cillian could reply, leaving the Alpha rumbling beneath me. "Did he just proposition me?"

"I think so." My lips twitched. "I guess that means he's starting to like you."

Cillian's expression told me he wasn't a fan of this development. "I don't need him to *like* me. I'm an Elite. He just has to respect me."

"He's my best friend. Him liking you is important to me," I pointed out.

Some of Cillian's irritation melted into an indulgent look. "Couldn't Quinnlynn become your best friend instead?"

I could hear the lightheartedness underlining that question, causing my smile to grow as I replied, "No. You're going to have to learn to love Benz."

His head fell back on a groan. "*Love*? That's too far, Omega. The only one I love is you. No one else."

My smile faltered. "No one else?" I repeated. "Not even Kieran or Lorcan?"

He considered it for a moment before saying, "I respect and care about Kieran and Lorcan. They're my brothers. But the way I love you is different from them. It's more intense. More consuming. Just… *more*."

My heart constricted in my chest, his words ones I'd never thought I'd hear from him. I'd hoped for a mating, maybe the opportunity to raise his pup.

But this?

Cillian admitting his love for me? Not just lust?

I…

"I love you, too," I breathed, clasping his face between my hands. "Gods, Cillian. I really love you, too."

His palm on my nape flexed, his gaze holding mine.

And then he was kissing me.

No, not just kissing me, *owning* me.

There was nothing tentative or restricting about this embrace. It was freeing. A new level of existence. A cataclysmic event.

"Gods, I want to bite you, Vana, but you need to eat first." He kissed me again before I could reply.

But fuck food.

I want you to claim me, I thought at him. *Please, Cillian.*

"I want to, macushla. Fuck, I *need* to. But you just passed out from my inherited power, and you haven't had anything since waking earlier. You have to eat, love. You need the energy. Because once I bite you, I'm going to rut you. *Hard.*"

I shivered at the mental image his words evoked inside my mind. *Yes, yes.*

He growled, his forehead meeting mine. "I asked Benz to bring your favorite—pizza with pepperoni and green olives. At least eat a slice, okay? If not for me or for yourself, then for our baby." His hand left my nape to palm my stomach over my sweater.

I stilled, the meaningful motion causing my heart to skip a beat.

Our baby.

I placed my hand on his, our fingers locking together as I glanced down.

Our baby, I thought again.

"Our baby," Cillian echoed out loud, pride underlining the words. "You're going to be an amazing mother, Ivana."

Tears pricked my eyes. "I don't feel very amazing."

His opposite hand reached up to cup my cheek. "You're an inspiration, macushla. You're just a little tired at the moment, and rightly so. Let's eat and see how you feel after, okay?"

I bit my lower lip, my insides seeming to spiral in twenty different directions at once.

Probably because I'd woken up with half a mate bond and a baby and thought my Alpha didn't want either of us.

Then I…

I can read minds, I marveled, wincing. *Sort of, anyway?*

I'd just learned that everything I thought I'd understood about Cillian earlier wasn't accurate at all.

Oh, and I was pregnant.

So yeah. I was a little dizzy. My eyes were leaking. My heart kept beating a weird rhythm. My stomach growled. And heat seared my belly where Cillian's hands and mine touched.

It was a lot to take in at once.

"Food," I said, my voice thick with a thousand competing emotions. I cleared my throat. "Food sounds good."

Cillian smiled, his thumb wiping away one of my tears. "Then let's eat."

I nodded and started climbing off of him, intending to grab some plates and set my two-seater table in the small dining area off the kitchen.

But Cillian caught my hips and gently sat me on the couch. "I'll get it," he told me, pushing away from the sofa and heading toward the kitchen.

He found the plates on the first try, as well as the silverware, confirming his familiarity with my space. *Probably from feeding me while in heat.*

My thighs clenched with the thought, and I cleared my throat again, my skin suddenly hot.

If Cillian noticed, he politely didn't comment and instead brought me a plate. The scent of gooey cheese mixed with spicy pepperoni made my mouth salivate. Add the salty kiss of the green olives, and I was practically drooling.

"Did Benz tell you this is my favorite?" I wondered as I accepted the platter of Italian goodness.

"No," Cillian replied before going to grab himself a slice.

Or that was what I thought he was doing, but instead he brought me a drink.

I would recognize that scent anywhere.

"Strawberry lemonade," I said with a sigh before taking a long drink. My insides practically rejoiced in response to both the flavor and finally imbibing something. "Did Benz pick this up on a whim?"

"Nope," Cillian murmured, grabbing himself a plate this time. Only, he didn't immediately return, causing me to frown at his back.

"Do you like strawberry lemonade, then?" I guessed. "And pizza with pepperoni and green olives?"

"Strawberry lemonade is fine." He turned around to join me, his plate holding a slice of mutilated pizza on it. "Pepperoni is okay, too. But I actually kind of hate green olives."

And that explained the murdered slice of pizza on his plate. "Then why did you order green olives?" I asked, confused.

"Because it's your favorite, at least when San Marinos makes it. I've noticed you forgo the olives from Eddie's down the street, but you definitely prefer San Marinos. So that's where I asked Benz to go." He took a bite of his food while I gaped at him.

"You know my favorite pizzas?" I asked, stunned.

"I know a lot of your favorites, Vana," he informed me with a wink. "Now eat, please. Before it gets cold."

I wasn't sure what surprised me the most—his admission or his use of the word *please.*

Regardless, I did what he said and nearly groaned at the flavor explosion on my tongue.

However, it only distracted me for a few bites before my curiosity was piqued again. "What other favorites do you know?" I couldn't help the suspicion in my voice. Mainly because I couldn't believe he actually knew these intimate things about me. I never thought he cared enough to notice.

"Hmm, let's see."

He set his mostly empty plate aside—I swore he ate that slice in, like, three quick bites. A small pile of olives was all that was left.

"Mint chocolate ice cream with chocolate sprinkles, not rainbow," he began. "Bourbon chicken is a go-to meal. You're also fond of grilled cheese, broccoli salad, and the occasional pierogi. And vodka tonic is your alcoholic drink of choice."

I gawked at him.

Every detail was accurate.

"You also like your steaks served rare, typically marinated with lemon and pepper, and you're not too keen on fish—which is unfortunate, given where we live. But you'll tolerate smoked salmon, and you'll eat white fish so long as there are condiments nearby to smother it in. And you're not fond of mushrooms, carrots, raspberries, or black olives."

All true.

"How do you know all that? From my thoughts?"

He shook his head. "No. I just pay attention."

"Oh." That made sense. He was in charge of guarding everyone in the sector. "I suppose you have to, with your job and everything."

"No, Ivana." He leaned forward, his hand cupping my jaw. "I've paid attention to you. I always have. And I always will."

Oh, I repeated to myself. *Oh.*

I really didn't know what to say to that. I'd always thought Cillian paid me little mind, choosing only to notice my presence when I stood right in front of him.

But this…

"I had no idea," I whispered.

His lips curled a little. "Now you do." He gestured his chin toward my plate. "Finish eating, macushla."

I shivered, the promise underlining those three words making my stomach clench in anticipation.

He's going to bite me.

Yes, I am, he agreed into my mind. *But not until you finish what's on your plate.*

Another tremble worked its way through me at the dominance in his voice, his Alpha tone speaking on an intimate level to my inner Omega.

I took another bite, followed by a sip of heavenly lemonade, all while he watched.

The darkening gleam in his gaze made his future objectives clear, but I couldn't help feeling a little curious about what he was actually thinking. What he was planning. *What he's imagining…*

His mind opened to mine in a blink, showing me just what he wanted to do to me.

How and where he wanted to bite me.

There were three—no, *four*—places he had in mind. And right now, he intended to indulge in all four locations.

My throat suddenly felt dry, forcing me to take several more swallows of lemonade. Gods, I needed a distraction, or I was never going to finish this meal.

Something grounding.

Something… something not sexual.

The baby, I thought, palming my stomach. *Yes. Think about the baby… not the process by which the baby was created… or my heat… or… or Cillian's desire to claim me…*

I shut my eyes.

And I swore I heard Cillian chuckle in response.

But when I peeked at him, he was the epitome of seriousness.

Which meant that laugh had been in his head.

Reading minds is… overwhelming. The words were meant for Cillian, but rather than think them as I usually would, I tried to speak directly to him. Like he could with me.

"Not quite," he murmured aloud. "That was still just a thought. But it's possible you won't inherit my telepathy at all, and just the mind reading."

"Just the mind reading," I echoed, picking up my pizza again. "Like that's some small detail." I bit into the cheesy goodness and forced myself to chew while I considered everything I'd overheard outside.

Every insult.

Every *thought.*

Although, I wasn't sure if they were all comments from their minds or if some of them had been uttered out loud. With Miranda, it was hard to say.

"*Oh. My. Gods. Pregnant and unclaimed. She's even more pathetic now than she was before.*"

I winced as I recalled her callous words, then cringed, as thinking about them seemed to pull me into her thoughts once more.

She was currently looking at a menu, deciding what to eat.

"Ivana," Cillian's deep tones brought me back to him, his gaze capturing and holding mine. "I'm going to have to teach you how to tune out the voices."

I swallowed, no longer hungry. "I'm not sure I like this new ability." Especially as I could still hear Miranda whispering in the back of my mind, her words cruel, her thoughts even crueler.

And it wasn't just her. I could hear… *more.*

My eyes closed again as an onslaught of voices suddenly poured into my mind, all of them seeming to talk at once.

Limus finally restocked the cheese. Thank the Gods.

Why is that Beta looking at me?

She has a pretty smile. Oh, but those lips would look far more interesting around my—

Ivana.

What's the code again? Three, five, six? No. Ugh. Three, four, six?

Ashlyn wouldn't run away.

I frowned. *Is that Quinn's voice?*

But before I could try to follow the strand, a dozen more

assaulted me at once. All of them about daily activities, or eating, or *sex*.

I clapped my hands over my head, no longer able to focus on anything around me. Nothing tangible. Just *thoughts*.

B positive is always so tangy.

Why is the milk always left out on the damn counter?

Countdown from ten. And breathe.

That little rebel left teeth marks in the table again!

Fuck, this is getting out of control. If they find out where—

Ivana!

I shuddered, that dominating voice drowning out all the rest.

Except it only lasted for a second.

Almost immediately, *more* voices assaulted me.

All of them spiraling into a chaotic mess of words and growls and noise that I couldn't comprehend. It was too much. Too overwhelming. Too—

A rumble reverberated through my head, the sound one that instantly calmed my mind and enclosed me in a sea of consistent vibrations.

Rhythmic.

Soothing.

Quiet.

I curled into the source of that repetitive thrum, realizing belatedly that it was Cillian's purr. His arms were around me, holding me to his chest, his lips at my ear as he hummed softly against my ear.

I'll teach you how to block them, he whispered into my mind. *It won't be difficult once you know how to form the mental walls, Ivana. You already have a natural inclination for it.*

I-I do? I asked, shivering.

Yes. You've used it around me countless times. It's why your mind is always so peaceful—you guard all your inner thoughts. Only the loudest ever escape your mind. His lips brushed my forehead. "We'll figure this out, love," he continued aloud. "I'll help you."

I leaned into him as another tremble worked its way down my spine. All I wanted to do was collapse into his purr and reside there for eternity.

My eyes were still closed, my insides nauseated from the onslaught of noise that had just assaulted my mind. But ever so slowly, I began to relax. At least a little.

I kept hearing all those statements on repeat, their owners a big blur.

Except for Quinn.

Her voice had stuck out.

Ashlyn wouldn't run away.

My eyes opened. "Ashlyn's missing." I'd forgotten Cillian had mentioned that previously, when he'd been talking about prioritizing me over finding her. I'd asked a few questions, but then I'd been distracted by his confession about why he'd gone to see Kieran.

About me. About the serum. About how it may have altered my ability to consent.

But now… now I recalled clearly what we'd been discussing before that conversation.

"You put me first, even though Ashlyn might be in trouble," I continued aloud. That was what he'd been saying when I'd interrupted him, asking about her whereabouts.

No, there was no *might* about it.

Ashlyn is *in trouble.*

And Cillian was too busy worrying about me to help Lorcan find her.

I'd realized a bit ago that I wanted to be his priority, but not at the cost of another life.

Ashlyn wouldn't run away, Quinn had thought.

While I didn't know the Z-Clan Omega well, I agreed with Quinn's assessment.

"Yes, I put you first," Cillian replied, making me frown.

What?

"It was the most natural decision in the world, Vana," he

went on, confusing me even more. "And it was the right one." He cupped my cheek, his thumb tracing the hollow beneath my eye. "But I understand now that I pushed you away because it was the only way I could focus on Kieran and on Blood Sector. Embracing this—embracing *us*—changes everything for me."

I blinked.

He'd said this to me before, while holding me in his arms.

Right before he mentioned Ashlyn.

I shook my head. "Stop distracting me," I told him, causing his lips to curl down like mine had moments before.

"I was explaining why I put you first, or rather, that I've always put you first. I—"

"No, I got that. I…" I closed my eyes for a moment, then opened them again. "Ashlyn's missing."

"Yes, I know."

"She wouldn't run away."

His mouth curved downward even more. "Okay."

"No, I mean, I heard Quinn thinking about it, and I agree with her." And I was definitely not making any sense right now because I kept changing topics on him.

With another shake of my head, I attempted to clear it.

Something about this was important.

Something about Ashlyn.

"She… she journals," I mumbled, thinking aloud. "I mean, she writes. And she wrote in my journal on the plane. But she also… she told me about her…" I trailed off, recalling our conversation from our trip to Glacier Sector.

Her words were always so cryptic, like a warning.

"As a Z-Clan Omega, she's prophetic," I said slowly. "And she writes her visions down in her journals." Which meant she should have seen this coming.

Maybe she did, I thought. *Maybe that's why she told me about her journals…*

"I have so many notebooks filled with musings back in my nest. But only someone who knows where to look can find my diaries."

I'd been confused by why she'd felt the need to tell me this, but I was starting to think there might have been a very good reason indeed.

"I hide my journals beneath my nest, under the floorboards. That's my secret."

"And you're telling me this because…?"

"In case you ever need to know something."

"Is there something I should know?"

"A great many things, I'm sure."

My eyes widened. "We need to find those journals."

CILLIAN

Lorcan? I called, engaging my telepathic link to my old friend and not waiting for him to reply. *Ivana says someone needs to search Ashlyn's nest for her journals. They're under the floorboards.* That last part hadn't been uttered aloud by Ivana, but I'd caught the location floating through her thoughts.

Journals? Lorcan repeated, not elaborating.

Yes. Like a diary. From what she told Ivana, Ashlyn often wrote her visions down in her notebooks. Which meant we might be able to find a clue as to where she was now by perusing her writings.

I had to believe she'd told Ivana for a reason.

And Ivana seemed to think so, too.

"She also warned me about Prince Cael," she said now, her gaze narrowing. "She said he was surrounded in darkness. I told her to tell Quinn, but she said Prince Cael wasn't dangerous, and to just be careful. I thought she was trying to play some mean-girl game with me, so I ignored her."

Guilt prickled Ivana's mind, her thoughts whirling into dangerous territory.

"This is not your fault," I told her sternly.

"I know, but I completely misjudged her." Her sad eyes met mine. "I just assumed she was like Miranda and the others. And I… I ignored what she was trying to tell me."

"Or you're remembering what she said at precisely the right time." I brushed my lips against hers, my arms tight around her as I held her in my lap. "From what you've told me, Ashlyn gave you information that she no doubt hoped you would use at the appropriate moment."

And now that I was thinking about it, Ashlyn might have left me a few clues as well.

I recalled our conversation from the day she fell into the ice pond, how she'd been startled by Grey's arrival.

"I just didn't see him coming, so his appearance… surprised me. Which is rather uncommon, to say the least," she'd said.

But that hadn't been all she'd voiced on the topic.

"Quinn asked me if I was okay with him joining," she'd murmured, talking about Grey being one of the Alpha candidates in the mating program. "I'm not one to fight destiny, so I agreed. Although, I thought our paths would cross later. Not today."

Does he have anything to do with this? I wondered, my lips curling down.

Maybe.

However, she'd also said, "Grey and Henrik don't mean me any harm."

The rest of our conversation had been almost as cryptic, with her basically chiding me for taking her back to her igloo.

Only, now I wondered if all those words had been about Ivana.

"I'm not yours to worry about, Cillian. While I appreciate your protective instincts, they're unnecessary."

"You do realize that you're not the only one being punished by your actions, yes?"

"Choosing to suffer out of some misguided need to repent doesn't just impact you, Cillian. That choice—the one where you put everyone else first—impacts her, too. If you remember anything I've said, please remember that."

At the time, I'd thought she was chastising me for leaving the other Omegas at the pond while I tended to her.

"I really have been stubborn," I muttered. "And maybe a little dense."

Ivana snorted, a string of sarcastic responses streaming through her thoughts.

I grabbed her waist, my fingers digging a little into her sides.

She shrieked in response, her gaze wide with indignation. "Did you just *tickle* me?"

I chuckled. "Yes, macushla, I did." And I proceeded to do it again, earning me a louder shriek from her as she tried to wiggle her way off my lap.

But there was no way in hell I was about to let her go.

She was mine, something I proceeded to show her by wrestling her onto the couch and pinning her body beneath mine.

"*Cillian,*" she huffed at me, squirming futilely.

"Ivana," I returned, settling even more firmly on her.

Her responding growl had me wanting to return the sound in kind, only with a much more erotic undertone.

Alas, Lorcan's voice in my head stopped me before I could start. *Kyra is looking right now. Did Ashlyn tell her which floorboards in her nest to look under?*

Let me ask, I replied as I repeated the question aloud for Ivana.

"No, she just said she hides her journals under floorboards

in her nest. So maybe directly under her bed?" Ivana suggested.

I relayed that message to Lorcan.

Silence met my comment.

"Kyra's looking," I informed Ivana.

"Yeah, I heard that in your mind."

I arched a brow. "You heard Lorcan's thoughts?"

Her lips twisted, her gaze contemplative. "No, not exactly. I… I heard you thinking about it?" She blew out a breath. "It's really complicated…"

I grinned. "Yeah, macushla, it is. But I'll help you."

She swallowed but nodded. "I can sort of see how you compartmentalize already."

"You can?" I asked, surprised.

"I think so." She chewed her lower lip, her brow furrowing. "Maybe *see* isn't the right word. But I… I could sense you favoring Lorcan while tuning out the others. And I think I know how you did it."

"Interesting," I murmured, prodding her mind a little to hear her puzzling through the process. Bits and pieces were basically incoherent, but I could hear her sorting out the chaos.

I couldn't understand most of it.

Actually, I couldn't fully hear it.

Because she was naturally blocking me from going too deep into her thoughts.

"I wonder if your innate immunity to me reading your mind has something to do with the construction of the mind," I mused aloud. "And now those gifts are blending to create something else entirely."

Her mouth curved downward. "What do you mean?"

"I mean, I can't comprehend the processes of someone else's mind; I hear their thoughts. But you seem to be not only aware of how I maintain my ability, but are able to mimic the concept as well. That suggests a unique form of mind reading that goes deeper than mental conversation."

"But I've felt your power, Cillian. You've leashed me before with your mind, and not just the other day in Glacier Sector."

I winced, the memory not one I wanted to relive. But it was very prevalent in her mind. "I should not have done that."

"No, you shouldn't have," she agreed. "But that's not the point. Your power basically controls the receptors in the brain that process free will. And you're able to apply restrictions to that free will. Which makes what you can do far more powerful than simple mind reading."

"I never said mind reading was simple," I uttered slowly, processing her words. "I've also never been aware of how I leash the wills of others; I just do it. However, it sounds like you not only sense it but can actually see it happening?"

She stared up at me. "Yes. I assumed everyone could."

"Sensing it, perhaps," I agreed. "But I don't think most wolves, if any, can see it. Are you saying you've been aware of me grounding Alphas before? Like when Quinnlynn was attacked a few months back?"

She nodded slowly. "You leashed all the Alphas in the sector that day, ensuring no one could shadow."

"And you sensed that or saw it?"

Ivana considered my question for a moment. "I think both? It feels the same to me. I was just aware of it happening."

"That's… fascinating," I marveled, gazing down at her in awe. "But you couldn't read my mind or actually see how it worked then, right?"

She shook her head. "No, I just felt it happening. And I knew what you were doing."

"Can you sense when Lorcan and Kieran evoke similar holds on others?"

"Yes. Their dominance is as powerful as yours."

"More powerful," I clarified. "But perhaps similar."

"The same, Cillian," she replied. "All three of you exude mental strength on the same terrifying wavelength."

I grunted. "Not sure about terrifying."

She gave me a look. "You know you're terrifying. I can hear confirmation of it in your head right now."

The ease with which she was peeling through the layers of my mind was both astounding and impressive. "You obviously possess a talent that involves understanding the intricacies of mental abilities, which explains your knack for thwarting them."

And now that she had access to my mind-reading powers, she was deepening her skills.

"Fascinating," I said again.

"Will the same happen to you when you bite me?" she asked. "I mean, you, um, *inheriting* my supposed gift?"

"There's nothing *supposed* about it, Vana. You have a gift." And an extraordinary one at that. I'd always wondered why her mind seemed so quiet. Now I somewhat understood.

As for whether or not I would adopt her unique talent when I claimed her…

"I don't know, but we'll be finding out very soon," I promised, my gaze sliding down to her mouth. "Or maybe now." Because I really wanted to claim her. Rut her. Make her mi—

Kyra found the journals, Lorcan interrupted, his timing leaving a lot to be desired. *There are hundreds of them, Cillian. Can Ivana give us any guidance on where to start?*

Suppressing a growl, I reiterated the question aloud to Ivana.

"I…" She blinked. "No. All she told me was where to find them." Her brow furrowed. "But… Did she go back to Night Sector before she disappeared?"

As I didn't know the answer, I asked Lorcan.

"Yes," I told her, repeating his response aloud.

"Then I wonder if the journal she was writing in that day is the one she wants us to find," Ivana said slowly. "It would make sense. She made sure I saw it. But I… I would need to see them to recognize it, as I wasn't paying enough attention that day."

More of that guilt pinged her thoughts. *Gods, why did I assume the worst of her?* she was thinking.

Don't, I whispered back to her. *You're helping now and that's what matters.*

She swallowed, her chin dipping in a subtle nod.

I relayed the information to Lorcan.

Kyra's shadowing them to Kieran's office. Unless you would prefer us to meet you there? A hint of sarcasm underlined that question.

Because my best friend knew my reply to that before even asking.

Stay away from my mate's nest.

Still haven't claimed her, then? he taunted.

Fuck you, Lor.

His responding chuckle served as a taunt that had me growling low in my throat.

Ivana shivered beneath me.

"Sorry," I muttered, doing my best to tame my inner animal. "Lorcan's goading me."

"You kind of deserve it, though," she replied, causing my eyebrows to lift.

"Do I?"

She nodded. "You should have claimed me during my heat. Instead, you chose to wait. So yeah, you deserve to be goaded by your friends. In fact, I'm rather pleased they're goading you on my behalf. I think they should have been doing this for years."

I gaped at her. "You're a sassy little traitor."

She shrugged, the picture of false innocence. "Just being honest."

"Hmm," I hummed, leaning down to nip at her mouth.

"I'll remember this later when you're begging me to let you come."

Her eyes widened. "What?"

"You heard me, my darling, sassy Omega." I nipped at her again, then slowly crawled off of her. "I'm going to teach you a lesson in delayed gratification."

"Because six years didn't already drive that lesson home?" she shot back without missing a beat.

Gods, I loved this female. "You're making me want to forget the journals and fuck you instead, Ivana."

She snorted. "Then maybe you need to give yourself that lesson in *delayed gratification*, Cillian. Because I no longer want your knot."

I laughed. "Your slick cunt says otherwise, Omega."

Her nostrils flared as she shoved her way off the couch, her hands landing on her hips. "I am not slick right now, *Alpha*."

Another laugh escaped me. "And now you're lying to me."

"I am not."

"You are," I assured her, catching her by the waist before she could even think to escape me.

A shocked gasp left her as I palmed her pussy, my fingers pressing into her alluring heat.

"Even through your jeans, I can feel you, Vana." I leaned down to place my lips at her ear. "And I can smell you, too." I gently bit down on her earlobe, my hand massaging her through her pants. "You're so fucking wet that you're going to have to change clothes."

I ground against her, ensuring she felt my responding need.

"Don't worry, Vana. I want you just as bad, perhaps even more." I licked a path along her neck, my teeth skimming her raging pulse. "Gods, I can't wait to be inside you again. To *bite* you. I want to do it now, say to hell with everything else."

Mark her as the most important being in my life.

Prove to her that she was my priority.

Make her mine.

"No," Ivana breathed, her palms landing on my shoulders as she tried to push me away. "We have to find Ashlyn."

I sighed. "Ivana—"

"No, Cillian." She pulled back and clasped my face between her hands. "I want you to put me first. I realized that the moment you left me to go to Kieran. So I can admit that much—I was wrong before about what I needed from a mate. You were right when you said I deserve an Alpha who prioritizes me."

"Which is what I'm trying to do right now," I told her. "I—"

She gently placed her fingers over my lips, silencing me.

"I wasn't done," she softly chastised. "I know you want to put me first, and I love you for that. But this is about who we are as a mated pair, Cillian. I just want to be included in your process, to know that you respect me enough to tell me what's going on. I want you to let me support you. So let me show you what that looks like. Let me show you who we can be."

Her thumb brushed my cheekbone, her gaze searching mine.

"Take me to Kieran's office," she went on. "Together, we'll find Ashlyn. As a team. As a united pair. As *us*."

I stared down at her, mesmerized by the strong Omega before me. "You're incredible, Ivana," I marveled, meaning every word. "So fucking incredible."

And I'd been a fool not to realize that before. To try to hide from her. To push her away.

This beautiful, fierce, amazing Omega had wanted to be mine from the moment we'd met. It took almost losing her to realize just how lucky I was that she'd chosen me to begin with.

"I'm going to spend the rest of our lives being worthy of you," I vowed. Then I sealed the promise with a kiss, one that had her arching against me as I wrapped one arm around her back and the other around her shoulders, my palm going to her nape.

She moaned, her mind completely open to mine. I could hear her wants. Her needs. Her *desires*. But underneath everything was a steel resolve to locate Ashlyn.

All Ivana wanted was to be my partner. To be my confidante. To be my mate.

And I was finally seeing what that meant.

It wasn't about prioritizing Kieran or the sector above my mate. It was about working with my mate to accomplish even more. It was about teamwork. About communicating. About supporting one another, no matter what.

This Omega had just taught me a lesson I never knew I needed to learn.

I thanked her with my tongue, worshipped her with my mind, and loved her unconditionally with my heart.

Let's go find Ashlyn, I whispered into her thoughts. *Afterward, I'm officially making you mine.*

IVANA

ASHLYN'S JOURNALS were spread out across the floor, their designs identical.

So much for recognizing one of them, I thought, blowing out a breath.

The only identifier on any of these was a symbol on the bottom right-hand corner of each front cover. But no one seemed to know what the symbols meant.

No one being me, Cillian, Kieran, Lorcan, Quinn, and Kyra.

Several of us had started scanning through piles of books while Lorcan and Cillian looked up the symbols in their data archives.

But three hours later, none of us had gotten anywhere.

"We're missing something," I said, looking at Cillian. "She told me about these journals. She told me to be careful with

Prince Cael, that he's surrounded by darkness. And she told me to tell you a new life is more important than an old one."

That last part still didn't make sense to me.

Was she talking about our baby? Or something else entirely?

And who is the old life? Her?

"What exactly did she say to you?" Kieran asked, his focus on Cillian as well.

"She called me stubborn, said my decisions didn't just impact my life, but someone else's, too—which I've since realized likely applies to Ivana. And she seemed pretty spooked by seeing Grey." Cillian frowned as he uttered that final reveal. "She said he didn't mean her harm, though. Just expressed surprise that their destinies were crossing this early."

Kyra and Quinn shared a look.

"She didn't join this program to find a mate," Quinn said. "You and I both know that."

Kyra nodded. "She's always been interested in Alphas, but not in a mating kind of way." She glanced at Lorcan as she added, "She wanted to know how to fight them."

"How to defend herself," he clarified.

Kyra shrugged. "Same thing."

Her mate grunted. "Only to you, little killer."

He talks a lot more now, I thought, blinking at Lorcan.

Yes, it's unnerving, Cillian replied into my mind, a hint of amusement underlining his words.

"But my point is, we knew from the beginning that Ashlyn joined this program for a purpose that had nothing to do with taking a mate," Quinn said. "And now I'm thinking it was to protect the other Omegas."

"Only, they were still dosed with the estrus party serum," Kieran replied, his gaze intent as he studied his Queen.

"Yes, but Sylvia was dosed first." Quinn's expression turned thoughtful with the words. "What if that was unintentional? And meant as a sign? A way to get the others out of Glacier Sector before everyone went into heat?"

"You think Ashlyn drugged her?" Kyra asked, incredulous.

"No… I don't know. I just…" Quinn paused to blow out a breath. "Look, everything Ashlyn does has a hidden purpose. It has always been that way. And she asked to room with Sylvia."

"So maybe she saw what happened to her, and whoever is behind this took Ashlyn to silence her," Kyra offered.

"Or maybe she already knew what was going to happen and wanted to make sure Sylvia was found," Quinn countered.

The pair of them studied each other for a long moment, their conversation seeming to continue with just their eyes.

They were best friends, and moments like this just drove that history home.

I let them continue their silent discussion and went back to look at the journals again. Specifically, the symbols.

"Do you think these relate to some sort of language?" I asked, talking to Cillian more than to the group. "Like maybe something Z-Clan wolves use to communicate?"

Because the letters looked a bit rune-like. Except they weren't a script I'd ever seen before, and given what little Lorcan and Cillian had found in their archives, it wasn't anything they recognized either.

Which said a lot, considering their ages.

But maybe we needed an outside opinion.

"We should ask Alpha Grey," I commented out loud, my eyes widening. "She told you their paths were destined to cross, right? Maybe that was a clue. Maybe she meant they were supposed to cross now. Like, *today*."

"Or she was hinting at Grey being the threat," Lorcan interjected.

"No, she very specifically said he didn't mean her any

harm," Cillian replied. "And I don't think she was solely talking about the ice pond incident."

"That sounds like the Ashlyn we know," Kyra mused. "Every comment is always a layered riddle."

"You usually like those riddles," Quinn commented dryly.

"Not when Ashlyn puts herself in danger," Kyra growled, her expression darkening. "I'm going to wring her neck when we find her."

"That sounds about right," Lorcan drawled.

Kyra narrowed her gaze up at her dark-haired, dark-eyed mate. "Do you want me to kill you?"

His lips curled. "I love it when you flirt with me, little killer."

"Stop distracting me."

"Stop propositioning me," he countered.

"You're infuriating." She uttered the words with conviction, then threw her arms around him and buried her face in his neck as he hugged her back. "Thank you."

I don't understand what just happened, I told myself, and Cillian by proxy.

But then I caught some of the answers in Kyra's and Lorcan's thoughts.

Lorcan had purposely goaded his mate to take her mind off Ashlyn. Just for a moment.

Because she was blaming herself for not pushing harder when asking Ashlyn about her intentions.

Actually, as I surveyed the group, I realized there was a lot of self-blame going on here.

Cillian, Lorcan, and Kieran all felt responsible as Ashlyn's protectors.

At the same time, Quinn and Kyra were chiding themselves internally for not making Ashlyn talk.

"She wouldn't have been able to say anything, even if you had tried to force her to confess," I blurted out. "She told me she couldn't *share* her visions. That's why she wrote them down." I held up two of the diaries. "And these are full of gibberish without timelines. Going through them all is going to take weeks. But if we can figure out what those symbols mean…"

"They might help," Cillian finished for me. "I agree. And I agree that we need Grey. I don't think Ashlyn was talking about the pond incident that day; I think she was trying to tell me something else."

"What about the darkness around Cael?" Kieran asked. "Was she warning us that he's somehow involved in all this?"

I slowly shook my head. "I don't think so. She purposely said *surrounded* by darkness. And she also told me he wasn't dangerous."

Kieran nodded. "Then we'll call Cael and Grey, see if they recognize these symbols, and go from there."

"Do you think we can trust them?" Kyra asked, her head against Lorcan's chest. He hadn't stopped hugging her, but her gaze was on Kieran.

"No," he replied. "But I'm willing to entertain the concept."

"As am I," Cillian agreed, his thoughts telling me why.

My eyes widened as he recalled everything Cael had said to him about me, how he'd called Cillian unworthy, telling him he needed to *do better*.

Apparently, Lorcan had done the same.

I gaped at him and then at Cillian. *They said all that?*

He glanced down at me, his lips twitching at the sides. *Surprised?*

Yes.

Why?

I… I don't know. I just… I frowned. *Lorcan never talks.* It was a lame excuse, but the first thing to come to mind. For Cael, I had no comment. I was… stunned.

As you already noted, Lorcan's a little more chatty these days, Cillian drawled, his arm coming around my shoulders. *And he cares about you. Me, too. Which is why I'm curious about Cael's motives.*

Out loud, he shifted topics, telling Kieran about Cael's growing power.

I listened intently, still surprised by everything I'd overheard in his mind, and even more stunned by what he said about Cael blocking him.

It sounded like what I'd been able to do. Sort of.

Only, my *gift*, as Cillian had called it, seemed to revolve around brain processes. Or sensing those processes, anyway. Or perhaps just sensing other mental talents.

All of it was very confusing.

However, I was intrigued to learn more about Cael and his potential abilities.

No, Cillian said into my mind, his hand catching my chin. "Stop thinking about Cael. You're mine."

I snorted. "You haven't bitten me yet."

"Ivana," he growled, low and with warning. "I will bite you right fucking here and rut you, just so I can ensure Cael gets the fucking message that you're mine."

A shiver traversed my spine at the possession underlining his tone. "I—"

"I assure you, that won't be necessary," Prince Cael interjected as he appeared without warning in Kieran's office. "While I enjoy a good bout of voyeurism on occasion, now isn't one of those moments." He turned to address the Blood Sector King. "We need to talk, O'Callaghan."

"Yes, it would seem we do," Kieran murmured, his head canting slightly to the side. "I was just about to call you."

Prince Cael smiled. "I know. That's why I'm here."

"You're going to need to explain that," Cillian growled, his protective instincts firing.

"Yes, that and a great many other things," Prince Cael replied. "But first, Alpha Grey needs to review those diaries.

There's an answer inside one of them that we all desperately need."

"You mean a confirmation," a deep voice rumbled as Grey materialized in the room, his long blond hair billowing around him in an ominous manner.

I didn't feel either of them arrive, Cillian growled, his words for Kieran and Lorcan, but I heard him thanks to my adopted talent.

"Start talking," Kieran said, his power punctuating the statement.

"We think we know where Ashlyn is," Prince Cael replied. "And we think we know who took her."

"Who?" Kieran demanded.

Prince Cael met his gaze directly and growled, "Prince Tadhg."

PART V

Dear Oracle of the Stars,

If you're reading this, then it's time to understand some of my choices. Some of my visions. Some of my...

No.

Don't react. Don't let them know what you've found. Do you understand?

Right, as I was saying... It's time. So I need you to listen closely, Stars.

If I'm right, your power is changing. You can feel things, yes?

Shh. No reacting. I mean it, Stars. Just focus and block out everything else.

And focus on your talent.

Does anything feel strange?

Weird vibes?

Potential puzzles to solve... or disassemble?

This is one of those moments where you have to choose your allies wisely.

Consider all potential paths.

And watch your step...

There are land mines afoot, Stars. Land mines that will alert our enemy that we're coming.

Be careful. Tread softly.

And remember...

Don't. Make. A. Sound.

I hope... I hope that's enough. I can't provide any more. We're at a crossroads, Stars. I... I see two ways this could end.

Maybe you'll find a third route.

Goodbye for now,
Ashlyn

PS: Congratulations on the little one. I send my blessing from the grave.

PPS: Our pasts make us stronger, not weaker. Remember that. Remember where you came from. And understand once and for all—you are not him. But sometimes you have to think like him to find the truth. To find... me.

CILLIAN

It took physical restraint to remain quiet and let Cael talk. His abrupt arrival had set off every alarm in my head.

Power.

Obscene *power.*

On par with Kieran. Me. And Lorcan.

A clear rival.

A potential threat.

But as he continued to speak, my sense of alarm shifted away from Cael's unexpected presence and toward the situation he spoke about now.

"That operation you and the X-Clan wolves took down in Bariloche Sector was just one of many," he was saying, shocking the hell out of me.

He'd just casually mentioned our involvement in the destruction of Bariloche Sector as though it were common knowledge, when in reality, we hadn't breathed a word of that outside of our very small circle.

We'd only been there for Quinnlynn, something Kieran, Lorcan, and I had definitely not told anyone else about.

"It was also taken down prematurely," Cael went on. "We had an in, someone working his way through the system, but then you all stormed in and burned the sector to the ground."

Grey grunted, his arms folded across his broad chest. He'd remained mostly silent since his abrupt arrival. However, his mind had whirred with strands of information. Internal comments regarding the *Omega slave trade* that he and Cael had apparently been researching for years.

"Working the system, meaning what exactly?" Kieran asked, his mind lethally quiet as he focused entirely on Grey and Cael.

"The Omega auction network," Cael clarified, his terminology differing slightly from Grey's internal monologue referring to it as a slave trade.

"What Omega auctions?" Kieran demanded. "I've never heard of such a thing."

"Because it's run by a secretive collective of Alphas. We've been trying to infiltrate their network for years." Cael heaved a sigh and ran his fingers through his dark hair. "We were trying to entice Tadhg into reaching out to our contact in Bariloche Sector so we could expose him."

"To prove he's one of the collective's members," Grey added in a rumble, his mind telling me it went far deeper than just establishing proof of Tadhg's involvement in the Omega auctions.

There was some other piece of this puzzle. Something he was trying to prove Tadhg had done. But before I could discern that piece, he shut me out, his glacial gaze cutting to me.

I've let you poke around enough, he thought at me. *I'm not here to hurt you or anyone else in Blood Sector, something you've already observed in your various sweeps through my head. So stop digging.*

There's more to the story than what you're saying, I told him.

Of course there is, but my personal reasons are none of your concern.

This is personal for us, too, I pointed out.

Not in the same way, he told me, his gaze boring into mine. Aloud, he said, "I need to see Ashlyn's journals. I can decipher them in a way none of you can."

Kieran bristled at that. "Not until I understand what's actually happening here."

"What's happening here is that a few high-ranking Sector Alphas created an Omega slave trade back when the Infected Era began," Grey summarized flatly. "They kidnapped fleeing Omegas of all kinds, put them into auction lineups, and sold them to the highest bidders all over the globe. They've continued that process for decades, only with fewer auctions due to limited supplies of Omegas. And their primary customers were assholes like Carlos."

Several other names peppered Grey's mind, all of them ones he allowed me to hear. None of the identities he listed were surprising. There were places like Bariloche Sector all over the world, all run by Alphas who saw Omegas as commodities to be used, not treasures to be worshipped.

"Oh, and your recent reveal of the Sanctuary has very likely piqued their interest," Grey concluded.

"Because we have no doubt that Tadhg has shared the information," Cael added.

"Right," Grey growled. "Hence, I need to review Ashlyn's journals to prove he's involved and see what she knows about it."

"How do you even know about the journals?" Ivana interjected, her bright eyes on Grey. "We didn't call you, and no one knew about the diaries until I told Cillian where to find them. Yet you and Prince Cael shadowed in here on a clear mission to read them. How? *How* did you know?"

Grey stared her down, his dominance heavy in the air and causing my wolf to stir inside. If he took a single step toward my Omega, I would be forced to intervene.

No one challenged Ivana.

No one except for me.

"Show her," he said, not taking his attention away from my female. "Show her the letter."

Cael slid his hand into his suit jacket and pulled out a small white envelope, then held it out toward my Omega.

I took it from him before she could move, not wanting my female anywhere near his princely touch. His lips twitched, but he didn't say anything. Just watched as I handed the item over to my female for review.

She eyed the name scrawled across it—*Grey*—and the symbol in the bottom left corner. It rivaled the ones on the journal covers.

Not uttering a word, she flipped open the flap and pulled out a plain white card.

They'll need your guidance, it read. *And she needs you, too. Don't give up, Grey. Count the days. Translate the journals. Review the visions. And remember that time is of the essence. Tick. Tock. Tick. Tock. Tick…*

Beneath it was a series of symbols that made no sense to my ancient eyes. Just like the others on the covers.

"It's a primitive language," Grey explained when Ivana glanced up at him with questions in her gaze. "Similar to hieroglyphics, only older and from a different region. *My* region. But that line there spells out Blood Sector, and beneath it is today's date, along with the time—which was roughly ten minutes ago."

"We guessed that you all would be here," Cael added. "But we weren't positive. Hence, we arrived a few minutes earlier than the time stamp on her card."

"How long have you had this?" I asked, gesturing to Ashlyn's cryptic note.

"Since this morning," Grey muttered, tugging on the

lapels of his leather coat. "I found it tucked into my jacket pocket, one I haven't worn since I was here last week."

Because the clever Omega must have seen that I wouldn't wear this coat again until today, he thought, the words seeming to be for himself. However, he didn't try to block me from overhearing these inner musings. Not even when he added, *And she must have done it after distracting me with that bloody kiss.*

My eyebrow rose. *Kiss?* I wondered.

But I didn't ask because Kieran was already speaking.

"This has all been very interesting, but where do you think Ashlyn is?" Kieran looked between Grey and Cael. "And why are you so sure that Tadhg is involved?"

Grey's jaw clenched, his mind shutting down once more.

There was definitely something there.

Some sort of history he didn't want me to hear.

Which only had me narrowing my gaze at him. *The more you hide, the more suspicious you appear.*

I'm not afraid of you, Elite, he returned, his gaze locking on mine. *I'm not afraid of anyone. So accuse me all you like. But you'll only be wasting your time.*

The door slammed between us again, almost sending me backward a step.

He's very powerful, Ivana whispered to me. *I… I can feel his energy wrapping around all of us, similar to when you leash the Alphas. But this… this is even more intense. Like he's doing something to us that none of us can feel.*

I didn't like the way that sounded, and I quickly relayed Ivana's findings to Kieran.

However, he was too busy listening to Cael's explanation—one I'd missed while talking to Grey.

Fortunately, I could catch up by listening to my best friend's mind.

Unfortunately, I didn't like what I heard there.

They're using fallen sectors as their trading playgrounds—fallen sectors like Eclipse Sector.

There is no tangible proof of Tadhg's involvement, but we know a powerful V-Clan Alpha is a member of this organization, and Tadhg's scent has lingered in several locations associated with the black market auctions.

Kieran glanced at his mate. "Is Tadhg the Alpha you scented in Bariloche Sector?"

She frowned. "No. I've seen him enough times lately that I can say with certainty it wasn't him."

"Correct. Tadhg never visited Bariloche Sector. Only my brother did." The unexpected comment caused Kieran's focus to instantly return to Cael. "Dixon was the one I mentioned who had infiltrated Bariloche Sector, our informant whose job was nullified when you and the X-Clan wolves took down Carlos's operation."

"Your brother visited Bariloche Sector? To rape Omegas?" Kieran asked, his quiet tone edged with simmering violence.

"He didn't rape anyone," Cael growled. "But he was forced to play some of Carlos's games. It wasn't a role he enjoyed."

Quinnlynn snorted.

As did Kyra.

Earning them both a sigh from Cael. "You don't know my brother like I do, but he values consent. Any of the Omegas he played with will tell you the same. I believe all three of them are in Andorra Sector now, if you would like to call them for a follow-up."

The fact that he knew their locations confirmed how much he'd been paying attention to the incident in Bariloche Sector.

An incident that shouldn't have concerned him at all.

Yet he'd felt the need to follow up on where the Omegas were taken afterward. *Interesting.*

"I healed some of those Omegas," Quinnlynn said through her teeth. "I know what was done to them."

"But not by him. You ran every time he came near

Bariloche Sector. He felt you leave." Cael stared at Kieran. "Which is how I know you helped the X-Clan Alphas take down Bariloche Sector—you went there for Quinnlynn. Took you long enough to find her, by the way."

Kieran took a step forward. "Careful, Prince Cael. I don't care for the accusation underlining your tone."

Cael narrowed his gaze. "We can posture if you want, *King Kieran*, but we're wasting precious time. If Ashlyn is where we think she is, then she's going up for auction soon. And once that happens, getting her back will be much more difficult."

"Look," Grey said, stepping forward and dropping his hands to his sides. "I get that a lot of this seems unbelievable. That's why we've been working for decades to try to catch Tadhg in the act. We need tangible proof of what he's done so we can hold him accountable."

"Which is what Dixon was attempting to do in Bariloche Sector. He was trying to get put on Tadhg's radar as an interested party so he could potentially be invited to a seat at the table," Cael added.

"Yes, Dixon and Cael assumed that if Tadhg found out another V-Clan Alpha was interested in Carlos's way of life, he would reach out and set a playdate." Grey sounded bored. "That didn't happen."

"You don't seem all that surprised by that outcome," Kieran noted, his observation rivaling my own.

"Because I'm not. Tadhg has spent a century, perhaps longer, hiding who he is from everyone in our world. He probably saw right through Dixon's intentions."

Cael blew out a breath and shook his head, his posture and expression suggesting this wasn't the first time he and Grey had exchanged these words. "We had to try."

"Sure," Grey drawled. "And now Ashlyn has taken fate into her own hands by offering herself up as bait. She's seen what's going to happen to those Sanctuary Omegas, and she's trying to stop it. Which is why I need to see those diaries. *Now.*"

"Shit," Kyra cursed. "Shit, shit, *shit.*"

"I know," Quinnlynn muttered.

Ivana frowned. "What?"

"This is just like Ashlyn," Kyra hissed, her catlike eyes flashing with annoyance. "Always putting herself in danger to protect others. We knew she didn't join the mating program to find an Alpha. We knew, and we didn't press the issue."

"It wouldn't have mattered," Quinnlynn argued. "You know how stubborn she can be."

Kyra shook her head. "I really am going to kill her when we find her."

This time, Lorcan didn't utter a response to Kyra's repeated threat. He just studied his mate intently, no doubt hearing a string of words through their mate bond. Or perhaps he was just sensing her mood.

Ignoring all that, I focused on Cael and Grey. "So you think she allowed herself to be captured, to try to stop the other Omegas from being hurt," I reiterated.

"Yes," Grey replied. "And it makes perfect sense, too. Tadhg would have learned about her prophetic abilities from Hawk or one of the other Alpha candidates from his sector. Or he likely knew because she's a Z-Clan Omega. Regardless, he would have seen her as a threat he needed to dispose of. And she placed herself in a position to be taken."

"By volunteering to come back to Blood Sector to help those who stayed here during their heats," Kyra muttered, shaking her head again and chastising herself mentally for not seeing it.

"She was one of the few who didn't go into heat, too, and had said it was probably because her kind didn't react to the serum," Quinnlynn grumbled. "But I bet she didn't imbibe the drink at all."

"Assuming a drink is how it was introduced," Kyra returned. "We still don't know how that happened."

"It was definitely the estrus party serum. I recognized it while trying to heal some of the Omegas." Quinnlynn's eyes narrowed at Cael. "A serum your brother would have had access to."

"True, if Bariloche Sector still existed," he replied, arching a brow. "I can bring him here for Cillian to interrogate if that would help the situation."

"He has a natural block in his mind, making that rather difficult," I pointed out. "Something I think you already know."

"It's a barrier he can remove." Cael proceeded to do just that, opening his mind to me so I could see the truth. "It's not difficult to do."

I didn't reply, instead poking around his thoughts and hearing the sincerity inside them.

As well as a worry for Ashlyn.

Because he knew all too well what was about to happen to her. So well, in fact, that it told me this had happened before.

To someone close to him.

No. Not to him.

To Grey, I realized.

Grey was the one who had exposure to this organization's auctions.

He'd experienced the pain of betrayal. The pain of *loss*.

All of this, the accusations surrounding Tadhg, the need to bring him down, was because of Grey. He somehow knew the Alpha Prince was responsible for whatever had happened in his past.

Tadhg kidnapped and sold Grey's sister into the slave trade, Cael thought at me, his turquoise irises swirling with barely restrained fury. *And he's been trying to prove it for over a hundred years. I only recently joined the fight in the last few decades.*

Why didn't you tell us? I asked, astounded by his reveal.

For the same reason you didn't tell us about Bariloche Sector, he fired back. *For the same reason you didn't inform us of the Sanctuary until recently. Trust takes time, Cillian. I think you know that lesson better than anyone.*

Hmm, I hummed, neither confirming nor denying that point. Because we both knew I understood it on a multitude of levels.

There is more we can share, he went on. *More we've discovered in our pursuit of Tadhg, specifically about this shadow organization known for their Omega auctions. But there's no point in continuing this conversation if you think we're lying.*

"Cillian?" Kieran prompted, causing me to glance at him. "Do we need Dixon?"

I returned my attention to Cael. This was the moment of no return. We either worked with Grey and Cael, or we chose to go against them.

Right now, I didn't see any obvious reason for the latter.

Because in Cael's mind, all I found was the desire for a new alliance. A respect for Kieran. Acknowledgment of our mutual powers.

And an acceptance that Ivana chose me.

That last realization hung between Cael and me, the genuine thought lingering on the cusp of his mind, ensuring I heard it.

You'd just better prove yourself worthy of her, he added. *Because she deserves the best. Not subpar. Not mediocre. Not even good. The* best.

I know, I telepathically replied. Then I looked at Kieran and answered his question. "No, we don't need Dixon. But we do need to give the journals to Grey. Because I think they're telling the truth. And as they've already mentioned, time isn't on our side."

IVANA

STACKS OF JOURNALS littered the floor as Grey organized them by date. Or that was what he'd said when Kyra had asked what the piles represented.

"These are from the last three years," he'd told us, gesturing to a tower of a dozen or so notebooks. I had one in my lap now, the insides filled with incoherent musings and bizarre illustrations.

I scanned the pages, searching for anything familiar.

She described various scenes, wrote cryptic phrases, and drew random bubbles all over her pages. Sometimes those bubbles had arrows. Other times they were just circles upon circles, reminding me a bit of a delirious black hole.

"Do these mean anything to you?" I asked Grey, showing him all the doodles.

He glanced at the page I held up for him and shook his

head. "No, not yet." Then he returned his attention to the item in his hand. His jaw ticked at whatever he read there.

I put up a block before I could hear it in his mind, my head already overwhelmed from all the thoughts whirling around in the room.

Hell, it wasn't even the room. It was the entire sector. I had no idea how Cillian lived with this every day.

Well, that wasn't true. I had some idea because I'd adopted this mental blocking trick from his mind. But it was taking serious focus to hold it up against the various musings floating around Blood Sector.

Closing my eyes, I stole a deep breath and calmed my own thoughts. Silencing everything and everyone around me.

Then I slowly returned to the task of trying to find hints within Ashlyn's chaotic writing.

There had to be at least three hundred passages in this journal, some of them sharing the same page, others scrawled across two papers.

I kept reading.

And reading.

Until I could swear hours had passed. Everyone else in the room had fallen silent, all of us engrossed in Ashlyn's cryptic words.

I rubbed my temples but kept pushing.

Dear Oracle,

We're close.

I miss my dreams.

Ashlyn

I glanced at the doodle beneath it, counting the circles. *Seventeen. Okay.*

The next page had twenty-seven circles.

And the one after had two.

Is it a pattern? I wondered, writing the numbers down on a blank sheet beside me.

The next page had seven.

Seventeen. Twenty-seven. Two. Seven.

Frowning, I flipped to the next entry and started counting, only to blink at the first line.

Dear Oracle of the Stars.

Stars had a circle around it.

But that wasn't why it caught my eye.

Shuffling a few papers back, I started reading the headings of everything leading up to this.

Dear Oracle.

Dear Oracle.

Dear Oracle.

I grabbed another notebook to glance through several entries. All of them started with *Dear Oracle*. Never *Dear Oracle of the Stars*.

My frown deepened.

I wrote *Dear Stars* in my journals, something Ashlyn knew because she had a problem understanding personal space and had watched me pen one of my entries on the plane.

A coincidence or something else entirely? I wondered, returning to her entry.

Dear Oracle of the Stars, I read again. *If you're reading this, then it's time to understand some of my choices. Some of my visions. Some of my… No. Don't react. Don't let them know what you've found. Do you understand?*

I blinked and glanced around, my brow furrowing. She couldn't possibly be talking to me. That… This…

I cleared my throat.

This is Ashlyn. Anything's possible.

I ran my gaze over her last sentence about understanding her, only to be distracted by a loud sigh across the room. "No," Prince Cael said, his finger pressing a button at his ear. "Everything's fine. I'll ring you if that changes."

Cillian and Lorcan were both staring at Prince Cael. Grey, too.

I couldn't hear who he was talking to, just a low hum of sound, and Prince Cael's responding grunt. "Okay, fine. If you're going to pout, then come over here and be useless for all I care." His hand dropped, telling me he'd just ended whatever call he'd been on.

"Dixon?" Grey asked.

"No. Granger," Cael growled. "He's insisting that I need an Elite present."

Kieran snorted. "Sounds familiar."

Cillian and Lorcan both arched brows his way. "You get lonely without us," Cillian drawled.

"Sure I do," Kieran drawled right back.

The air shimmered as Granger appeared in the office, his stoic expression taking in the scene before him. "What the bloody hell are you even doing?" he asked.

"Reading," Grey told him, then returned to the item in his hand.

"Reading what?" Granger asked.

Prince Cael sighed and started explaining about Ashlyn's journals, causing me to look down again at the entry I'd been reading before his conversation had distracted me.

Right, as I was saying was the next line, causing my eyebrow to arch upward. *It's time. So I need you to listen closely, Stars.*

Okay, now I was… about eighty percent sure she'd written this to me. Maybe.

If I'm right, your power is changing. You can feel *things, yes?*

I blinked. *This can't be real,* I whispered to myself.

Vana? Cillian asked as I read the next line from Ivana's journal, which said, *Shh.*

Holy stars, I thought.

No reacting was what came next. *I mean it, Stars. Just focus and* ***block*** *out everything else.*

The word *block* had been written over several times, giving it a bold-like appearance. Seeing it and thinking about it had me putting up walls all over my mind on instinct, but not with Cillian.

Instead, I left my thoughts open to him and whispered, *I think I found something, but we can't tell anyone. Not yet. Not until I understand what this means.*

In my peripheral vision, I saw him take a step toward me. *No, you can't react. Just let me… let me see what Ashlyn might be trying to tell me.*

He continued toward me anyway, causing me to grit my teeth. But all he did was clasp my chin and pull me up for a kiss.

They already saw me looking at you, he whispered into my mind as his tongue slid into my mouth. *Now I'm just distracting them from wondering what caught my attention.*

He deepened the embrace by sliding his palm to my neck and squeezing my throat.

For a split second, I forgot what I was doing. Hell, I was pretty sure I forgot my own name.

Because Cillian was kissing me.

In front of his friends.

In front of their mates.

I'll kiss you in front of the entire fucking world, Vana, he told me softly. *Whatever it takes to prove you're mine.*

All you have to do is bite me for that to be true, I reminded him.

He growled low in his chest, the sound vibrating through me in a wave of possession.

I would do it right fucking now, macushla, but I don't think you want me to rut you in front of an audience. And I'm not quite sure I want to share you in that way, either. He nipped at my lower lip before pulling away. *Go back to reading. I'll be listening. And keep your walls up.*

His jarring change in topic left me winded and a little flustered as I glanced around the room.

Everyone was gaping at Cillian.

Well, not everyone.

Prince Cael was grinning. "Trying to convey a point?"

Cillian abruptly turned around and kissed me again, startling me even more. *Get back to work,* he demanded into my mind. *I want to know what else that passage says.*

I almost asked him, *What passage?*

But then I remembered what I'd been doing before his erratic behavior had begun, and I jolted against him in response.

Easy, love, he murmured. *No reactions, remember?*

His teeth skimmed my lower lip again, his dark eyes burning into mine. "How's that for a message, Prince?" he asked, still looking at me.

"I would have added more tongue" was Prince Cael's succulent reply.

A fire lit in Cillian's gaze, one I felt searing me to my very soul.

"If you two are going to fight, take it outside," King Kieran interjected. "My office is too crowded for this shit."

"But this is what you wanted, wasn't it?" Prince Cael said, his silky tone causing both Cillian and me to look at him. "You asked me to join the mating pool to prod your Elite into action, yes?"

King Kieran stared at him, one dark eyebrow arching. "Did I say that?"

Prince Cael smiled again. "No, but we both know that was your intention. And it looks like it worked."

Go back to Ashlyn's passage, Cillian whispered into my mind. *And ignore the conversation we're about to have.*

What?

Take advantage of the distraction, Vana, he told me, then released me to join the two men as King Kieran asked, "Would I do that?"

"You would absolutely do that," Cillian muttered. "Just

like you would fuck with sleeping arrangements to ensure Ivana and I shared an igloo. Oh, wait, you *did* do that."

King Kieran snorted, but I caught the amusement dancing in his thoughts.

He was playing a game.

One Cillian must have asked him to play.

As a distraction, I realized, recalling what Cillian had just said. *They're distracting everyone so I can focus on what I've found.*

Glancing down, I reread a few of Ashlyn's lines.

I mean it, Stars. Just focus and ***block*** *out everything else.*

Swallowing, I did what she asked once more and continued scanning downward.

And focus on your talent.

Okay, I thought at her.

Does anything feel strange? was the next line. *Weird vibes? Potential puzzles to solve… or disassemble?*

My brow crinkled as I reviewed her riddles. The only *weird vibes* in the room were coming from Cillian and Prince Cael as they appeared to be squaring off with one another.

Which had Granger and Lorcan both tensing in the periphery.

But not Grey.

Grey was fully immersed in something else.

That strange power still emanated from him, the one I couldn't decipher before. Only it wasn't his ability that grabbed my attention as I scanned the room, but Granger's. His mind… his mind was like…

A puzzle, I realized, blinking back down to the diary and catching that word on the page once more.

This is one of those moments where you have to choose your allies wisely, she continued. *Consider all potential paths. And watch your step…*

Okay… Was she talking about solving the puzzle? Being careful with how I unwove it? *Potential puzzles to solve or to disassemble* was basically what she'd said. So it would make sense that she was providing caution over how I *disassembled* it.

There are land mines afoot, Stars, Ashlyn had written next. *Land mines that will alert our enemy that we're coming. Be careful. Tread softly. And remember… Don't. Make. A. Sound.*

I swallowed, her warnings feeling ominous. But as I prodded Granger's thoughts, and noted the layers of his mind, it… it made sense.

He was masking behind a thick veneer of power, one that allowed only his surface-level musings to escape. But I could sense the darkness beneath.

My eyes nearly widened. *Be careful of Prince Cael,* she'd written to me on that plane. *He's surrounded by darkness.*

Darkness being Granger? I wondered now.

He wasn't who Prince Cael and Grey had accused of taking Ashlyn, but maybe… maybe they had it wrong?

Swallowing, I kept reading.

I hope… I hope that's enough. I can't provide any more. We're at a crossroads, Stars. I… I see two ways this could end. Maybe you'll find a third route. Goodbye for now, Ashlyn.

Beneath her name were two postscripts, the first of them giving me chills. But it definitely felt like it was for me.

PS: Congratulations on the little one. I send my blessing from the grave.

The second, I wasn't sure about.

PPS: Our pasts make us stronger, not weaker. Remember that. Remember where you came from. And understand once and for all—you are not him. *But sometimes you have to think like him to find the truth. To find… me.*

Maybe that part would make more sense once I solved the puzzle in Granger's mind.

Unless it's Grey I should be deciphering, I thought, considering the other male.

This is one of those moments where you have to choose your allies wisely, Ashlyn had written. *Consider all potential paths. And watch your step…*

I… I wasn't sure which *path* she wanted me to take.

Glancing back down, I reread the line that said, *I see two ways this could end.*

But then she mentioned a third route.

What's the third route? I wondered.

I don't think it's Grey, Cillian told me. Yet aloud, he was in the process of lecturing King Kieran about his *meddling.*

"What the hell has gotten into the two of you?" Quinnlynn demanded.

"Your *mate* keeps concerning himself in my affairs," Cillian told her. "And don't chuckle, Cael. You're just as bad."

Stop listening to me, he added mentally. *See if you can poke around Granger's mind. I'm about to really distract him.*

By doing—

My eyes widened as his fist connected with Prince Cael's jaw. "*Cillian,*" I hissed out loud.

See what he's hiding, he demanded in my head. *Now.*

Prince Cael lunged forward with a growl, the two men crashing to the floor in a heap of testosterone and snarls.

I jumped up from my chair, the journal clutched in my hand, and darted backward to brace against a wall while King Kieran ushered Quinnlynn out of the room.

Kyra just shook her head.

As did Lorcan.

And Grey… Grey was too engrossed with his reading material to care about the chaos behind him.

I frowned, my curiosity piquing as I considered his mind for a moment.

That power he was exuding had waned, his focus intent on Ashlyn's words. *Did you find something?* I wanted to ask him.

But movement out of the corner of my eye drew my gaze back to the brawl happening next to Kieran's desk. Granger had pulled a knife, his gaze intent on Cillian.

My lips parted, a warning ready to leave my mouth, when Granger's murderous thoughts yanked me in. No, it wasn't just his thoughts, but his… his *power.*

It was pulsing.

Swirling.

Regenerating with every second to create a new layer to swim through.

What a unique ability, I marveled, losing myself within his mental process. He was constantly masking, and not just his musings but everything else, too.

Everything that made him a wolf.

Like his voice.

His growl.

His scent, I realized, finding that strand whirling around him.

He was literally a puzzle, one where he rearranged pieces around himself to create a new version for every situation.

All while hiding beneath a series of iron-clad protections. They reminded me of steel ribbons, flexible to an extent, but mostly unbreakable.

I wove beneath them carefully, longing to go deeper, to hear his inner confessions. Because he was definitely hiding something.

Everyone around me fell silent as I focused intently on my target, my fingers clutching the journal to my chest.

What are you holding back? I wondered. *Who are you really?*

Because everything about him was a lie. A mask. An alter ego.

He'd spent decades perfecting this identity, living in this voice, this growl, this *scent*. But another version lurked beneath all these barriers.

I kept pushing, gently moving strands out of the way, and searching for the true identity underneath all his mental barricades.

Show me, I demanded, swimming through the mental

minefield. *This is what Ashlyn meant about watching my step, to tread carefully, to not alert—*

The air whooshed out of my lungs as a concrete boulder slammed into me, cutting off my ability to breathe.

Everything spun.

Throbbed.

The world… the world… was too dark. Too black. Too—

Ivana! Cillian shouted. Was that in my mind? Out loud? I… I couldn't tell.

I… I don't know where I am…

I waited for his reply.

Nothing came.

Just silence.

Darkness.

Nothingness.

Death.

CILLIAN

A Minute Earlier

Fuck, Cael could throw a punch.

I flexed my jaw and ducked as I narrowly avoided getting hit again.

He growled.

I returned the growl.

And both of us went to battle with our minds, trying to force the other to submit.

This distraction wasn't going to work for much longer. Cael knew I was up to something. He'd said as much with a thought right after I'd hit him the first time. *I don't know why we're doing this, but I'll play, Elite. Give me your best.*

I'd responded by introducing my fist to his face again.

Which had infuriated Granger.

But Cael had demanded that he stand down. "I'm fine. I can handle this."

"He just disrespected you," Granger had said through his teeth.

"I said, *I can handle this*."

And handle it, he had.

Shadowing all over the fucking room for the last few minutes. Throwing punches. Kicks. Verbal insults. *And the occasional mental laugh*.

The asshole was enjoying this far too much.

Begrudgingly, I could admit that a part of me felt the same. And I very much hated that we were both so well matched. If I liked him, I'd ask him to spar more often.

Alas…

My foot met his lower back as I shadowed around him in a quick move to try to knock him down. The kick sent him right into Kieran's desk, toppling several items onto the floor.

If you fuck up my office, I'm going to be very annoyed, Kieran informed me flatly as Cael shoved off the wood with a growl.

I would take it outside, but I need access to Granger's mind. Ivana is close to breaking through his final mental layers. I could almost hear his true thoughts now, see whatever it was that he—

I shadowed to the opposite side of the room, narrowly avoiding Cael's claws.

Because the bastard had just transformed his hand into a wolf's paw.

"That's an impressive talent," I admitted with a huff.

The bastard smirked, then vanished.

I spun, attempting to anticipate his reappearance.

"I could rip you right open," he said near my ear, his claws digging into my throat in the next blink. *Because you're barely trying*, he added mentally, his chest rumbling with a growl against my back. *What the fuck is going on, Cillian?*

I muttered a curse.

He knew I wasn't serious about this attack. I would never

have done this with Ivana in the room. His mind said as much.

And he was right—I wasn't trying. Not even a little bit.

Only a few minutes had passed since I'd first hit him, my momentary distraction short-lived.

But it seemed to have been long enough for Ivana to find her way into Granger's mind.

Show me, I heard her demand as Cael's claws dug into my throat.

Start talking, he thought at me.

But I was too busy listening to Ivana thinking about the minefields in Granger's mind. *This is what Ashlyn meant about watching my step, to tread carefully, to not alert—*

An explosion erupted, causing me to grab my head as agony sliced through every nerve ending.

Pain erupted through my neck as my knees gave out, the ground suddenly embracing my fall. Or halting it, anyway. Harshly. Coldly.

Oh, Gods, what the fuck? I couldn't breathe. I was choking. Drowning. Lost in a sea of perpetual darkness.

Except…

Except there were growls all around me. Reverberations. *Power.*

My eyes flew open as Kieran hit me with a dose of his healing gift, my world suddenly right again.

Only nothing was right about what I was seeing.

Granger had his hand locked around Ivana's neck, her body limp against the wall from whatever the fuck he'd just done to her.

Ivana! I shouted into her mind.

Nothing.

Not a single sound.

No sign of life.

I was on my feet in an instant, my gifts locking on Granger

as I roared into his thoughts. Every ounce of my wolf's dominance went into that sound as I *demanded* that he submit.

His legs shook, but his hand remained around my Omega's neck.

I didn't think; I acted, sending another thunderous rumble into his head. My chest echoed that sound, causing the entire room to quake around me.

Or that was how it felt, anyway.

I wasn't actually looking at the room or anyone nearby. My entire focus was on the Alpha holding my female captive. And her limp form. Her pale cheeks. *Her lifeless state.*

A third growling howl ripped from my mind to his, ordering him to obey. To release my Omega. *To kneel.*

Beads of sweat dotted his brow, his mental walls wavering beneath my oppressive commands.

Cillian? Ivana whispered, her mental voice stirring a wave of primal need inside. *I… I…* She trailed off, her mind seeming to seek mine out for comfort and support.

No.

Not just comfort and support.

Knowledge.

I felt her absorbing it, using it, and applying it with a soul-deep determination.

Then she released her own growl, her newfound ability flourishing to life as she blasted through Granger's consciousness and demolished the barriers protecting his true thoughts.

I seized the advantage, taking hold of his mind with my own and leashing him with my power. My strength. My *dominance.*

He snarled in response, releasing Ivana. I shadowed forward to catch her, my arms instantly locking around her before Granger landed in a heap on the floor. Another potent blast knocked him out, allowing my focus to fall to Ivana.

She shivered in my arms, her eyes still closed, her skin clammy. *Kieran*! I called with my mind.

He was beside me in an instant, his palm ghosting across Ivana's form. *She's okay,* he told me. *The baby is okay, too.*

Then why isn't she awake? I asked, my mental voice resembling gravel. *Why is she barely breathing?*

"She's breathing just fine," he said out loud. "Give her a moment, Cillian."

I didn't have a moment.

I needed her awake right fucking now.

I needed her to be mine.

Alive.

My mate.

Gods, the power she'd just exuded, the beautiful talent, the way we'd just taken Granger out together… I held her closer, my lips near her ear. "Wake up," I demanded. "Wake the fuck up so I can bite you."

Because I couldn't wait a second longer.

This female was mine. And I needed her to finish this. To complete us. To embrace our future together.

Please, Vana, I whispered into her mind. *Please wake up.*

Kieran and the others were talking around us, but I didn't listen. I didn't fucking care. All that mattered was Ivana. Our incomplete bond. Our stranded souls. We needed to be united, to become one.

Her lashes fluttered, her thoughts seeming to brush mine. *Granger?* she asked.

Is a fucking dead man, I vowed, sending another blast through his broken mind for good measure. Someone was binding him physically.

Grey, I realized.

But I immediately disregarded his actions and focused on my beautiful Omega. Her pretty blue eyes slowly peeked up at me, her cheeks still a pale shade that made my heart race.

"Vana," I whispered, my voice holding a note of reverence to it.

This female was everything.

Powerful.

Gorgeous.

Determined.

Confident.

She'd fought for me for so long, and I'd repaid her with rejection—something I'd denied before but now saw how right she'd been to use that term.

I had rejected her at every turn.

Told her to find another Alpha.

Someone worthier. Someone better. All while ignoring that I could be that Alpha.

Because I feared becoming my father. I feared extending his familial line. I feared letting everyone else down by prioritizing a mate over their security.

But by doing so, I gave all those fears purpose. I lived in the past. Let my father's ghost haunt me for over a thousand years.

No more.

I was done letting a dead man dictate my wants and needs.

Done listening to that voice in my head that claimed I wasn't good enough or deserving of a mate.

Ivana and I were more powerful together than we were apart. Today proved that. Hell, the last six years had proved that.

I'd been alone without her. Lost. Unconsciously miserable.

And it'd taken her calling me a coward to set me straight.

It'd taken me watching her with other Alphas, realizing that I might just lose her once and for all, to wake the fuck up and claim what had been mine for years.

Then I'd messed up again during her heat. After her heat. Even right fucking now.

I threaded my fingers through her hair, my gaze holding hers. "You're mine, Vana."

She swallowed, her eyes searching mine as I unleashed every thought into her mind. All my anguish. All my longing. All my unfulfilled desires. All my frustration. All my fears. All my *everything*.

But most importantly, I shared my love. My devotion. My intention. *My claim.*

Tears formed around her irises, making the blue depths glitter.

Then she subtly tilted her head to expose her neck, the invitation clear. "Bite me, Alpha," she whispered, her full lips moving with the words.

I hadn't realized how much I needed her to say that. To *demand* it. Because it only further proved that we were meant to be. "Always telling me what to do," I murmured back to her.

She stole a breath, suggesting she was about to say something else, maybe utter another command.

But the air escaped from her on a gasp as I sank my canines into her neck.

Her blood touched my tongue in the next instant, stirring a possessive growl from my chest, one that immediately morphed into a purr. Because her essence was *heaven*. Citrusy yet tangy. Alluringly seductive. And one hundred percent *mine*.

I swallowed three pulls before I finally moved away to stare down at my stunning mate. Her blissed-out expression told me she'd liked that bite and very much wanted to feel it again.

I obliged by leaning down and nibbling on her lip just hard enough to break the surface. Then I laved away the hurt and claimed her with my mouth.

Kissing her to my heart's content.

Owning her with each swipe of my tongue.

All while she writhed and moaned in my arms.

It took significant effort to pull away, to press my forehead to hers, but I needed to confirm that she was truly okay. Truly healed. Truly *alive.*

Because those few short seconds without her had felt like an eternity of loss.

Part of me recognized the insanity of that need—*of course she's fucking alive*—but I had to make sure this wasn't a dream. It felt too fantastic to be real life. To be *my* life.

However, as I stared down into her lust-filled gaze, all I found was my future. My renewed existence. My *world.*

"I love you," I told her. "I love you so fucking much."

Her palm caressed my cheek, her thumb drawing a line beneath my eye. "Good, Alpha. Now tell me you'll love me forever."

Her cheeky reply had me laughing outright, her penchant for telling me what to do in full form. "Who am I to deny such a beautiful Omega?" I mused. "One I will absolutely *love forever.*"

Ivana's gaze sparkled. "Finally," she said with a sigh as I slowly lowered her to her feet with my hands holding her hips. "You're *finally* listening to me."

I chuckled, pulling her against me in a hug. "I've always listened to you, Vana." That had never been the problem. "I just had to learn to *hear* you."

She tilted her head back to reveal a flirtatious grin. "It helped that you took your head out of your ass."

I laughed again and shook my head. "You're lucky I love you, Omega, or I would be tempted to spank *your* ass for talking to me like that."

She shivered. "That sounds more like a reward than a—"

Someone cleared their throat, causing my wolf to growl at the unexpected—and very fucking *unwelcome*—interruption.

"While this has been entertaining and all, I'd like someone to explain to me what the fuck just happened to my Elite," Cael said, a hint of waning patience in his tone.

"He attacked my mate," I returned without looking at him. "So Ivana and I attacked him."

"Yes, with impressive power," Cael drawled. "But I would like to understand what led to that bout of insanity. I assume it has something to do with your lackluster fighting skills?"

I grunted, finally looking at him. "There was nothing wrong with my fighting skills."

"Please don't treat me like I'm an idiot, Cillian. Eventually, I will become offended and we'll engage in a real fight. Outside. As wolves. With our teeth and claws." His eyes seemed to narrow more with every word he spoke. "Tell me what the fuck is going on."

"Granger's been playing us," Grey growled as he dropped a stack of journals on the ground beside Granger's prone form. "And I've confirmed Ashlyn's location."

"Where is she?" Cael demanded.

Grey's glacial eyes met mine as he replied, "Eclipse Sector."

CILLIAN

"Eclipse Sector?" I repeated. "Is that in one of Ashlyn's journals?" Because, based on what I'd seen of her entries, it seemed unlike her to be so forthcoming.

"No," Grey replied.

No elaboration.

No context.

No explanation.

"How did you find her location?" I tried again, needing more than just his confident statement.

"My gifts are irrelevant to this conversation," he informed me in a bored tone. "Use your own talents to verify what I've said. Search Granger's mind. The information is right there."

My jaw clenched. I didn't care for unknowns, and both Grey and Cael were proving to possess *unknown* powers. Powers that could be a threat.

We've severely underestimated Lunar Sector, I told Kieran.

Yes was his only reply, his mind otherwise occupied by evaluating the scene. Grey had done something to bind Granger. Not something tangible or even visible, but a mental restraint that was akin to leashing a wolf's shadowing ability.

Except Grey's energy felt thicker. Heavier. More intense.

I was about to ask Ivana what she sensed, when I realized her focus was entirely on Granger as she tried to delve through his thoughts in search of anything to do with Ashlyn.

Her trajectory served as a kick to the ass, forcing me to follow her into his mind as well. Learning more about Grey and his unknown abilities could wait. Ashlyn could not. She was out there somewhere, likely suffering, and waiting to be saved.

I just hope it's not too late, Ivana was thinking, her determination turning desperate. *I don't even know where to start looking.*

In his memories, I murmured telepathically.

Then I showed her what I meant by pushing into the parts of his brain that held his past. His secrets. His *identity*.

A deep mental growl echoed through my mind, drawing my attention to the source of the sound. *What is it?* I asked, meeting Kieran's gaze.

The scent, he snarled back with his thoughts. *Quinnlynn recognizes it.*

I arched a brow. *Granger's scent is the one she picked up on in Bariloche Sector? Not Dixon's?*

Yes was his confirmation, his need to rip the bastard apart stirring a violent warmth in the room. However, his expression remained neutral. He was the epitome of calm and collected. But inside, he was planning a slow and painful death for the wolf on the floor.

"Do you think he planted Tadhg's scent at those scenes?" Cael asked quietly, the question seeming to be for Grey.

"I don't know," he replied. "But I intend to find out. After we locate Ashlyn."

Cael nodded, his turquoise gaze landing on me. "Have you verified Grey's confirmation on Eclipse Sector?"

"Not yet," I told him, then went back to sifting through Granger's memories.

Ivana listened quietly, observing as I searched for the information we needed.

It didn't take long to discover a recent recollection of his dark intentions regarding Ashlyn. *That bitch is going to ruin everything,* he'd thought. *I have to get rid of her.*

I couldn't see his past, just heard bits and pieces of events.

But as I stumbled upon him thinking about Eclipse Sector and the vast zombie-filled land that existed there, it became quite clear that he'd shadowed Ashlyn there and left her to fend for herself.

"Fuck," I muttered. "Grey's right."

The male in question simply grunted.

I ignored him and tried to determine from Granger's mind where exactly he'd dropped the Z-Clan Omega, but the details were murky. Like he hadn't truly paid attention to where he'd taken her, just popped over into one of the various places he'd visited in Eclipse Sector in the past, tossed her onto the ground, and vanished before he could process much else.

He'd clearly been in a hurry to just dispose of her.

"Do you have any idea where in Eclipse Sector he took her?" I asked Grey, wondering if his mysterious talent came equipped with more details.

"No, I was hoping you could help with that part."

I shook my head. "Granger didn't focus on anything other than the sector as a whole." Which basically meant he could have left her anywhere in Ireland.

"What about her journal entry?" Ivana asked, glancing

around for the notebook. "The one I was reading. It had…" She trailed off as she spotted it several feet away.

I released her hips so she could move, then watched her bend to retrieve the item in question. She quickly started flipping the pages, searching for *Dear Oracle of the Stars* at the top of each entry.

"There was something at the end," she said while continuing to scan. "Something I didn't quite… Here. This." She started reading again, her eyes skimming the words until she found the postscript. "This part proved she was talking to me."

Ivana walked back to my side, her finger pointing at the first part congratulating her on the *little one*. I frowned at the last line.

"I send my blessing from the grave," I read out loud. That was certainly morbid. "What do you think it means?"

"I don't know, but look at the next part."

Grey joined us as I reviewed the post-postscript, reciting the words for everyone to hear. "Our pasts make us stronger, not weaker. Remember that. Remember where you came from. And understand once and for all—*you are not him*. But sometimes you have to think like him to find the truth. To find… me."

That was definitely a clue of some kind.

But what did it mean?

"Remember where you came from," I repeated. "Okay, given that we know she's in Eclipse Sector, I would say this line is for me, Lorcan, or Kieran."

However, the next part…

"You are not him," I echoed. "But sometimes you have to think like him to find the truth. To find… me."

Your father, Ivana thought at me. *You're not your father.*

I frowned. Could it be that simple? I'd just come to that conclusion myself when claiming Ivana. I wasn't my father. Fuck, I was nothing like him.

But sometimes you have to think like him to find the truth.

My brow furrowed even more. *What would my father have done in this situation?* He wouldn't have cared, and he would have left Ashlyn to die.

Except, that couldn't be what she meant.

Is she comparing Granger to your father? Ivana wondered.

Possibly. Only, they weren't all that alike either. My father would have just thrown Ivana into a pit and left her to die, not bothering at all to shadow her to another location. That would have required too much energy. And he would have wanted to make a statement by forcing everyone else to watch her suffer. Starve. Wither away to nothing.

I'd seen several wolves perish in those holes.

He'd eventually burn their remains and sever their heads, again as a public display.

Because he was a fucking monster.

Gods, just thinking about him made me want to find his corpse and burn his remains. Only there was nothing left of him. Kieran, Lorcan, and I had seen to that ages ago.

So what are you trying to tell me, Ashlyn? I wondered, studying her text. *Are you in one of those old holes?* That seemed impossible, given how many centuries had passed since they'd been in use. But maybe she was left near my father's favorite torture location.

Or near the place where he died.

I send my blessing from the grave.

All right, little psychic, I thought. *I'll entertain your riddle.*

"She might be hiding underground, perhaps near the old hills," I told Kieran. "Where Abbán used to deliver his messages."

"And what hills would those be?" Grey demanded.

I blew out a breath and palmed the back of my neck. "It's near the Giants Causeway, but not." Fuck, I couldn't just draw a map for him. If he hadn't visited the specific area of Eclipse Sector, he wouldn't know where to shadow to.

Show him, Ivana told me.

What?

Take him there, she reiterated, causing me to glance down at her.

I'm not leaving your side, Vana. I'd just claimed her. Hell, all I should be doing right now was fucking her in her nest. *Our* nest.

Shit. This whole thing was a bloody nightmare.

My palm fell from my nape to cup her face. *You're my priority*, I reminded her. *I'm not leaving you.*

She placed her hand on top of mine. *You're not leaving me,* she agreed. *But this is who we are together, Cillian. You're going to go with Grey, Cael, and Kieran or Lorcan, and find Ashlyn.*

"You're telling me what to do again," I said aloud.

"You're mine now, Alpha. You'd better get used to it," she returned. *Now go,* she added with her mind. *We're a team, Cillian. And Ashlyn is your*—our—*priority at the moment. So go find her.*

I leaned down to brush my lips over hers. *Just so we're clear, Omega, I will be knotting you for days when I return.* Because her insistence that we do this together, her continued lessons in what it meant to be a mated pair, was making me burn that much hotter for her.

I'm holding you to that promise, Alpha, she whispered as she returned my kiss. *Hurry back.*

Pressing my forehead to hers, I held her for a long moment, then looked at Kieran and Lorcan. They were standing beside each other, their gazes focused on me. "Who wants to go on a field trip?"

"Me," Lorcan replied instantly.

Kieran glanced at him. "You do realize I can handle myself, yes?"

"I do," his cousin drawled. "But I'm in a zombie-killing mood."

"And I'm not?"

"No, you're not. You're in a torture mood," Lorcan informed him. "So take it out on Granger while we're gone." He stepped forward. "To the burial ground first?"

I nodded. "Yep."

"Keep him alive," Cael interjected, his focus on Kieran. "We need answers from him."

Kieran shrugged. "I'll try."

"Do better than try," Cael growled. "You have no idea what he's done."

"Perhaps you should enlighten me upon your return," Kieran suggested.

"Perhaps I will," Cael bit back, his anger very unlike the charismatic, easygoing Alpha Prince persona he so often put on.

Beneath all that glamour and circumstance was a cunning, powerful wolf.

Ally or foe? I wondered. *Time will tell.*

"We're going to need guns," Lorcan said.

I nodded. "Yeah. And a distraction."

"Yep." His eyes glittered. "Wanna hunt some zombies with us, little killer?"

Kyra snorted as she slipped into the room. Her thoughts told me she'd been lurking in the hall for the last few minutes, waiting for an opportunity to enter. Lorcan must have sensed her, too. Or maybe he was just asking her out on a date. Who the hell knew?

She twirled a pair of knives in her hands and grinned. "Just tell me where to go."

"Likewise," Grey added. "And I don't need a gun. You all can handle the zombies while I hunt the little riddler."

I assumed *little riddler* meant *Ashlyn*.

"I also don't require weapons," Cael murmured. "I'll be using other talents."

Lorcan shrugged and shadowed off without a word. His mind told me he was raiding the armory. Not sixty seconds later, he reappeared with two of our go-bags. He tossed one to me, which I rifled through to find my holsters and favorite toys.

I was in the middle of adding a bulletproof vest over my sweater when I heard Ivana checking me out from behind.

Like what you see, Omega? I asked, engaging the link unique to our new bond. We hadn't used it yet, primarily relying on my telepathic and mind-reading abilities instead. But it felt right to engage her like this now. More intimate. More… *us*.

Yes, I do, Alpha, she murmured back, easily connecting to me via the same link. *Very much.*

Hmm, I hummed. *I'll remember that later.*

Then I nodded at Lorcan. "Let's go."

IVANA

Kieran took in the sight of his disheveled office and shook his head. "What a bloody mess."

My lips twitched. "It could be worse."

"Hmm," he hummed, glancing at the items scattered about the floor before shifting his attention to Granger's prone form. "You should be resting in our nest."

I blinked, confused by his words for a split second before Quinn slipped into the room with her hand on her rounding belly. "And you should stop telling me what I should and should not do."

"I'm an Alpha, darling. It's who I am."

Quinn snorted and walked over to me, her lips curling more with each step. It wasn't until she was right in front of me that I started to understand her smile because she leaned forward and sniffed my neck. "He bit you!"

I arched a teasing brow. "That's a very strange way to greet someone, Quinn."

"I'm a wolf. I'm pregnant. Every part of me aches. Give me this, Ivana. Because one day, you will understand. Trust me." Then she opened her arms and threw them around me in an unexpected hug, all while squealing with excitement. "It worked! I'm so excited that it worked!"

I hugged her back, a bit alarmed by her wild emotions and bizarre behavior. Primarily because I feared she was right and that I would soon be acting just like this—sniffing people at random and spouting strange exclamations. "What worked?" I asked her.

"The mating program!" She released me and spun toward an amused-looking Kieran. "I told you this would work."

"I'm the one who coaxed Cael into joining," he drawled.

"Yes, because I suggested they would make a fine couple."

"Indeed," he agreed.

I frowned. "Hold on, so you did get Prince Cael to join to try to make Cillian jealous?" I demanded. They'd been talking about it while I'd been scouring Ashlyn's journals earlier, but Kieran had feigned innocence.

Now he looked smug as well.

Meanwhile, Quinn just appeared to be pleased. "It's about time he claimed you."

I shook my head. "You two really are meddlers. What if I'd fallen for Prince Cael?"

"Then you would have made a fine couple," Kieran reiterated. "And Cillian would have regretted losing you for the rest of his long, lonely life."

I winced at the thought, not liking that notion at all. "He carries a lot of responsibility on his shoulders."

Kieran sobered a little. "I know. A lot of it is undue, too."

I swallowed and nodded, not wanting to talk about this anymore. It felt wrong to discuss my mate with his best friend.

Mate, I repeated to myself. *My mate.*

Because Cillian had bitten me. *Twice.*

I shivered at the heated promise he'd left behind, the very wicked intentions underlining his words.

Gods, I wanted him.

I wanted him so badly that I could barely think straight.

My thighs clenched, causing my cheeks to warm in response. I needed a distraction. Stat. Something to help cool the inferno building inside me.

Cillian's claim still hummed through my blood, causing my body to react in kind.

We needed to finish our vows. Tie ourselves together in literal knots. *Pleasure one another for days.*

It was like my estrus all over again.

Except I wasn't in heat at all, just very, *very* turned on.

Clearing my throat, I glanced around the office again, searching for something else to focus on.

Granger instantly caught my attention, his lifeless body taking up residence on the floor. "Do you think he gave us the estrus serum?" I blurted out, grasping for anything I could possibly think of that would turn my hormones off.

My change in topic also seemed to work on Kieran and Quinn because they both instantly scowled. Only the latter finally looked at the male in question, her nose curling in disgust. "He's definitely the one who visited Bariloche Sector, so he would know all about the serum."

"And not Dixon, then?" Kieran asked her, falling into work mode.

"There was only one V-Clan wolf I ever scented, and it was this Alpha." She glared at him. "But what I don't get is, why didn't I recognize him the other times I've met him? Why does his scent suddenly register as familiar now?"

"Because Ivana did something to unmask him," Kieran explained.

Quinn gaped at me. "What did you do?"

"I…" I trailed off, my lips twisting to the side as I

considered how to phrase what I'd done. "Cillian says I have a natural understanding of psychic processes, so I… I just sort of maneuvered through Granger's mental barricades to look for the truth beneath all his layers."

Which gave me an idea now. Cillian had shown me how to access Granger's memories. Maybe I could find one associated with the estrus serum.

Rather than voice my intentions aloud, I simply prodded Granger's mind again, curious as to what kind of state it was in after whatever Cillian had done to him. It'd felt like a psychic blast, one I never wanted to be on the receiving end of. It probably felt like being shot in the head. Or perhaps having one's head blown off entirely.

Shivering, I ignored the underlying sensation that thought stirred inside me and focused on Granger.

Everything seemed murky, which was strange. It'd been categorical and layered before, but now… now it was… almost foreign. Like this wasn't his mind at all.

That's odd, I thought, poking a little more and stilling when I found something somewhat familiar.

Only not familiar at all.

That bizarre energy Grey had been omitting earlier was all over Granger. I couldn't define it or really understand it, but I could *feel* the potency of it. The danger. *The ill intentions.*

My eyes widened.

Kieran and Quinn were talking about what she'd experienced in Bariloche Sector, how she used to hide whenever the V-Clan Alpha visited. But she knew his scent. It lingered on some of the Omegas he'd played with there.

"You're sure it's Granger?" I asked unsteadily, causing them both to frown at me as I'd interrupted Quinn mid-sentence.

"It's definitely that scent," she said slowly. "Why?"

Because I'm no longer convinced it's actually his, I nearly replied.

But a flicker in his mind—a hint of something *more*—had me not saying a word.

There was something else going on here.

I followed that flicker, searching for the source, only to come up against a wall of massive energy. I jerked back, the wall breaking my fall behind me.

"Ivana?" Kieran prompted.

I gaped up at him. "Something's coming, Kieran. Something—"

He stiffened, his gaze swinging to the windows framing his desk. "*Fuck. Run!*"

Quinn grabbed my hand before he even finished the demand, but another hand captured my opposite wrist before I could follow her.

That hand yanked me back down to the ground, causing me to land with an *Oomph*.

Granger was suddenly on top of me, his gaze wild as he wrapped his palms around my throat like he fully intended to rip my head off.

My yelp was silenced by my inability to breathe, his nails digging into my skin and drawing blood.

Gods, he really is going to rip—

"You fucking cunt," he snarled, his expression holding a touch of insanity to it. Almost as though he'd lost his mind.

To something else? To someone else? Is it even him?

I clawed at his wrists, trying to dislodge him, but he was too big. Too massive. *Too strong.*

He released a sound that reminded me of a rabid dog, his eyes seeming to clear for half a beat as a hint of horror struck his features.

It was jarring compared to the murderous rage from a second ago.

Then suddenly he disappeared.

Vanished.

And Kieran stood above me, his hand wavering in front of me.

I glanced to my left, searching for Granger's body.

But he wasn't there.

He'd… he'd *shadowed* out of the office before Kieran had even been able to reach him.

Over and done that fast.

I gasped in air, my fingers touching the gouges in my throat. Only to yelp as Kieran reached for me and pulled me to my feet. His gaze went to my abused neck as a blast of healing energy swam over my skin, the source of it him.

Then he abruptly pushed me toward Quinn with a snapped "*Go!*"

Confusion billowed around me, the world spinning.

Everything had happened so quickly, maybe within the breadth of a few seconds.

And I was suddenly experiencing déjà vu by Quinn grabbing me again. Only this time, she jerked me forward, wrenching me out of Kieran's office a mere instant before glass exploded everywhere in our wake.

I shuddered and tried to keep pace with a now sprinting Quinn. She was quick for someone so far along in pregnancy.

She started toward one of the rooms, only to pause and double back toward the stairs.

Chaos erupted behind us, Kieran's growls thundering through the building as the scent of metallic tang hit my nostrils. *Blood.*

His bellow soon followed, causing Quinn to skip a step.

I caught her by the arm, hoisting her back up before she could fall. But she halted entirely, her expression contorting with terror as she glanced over her shoulder.

Then Kieran howled, a warning underlining that single haunting sound.

And Quinn began to run again.

No words. No cries. No hisses or growls. Just quiet feet up the stairs and down the hallway toward their quarters.

I'd been in this corridor before, but not in their actual nest.

However, Quinn yanked me right inside and slammed the door behind us with a thunderous click.

Then bolted for the wall.

Ripping a panel away, she revealed a keypad beneath where she punched in a series of numbers. I gaped as a secret room appeared filled with security consoles that all fired to life upon her entry. "What…?"

She ignored me, sitting down to pull up an image of Kieran's office and the violence unfolding inside it.

Kieran was in the process of fending off three or four Alphas. I couldn't quite count, as it was all a blur of men that were moving too fast for the camera to focus on.

But his growls could be felt and heard all the way up here, almost as though he stood beside us.

Quinn cursed, then pulled up a few other images within their compound to see several Alphas running up the stairs.

The same stairs we'd just climbed.

"Inside!" she shrieked at me, that single word sending me sprinting forward. I turned toward the door and trembled as the front entry to her nest caved beneath one solid kick from an Alpha.

His multicolored irises met mine a hairsbreadth before I slammed our iron door closed. Quinn leapt up to flip some sort of automated lock just as that hulk of a male crashed into the entry from the outside.

The iron held.

And another series of locks clicked into place.

Followed by a thin metallic shield that covered the entire wall.

"We'll be okay in here," she whispered. "There's a protective enchantment that prevents them from shadowing in, and the iron should hold. For a while, anyway."

I swallowed. "What the hell is going on?"

Obviously, we were under attack. But by whom? And why?

She just shook her head. "I don't know, but I need to warn the others."

I was about to ask who she meant by *others* when she pulled up a screen and typed out a message that read, *BSUA*. Then she selected Jas's name and hit Send.

"BSUA?" I repeated out loud.

"Blood Sector under attack," she replied as a buzzing sounded from her wrist. She tapped it, showing me Jas's reply of *P*. "And that means they're preparing."

"To come help?"

"No. To defend the Sanctuary," she said. "In case something happens to me. Or to Kieran." She glanced at the screens as she uttered that last line, her jaw tightening. "There are too many of them."

But just as she said it, Kieran roared and threw several wolves back out the window and onto the street.

Then he *leapt* after them.

"Shit," Quinn muttered, pulling up another screen just as Kieran appeared on the ground. He must have shadowed to the street from midair—an impressive trick—and was already healed from whatever had happened before.

His power warmed the air, commanding every aspect of the sector and proving his place as King.

Quinn shivered, then slumped in her chair and pressed her palm to her belly. "Yeah, your daddy is kind of a badass," she whispered. "But I need you to calm down and let Mommy think, okay?"

"Can you message Cillian or Lorcan?" I asked.

"Yeah, I—"

Another wave of energy pulsed through the sector, cutting off her response and causing the screens all around us to freeze before burning out.

She tried to click a button, to turn it back on.

But in the next moment, the power died completely, casting us into darkness.

"The generators will kick on in a few minutes," she whispered, her voice holding an edge to it.

An edge I understood all too well.

Because a lot could happen in a few minutes.

"But I should be able to call Cillian." Quinn flicked her watch, bringing up a message screen. However, the disconnected sign hung in the top right corner, confirming what we both knew had really happened.

That surge hadn't just taken out our electricity; it'd disconnected us from the satellites above.

Which meant whoever was attacking Blood Sector had arrived with destructive weapons.

And a whole hell of a lot of supernatural power…

CILLIAN

Several Minutes Earlier

A CHILL SWEPT down my spine as I arrived in my birthplace. A land I'd both loved and hated. Loved because it was my home. Hated because of the man who'd raised me here.

My father.

Alpha Abbán.

Fuck, I swore his ghost existed here. I could feel his icy breath on my neck, hear his cruel taunts in my ear. It was sickening. Gut-wrenching. Nearly overwhelming.

And exactly why I never came here.

Exactly why I *loathed* this place.

It hurt to breathe here. To exist. To *think*.

Only... that cold breeze of familiarity soon dissipated. Much faster than it ever had before. And behind it all, I felt a foreign warmth. A heat radiating from my heart, burning through my very soul.

Ivana, I realized, palming my chest.

She wasn't here, but she was with me. Tethered *to* me. My new purpose. My lifeline. *My present and my future.*

I shook my head, clearing the haunting past from my thoughts, and focused on the now.

That was what Ashlyn's note had said, right? Our pasts made us stronger. Realize I wasn't my father. But think like him to find her.

Lorcan and Kyra shadowed in a few feet away, my old friend clearly knowing exactly where I'd intended to land. Then I heard Cael and Grey both trying to find me from somewhere near the cliffs.

"They're by the water," I told Lorcan quietly.

He nodded and left without a word, intending to bring them here—to the place where it all began.

Oh, the landscape had changed over the last millennium, and the scents were different. But I recognized the soul of this place. The history. The stories embedded into the very earth.

I started prowling, a gun at my side.

It was still night, making it a prime time for me to hunt. But the early morning hour was coming, and soon, the sun would creep up over the horizon.

Not that it mattered.

I wasn't impacted by sunlight. Alas, neither were the Infected. Or *zombies,* as Lorcan had called them.

I didn't hear any nearby, though. Just the sounds of gentle waves rolling against the shores, reminding me of another life. An old one.

All right, Ashlyn. Where are you? I wondered, searching for her mind.

When I didn't find her, I shadowed deeper into the hills and paused once more to listen.

Still no sign of the Infected or Ashlyn's thoughts.

I cast my power in a wider net but came up with nothing. Ashlyn was either unconscious or not here.

Grinding my teeth, I focused on her note again, trying to figure out how to *think* like my father.

Assuming that's who she even means. But who else could it be?

Frowning, I tried a new tactic and shadowed to the place I literally came from—the spot my Omega mother would have given birth.

It wasn't far from where I'd met Lorcan and Kyra, just higher up on a hill. While I couldn't recall where I'd actually been born, I knew this was where Omegas from Eclipse Sector used to go to give birth. My mother would have done the same.

I swallowed, thinking about the female who once gifted me life. I didn't remember anything about her. She'd died when I was young. Maybe a few months old.

I learned in my early childhood years that my father had killed her. Knowing that had made me want to kill him more.

But in the moment, I froze, I thought, my eyes narrowing.

It was a moment I'd long hated. A moment I regretted. A moment I *feared* made me a lesser Alpha.

However, considering it now, I wondered if that was the past Ashlyn had referenced. The night I'd failed to kill my father.

"You mentioned Eclipse Sector being part of this Omega slave trade before." Kyra's voice reached my ears from somewhere to my left. I couldn't see her, and her words were faint, but my enhanced hearing allowed her soft tones to reach me. "How?"

"As a trading ground or a potential auction site," Cael replied. "Or that's what we think. It's possible they've also hosted hunting parties out here."

"Hunting parties?" she repeated, the term sending another chill down my spine.

Because I absolutely knew what a hunting party was. My

father had loved them. *Craved* them. He'd fucking loved making his females scream.

"Where the Omegas run and the Alphas hunt," Grey growled, his crude summarization making me grunt. "We've never seen it happen; we've only heard of them. But we know they're real."

"And you think they host them here?" Kyra pressed, asking a question I was dying to know the answer to as well.

"Not regularly." Cael's reply was louder, his scent curling around my senses and confirming they were close. "But at least once. Unless it was an auction or a trade."

"Too many scents for a trade," Grey muttered. "An auction, perhaps. But most likely a hunt. This land is perfect for it."

"And the hills have a history associated with it as well," I added as they appeared to my left.

Grey nodded. "That they do."

I wasn't sure what he knew about it other than maybe rumors. But the haunted gleam in his gaze made me wonder if it was something more. Something to do with whatever he was hiding. His talent, perhaps?

I didn't have it in me to press him, not when it was clear we needed to focus on Ashlyn.

"I don't hear her anywhere," I told them, getting right to the point and changing the topic away from the *Omega slave trade*. We'd… deal with that issue after we handled this one. "Do you smell her?" My question was primarily for Grey. I suspected that of all of us, he would be the one most familiar with her natural perfume.

Unfortunately, he shook his head.

Sighing, I was about to suggest splitting up on different parts of the isle when he rumbled out, "But she's definitely here."

"You can sense her?" Cael asked.

"No."

"Then how do you know she's here?" Kyra asked, her exasperation rivaling my own.

"I just…" He trailed off and cleared his throat. "Trust me. She's here."

Trust you, I thought, grunting internally. *Right.*

Where are all the Infected? Lorcan thought, his gaze flicking toward me. *I don't smell any of them.*

They're probably in the old cities, I replied telepathically. It'd been a long time since we'd been back here. Maybe four or five decades. There just hadn't been cause to visit after we'd moved everyone to Blood Sector.

But not to smell a single one? He glanced around, his gaze narrowing. *I don't know, C. I don't like it.*

I didn't like it either. I didn't like any of this. The cryptic journal entry. Granger's unexpected betrayal. Cael's and Grey's mysterious powers. The Omega slave trade. Leaving Ivana behind. Being *here.*

Something wasn't adding up.

What am I missing?

I'm embracing my past, just like you said. I'm here. I'm not my father. But you want me to think like him…

He left Omegas in holes. Ashlyn sent her blessing from the grave.

But she's not here.

My brow furrowed, my mind whirling with nonsense. It almost felt like…

My eyes widened.

It feels like a distraction.

One used to derail all of us from the truth.

Not too dissimilar to the night Kieran had killed my father. We'd lured him out into these hills with an Omega in heat. Or so he'd thought. We'd tricked him with the scent, then cornered him.

And Kieran had finished the task.

Now we'd been lured out here to track another Omega. A

Z-Clan Omega. All on the basis of Grey knowing she was here.

"How?" I asked Grey, facing him. "*How* do you know she's here? You can't sense her. None of us can smell her. So tell me how you know. Is it your gift? Is she your mate? Or is it something else entirely?"

His icy gaze seemed to frost over even more. "I don't need to explain myself to you."

"Yes, you do," I told him. "Because I don't think she's here. I think we've been set up."

"You think we've run away with the fairies?" Cael interjected. "That we're playing some sort of game?"

"No," I replied. "I think Grey's head has been fucked with." It would explain the strange air of power that Ivana and I had picked up on. We'd assumed it was his gift. But what if it wasn't his at all? What if someone had clouded his judgment?

And what if Granger was just another distraction? I thought in the next breath. *Did he lie about Ashlyn being here? Is that why the memory was so vague about where he left her? Was it even real?* My eyes widened. *What if he's the proverbial Omega in heat, the red herring that lured the prey right into a trap?*

Kieran.

No. Not Kieran.

Quinnlynn and the Blood Sector heir growing in her belly.

Taking them out would end the MacNamara bloodline, and the enchanted barrier around Night Sector—as well as the Omega Sanctuary inside—would fall.

If Cael and Grey were right about this secret network of Omega auctions, then the Omegas were the target all along. And all these episodes with the estrus party serum were just distractions.

Ashlyn disappearing was another distraction.

Granger was a distraction.

This was a distraction.

"We need to get back to Blood Sector right now," I told Cael and Grey before looking at Lorcan and Kyra. "And you two need to go to Night Sector." Because if someone was trying to end the MacNamara line, then others were waiting for the opportunity to attack the Omegas under Quinnlynn's protection.

"What about Ashlyn?" Grey demanded.

"She's not here," I told him. "There's nothing fucking here." Which should have been our initial clue.

The Infected hadn't ventured out here in a long while, which confirmed there hadn't been any signs of recent life.

"She was never here," I added. "Look deep down; you'll find I'm right."

Grey's glacial gaze glittered with fury, immense power pouring off him. But rather than rage at me, he took a deep breath.

Then he tilted his head back and *howled*.

I took a step back, his explosion of energy unlike anything I'd ever felt. Lorcan grabbed Kyra, his mind telling me he was about to shadow her to safety.

Only nothing followed Grey's ripple of intensity.

It died almost as immediately as it had appeared.

And all that happened next was Grey saying, "I'm going to fucking kill Tadhg."

He disappeared in the next instant.

"Fuck," Cael breathed. "*Fuck*!"

I caught his intentions in his mind just as he followed Grey.

"They're going back to Blood Sector," I told Lorcan. "I'll message you as soon as I know something."

"Likewise," he said, referring to Night Sector.

I shadowed in a blink, going right to Kieran's office.

Where I discovered it covered in shattered glass and blood.

Ivana's terrified scent lingered in the air, causing my wolf to rage inside me.

I snarled her name, my mind instantly locating hers. *Where are you?* I growled.

Quinn and I are locked in a safe room in her nest.

A part of me relaxed. Not entirely, just marginally. *Are you hurt?*

I'm okay. But Kieran—

Are you hurt? I repeated. Because I could smell her blood in the air.

I'm fine, Cillian. Go help Kieran!

My grin felt feral on my face. If Ivana was issuing demands, then she really was okay.

But someone had made her bleed.

Someone had to pay.

Who hurt you? I demanded.

Oh my Gods, Cillian, go—

Who? I echoed, ensuring she felt the impatience underlining that single word.

Granger, she whispered, her submission a gift I cherished in that moment.

Because I'd needed that name.

He will die, I promised as I shadowed to the street outside.

Kieran stood in the middle of the road, his suit in tatters, his dark eyes glowing as he focused on Tadhg.

Fucking traitor, I thought, glaring at the bald Prince of Alpha Sector. Soon to be the *former* Prince of Alpha Sector. Because Kieran looked ready to rip him apart.

If Tadhg noticed my arrival, he didn't show it, his entire focus on Kieran.

"You dare attack me, the V-Clan King, in my own fucking home?" he seethed. "And you think to try to touch my Queen? My Omega? *My fucking mate?*"

The entire fucking sector shook beneath Kieran's growl, his power emanating with such ferocity that it made it hard to breathe.

Several wolves fell to their knees nearby, their heads bowed.

But Tadhg simply smirked. "Your bark doesn't scare me, *King*."

A wave of power emanated from the Alpha Prince, the force of it hitting me square in the chest and knocking me a step backward.

However, Kieran maintained his ground, his eyes narrowing even more. "You'll need to do better than that, *Prince*."

Cillian.

The voice didn't belong to Kieran, but to Cael.

I met his gaze from across the street, somewhat surprised to see him just casually leaning against a wall.

Cael, I returned.

Where's Queen Quinnlynn? he asked.

I narrowed my gaze. *Safe.*

Are you sure about that? He glanced around, a tic forming in his jaw. *Because this feels like a redirect. These mutts were all too easy for me to put down. And now I can't find Grey.*

It took me a second to see what he meant—to *feel* him controlling the other Alphas lurking in the street. A lot of them were bloody and breathing heavily, their attire rivaling Kieran's.

His mind helped me put together the pieces, telling me how he'd fought several of them in his office before taking the party outside.

Where he'd run into Tadhg.

However, Cael was right. This… this was too easy.

Tadhg had lured us all away from Blood Sector for a reason. Perhaps I'd discovered his intentions faster than he'd anticipated, but he still seemed far too calm.

So where is Grey? I wondered, my mind instantly searching for the Alpha in question. Murderous intent rolled through the male's thoughts, causing me to glance sharply back at the darkened building behind me.

I didn't think; I just shadowed directly to Kieran's personal quarters.

And found Grey in the middle of three Alphas, showing them the true meaning of Z-Clan Alpha strength.

Vana! I shouted via our bond, her scent wrapping around me like a warm embrace. Only that hint of iron underlying her natural perfume had me rumbling in fury. I already knew she'd been hurt. But now I wondered—

I'm okay, she replied before my concerns could grow. *But something's happening to Quinn. That weird fog I sensed around Grey and Granger is… it's doing something to her.*

Granger? I repeated.

Yeah, right before the attack, I sensed it in Granger. But now it's in Quinn, and I… I don't know what it means. But she's acting strange.

Can you figure out how to undo the fog? I asked her.

I'm trying, but every time I unweave part of it, more appears.

Can you trace the source of it? The question left me as I surveyed the rest of the room, searching for any other threats. But all I found were some dead Alphas that Grey had already handled—or I assumed he was their executioner, anyway.

He confirmed that assumption in the next beat as another Alpha lost his head and collapsed to join the macabre scene on the floor.

Nice, I thought before refocusing on Ivana.

She hadn't replied, but I heard her trying to locate the source of the fog clouding Quinn's mind.

While she worked, I searched all of Blood Sector, scanning the minds of everyone here for any signs of ill intent.

There were several assholes outside with Tadhg who were waiting for an opportunity to strike. But it seemed Cael had already wrapped his own powers around them, holding them back while Tadhg and Kieran squared off in a show of Alpha energy.

However, there were a few stragglers who had escaped Cael's notice. I heard them moving through the building, up the stairs, slowly creeping up here to reach their prize.

You were right about it being a distraction outside, I told Cael. *Grey's up here handling three of the rogues. There are six… no, make that seven, more making their way up here.*

Do you need me?

I smiled. *Nah, I can handle these jackholes.*

Because one of them was Granger.

And we had a date planned.

A very bloody, violent fucking date.

IVANA

"We should open the door," Quinn said suddenly.

"What?" I asked her, startled by her suggestion.

"It's too dark in here."

"We're wolves. We can both see just fine," I reminded her. "And the power will be back on any minute, right?" That was what she'd told me after the initial electrical surge. But ever since that had happened, she'd seemed a little off.

Which was how I'd noticed the mysterious fog clouding her mind.

Just like with Grey.

And Granger.

Cillian, Quinn wants to open the door.

Absolutely fucking not, he hissed back at me via our bond. *There are several hostiles on their way up, including Granger.*

I'm not so sure he's a hostile, I told him, frowning. *I… I don't know what he is.*

A dead wolf, Cillian informed me. *That's what he is.*

Just hold your judgment until I figure out the source—

"Quinn," I hissed out loud, abruptly ending what I'd been mentally saying to Cillian. She'd stood up and was near a panel by the metallic barrier.

"We need to leave," she told me flatly.

"We need to stay right here," I growled at her, pushing away from my chair to meet her at the panel. I gently moved her hands away from it and focused on her mind, trying again to track the source of the strange fog. The power had thickened, creating a murky layer that hummed with electrical undercurrents.

Who is doing this to you? I wondered as I unwound the strands again.

She blinked. "What's happening to me?"

"Someone is… I don't know how to describe it. Compelling you, maybe? Or forcing you to believe false information?"

"Like how I should open the door?" she asked.

"Yeah, like that," I muttered, capturing the cloud forming in her head and blowing it away with my mind before it could latch on.

Then I jolted as that fog came at me, trying to fuss with my own sense of right and wrong.

I don't think so, I thought at it, throwing up a mental wall to keep it from clouding my judgment.

Electricity zipped down my spine, the magic intensifying as the psychic energy demanded that my barrier crumble.

"Oh," I breathed, my palm slamming against the wall as my knees threatened to buckle.

Cillian said something, but I couldn't hear him, my mind fighting to protect itself from any and all intrusions.

Only one Alpha could make me submit, and he wasn't the

owner of this intrusive power. This manipulative cloud. This compulsive nonsense.

Back off, I growled at it, my mental barrier vibrating with resistance. Determination. An unwillingness to bow.

I gasped as the power hit me again, this time like a blade to my head, stirring an ache I felt to my very soul.

But my shield held.

It didn't even crack.

Or had it?

I… I wasn't sure.

The world felt dark.

Unfamiliar.

Cold.

Why am I so alone here?

I shivered, my eyes blinking into the inky night. *What happened? Where am I?*

Ivana! Cillian shouted, making me blink.

Cillian?

Fuck, Vana. Come back to me, macushla. Fight!

I frowned. *Fight what?*

But in the next instant, I felt it. That oppressive presence. The power that had blasted through my mental blocks, threatening to take control of my mind. *No!*

The black curtain fractured, then detonated into a pile of obsidian blocks.

And my sight returned.

I was still in the room with Quinn.

But she was trying to open the door again, her fingers flying over the panel keypad.

I caught her wrist, yanking her back just as a click sounded.

"Quinn!" I shouted, both aloud and in her mind. Then I shoved that damning fog from her thoughts once more and sent it right back to the owner.

To the culprit outside.

Only, it wasn't who I expected.

It… it wasn't even an Alpha. But an *Omega.*

I felt her stumble. Heard her cry out in response. Then sensed her recharging to strike again.

However, this time I was ready. I caught her incoming assault with a mental fist and returned fire with her own power, pelting her mind and forcing her to her knees.

Then Cillian followed up with one of his psychic blasts, knocking the female out entirely.

A howl sounded, one that reverberated the very floor beneath me, as well as the walls around us.

That howl demanded attention. Required submission. Mandated *respect.*

King Kieran, I thought, trembling as he howled again with even more ferocity underscoring his roar.

I grabbed on to the nearby desk for support as the door to the safe room began to open.

I hadn't stopped Quinn in time. She darted forward, intent on fixing it.

But it was too late.

The wall opened to reveal her bloody nest. Death littered the floor. And Grey stood on the other side, covered in the remains of the Alphas at his feet.

He growled, the rumble menacing in nature and causing Quinn to stumble backward several feet.

His eyes were pitch black, bloodlust painting his features in harsh lines. *A Z-Clan Alpha in a rage,* I thought, swallowing.

I'd heard rumors of their kind, knew them to be brutal and cruel. But in a blink, Grey's irises turned back to their icy color, and his expression marginally softened.

Cillian shadowed into the room, his dark clothes stained with evidence of his fight, his hands covered in blood. But that didn't stop him from grabbing me by the nape and yanking me into his hard form. His mouth crashed down on mine in the next instant, his kiss hungry and demanding and *confusing.*

There was a battle going on.

A war raging all around.

And he was kissing me like he fully intended to fuck me right here, in Quinn's ravaged nest.

By the time he finished, I could hardly breathe, my body and mind so utterly consumed by him that I was starting to question my own reality.

Only then did he say, "Gods, I love you." He nipped at my bottom lip before I could return the sentiment, then started pulling me out into the hallway where Quinn was waiting.

Grey was nowhere in sight.

Another howl bounced off the wall, an Alpha calling his pack to the center. It was loud. Intense. And had my knees threatening to buckle again.

But a purr from Cillian held me steady, his fingers lacing with mine. "We need to go to Kieran."

Quinn was already walking that way, her steps not nearly as wobbly as my own. Maybe because it was her mate releasing that sound. Or perhaps it was because her power rivaled his own. She was our Queen for a reason.

When she reached the stairwell, she paused. "Where are all the bodies?"

I wasn't sure what she meant until we reached the same point and I saw all the blood smearing the walls. My eyes widened. *Was this you?*

Yes, Cillian confirmed. "I shadowed the unconscious Alphas out to the street for Cael to hold. The dead ones were dropped in a pile next to Tadhg."

I swallowed. "And where's Tadhg?"

"On his knees outside," Cillian replied. "Kieran is making a statement. One that doesn't require words."

Quinn visibly shivered, her pupils dilating in response to Cillian's comments. Whatever Kieran was doing, she no doubt felt it. And the slight curve of her lips told me she approved.

Where's the Omega? I wondered.

Sylvia's unconscious, he replied, making me freeze mid-step.

"*Sylvia*?" I repeated aloud, causing Quinn to falter as well. "The one with the compulsion power is *Sylvia*?"

His jaw clenched as he nodded. "Yeah."

"How is that possible?" Quinn demanded. "She's from the Sanctuary."

"How long has she been there?" he asked. "Is she a more recent addition? Do you know where she came from?"

"I…" She trailed off, frowning. "Jas vetted all the Omegas. She just re-vetted them recently, after everything that happened with Fritz."

Cillian nodded. "And she probably assumes she vetted Sylvia. That's what Sylvia would have forced her to believe."

Quinn's jaw clenched, her gaze hardening as she resumed her trek down the stairs. Only, she wasn't stepping now so much as marching.

"But Sylvia was drugged, too," I said, frowning. "Why would she drug herself?"

"To have access to Blood Sector," Cillian replied. "Access to Kieran and Quinn. To their powers. Their *minds*."

My eyes widened. "Oh, shit."

"And then Granger dosed everyone else with the same serum to create a distraction. He slipped it into the refreshments Cael and Dixon were handing out after Sylvia's attack."

My eyes widened even more. "I helped distribute that drink."

"You had no way of knowing, Vana."

"Yeah, this is not on you," Quinn echoed. "This… this is about *them*."

Her stomping grew even louder, her anger a palpable presence that had me wincing. Pregnancy emotions were… intense. However, I shared those emotions right now.

Because I'd helped Granger.

Unknowingly, yes.

But that didn't change what had happened.

"What was the point of it all?" I wondered out loud. "Why did they drug us?" Because they clearly hadn't benefited from the "estrus party" they'd created; it'd started after we'd arrived in Blood Sector.

"They originally planned to attack us while we were all busy taking care of the Omegas in heat—but Ashlyn did something to stop them. I don't know what yet, just that she'd posed a problem that required their plans to shift."

"You gathered all of this from Sylvia's mind? Or Granger's?"

"Both," he replied. "And Tadhg's thoughts have confirmed some of it as well."

"I'm going to enjoy watching Kieran kill Tadhg," Quinn seethed. "But Sylvia is *mine* to handle."

"It's possible she's still a victim here," Cillian hedged. "From what I saw in Granger's mind, Tadhg groomed her to become his personal weapon, one he deploys at will."

"But… but how did he know to send her to the Sanctuary?" I asked. "You all didn't share information on it until recently, right?"

Cillian's jaw clenched. "The shadow organization Cael and Grey mentioned has clearly been aware of the Sanctuary for quite some time, but they haven't known how to get through the barrier. They set Sylvia up as bait, and potentially others, too."

Quinn snarled at that, her boot landing hard on the final step before reaching the main floor. Had she been wearing heels, she probably would have broken one with that final stomp.

"So the slave trade is true," I whispered.

"Yes," Cillian muttered. "Definitely true." His annoyance trickled through our bond. Not annoyance at the existence of such a concept—Omega slaves were nothing new in our world

—but annoyance at not having known about this particular agency.

Whoever they were, they had excelled at keeping their existence a secret for a very long time.

And that concerned Cillian.

It concerned me, too.

Swallowing, I followed him and Quinn out of the building to the massacre outside.

There were Alphas and Betas everywhere, most kneeling with their heads bowed, others unconscious on the street, and a handful of them standing with their attention focused on Kieran.

Well, not quite focused.

No one was meeting his gaze directly.

Only Cillian seemed capable of that, and even he winced a little at the power pouring off Kieran's vibrating form.

It was impressive.

Almost as impressive as Benz being among the standing Alphas. He was the only Beta not kneeling in submission. His turquoise gaze met mine, relief shining bright in the depths of his eyes. I returned the look and gave him a little nod. It felt like a million years since I'd last seen him. There was so much to say, to catch up on.

Later, I thought, knowing Benz would understand even though he couldn't hear me. The telepathy gift was clearly one I hadn't inherited through my new bond to Cillian. I wasn't upset by that. Mind reading was… enough.

Kieran took one look at Quinn and held out an arm, his unspoken command clear.

She went to him with confidence fueling her steps and slid right into his side. His opposite hand came over to palm her protruding belly, his growl softening to a subtle purr.

At least until he looked down at Tadhg's bald head.

The Alpha was on his knees like several others, but the way his body twitched and pulsed told me he hadn't taken that position willingly. Everyone else seemed to be kneeling out of respect. But not Tadhg. He was being held there by Kieran's will.

Grey shadowed in a hairsbreadth of a moment later, holding an unconscious Sylvia in his arms.

He slowly and gently set her on the ground, his Alpha instincts taking over when it came to handling someone so much smaller than him.

That same *kindness* didn't exist inside me.

When I looked at Sylvia, I saw a traitor. A villain. Someone who had fucked with the minds of others all for some unknown gain.

Except Cillian's words from a few minutes ago whispered through my mind.

It's possible she's still a victim here.

Possible, perhaps. But her power hadn't felt all that innocent. It'd felt purposeful. Intrusive. *Deadly*.

"Prince Tadhg of Alpha Sector, you and your cohorts have committed the highest level of treason today," King Kieran announced in a voice that carried for miles, his Alpha prowess in full force. "There will be no trial. No pleading your case. The lives of you and your co-conspirators are forfeit."

He paused, like he was waiting for anyone to try to argue.

But all Tadhg did… was *laugh*.

The rumble of sound seemed to rival King Kieran's, the mocking tone traveling for miles.

"You're a fool," Tadhg gritted out.

"I'm a fool?" King Kieran repeated, canting his head to the side in a manner that came off as far too threatening to be innocent.

"You're all fools," Tadhg reiterated. "Ask Grey. He knows."

The Alpha in question glared, his eyes darkening to the same shade I'd seen when leaving the safe room. But he didn't make a sound. Didn't utter an explanation. Just stared down at

Tadhg with such immense hatred that it left no question as to whether or not these two had history.

Tadhg's head jerked as he fought whatever control Kieran had exuded over him, and managed a glance up at Grey. "You just keep your relics, don't you? First Nikiski. Now Ashlyn." He huffed another laugh. "You just keep failing your Omegas, don't you, Grey?"

Grey's fists clenched at his sides. "*Where* is my sister?"

"So you choose her over Ashlyn, then?" Tadhg taunted. "Your own blood over a potential mate? I'll be sure to let her know your choice."

A growl left Kieran. "You won't be letting anyone know anything." A wave of power slammed down on the prince in the street, causing his neck to strain and his jaw to clench as he snarled in response.

"Where is she?" Grey demanded, taking a step forward. "Where the fuck did you leave her?"

Blood trickled from Tadhg's mouth, the weight of Kieran's energy seeming to act as a physical blow. "I dropped her in Kodiak Sector," he gritted out. "That meddling little bitch is no doubt dead by now. Good fucking riddance."

Grey stared at him for a long moment, his expression seeming to smooth out, all signs of his fury dying as he shifted his focus away from Tadhg to Prince Cael.

He stood on the sidelines, arms folded with a shoulder braced against a building wall. He was the epitome of boredom. Yet I could feel the presence of his gift all around us.

Cillian had said he'd dropped all the Alphas off for Prince Cael to hold.

I now understood what that meant.

He seemed to have them all under his mental fist, holding them in a way similar to how King Kieran imprisoned Tadhg now.

“That final note was never for Cillian or Ivana; it was for me,” Grey said, making me frown.

“What final note?” Cillian asked before I could voice the same question.

“The one about our pasts making us stronger and remembering that I’m not him.” Grey looked at Cillian. “That post-postscript was for me. And now I know where Ashlyn is.” He looked down at Tadhg. “Thank you. You’ve been most helpful.”

With that cryptic comment, he disappeared.

CILLIAN

Kieran's mind whirred with the need to *kill*.

He was livid. More livid than I'd ever heard him.

But he was practical, even in his anger.

Destroy his mind, he told me. *Find every fucking detail about this shadow organization that—*

A scream cut through his mental command, the source of it suddenly writhing on the ground.

Feminine. Pained. *Furious*.

Quinn jolted forward, ready to intervene when the Omega's body on the ground twisted in agony, the shriek having come from her parted lips.

Tadhg winced, then started convulsing right along with her.

Ivana gasped beside me, her mind instantly working as she tried to undo what she'd just realized was happening.

No! Ivana screamed, reaching forward with her own mental gifts.

But it was too late.

The damage was done in an instant, this fail-safe one I could never have seen coming.

A suicide sequence. One meant to destroy the mind.

Sylvia instantly stopped screaming, her body going eerily still as Tadhg collapsed beside her, the two of them… brain dead.

Kieran cursed, kneeling down to heal them. But even he couldn't bring them back from death.

Whatever trigger that Omega had just flipped was one that had been programmed long ago to take both her and Tadhg out.

Cael growled, as did Kieran.

Quinn and Ivana just looked shocked.

And Granger… Granger had gone white, his thoughts chaotic. Because he just realized they'd left him as the only one alive with information we desperately needed.

But he didn't know enough to be of any use.

I could hear it deep down that he'd already given me everything he knew about what had happened. The shadow contacts were all Tadhg's. He'd been the one at the table, taking the calls, attending *hunts*, never once allowing Granger into his inner sanctum.

He was effectively useless to us now.

And as good as dead.

"Fucking craven," Cael muttered, stepping forward to spit on Tadhg's corpse. "At least Grey had one win before that bastard offed himself."

"But his sister…?" Quinn whispered, glancing up at Cael from where she hovered over Sylvia. She'd tried to heal her while Kieran had gone to Tadhg, but neither of them had been able to make a difference. Whatever mind trick Sylvia had pulled had been permanent.

"He used Tadhg's expectations against him," Cael told her, his voice softening a little. "Tadhg knew Grey's been hunting for Nikiski for decades. He assumed Grey would ask about his sister, not Ashlyn. So Grey played the game, knowing full well that if he did, Tadhg would give him the opposite information."

"Ashlyn's location, not Nikiski's," I translated, understanding what had happened.

"Exactly. He made it sound like he was still holding Ashlyn, which we all know isn't true. Granger made it look like he dropped her in Eclipse Sector, but our noses confirmed the lie. I'm betting Granger never even had her." He turned to look at his former Elite. "Am I right?"

Granger simply clenched his jaw in response, saying nothing.

However, his mind confirmed it for me.

That *memory* had been Sylvia's doing, the powerful Omega having had far too much manipulation power of the mind. Although, I could see everything clearly now that she was gone.

Sylvia had been one of Tadhg's acquisitions through the slave trade, an Omega of extraordinary genetics. Mostly V-Clan, but with a touch of vampire. Similar to Kyra in that way, yet so incredibly different, too.

Tadhg had acquired her when she was a child and groomed her as a weapon, just like I'd told Quinn and Ivana.

She was innocent to an extent, having been basically brainwashed by her owner.

But that didn't make anything she'd done any less evil.

"What did Ashlyn do to foil your plans?" I asked Granger.

He glared mutinously back at me.

That was fine.

I didn't need him to speak. I could just break his mind with a little help from my mate.

Vana, I murmured. *Can you help me get around his barriers?*

Because those were very much him. I had no doubt that gift for being able to mask his identity was exactly why Tadhg had recruited him.

Ivana squeezed my hand and leaned into my side, then closed her eyes and went to work.

Granger fought back at first, trying to shove her from his mind. But she sidestepped him with ease, her confidence growing with each step.

She'd spent her entire life hiding behind shields without ever realizing that was a special talent, not just a normal skill. It didn't surprise me at all how easily she'd embraced this extension of her power. She was a natural. Intelligent. *Beautiful.*

Power hummed between us as she worked, her mind so focused on Granger that she didn't seem to notice anything else. Not the grunts or groans of the Alphas as Kieran began walking around and killing them one by one—with his hands.

Not the shudders of the observing crowd.

Not the rumble of Kieran's growl as he exuded his strength and reminded every V-Clan wolf present of just what he could do.

Not the fire that ignited to start burning their bodies.

Nothing.

Just Granger.

Yet Granger was *very* aware of the death surrounding him, his future lurking on the wind.

He was going to die. But Kieran wouldn't be the one killing him. That pleasure would be mine, just as soon as I dug every piece of information from his mind that I could.

There, Ivana thought at me, her head against my shoulder. *He's ready.*

Thank you, macushla. I rolled my neck, then met Granger's gaze. *Time to get to work.*

Granger gritted his teeth, his mind instantly trying to battle my intrusion. But Ivana kept his power at bay while I delved deep into the recesses of his mind, searching for anything useful.

I found the day he first met Tadhg. Their friendship had formed over their mutual agreement that Omegas should be property, not mates. At first, Tadhg didn't use Granger. It wasn't until much later when Granger went to him one night to share what Cael and Grey were up to, how they suspected Tadhg of taking Grey's sister.

Tadhg had denied it at first.

But Granger hadn't believed him.

Rather than report back to Cael—where his loyalty should have fucking lain—he'd kept feeding updates to Tadhg. He'd wanted Tadhg to take him on as an Elite because he'd stupidly believed that Tadhg would give him more power.

No, not just power.

Omegas.

There weren't many in Lunar Sector, and those who were there were very much under Cael's protection. Granger knew he'd never be given one to play with. Because Cael believed in mate bonds and giving Omegas a choice.

Granger was disgusted by the concept.

And jealous that Dixon received favoritism, too. Favoritism as Cael's brother, even though he was clearly the weaker Elite.

I snorted at that last discovery. Granger didn't understand the meaning of *weak*; otherwise, he would have known just how wrong his assumption was. Granger considered himself to be superior because of his mental abilities. While yes, his talent was impressive, how he chose to use that talent marked him as the weakest of men.

Alphas shouldn't take from those they saw as weaker than them; Alphas should *protect* those who needed it.

And Omegas weren't weak or meant to be owned. They were powerful, something Ivana proved time and again.

But I didn't comment on any of that in Granger's mind, just continued processing his thoughts and experiences.

As I'd already discerned, he didn't know anything useful about the shadow organization, just that it existed. He'd been waiting for Tadhg to invite him to the table, hoping for a reward for all his insider information sharing.

Pathetic, I muttered, then continued digging.

Hours seemed to pass as I went through every aspect of his mind, searching for whatever he knew about Ashlyn. About how she'd interfered.

When I finally found it, I couldn't help but laugh out loud.

The little psychic had been waiting in Sylvia's room when he and Tadhg had shadowed in to begin their attack.

She'd given them a little wave and murmured, "I hope you weren't relying on Sylvia to wake up anytime soon. I may have used some of those drinks from Glacier Sector—you know, the ones meant for me and the others—to keep Sylvia hydrated during her heat. As you can see, she's still, well, in the throes of it, as it were."

Tadhg had lost his shit, snarling right in Ashlyn's face, telling her she was a fucking menace.

To which she'd just shrugged and replied, "I've been called worse."

Furious, he'd grabbed her by the arm and disappeared.

Granger had waited over an hour for him to return, but when he never did, he slunk back to Lunar Sector in a huff.

It wasn't until a few days later that Tadhg had reached out with a revised plan.

"That psychic cunt will play a part in this after all," he'd said, pleased with himself for his new idea. "We'll send them on a hunt through Eclipse Sector—fitting, given recent events there—while we take down Quinnlynn MacNamara and that damn shield around the island. Then I'll notify my contact that the fun can begin."

Granger had asked about the contact and what *fun* he meant, but Tadhg hadn't elaborated beyond replying, "Let's just say, it'll be the most impressive estrus party yet."

Granger, the idiot, hadn't asked any additional questions.

A follower through and through.

"Why this asshole was your Elite, I will never understand," I said to Cael, aware that he'd come to stand beside me a while ago. He hadn't interfered with my work, just waited quietly while Ivana and I ripped through his Elite's mind.

Rather than reply, he simply asked, "Learn anything useful?"

Kieran joined us, his gaze and thoughts telling me to answer Cael's question.

So I did, elaborating on everything I'd just discovered, including how Ashlyn had thwarted their plans.

"Was he ever faithful to me?" Cael asked, sounding tired.

"Yes," I admitted. "He just doesn't share your morals. Tadhg's appealed to him more."

Cael nodded. "Dixon has never cared for Granger. I'll have to inform my brother that he was right and I was wrong." His tone deepened with that last part, suggesting he wasn't used to admitting to making errors. But the fact that he could state it so plainly out loud spoke volumes about his own personal character.

"Kill him," Kieran demanded, the words seeming to be directed at Cael.

The Alpha Prince glanced at me. "I smell Ivana's blood on him."

"He attacked her."

He nodded, as if he'd already gathered as much. "The bastard betrayed me in the worst way. But I wouldn't have known about it had you and your mate not discovered the truth. So how about we… work together?"

I arched a brow. "What are you suggesting?"

"You remove his head. I'll burn the body." He uttered the words so casually, like he wasn't announcing Granger's future death right in front of him.

"I want to use my hands."

"That's fine." Cael smiled, and a hint of the predator beneath glimmered up at me. "I'm all for making it hurt."

Ivana made a sound, causing me to glance down at her. She wasn't disgusted by the notion, as it hadn't been a gag or even a note of disapproval. It'd been a *yawn*.

One glance at her face told me why.

It'd been a fucking long day, made even longer by however much time had passed while I'd been inside Granger's head. Given that all the other Alphas were already burned to ash in the street, and the sun was high in the sky, it'd definitely been hours, just like I'd suspected earlier.

My Omega—my beautiful, *pregnant* Omega—was exhausted.

I'm fine, she whispered into my mind.

You're tired.

She shrugged. *We'll go back to our nest after this.*

Our nest? I echoed, loving the sound of that.

Yes. You owe me a good knotting session.

I arched a brow. *I'm covered in blood, macushla.*

I'm very aware. Her gaze ran over me with interest. *My deadly, sexy, violent Alpha.*

Hmm, I hummed, enjoying the look in her eyes.

I wanted to darken it.

Which gave me an idea.

One I acted on by releasing her hand, walking over to Granger, and twisting his head clean off without even blinking. *I will kill anyone who ever thinks to hurt you,* I told her. *Remember that and believe that.*

Her pupils dilated even more. *I've always trusted you, Cillian.*

I'm sorry it took me so long to trust myself, too, I replied, walking back to her and grabbing her by the nape to kiss her soundly on the mouth.

Cael grunted. "I get it, Elite. She's yours."

"Prince," Kieran corrected, causing me to freeze against Ivana. "Assuming he wants Alpha Sector, anyway."

I slowly pulled back to look at him. "Fuck. You."

Kieran threw his head back and laughed.

I did not join in.

"I am not fucking taking over Alpha Sector. Give it to Hawk. Or, hell, give it to Grey." I assumed he'd be back with Ashlyn soon.

He seemed to know exactly where to go, which was good because Kodiak Sector was no-man's-land for V-Clan wolves.

It was filled with Z-Clan Alphas that none of us wanted to fuck with.

But that wasn't the point of this current conversation.

"I am not interested in leading, Kieran. I know I could do it. I'm powerful. But I don't fucking want to be an Alpha Prince. It has nothing to do with my lack of qualifications or my lineage. It's because I like being your Second. So stop fucking pushing this."

His eyes glittered with amusement. "My Second, hmm?"

I rolled my eyes. "Elite. You know what I meant."

"Oh, I think I do, yes," he replied. "And *Second* sounds right. Or temporary King when I need a break. Like, in, say, a few months when my mate gives birth?"

I narrowed my gaze at him. "Did you just trick me into agreeing to take on Blood Sector for you so you can go on holiday?"

"Paternity leave isn't a holiday, from what I understand."

Fucker, I thought at him.

Which, of course, resulted in him laughing again.

For just annihilating a horde of Alphas, he was sure in a good fucking mood.

"Oh, Night Sector is secure, by the way," Kieran added conversationally, his change in topic giving me whiplash. "If you're going to be my Second, you should check your watch more. Lorcan's been messaging you for hours, and you know how much he doesn't like to talk."

He started walking away after that, all while thinking, *"King Cillian" does have a nice ring to it.*

"Dead Kieran" does, too, I thought right back at him.

He chuckled again. *I don't die easily, King Cillian. I believe I just proved that.*

We'll see next time we spar, I told him.

I'll add it to my calendar for sometime next week. You have an Omega to see to first. And I suspect you're going to require some days off to tend to her needs.

I really wanted to tell him not to comment on my Omega's *needs* but decided it wasn't worth the response. He would just fire something witty back at me.

Besides, he was right.

Ivana did need me.

And I needed her.

"Do you think Grey will find Ashlyn?" she asked, her question seeming to be for Cael, as she was looking at him now.

He'd already begun burning Granger's remains, ensuring the asshole fully embraced death. Typically, V-Clan wolves had to be beheaded and burned to die.

Apparently, frying the brain also worked, as Tadhg and Sylvia had proved.

She really was a weapon.

One that had been used wrongly, a fact that saddened me. Yet I couldn't help but feel relieved that she couldn't cause any more destruction.

"Yes," Cael said, drawing my attention back to him. "It may take him some time, but I believe she's left him enough clues to go off of."

"From the note she wrote to Ivana?" I asked.

"Among other entries, yes," he murmured. "There's a lot more going on between him and Ashlyn than he's telling anyone. Those two cryptic wolves deserve one another."

"You're not at all concerned?" Ivana pressed.

Cael smiled. "I'm always concerned, sweetheart. But there's a reason I trust Grey with my life and my sector. He's the most resilient bastard I've ever met. If anyone can get Ashlyn out, it's him. You'll see."

Ivana swallowed but nodded. "I hope you're right."

"I usually am," he replied, glancing at me. "Just ask your mate."

I simply stared at him. "You play dangerous games, *Prince*."

"Right back at you, *Second*."

"That'll be *King* to you soon," I taunted him.

He grinned. "I'll start working on my formal bow."

"Do that," I told him. "And let us know when you hear from Grey."

Ashlyn's disappearance would weigh on me until I heard from him. But I acknowledged that there was nothing I could do here.

She'd told Ivana to tell me that a new life was more important than an old one and that she would be fine.

I finally understood what that meant.

She'd been talking about *my* new life, the one Ivana had given me. All while promising she would survive.

"Choosing to suffer out of some misguided need to repent doesn't just impact you, Cillian. That choice—the one where you put everyone else first—impacts her, too. If you remember anything I've said, please remember that."

Ashlyn was right.

Choosing to try to go after her now would put me at risk. Which would put Ivana at risk, too.

My choices were Ivana's choices, just as hers were mine.

We were a team now.

A pair.

I had to put her first. Always.

But as Ivana had shown me, that didn't mean I had to

forgo my other priorities for her. We functioned best as a unit. As *us*.

And I looked forward to finding out what all that meant.

For the first time in my life, the future was bright.

Because of the Omega by my side.

My Ivana.

My love.

My mate.

IVANA

Droplets of red water streamed down Cillian's chest, exciting my inner beast.

It was wrong.

Depraved.

Yet it made me burn all over.

My Alpha had shown his strength today. He'd fought. He'd killed. He'd *won*.

And something about that stirred a primal need inside me, one that had me wanting to bite him all over again. To ensure he knew he was mine. That everyone *knew* he belonged to me.

That same possessive urge was reflected in his gaze, his mind mirroring my own. I could hear his yearnings, his intentions, his dark desires.

He wanted to knot me like this, to claim me while the water washed away the remnants of death. To come inside me in a joyous union of new life. To show me that he'd chosen me —*us*—over everything else.

"My Omega," he whispered against my mouth.

"My Alpha," I whispered back, then moaned as he kissed me.

It felt like we'd been apart for years, not hours. Like we'd claimed one another a decade ago, not within the last day or so.

Kissing him felt like coming home.

Being alive once more.

Fully embracing my future in this world.

Stars, I'd wanted him for so long. So very, *very* long.

To finally have him in my arms… it almost resembled a dream. But it was real. Oh, so *real.*

He pressed me into the marbled wall, his knot a brand against my lower belly. "This is going to be hard and fast, Vana," he warned me. "We'll take it slow back in the nest. But I've been without you for too fucking long, and I haven't had nearly enough of you."

"And whose fault is that?" I breathed, arching into him.

He nipped my lower lip. "Always sassing me."

"Never going to stop," I promised as he lifted me into the air.

He didn't give me a moment to brace or to even consider what was coming, just entered me in a single thrust. I screamed, the intrusion painful yet absolutely what we both needed.

I wanted to feel this.

To know he was the one stretching me. Claiming me. *Fucking me.*

"Gods, I love you," he murmured, his breath minty against my mouth. "I love you so fucking much, Ivana."

His tongue silenced my response, forcing me to think it at him instead. *I love you, too.*

He growled, seeming to like that proclamation. Perhaps I hadn't said it enough.

So I repeated it.

Again.

And again.

All while he fucked me just like he'd said he would. *Hard. Fast. Thoroughly.*

His hands gripped my hips so tightly that I knew there would be bruises. But I was too busy drawing my nails up and down his back to care.

This was a savage claiming.

A primal *need.*

A long-awaited union between freshly mated wolves.

"Bite me," he demanded. "Make me bleed, mate."

I sank my teeth into his lip, causing him to grin against my mouth.

Then I went to his neck and bit him again. Harder. Right over his pulse point. His blood coated my tongue, forcing me to swallow his essence. He tasted so divine. Like my own personal treat.

Because that was exactly what he was—*mine.*

He rumbled in approval, his hips grinding against mine, forcing me to climb to new heights of pleasure. I clawed at him and bit him once more, this time on the other side of his neck.

One hand left my hip to fist my hair as he held me to him, silently commanding me to drink.

Stars, it was wild. Untamed. Everything I'd ever dreamt of.

Only he made that dream burn even hotter as he yanked my head away and back so he could return the favor. I jolted as his teeth met my pulse point, his lips hot against my throat.

It was feral.

Beautiful.

So vicious that I couldn't help but scream again.

Yes, he praised into my mind. *Make them hear you, Vana. Tell this entire fucking sector that you're mine. That they were wrong to ever think or say otherwise. You. Are. Mine.*

I shuddered, his claim so bold and true that I could barely breathe.

Then he tipped his head back and *howled.*

The suddenness of it had me writhing against the wall, his domination so utterly devastating that every part of me clenched against him.

He was telling the sector exactly where he was.

In my nest.

Our nest.

Fucking me.

Taking me.

Claiming me.

It left no doubts as to his intentions, his possession, his *love.*

He wanted the entire world to know I was his and ensured they did by howling a second time.

Oh, Gods… The vibration of that sound… it was so loud. So primitive. So *Alpha.*

He followed it with a growl that had slick pouring out of me, his commanding rumble instantly calling upon me to submit.

I'm yours, I told him.

Then I repeated it aloud.

And *screamed* it from the top of my lungs.

His hand slid between us, his thumb stroking my clit as he growled, "*Prove it.*"

Every part of me lit up in flames, his body stoking mine to an inferno of sensation and bliss. I gripped him with my thighs as my arms encircled his neck.

Then I let myself go. All my worries. My pain. The past. Every hurt. I just… released everything. And allowed myself to fly into an oblivion of *us.*

Pleasure.

Heat.

Love.

It all existed here. Thriving. Pulsing. Vibrating with life.

A bright future.

A forgotten past.

And a sector full of wolves who knew exactly what had just happened between us.

I could hear their thoughts, but I tuned them all out and focused on the only minds that mattered—mine and Cillian's.

His chest rumbled with approval, his thoughts praising me for being his, thanking me for choosing him, for my unending patience, for *sassing* him.

I smiled at that last part, my lips parting as I panted, "*Knot me, Alpha.*"

"Mmm, always telling me what to do." The phrase seemed to be one of his favorites now.

I didn't mind it; I enjoyed it, too.

Because he almost always did exactly what I wanted.

And now was no different as he took me even harder against the wall, his thumb stroking my sensitive nub with a vengeance, forcing me to continue climaxing around him.

"Gods, I love the way it feels when you come all over my cock," he told me, his teeth skimming my lower lip. "Keep squeezing me, macushla. Yeah, just like that."

His grip tightened in my hair as he yanked my head back once more, only this time he sank his teeth into my breast.

I shrieked, the sensation sending a hot kiss of need through my veins despite my current orgasmic state.

Gods, this man.

This wolf.

This Alpha.

He released me and let me see the blood painting his mouth, then captured my lips with a fierceness that made it impossible to breathe. To think. To… to *exist.*

I lost track of time and space, only to come back as his

knot slammed into me, claiming me from within while he released pulsing waves of his hot seed.

He exhaled into my mouth, reminding me to inhale, and then kissed me again. His tongue exuded dominion over my very being, dominating me in a way that left me feeling safe and protected in his arms. Yet equally cherished and pleasured.

Ecstasy rippled over me, my orgasm seeming to never end while his knot continued to pulse. Hours might have passed. I wasn't sure. I didn't care. I was with Cillian. He was all that mattered.

And the life inside me, I thought, sighing as a cloud of warmth engulfed my skin.

Cillian had somehow finished our shower, all while remaining inside me, and now we were heading to our nest to begin again.

Because his knot was starting to subside.

Yet he was still rock hard.

"I'm going to fuck you until you pass out, Vana," he informed me. "Then I'm going to wake you with my knot."

I shivered. "Okay," I told him. Because I liked the sound of that. "Now tell me that you're going to do that every day for the rest of our lives."

He chuckled as he pressed me into the soft mattress, his arms caging me in from above. "I'm going to knot you every fucking day for eternity, Vana."

My lips curled. "Good Alpha."

"You have no idea how good, but I'm going to show you, Omega." He pulled out to the tip, just to slam into me. "I'm going to worship you." He repeated the action. "Knot you." Another thrust. "And love you with everything that I am."

Another quiver worked its way down my spine. "You're worthy, Cillian," I breathed, needing him to hear the words. Because I'd overheard that part of his mind whispering that one day he would be worthy of me. That he would do whatever it took to be *enough*. "You're so incredibly worthy."

I kissed him before he could reply this time, taking a page from his playbook and returning the favor.

Then I continued speaking into his mind, repeating over and over that he was worthy, until he made me come again and I lost all manner of coherent thought.

Much, much later, as I slowly lost consciousness beneath him, I heard him whisper, "The next time you ask me to dance, Ivana, I promise I'll say yes. I'll always say… *yes*."

PART VI

Dear Stars,

I have a mate, and not just any mate, but Cillian. Elite Cillian. Alpha Cillian. My Cillian. My Alpha. Mine. Mine. Mine.

He's watching me write this.

He thinks I'm cute (even if his eyes say otherwise right now).

I think I'll straddle him. Naked. See how he looks at me th—

(Cillian knotted me before I could finish this entry).

Anyway... I'm in love with an Alpha named Cillian. He is now mine and I am now his.

The end.

Love,
Ivana
PS: Grey found Ashlyn. It's quite the story. I'll share it in my next entry...

EPILOGUE

ASHLYN

I've always known how I would meet my mate.

Or I thought I did.

Until it actually happened in Glacier Sector.

But I always assumed it would be here, on the chilly shores of Kodiak Sector.

I've dreamt of this moment so many times, always waking with both excitement and regret.

Because I know how much this is going to hurt. How our story is going to begin and potentially end.

It's not for the faint of heart. Sometimes I wonder if I can really handle it.

However, I wouldn't change the decisions I made that landed me here. The alternative paths were far worse for everyone else. Too much death and pain.

If I have to endure this for everyone else to be safe, so be it.

I just hope Grey hurries up.

Glancing up at the sun, I note the afternoon time.

Should be soon, I think. *Assuming he understood the messages I left for him.*

I don't mean to be cryptic, but I've learned that's the best way to convey hidden meanings without altering futures.

Messing with fate comes with severe consequences, consequences I have no interest in facing.

I shiver as a chilly wave assaults my bare skin. It's the only way to keep my scent from spreading, from alerting the Kodiak Alphas to my presence.

But Oracle, I'm exhausted.

I've been awake for days. Sitting in this chilly water while my body fights to stay warm enough to survive. I resemble a blue waterlogged alien right now. Grey probably won't even recognize me.

If he even comes for me, I think.

Closing my eyes, I refuse to consider that alternative.

That path isn't good for either of us.

This is the only right way. The best—

"All right, little riddler." The deep voice washes over me, causing my eyes to spring open.

Grey stands a few feet away, covered in blood, just like in my visions. I tremble, both terrified and elated. "Y-you're h-here," I stammer out, my voice barely resonating above the waves.

He frowns, then holds out his hand. "Let's get you somewhere warm."

I consider it for longer than I should, then reach up to grab him just as howls sound in the distance.

Grey lunges forward to grab me, then shadows us out of Kodiak Sector before anyone can stop us.

But he doesn't take me back to his lair.

He takes me somewhere else entirely.

To a place I've dreaded since the first time I dreamt of this moment.

I know what comes next. The words. The irritation. *The pain.*

He instantly pulls me into his arms, a wool blanket wrapping around me. But his eyes are hard as he tilts my head up so I'm forced to meet his gaze.

"I'm going to warm you up," he tells me. "Then we're going to talk about those little notes in your journal about Nikiski. And afterward, you're going to help me find her."

There it is.

Our fate.

The one that's going to either make us… or break us.

Because it requires us to go back in time.

To visit a past neither of us wants to consider.

To embrace a potential future that could destroy us both.

To return to… *Kodiak Sector.*

Ashlyn's story is next in *Kodiak Sector*…

Kodiak Sector

Welcome to Kodiak Sector, home to the most vicious Alphas in the Z-Clan world.
It's a deadly place for an Omega like me.
But my intended mate is determined to drag me back to the hell I came from, all to save his sister.

He thinks I know how to find her.
I don't.
I just *see* things. Like the future.
And right now, it's full of savagery and pain.

Until suddenly, my visions disappear.
Suggesting a fate worse than death.
One I begin to understand when I go into heat in the underground caves of Kodiak Sector.

My intended mate is suddenly forced to choose—me or his sister?

For once, I can't see what will happen.

But in my heart, I know who he'll save.

Because no one ever picks me.

Author's Note: *Kodiak Sector* is a standalone shifter romance featuring a dark world with knotting, nesting, growling, and a whole hell of a lot of purring. Because while Ashlyn might not "see" it, Grey is obsessed with her in the best way. She's his, and he protects what's his…

USA Today Bestselling Author Lexi C. Foss loves to play in dark worlds, especially the ones that bite. She lives in Chapel Hill, North Carolina with her husband and their furry children. When not writing, she's busy crossing items off her travel bucket list, or chasing eclipses around the globe. She's quirky, consumes way too much coffee, and loves to swim.

Want access to the most up-to-date information for all of Lexi's books? Sign-up for her newsletter here.

Lexi also likes to hang out with readers on Facebook in her exclusive readers group - Join Here.

Where To Find Lexi:
www.LexiCFoss.com